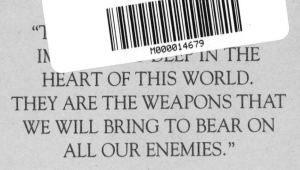

"T
IN   P IN THE
HEART OF THIS WORLD.
THEY ARE THE WEAPONS THAT
WE WILL BRING TO BEAR ON
ALL OUR ENEMIES."

Zellorian smiled horribly and began to compress his hands, forcing Wyarne to his knees. Blood spurted through his fingers as the hands gripped bone.

Wyarne screamed, but he could not break free. He felt himself being crushed, his chest constricting until the ribs snapped and closed up. Still the merciless release of power went on.

No one in the company dared to interfere. Zellorian exerted fresh power, squeezing the deformed flesh, compacting it as though between the immense wheels of a stone mill. The ruined flesh and bone before him toppled as he released it, the corpse no bigger than a child's.

Zellorian lifted his bloody hands. "This is how you die, those who would betray us now. Look down upon this bloody wreckage. The dark is hungry for such sacrifices, but we have enemies enough to sate it."

Other Avon Books in the
STAR REQUIEM *Series by*
Adrian Cole

Book 1: Mother of Storms
Book 2: Thief of Dreams
Book 3: Warlord of Heaven

THE OMARAN SAGA

Book One
A Place Among the Fallen

Book Two
Throne of Fools

Book Three
The King of Light and Shadows

Book Four
The Gods in Anger

Other Books Coming Soon

Blood Red Angel

Avon Books are available at special quantity discounts for bulk purchases for sales promotions, premiums, fund raising or educational use. Special books, or book excerpts, can also be created to fit specific needs.

For details write or telephone the office of the Director of Special Markets, Avon Books, Dept. FP, 1350 Avenue of the Americas, New York, NY 10019, 1-800-238-0658.

STAR REQUIEM

BOOK 4

LABYRINTH OF WORLDS

ADRIAN COLE

AVON BOOKS • NEW YORK

AVON BOOKS
A division of
The Hearst Corporation
1350 Avenue of the Americas
New York, New York 10019

First AvoNova Printing: July 1993

AVONOVA TRADEMARK REG. U.S. PAT. OFF. AND IN OTHER COUNTRIES, MARCA REGISTRADA, HECHO EN U.S.A.

Printed in the U.S.A.

RA 10 9 8 7 6 5 4 3 2 1

CONTENTS

BOOK FIVE – THE UNLEASHING

EPILOGUE

PREFACE

THE LAST DAYS OF MAN

Man once ruled over an Empire that stretched throughout countless worlds, worlds that formed a complex cycle, a self-contained chain.

In his hunger for knowledge, Man unlocked the door to another realm, that of the alien race, the Csendook, and thus began a thousand year war in which these ferocious aliens, faster and stronger than Man, began the inexorable conquest of his Empire.

In desperation, facing extinction, Man's Imperator Elect and his Consulate sought to escape the Csendook tide. On the world of Eannor, the Imperator's Prime Consul and principal scientist, Zellorian, used dark and forbidden powers to create a gate into a separate cycle of worlds, a feat thought to be impossible. Zellorian brought the Imperator Elect, his remaining Consulate and the last of Man's army through to the world of Innasmorn, the Mother of Storms.

Innasmorn is a world of elemental forces, where the storms are worshipped as gods by its inhabitants. They, who are themselves partly elemental, have no use for technology and have almost completely outlawed the use of metals. When they learn of the arrival of the intruders, the Men of the Imperator, they begin preparations for a war.

However, a small group of Innasmornians under Ussemitus, a woodsman, question the decision of the the Windmasters to carry war to the intruders, about whom little is known. Ussemitus meets Aru Casruel, a girl who flees the Sculpted City, where the Imperator has built a base in the mountains. Aru warns Ussemitus that Zellorian is prompting the Imperator to subdue the people of Innasmorn. Those in the Sculpted City who would prefer an alliance and peace with the races of Innasmorn are being eliminated by the ruthless Zellorian.

Ussemitus and Aru search for a forbidden land far in the west of Innasmorn, which is said to contain ancient powers. They fear that Zellorian will seek out these powers and attempt to harness them in his new thirst for control. With the help of Quareem, a renegade Windmaster, Zellorian attempts to release the storm-of-the-dark, terrible destructive forces chained by the gods of Innasmorn, but Ussemitus and his companions enlist the help of the Windmasters and thwart Zellorian's ambitions.

As the shadow of a new war threatens to embroil Man on Innasmorn, the victorious Csendook declare their own Crusade against Mankind ended. A Supreme Sanguinary is appointed, Auganzar, and he is given the task of subduing the last surviving Men in the original world cycle. Auganzar creates gladiatorial schools, where Men are trained as *moillum*, human gladiators who have exchanged their freedom for service to the Csendook. They perform in the Games and are used in hunting down their own fellow Men who will not capitulate, for which the *moillum* are well rewarded.

But Auganzar is obsessed with the belief that the Imperator Elect is still alive and that somehow he has evaded the Csendook and achieved the unthinkable, breaking through the very fabric of the world cycle to whatever lies beyond. When the Csendook military rulers, the Garazenda, learn that Auganzar may be seeking the Imperator Elect, some of them, led by the Marozul, Zuldamar, embark on a secret plot to assassinate him, as they have no desire to renew the costly Crusade.

Auganzar sends one of his loyal commanders, Vorenzar, to the world of Eannor, where it is believed by most Csendook that the Imperator Elect perished along with Zellorian and his principal supporters. But Vorenzar is charged by Auganzar with searching for any trail that might lead to the Imperator: he is told to find him at any cost.

Using an Opener, one of the Csendook sub-races bred for the creating of gates between worlds, Vorenzar finds a way through to Innasmorn, aided by a strange, ghost-like guide that promises him power. With a handful of survivors from the carnage of the Crossing, Vorenzar hears of and searches for a land in the far west of Innasmorn that is said to contain absolute power, the World Splinter.

Meanwhile, Ussemitus and his companions also journey to the lands of the west in search of the fabulous land, knowing that Zellorian will be seeking its powers for his own ends. The gliderboat of Ussemitus is pursued by another similar craft, the quasi-human death machine, a black gliderboat, created by Zellorian.

Ultimately Ussemitus and his companions reach the World Splinter, an immense fragment of a lost world of power, and in a grim struggle defeat Vorenzar and his minions and turn aside the corrupt power of the black gliderboat. The dark powers that Innasmorn once chained are now embroiled in the conflict, using the evil in Vorenzar and in Zellorian's terrible servant to release a Malefic, a nightmare force that prepares to unleash the old powers of the night.

As Ussemitus prepares to defend Innasmorn from the ravages of these forces, Zellorian determines to crush the remaining resistance to his control of the Imperator Elect. He foils a plan of Consul Pyramors to get rebel aid to the outlawed Gannatyne, and reveals to Pyramors that his lover, Jannovar, is not dead as he thought, but alive in the old world cycle they have left.

Zellorian sends Pyramors back to Eannor in exchange for the safety of his rebels. As he travels through the gate between world cycles, Pyramors meets an Accrual, a parasitic being that feeds on the blood and sacrifices that create gates. The Accrual promises Pyramors a return to Innasmorn if he acquires sacrifices for it.

On Eannor, Pyramors is captured by servants of the Csendook Marozul, Zuldamar, and his presence is kept a secret from those who serve Auganzar. Zuldamar's Csendook persuade Pyramors to help them in the assassination attempt on Auganzar, in return for which they will find Jannovar.

Pyramors progresses through the gladiatorial schools, the warhalls, preparing for the Testament, the ultimate gladiatorial games held on the Warhive, where he will have the chance to kill Auganzar. While he moves upward through the system, Pyramors is hunted by Auganzar's servants, Zemaal, masters of the hybrid tigerhounds. He is also being searched for by a spectral, a spirit being of Innasmorn, sent to the world cycle by Ussemitus.

Helped by Jannovar, Pyramors triumphs at the Testament, but before he can destroy Auganzar, is forced to flee with Jannovar down into the depths of the Warhive. They find their way back to Eannor and the zone of sacrifice, readying for a return to Innasmorn, but are confronted by Auganzar. A bargain is struck : in exchange for the secret of the way to Innasmorn, Auganzar agrees to let Pyramors warn his allies that the Csendook are coming. Auganzar seeks only the Imperator Elect and Zellorian. He gives Pyramors six months to take his allies to safety.

And on Innasmorn the armies of Vittargattus and Ondrabal are about to unleash the storms of Innasmorn upon the Sculpted City. Ussemitus and his allies seem powerless to prevent wholesale chaos.

BOOK ONE

WAR WOLVES

1

THE RENEGADES

Silence and darkness.

They were one, like the great emptiness before time, before the birth of the first world. Complete and utter, infinite. Ussemitus was barely conscious of himself within it, like a lost thought, in danger of being smothered by the infinity that surrounded him. Used as a lens for the powers within the World Splinter, he had focused the Mother's power, directing the course of the servant spectrals out beyond this place, beyond Innasmorn itself, to Eannor and further, to the Warhive.

The first spectral he had sent was lost, damaged in the arenas of the Csendook world, absorbed somehow into the sword of their Warlord, Auganzar. But the other had succeeded in its task and guided Pyramors and the girl, Jannovar, back through the bloody path between world cycles to Innasmorn. There was terrible danger on this path: the blood-hunger of the Accrual, the monstrous parasitic being that stalked the path. It was aware of Pyramors, and what had been promised it. But the spectral had evaded it.

Even so, Ussemitus felt his own powers drained, his mind and body weak, in need of long rest. Somehow he had brought Pyramors back, but only just. He would have brought him here, to the World Splinter itself, to safety, to a haven where he could prepare him for what was to come. But the energy of the spectral was all but burned up. In desperation, a gate had been opened, somewhere far short of these western lands: in the mountains, east of the Sculpted City. There, at least, there should be a degree of safety from Pyramors's enemies, and possibly a way to the rebels that had fled the city.

But for now, Ussemitus had fallen again into the exhausted sleep, deep down in the womb-like retreat of the World

3

Splinter, where fresh power could be tapped, pumped into him. He had no contact with Pyramors. There was no way that he could offer him further help. Not yet.

The dark closed in. The Mother gave him deep rest: there were so many things he must do for her if he were to fulfil the destiny she had planned for him. But she felt a tremor of unease. There was something within him, a fierce will, that would wake with him, and question. Would he accept the answers?

They had been travelling through the rugged mountains for almost two months. At first they had no real idea where they could be, but Pyramors calculated that they were in the eastern mountains, north and east of the Sculpted City. The spectral that had guided them so heroically through the paths of the Accrual's lair, had not been able to take them further, to whatever destination it had wanted to find. When its energy had been spent, it dissolved into the air as if it had never been. With it had gone all hope of contact with whatever controlled it.

Pyramors found it difficult to control his frustration. This was Innasmorn, in a totally different world cycle to Eannor, yet he was countless miles away from the city. But Jannovar was thrilled to be free of Eannor and the Csendook worlds, and said so repeatedly. She knew the urgency of Pyramors's quest, but to be here was, to her, like a part of a dream she had never expected to fulfil. She did nothing to hold back their journey, but she would have been perfectly content to remain with him in these mountains, alone and wrapped up in the love that had grown between them. She could never be the woman who had once been his lover, her own sister – Jannovar, whose name she had taken, and which she would always insist on keeping.

Pyramors came through the tangle of undergrowth as lithely and as silently as a cat. Strapped to his shoulder was the recently slain carcass of a creature not unlike a young buck deer. They were mercifully plentiful in this part of the mountains, and he and Jannovar had been able to eat well.

He parted the branches in front of him to see the rock pool. It was one of the most suitable places they had found since beginning their trek through the mountains, naturally sheltered from predators by the rock wall behind it and the drop down to the valley below, with tightly packed copses on either side. The pool was fed by a tumbling stream that ran out at its far end as an overspill and dropped in a fine spray to the lands below.

Pyramors smiled. Jannovar had stripped off her clothes and bathed in the icy pool. Now, with the sun at its zenith, she was standing on a smooth rock at the edge of the pool, her hair flung back. She twisted it to wring the water from it, the sunlight gleaming on her naked body.

Pyramors drew in his breath. He knew that body now, every line of it, its texture. So like the Jannovar that had been, and yet not her. He accepted it now. They were not the same. At first he had made her a substitute, and she had encouraged it. But they learned quickly that it would be impossible to persist in this illusion. She must be loved for who she was.

Looking at her now he knew that he loved her, not as her sister. Their time in these mountains had opened a new way for him. Though his life was mapped out ahead of him, his time not his own, she was an intrinsic part of it. Did she understand? Could he ever make her believe that, although his past could never be wiped away, she meant so much to him now? It had taken him a long time to realise it himself.

He slipped from the bushes, confronting her with a grimace as if he were a bandit.

She gasped, not having heard him approach, and almost tumbled back into the waters.

He was beside her at once, arms about her, laughing. He bent to her and kissed her, and for a long moment they clung to each other above the valley.

'A beautiful creature like you should take more care,' he laughed softly. 'If you were attacked in such a remote place,

5

who would come to your aid?'

Her arms tightened about him. 'Then I'm safe from attack, now that you've arrived?'

'That isn't what I said.' He kissed her again, but a moment later his head jerked up.

She knew at once that something was wrong. She had come to understand and trust his uncanny sense of hearing. He gestured to her clothes and she bent down to them, dressing swiftly while he dropped the carcass and slipped his sword from its sheath. She knelt among the rocks, eyes scanning the bushes around them and the rocks above. She saw nothing.

Pyramors had noticed a subtle change in their surroundings: she saw him tense. He held his blade ready. Were there men in these forests?

'D'you have a name, fellow?' came a gruff voice.

Pyramors did not react, but his pulse throbbed. The man had spoken in his own tongue. He was no Innasmornian.

'There are half a dozen arrows aimed at your chest, fellow. Spit out your name,' came the voice.

'Pyras,' said Pyramors, using the alias he had used among the Csendook.

'Never heard of yer. Who d'ya serve?'

Pyramors knew from the man's tone that he was not one of the Imperator Elect's guard, nor part of any unit of Zellorian's. He must be one of the rebels. But he had to be sure.

'Myself.'

'What about our illustrious Imperator?'

'I love him as deeply as you do.'

There was silence for a moment, and then the first of the branches were pulled apart. A weatherbeaten face poked through, the man's beard thin and ragged, his eyes as sharp as a hunting bird's.

The man grunted as if he recognised Pyramors but could not place him. It would be true of many of the rebel soldiery, who would never have met the Consul or been close to him. The man's attention strayed to the girl among the rocks.

Behind him another warrior emerged. 'Pyras my arse,' he said under his breath, his own face splitting in a grin. 'It's Pyramors.'

Pyramors knew him at once. It was Lascor, one of the soldiers from the Sculpted City whom he had helped to escape.

Lascor came forward, bowing. His wide grin suddenly changed as he straightened. 'Sire, I must apologise. For myself and for Kelwars here. Our life in the mountains has roughened our tongues.'

Pyramors nodded, though he did not mask his relief. He studied the two men critically. Lascor was of medium build, as fit and muscled as any of the *moillum* Pyramors had left on Eannor, his face clean-shaven and deeply tanned. There was something in his manner that spoke of his freedom, something that was missing in a *moillum*, as though he had been born to this terrain.

Kelwars, whose smile had become an unwitting scowl, was much the leaner of the two men, his chest thick with hair, his arms bare but tattooed exotically. The bow slung over his shoulder looked as if it would take two ordinary men to draw it, and his hands were scarred and calloused.

'How far is the city?' said Pyramors.

Lascor was puzzled by the question. Pyramors guessed that he would have assumed Pyramors had come from the Sculpted City. But the warrior pointed across the valley to the next range of peaks. 'Fifty miles or more.'

'And Gannatyne?'

Lascor gestured back beyond the woods. 'Ten or so. In the fortress of Starhanger. But it's not safe to go there. Zellorian has strengthened its defences.'

'I've arrived here by a somewhat tortuous route,' Pyramors told them. 'All of which I will explain in good time. Who commands you? Are you directly under Jorissimal?'

Lascor nodded. 'Yes, sire. He controls all our units. Sire, have you left the city altogether?' He glanced at Kelwars, but the latter looked away, as though uneasy.

'I have. It is no longer safe for me, nor for any of our sympathisers. Zellorian is conducting searches designed to destroy all who oppose the Imperator Elect.'

7

Kelwars was listening, but his eyes could not keep from Jannovar, who had risen up from her place of hiding. She tossed her head, freeing her hair of more water, unaware of how stunning she looked.

'This is Jannovar,' said Pyramors, holding out his hand to her, though his eyes remained fixed on the two men. They both saw the challenge in them, as if Pyramors expected them to comment.

Both Lascor and Kelwars inclined their heads as Jannovar took Pyramors's hand, but Pyramors could see the sudden tension in them. Her presence here would undoubtedly pose questions, if not to them then certainly to their stern leader. But maybe they would not know about Jannovar, and what had occurred on Eannor at the time of the Crossing. Possibly her name might mean nothing to any of them. Better if it did not.

'A pleasure to meet you, my lady,' said Lascor.

'Her father was an Ekubal,' said Pyramors. 'So you will accord her the respect that noble house is due.'

'But of course, sire,' said Lascor, and both he and Kelwars again inclined their heads.

Pyramors casually picked up the carcass of the creature he had slain and slung it over his shoulder, sheathing his sword. 'Will you take us to Jorissimal?' It was an instruction, not a request, and the men recognised it.

If they were curious, they kept their feelings to themselves, but the power of Pyramors was known to them, and their men, all of whom showed their delight at having the Consul among them, knowing that he was Gannatyne's strongest ally, the centre of the rebellion.

As the party made its way up through the forest, Pyramors asked for reports, and Lascor brought him up to date on their situation. Apparently there were a number of rebel nests, places hidden high in the mountains where patrols from Gannatyne's prison could not find them. Zellorian's guards spent as little time out of the garrison as they could, knowing that it was secure from any attacks. It seemed unlikely that Gannatyne could be freed. No one had been able to get into the garrison to find out anything about him although word from the Sculpted City had filtered back to the rebels that he was alive, living the life of a hermit within his prison. Lascor explained that the Sculpted City had fallen silent for some months and that there had been no fresh escapes, which seemed strange. He wondered if the rebellion there had ended somehow.

Pyramors was reluctant to say much about it.

Lascor told him that Jorissimal was undecided as to what to do. Should he make an attempt on the garrison and free Gannatyne if at all possible? If he succeeded, it would mean that more of the men of the Sculpted City would rally to the rebellion. Or should the rebels use their strength to help others out of the Sculpted City? Jorissimal had decided it must be one thing or the other: the rebels were becoming exasperated at the lack of decision.

'It's our families,' said Lascor. 'Many of us have wives, children, in the Sculpted City. They cannot be safe. We have always assumed Zellorian would not dare take action against them. He'd only be fuelling the rebellion, would he not? But at the moment it seems as if the rebellion is at a standstill.'

Pyramors listened to all that was said, encouraging the rebels to speak openly. He did not speak his own mind, offered no solutions, but promised them that when he sat down with Jorissimal, something positive would be done.

Out of hearing of the Consul, Kelwars spoke softly to a companion. 'The whispers I hear speak of betrayal. That Pyramors himself ended the rebellion in the city. Guard your back, Tennegar, and watch every shadow from now on.'

They sat alone, looking out from the high place at the mountains, the twilight glow beyond them. In the camp below them there was little sound, and the fires were carefully shielded. Pyramors had to remind himself that this was Innasmorn, an alien world, a world of other races, beings who were outside the wars of man. But how long could they remain so?

Jorissimal sat with him, equally thoughtful after their long, private talk. He was a sound warrior, a man in his early fifties who had seen considerable action in the Csendook wars, and Pyramors would trust him with his life. But even Jorissimal had frowned at the news his Consul had brought with him from Eannor. He had listened thoughtfully as Pyramors had explained all that had happened to him since being sent through to Eannor by Zellorian. But he had deliberately played down the fact that he had told the rebels in the city to give up their rebellion.

'Csendook,' murmured Jorissimal at last, breaking the silence of the night air. 'Coming here.'

'In less than four months,' said Pyramors.

Jorissimal shook his head. 'You lead us. No one will deny you that, sire. But to bring Csendook to this world, this haven – '

'I have brought Zellorian's doom, no more than that,' said Pyramors curtly. He was well aware of the horror his decision would have for his people. It would seem like a betrayal. But he must teach them it was to be revenge for Zellorian's betrayals.

'Can you be sure Auganzar will keep to his bond? He is, after all, a Csendook. They are sworn to destroy all mankind.'

'I trust him to do what he promised me. But we have only a few months to save our own people. When Auganzar arrives with his Swarm, he will obliterate the Sculpted City and anyone he finds there.'

'And after that? When he has the head of the Imperator on one pole and that of Zellorian on another? What is to prevent him seeking mastery of this world?'

'He'll leave it. We'll be spared.' Because I could have had him and his Swarm killed, Pyramors told himself. I could have given them to the Accrual, though Auganzar found that out. I did not know, but Auganzar understood. How can I explain to my people the bargains that were struck? That he gave me Jannovar. How could they see that as anything but just another deceit, a betrayal? But how much do they know about her? The question burned, but he dared not ask it.

10

Jorissimal would have pressed Pyramors on this, but he could see that he would unlock no more detail than he already had. But Pyramors seemed assured. For whatever reasons, he *trusted* the Csendook. It was unprecedented. No treaties had ever been struck with the aliens before.

'Our position is critical,' said Pyramors.

'If we could free Gannatyne – ' Jorissimal began.

'We don't have enough men yet. I've not seen the garrison, but we could destroy ourselves trying to get in. We need a stronger force.'

'Then you've decided to return to the Sculpted City?'

'We must get our people out, their families. Call all the rebels together, Jorissimal. Bring their leaders to me. We have to do it soon.'

Jorissimal rose, studying the black skies overhead as though they had been lowering, intent on listening to what had been said. He nodded. 'I'll send runners out within the hour.'

Some time later, in the shadows of the cave that had been provided for them, Pyramors and Jannovar held each other. He kissed her gently, meaning to talk softly of the things to come, but she silenced him and drew him down beside her on the skins and furs. They made love gently, forgetting for a brief time the fears they both felt about the coming weeks. Jannovar knew well enough that the conflict would begin soon.

'You must remain here,' he told her at last. 'You have endured enough terrors with me.'

She would have argued, would have told him she would gladly remain with him even at the head of his warriors, but she knew him well enough to know that it would be pointless. He would not take her. She had known the moment would come.

'Is it to be soon?'

'The leaders will gather. I'm taking them to the Sculpted City. We have to bring our people out, even though Zellorian may believe the rebellion to be over. Even though he no longer persecutes them, they will not survive the coming of Auganzar.'

She shuddered in his arms. She would never forget the terror of the zone of sacrifice on Eannor, the confrontation with the Supreme Sanguinary. She could never share Pyramors's trust of the alien warlord.

'But it will end,' he avowed. 'Then our lives will be our own. There'll be no more hiding, no more slavery.'

Again she kissed him, holding him with a barely concealed desperation. They loved again, until the dark, brooding stillness of Innasmorn drew over them both.

2

VOICE OF THE NIGHT

The two men stood on a balcony that overlooked the city. As twilight fell, darkening the mountains that pressed close to the very walls, lights blazed in the streets below. Innasmorn, with its strange winds and temperamental storms, had made the citizens cautious. They had no liking for ambiguous shadows or for the darkness of this world's night. And in the Sculpted City there were other reasons for a man to be wary of the silent hours.

Both men were dressed in the robes of the Consulate, white and flowing, though they were ready to make for their homes and their families, where they would be glad to put off the responsibilities of their posts for another night. But they could not slough off their concerns so easily.

Inevitably, as they looked at their city, they turned to stare at the rock wall that rose up from its eastern extremity, the wall that was the beginning of another range, rising sheer to the clouds. There were buildings cut into its base, for the city had been cleverly constructed within the valley, using as many natural features as possible. But there were no lights in those buildings, and in the face of the mountain the openings were unlit, as though they might be the caves of huge bats or other aerial creatures. Occasionally something seemed to pass there, insubstantial as a shadow, and both the Consuls frowned in thought. Somewhere high up within that rock wall, the Prime Consul worked on whatever new design he had for the future of the city. While in the palace, a fortress that rose up in the heart of the city, dominating it in a tradition that went back to the remotest beginnings of man's history, the Imperator Elect and his immediate servants thrived, careless of Zellorian's work and the city's needs.

The first of the two Consuls, Tremazon, shook his head in an exasperated way. 'Innasmorn is not a haven, Gratello.

13

It has become a prison.'

Gratello, the elder of the two by a dozen years, looked about him cautiously, although there was no one likely to be near them in this private place. He ran scrawny fingers through his white hair. 'You're beginning to sound like one of Gannatyne's supporters,' he replied with a nervous laugh.

Tremazon grunted. He was in his mid forties, though the events on Eannor, the Crossing and the settling on Innasmorn had taken a premature toll. 'I'm not a young man. I've had my fill of wars.'

'You think Zellorian plans war? But surely the so-called rebellion is over.'

'We're his fools, Gratello. His fodder.'

'Have you only just begun to realise?'

'Of course not. But I've never thought rebellion sensible, not while Zellorian holds such power.'

'But you do now?'

Tremazon looked closely at his companion. They had been friends for many years. But no one spoke of rebellion, treason, without putting his life at stake. Zellorian ruled this city. It was easy to lose a friend, no matter how old, when one courted rebellion.

'I have tolerated many things, even the casting out of strong men like Gannatyne, for the good of the city. For the safety of my own family.'

'Judgements we have all had to make,' agreed Gratello.

'But we are not free men.'

Again Gratello looked about him. 'You know what you are saying?'

Tremazon nodded to the far rock wall, the towering fist of Zellorian's power. 'What does he do there? What control do the Consulate have? None! The Imperator is quite content to revel in his freedom here. He does nothing but amuse himself. He has never had so much freedom. Affairs of state no longer matter to him. They are left to the Consulate, or rather, to select members. What responsibilities do you and I have now? Duties that could be performed by clerks! We are on the Consulate to govern, Gratello. Not to organise the building of houses! To supervise the storing of grain!'

14

'Not all of the Consulate have such minor duties.'

'No. They do not. Some Consuls have grown greatly in power. Men who have no business being on the Consulate at all. How can we possibly tolerate the likes of Onando? That little pig of a man! He would sell his own mother if it meant another step closer to Zellorian.'

'He spends much time with the Prime Consul, as do others who are as uncouth and unsuitable,' Gratello agreed.

'I regret my past weakness,' Tremazon told him abruptly. 'I acted from cowardice – '

'We all have our people to think of – '

Tremazon glared at him. 'No. We should have had more spine.'

Gratello drew in his breath. 'Tremazon, we must trust each other. If we speak our minds fully on this matter – '

'Betrayal is death. If you spoke of this to Zellorian's supporters, I am already marked.'

In the light from the brands below, Gratello's face was glistening, a sheen of perspiration coating it. They were toying with fire. But Gratello could not believe Tremazon had come to test his faith: he could not really be one of Zellorian's fools, seeking to trap him.

'I'm with you, you know that.'

Tremazon breathed a sigh of relief. He could see that his words had frightened his old friend. 'We've trod the safe path for long enough. It's no longer safe. You know that Gannatyne has allies in the city?'

'Even now? Well, I had guessed as much. But since Consul Pyramors left us, there have been few reports of men slipping away into the mountains. If there is insurrection, it is well hidden.'

'Have you talked to any of the other Consuls?'

Gratello paled. 'No! It is dangerous.'

'We may have to now. There *must* be others like us, who secretly long to bring Zellorian down. Not those who we suspect of being Gannatyne's allies, as Pyramors was, but others who have never dared even to whisper their misgivings. We must find them, Gratello, whatever the dangers.'

Gratello dabbed at his face. The night had become oppressive. 'You're right, of course. We must find them.'

As he took his leave of his friend, he heard him speaking as if to the strange night air of this world. One word still hung in the air and seemed to drift back to him. Prison. How many more were there like Tremazon who had not dared even to breathe their loathing of the Prime Consul?

High above the tower where the two Consuls had secretly spoken to each other, the wall of the eastern range rose up, a dark threat above the city, a symbol of the power of the man who roamed its inner passages and complex mazes, constructions that his arts had built for reasons he alone knew. No one came here to these upper bastions apart from his most trusted warriors and servants, creatures who were utterly bent to his will. There was no question of their lack of faith; they revelled in his power, their own lusts and greed.

Zellorian had not slept for many nights. He sat in his wide central room, staring at the huge charts that were spread out on the marbled floor before him. His gliderboats had been far across the skies of this alien world and had brought back to him the fragments of knowledge that had enabled his cartographers to make some sense of the lands of Innasmorn, though there were countless gaps in the picture.

Always the World Splinter beckoned him. A huge source of power, closed in and dangerous, it mocked him across the vast wastes of a world. He would assault it, raid its treasures. When he was properly prepared. His fleet was growing: Wyarne, the Artificer whose constructive powers were second to none, worked incessantly on refining and enlarging the fleet. Surely the moment would soon come when the World Splinter could be taken.

Zellorian slumped back in the carved chair, hand over his eyes. His head roared with inner sound, the darkness at the back of his thoughts heaving like a sea, the waves rising and falling urgently, as though they would break on the shores of his consciousness, revealing to him whatever secrets they

16

held, the shapeless thoughts he had only glimpsed in his dealings with the powers of this diabolic world. Mother of Storms? Of nightmares.

One of the uneasy thoughts rose up from the murk and would not be shut out. Its features shaped themselves from the black foam. Zellorian recoiled in surprise, but he could not dispel the vision, even by opening his eyes. It hovered before him like a mist.

The air in the chamber trembled, then began to spin. Zellorian made to rise from the chair, but the force of the air held him down. It was as though a wind had entered the room, spinning and rising in pitch, though the chamber was buried deep in the heart of the mountain.

In the centre of the chamber, above the outspread charts, the face from his inner vision formed. It writhed as though unseen hands pulled at it, twisting it, moulding it, and the eyes were filled with pain and then with fury, with hatred. He knew them, as he had known them for months. They were a curse, a haunting, unavoidable, following him down into his dreams, and now, it seemed, back from them.

Vymark.

He had been a warrior, one of his best. But he had been crippled in the Dhumvald, and after that the best of him had been used by Wyarne to create a gliderboat with terrible powers, powers that Zellorian had controlled from here. But something darker had fused itself with the gliderboat, a power too great for Zellorian to control. And that power had taken over.

For a moment it was Vymark, the former warrior who stood before Zellorian. He might have been alive, resurrected and restored. The Prime Consul gaped. Could the power of Innasmorn have done this? This was flesh and blood, real.

'Do you know me, master?' said Vymark. It was his voice, every syllable perfect. He stood arrogantly, with a confidence that Zellorian recognised.

Zellorian rose. 'You are whole?'

But to his horror, Vymark shook his head and laughed, though this was no familiar sound. It grated, became a

17

horrible mockery of laughter. Vymark's face again began to change, as did his body, rippling and undulating, stretching, becoming something other than flesh, a machine, a dark and sleek craft.

'Is this not what your arts did to me, master?' said the voice of Vymark within Zellorian's mind. It was true, for this was the gliderboat that Wyarne had created – the craft that had flown far to the western lands, only to be smashed from the skies by the storms of Innasmorn over Shung Nang.

'Destroyed, you assumed?'

Zellorian had no need to answer. The thing before him read his thoughts, plucked answers from them at will.

Again the air trembled, and this time one of the gliderboat's wings altered dramatically, becoming something that resembled the claw of a giant bird of prey, a savage instrument of torment. It reshaped itself in an instant, the whole craft squeezing up into darkness that spread to become a warrior again.

Zellorian gasped in horror, recognising that this was no longer Vymark. Far taller, stockier, it wore the black armour of the hated enemy. *Csendook.* The war helm formed itself, a symbol of the power and indomitability of the aliens. The warrior lifted its arm and pulled off the great helm, revealing its face.

'I was Vorenzar, a Zaru under the direct command of Auganzar, Supreme Sanguinary of the Csendook nation,' snapped the creature in its own tongue, though Zellorian understood it well enough. 'You wonder why I am a part of this hybrid thing before you.'

Part of it? Zellorian's mind cried out. How could this creature possibly be part of the thing Wyarne had created?

'Oh, but I am,' said the Csendook. 'You may have thought yourself secure on Innasmorn. But I came through, and I was not alone.'

Out of the gathered darkness behind Vorenzar, other beings formed, more of the Csendook warriors.

'A small party of us came through. We were guided by servants of the Mother of Storms.' Vorenzar spoke the name with utter contempt. 'The Mother intended to interfere with our race. But other powers as great as hers deterred her. Her plans were maimed.'

Zellorian watched, unable to move, as the Csendook shapes began to merge with that of Vorenzar, until they had all become one being. Flickering with power, the lone warrior glared at the Prime Consul, face a mask of livid hatred.

'You came through?' Zellorian mouthed the words, appalled.

'Oh yes! Through the world gate. Thousands of my people were slaughtered so that we could achieve this goal. The Mother brought us here as part of her scheme to destroy the Csendook race. Something that would appeal to you, Prime Consul.'

Zellorian could not hide his inner loathing of the Csendook, his ultimate dream of taking back from them the Empire they had snatched, in their lust for genocide.

But Vorenzar did not fall on him for his black thoughts of slaughter. Instead he laughed, an unnatural sound. His mouth twisted, and his body began to heave, changing shape once more, becoming a shapeless mass, a pitch black entity. The eyes of Vymark looked out from that shape, eyes filled with fresh suffering, then malice, then a new hunger. They were the eyes of a force that Zellorian did not recognise, a being from the deepest reaches of his nightmares.

'We share common goals, Prime Consul,' came a new voice, and it was as though the evils of a dozen worlds shaped themselves into that voice.

'I. . .do not understand you.'

'Oh, but you will, you will. There are so many things we must share. So many goals we must work towards. I know what it is you crave. I have tasted your desires, I have supped at the very same table. Your lust fattens me.'

An inkling of the truth struck Zellorian as he thought of the renegade Windmaster, Quareem, who had first taught him of the powers of Innasmorn, of her dark side, the storm-of-the-dark, and powers beyond it.

'Ah, you begin to understand. I am an envoy of those powers. They have been chained for an eternity. Those Malefics. But know this, one of them is free. I am its mouthpiece here.

And already I have seen so much. Beyond Innasmorn. The world cycle is a duplication of another, of more, perhaps. You, Prime Consul, understand these things. You have *traversed* the paths between them. As the Malefics would.'

The darkness throbbed in the chamber, as if it would swallow Zellorian, but he could not resist it. Like a man driven to the need for sexual release by his lover, he could not refuse what was being given to him.

'I do not ask you to serve us. You will become one with us. You will have power absolute. All that you have ever craved and more. You will restore your Empire, slaughter your foes. We will feed on them. We will use them to engorge ourselves, and the Mother will be humbled before us. Innasmorn will be ours, the storms our breath.'

Zellorian felt giddy. His mind had already been invaded. He had felt the intrusions for a long time, the seeds that had been sewn and which made it impossible to reject anything now. But the power offered to him!

'There are things that must be done if the Malefics are to be freed. Powers to be tapped. Enemies to be destroyed.'

Zellorian nodded at the balled darkness, the eyes that were not human eyes. 'Name them.'

'This city in which you dwell is under threat.'

'From whom?'

'The people of Innasmorn have drawn up their armies. Already they are in the mountains, bearing down on your city. They have many Windmasters with them, and these beings can gather much power. They have already used it to mask the progress of the armies from the eyes of your people.'

'Armies?' said Zellorian, shocked. 'What armies?'

'Vittargattus, clan chief of the Vaza nations. And Ondrabal, King of the southern tribes. An uneasy alliance, and yet both are bonded by their hatred of Man. Thousands of their warriors are camped in the foothills.'

'Innasmornians!' snorted Zellorian. 'They *dare* to bring war to the Sculpted City!'

'Their Windmasters will hurl chaos upon you. Many of your people will die in the confusion. The Innasmornians will wait until the deluge is over before they swarm upon you. Your people will be reduced.'

'I, too, have powers,' snapped Zellorian, but the darkness before him laughed in scorn.

'Does this city matter? It is an outpost, a useless gesture. Man that was is a spent force. Why should you protect this shell? You have what powers you need. You have your gliderboats, your technicians. If you stay here when the seige begins, you will suffer.'

Zellorian looked aghast. 'Are you telling me that I should *flee*? Withdraw from this place?'

'Withdraw, yes. Abandon this city to the Innasmornian rabble. Once they have destroyed it and put your people to the sword, they will disband and go back to their forests and lowlands. But you will have another sanctuary, where you will not be found. And where you can begin to learn, to create new gates. The sweet powers you crave will be open to you.'

A slow smile crept over the features of Zellorian. It was quite true. Why should he waste his energies on the last of his race? They were no better than the Innasmornian peasants. While the Malefics. . .ah, but they were so much closer to the heart of real power. To his own desires. Empathy with them would lead to greater voyages of discovery. Perhaps it would open up paths to the world cycles, make them as accessible as the rooms of a house.

'You are already beginning to understand,' said the voice of the Malefic, hearing every thought.

'How do we begin?'

'Prepare to leave,' said the voice at once, pouncing on Zellorian's words. 'Another city will be ready to receive you, a far place, where even the boldest of Innasmorn's adventurers do not stray. You will be summoned.'

The wind rose afresh, and in its coiling powers, Zellorian felt the departure of the shadow being. He sagged back, exhausted.

He may have slept, he could not say. But hours later he rose from his seat and left the chamber. There was no evidence to show that anything had been here, any dark force. But he knew it had not been an illusion. The whispers in his mind were there yet. If he summoned them, they would answer.

Outside, in one of the many corridors, he was met by one of his guards, a man whose face was without emotion, one of a new breed of creatures who never allowed his personal views to surface and who reacted to Zellorian's commands as aa machine would. Consequently the guard ignored Zellorian's harrowed features, which were ravaged by lack of sleep, the eyes sunken and dark, the skin stretched taut over the bones beneath. The lips were similarly tight, bloodless, and there was the coldness of stone about the Prime Consul, the wild look of the fanatic.

'I want new instructions sent out to certain of the Consulate,' Zellorian told the guard.

'I will despatch them with all haste.'

'The restrictions on leaving the city are to be tightened. No one is to leave until further notice. *No one.* Tell the Consulate that it's because of an investigation into a fresh rebellion. I'll give you the names of those who are to be told.'

As they walked down the echoing corridor, Zellorian spoke the names that came easily to his lips now, the names of the men who he could trust to undertake whatever instructions were given to them. Perfect puppets, their strings the strings of fear as much as they were strings of avarice.

Zellorian smiled to himself. He'd leave them all to rot when he left for this new destination promised to him.

'Onando,' he said, adding the name to his list.

'Will that be all of them, sire?'

'Yes. Oh, there is another.' Mustn't forget that particular fool. He was too old to do anything other than what he was told, and his wife's health had not been too good since arriving on Innasmorn. The old fool would do nothing to jeopardise his beloved family.

'As you command, sire. Gratello.'

3

GRATELLO

'We simply can't wait any longer, Jubaia. Three days ago I told you that was all we dare stay.' Aru tried not to sound tired, but the days of waiting, of uncertainty were closing around her like a palpable thing. The mountains oppressed her, the skies of Innasmorn hanging like a threat, no longer offering the shelter they had come to represent. And she could feel Jubaia's gloom, his deep fear of the city below them.

'Where are the spectrals?' Jubaia said, thinking aloud. 'I was sure Ussemitus would have sent them back to us by now. But in the west I can detect only silence, darkness.'

'Do you think anything has happened to him?'

Jubaia understood her feelings for Ussemitus, but discreetly did not refer to them. 'There must be so much for him to contemplate in that place.'

'And Pyramors? Can the spectral really bring him back from Eannor?'

Jubaia shrugged in the darkness. 'I cannot say, my lady.' After all they had been through, he still insisted on calling her that. She wanted to admonish him for it, but she knew it was only her nerves fraying.

'Look, I can't sit here like this. I have to enter the city.'

Jubaia knew that she could not be stalled for too long. He was surprised she had been as patient as she had, her anger of earlier gradually subsiding, though her fierce desire to act had not. 'It will be too dangerous –' he began, but it was a token protest.

'No more dangerous than when you were dropped into Shung Nang.'

'Well, I –'

'Yes. You put your life at risk, little thief. There are hundreds of my people in the Sculpted City, and if the

Windmasters attack, they may all die. Come on, wake the gliderboat.'

'What will you do?'

'I'll get to as many as I can. Warn them that they mustn't resist the invasion. If they give themselves up to Vittargattus and Ondrabal, they'll be spared.'

Jubaia grimaced, gargoyle-like, in the shadows. 'Are we certain the Vaza clan chief will be merciful?'

'You go back to him and meet up with Armestor and Fomond. Talk again. Do what you are best at doing.'

'Which is?'

'Persuading,' she laughed.

In spite of himself, he grinned. He knew that Ussemitus would have been furious with him if he had known that he was considering agreeing to Aru's almost suicidal request. But she was right. There was very little else they could do.

'The best chance I have,' Aru went on, 'is with the gliderboat fleet. When the storms break, the last thing the people in the city will do is try to take to the skies.'

Jubaia gasped. 'But, my lady, that will be even more dangerous!'

'That's why you'd better come back here with the gliderboat. I'm going to need both of you when I break out. Meanwhile I'm just praying that Ussemitus will send spectrals. But the gliderboats will be our only hope of getting the families out of the city.'

Jubaia's last shreds of humour were gone. He shook his head slowly, though he could not hope to dissuade Aru from her intention, even though Ussemitus would be furious.

'Let's go while it's still dark,' she insisted.

Jubaia could feel the inner dark of Circu, her own fear of this place, this city with its harrowing memories, forcing her deep within herself. Softly he spoke to her, rousing her. She resisted him, as though she would sleep on, no longer a living entity, merely a machine. But he knew it was a facade to protect her.

'We must do this,' he whispered to her mind, probing deep down into the fear, the sorrow that also gripped her.

It will be swift, she told him. *I will not linger in that hated place.*

Jubaia turned to Aru. 'Hold on tightly. We will make a pass low over the city. Where do you wish to land?'

Aru clung to the prow of the gliderboat as it hovered above the ground. 'Make for the western wall. I'll tell you when.'

As they left the safety of the ledge, high up in the mountains, and dropped down into the darkness of the wide valley of the Sculpted City, they were aware of the night skies overhead, the writhing clouds. A storm gathered there, and they wondered if the Windmasters had already started to commune with the wild elements, the gods of Innasmorn, exhorting them to muster for the assault on the city. Aru would once have scorned such a notion, but she knew better than that now.

Jubaia could feel Circu's tension, and again she closed herself off, not speaking inwardly to him. Her fears transmitted themselves to him and he shared them. This city of Man did not belong on his world, even though some of its people were to be allies. The towers loomed up, monuments to the power of an alien nation, conquerors, under the will of Zellorian, the monster who would suck Innasmorn dry if it suited his designs.

There were no other craft in the night skies. Aru thought it unlikely that any would be patrolling after dusk. Man probably thought himself secure in this remote haven. Circu moved with tremendous speed, dropping almost vertically before levelling out almost at valley bottom level, approaching the walls of the city as if she would smash into them. Jubaia and Aru clung tightly to the craft, their eyes streaming, the wind almost forcing the breath from their bodies.

'Slow down,' Aru tried to shout, but the words were flattened in the rush of air.

The gliderboat swooped up and over the wall, but if there had been knights on patrol, they would have seen only a shadow, a cloud. Within the city, the craft slowed, arcing round and dropping to the level of the towers and parapets. Aru found a place that she thought would suit her, a maze of little alleys, poorly lit. She nodded and Jubaia talked the craft down into one of the wider streets, hovering yards above its dark throat.

'You'd better come back for me,' Aru grinned, then put her sword between her teeth.

Jubaia felt a stab of remorse at letting her go alone, but he knew there was no alternative. He merely nodded, feeling foolish. Then she was over the side, immersed in darkness.

Circu knew she had gone and did not wait for a command to leave. She aimed her nose at the skies and rose up at a speed that nearly punched Jubaia out of the craft.

'Do you wish to eject me, too?' he shouted, but his gladness at getting away from the city at least tempered his cry.

I'd have caught you, came the soft retort, a reminder of how she had been, but afterwards Circu fell silent again, and Jubaia was left to reflect on what it was that had so disturbed her. This city, he guessed, had much to answer for. Already it was falling away far below them, and he wondered at Aru's safety.

Armestor groaned in his sleep, about to be carved up by whatever creature it was that had him at its mercy. But Fomond jerked him out of the nightmare, sparing him from the crushing jaws.

'Come on. Up! Armestor. They're back.'

Armestor rubbed at his eyes, gazing sleepily at the fabric of the tent. The air inside was thick and clammy, despite the fact that the armies were now high up in the mountains. Fomond looked as though he had slept soundly and without a care. He grinned at his companion, bow slung over his shoulder.

'Who is it?' grunted Armestor, shedding his pelts and reaching for the water pitcher. 'Ussemitus?'

A brief frown crossed Fomond's features. He shook his head. 'No. The gliderboat. News from the Sculpted City.'

When they emerged from the small tent, which had been deliberately pitched near that of Vittargattus and his principal Windmasters, it was to see the clan chief, Azrand

and Ondrabal all staring up at the skies. The unmistakable shape of the gliderboat was dropping slowly towards them.

'I see Jubaia,' whispered Armestor. 'But unless Aru is hiding within, he's alone.'

Vittargattus turned, and seeing the two Innasmornian woodsmen, waved them over to him. Azrand bowed slightly, the least hostile of the three, but Ondrabal's eyes were fixed on the gliderboat, the craft fascinating him.

'Tell your friends to join us,' said Vittargattus. 'They'll not be harmed.'

Below the outcrop of rock where they stood, the tents of the twin armies were wedged into a long valley, disguised from the skies by their colours, pale greys and drab browns. Many of the warriors had emerged into the early morning light to stare up at the strange aerial intruder, and more than a few arrows had been nocked in case this was the beginning of an attack. But no one would release an arrow until either Vittargattus or Ondrabal gave the word. Their power was absolute.

Fomond bowed to the clan chief. He stepped forward and stood at the very lip of the outcrop, waving up to the gliderboat. Armestor was quite right – only Jubaia sat in it.

'Come down to us, Jubaia,' Fomond called.

Above him, some thirty feet overhead, the gliderboat hovered, absolutely still, and Vittargattus marvelled at the control exercised by the machine. Surely, though, this was an unnatural thing. There must be an evil in it for it to be thus. Did the Mother not warn of the Curse of metal artefacts?

'You must step down to us,' Fomond told Jubaia. 'You will not be harmed.'

Armestor watched, but he was also glancing behind him to see the gathered Windmasters and Seers. To his horror he saw Kuraal among them, the Blue Hair who had once sought the lives of Ussemitus and his companions. Kuraal's eyes had narrowed to slits, his loathing of the alien craft printed clearly on his face.

Jubaia persuaded Circu to drop within feet of the rocks, though she promised him she would wreak havoc among these arrogant warriors as she called them if they attempted to harm him. But Jubaia alighted and the craft lifted slightly, still hovering. This caused an even greater stir among the warriors, for they knew then that the strange craft had a life of its own.

Fomond gripped Jubaia's hand and pumped it. 'Where is Aru? Is there word of Ussemitus?'

Behind him the shadow of the clan chief fell over them both.

'Tomorrow we will be at the south of the valley that opens out on to the city of Men,' said Vittargattus, raising his voice so that his gathered warriors could hear him. He turned to Ondrabal. 'My brother from the southlands and I will wait no longer. Windmasters and Seers will begin their workings. They will send the storms upon our enemies. Disaster will smite this city. It will know again the Falling Sky of its birth, but this time the city will not rise up.'

Jubaia felt like a small creature about to be crushed to a pulp by the sheer force of the huge clan chief. And Ondrabal looked as though his very expression could shrivel his opponents' resolve.

'What news have you brought?' prompted Fomond.

Jubaia bowed. 'Sires, we understand your eagerness to smite your enemies. They are not aware of your presence in these mountains. Their city is at your mercy.'

'I trust this is no trap,' said Ondrabal, his voice cutting the air like a blade.

Jubaia grimaced. 'Indeed not, sire. No trap.'

'You begged us for time,' interrupted Vittargattus. 'What have you achieved? Where are the people you wished to rescue? Are they ready to meet us and throw themselves on our mercy?'

'We have not yet been able to bring them out of the city,' said Jubaia, swallowing hard. 'Aru Casruel has gone into the city in an attempt to bring them out – '

Ondrabal stiffened. 'The woman has gone into the city?'

'Sire,' said Fomond, 'I say again to you that we pledge our lives on her trustworthiness. She will not betray you.'

'So you have said,' nodded Vittargattus. 'But what does she intend? How will she get her allies out?'

Jubaia's expression contorted into an even more pained one. 'She has a reckless plan, I fear. But she understands your intention to release the storms and follow them up with an assault.'

'Even though that may mean her death?' said Azrand.

Jubaia nodded. 'The destruction of the city and its Imperator Elect is uppermost in her mind. She would gladly sacrifice herself if she had to in order to achieve that end.'

Vittargattus grunted. 'Whether she lives or dies, she will be assured of that. These intruders will die. And what of Ussemitus? His hunt for powers in the west?'

'Is there word?' said Azrand, with some eagerness.

Jubaia nodded. 'There is. He has communicated with us, and shown us something of the powers he has tapped. From the World Splinter he has sent out spectrals, spirit beings that do his bidding.'

'And where are they now?' said Ondrabal.

'Recalled, sire.'

'Recalled?' echoed the King. 'Will they not help us, or your allies?'

'It seems that their exercise requires great energy. I fear that Ussemitus needs to rest. But he will send them again.'

Ondrabal turned to Vittargattus. 'We have been tolerant and patient with this strange alliance. But now that the day of war comes upon us, we cannot deviate from our intent. When we begin the attack, we spare no one. Otherwise we risk both armies.'

Vittargattus faced Fomond. 'Well? You understand?'

'The death of the Imperator and his Prime Consul are paramount. Ussemitus would agree,' said Fomond.

Armestor, whose throat had dried up, managed to speak at last. 'That is understood, sire.' He could not bring himself to look at Jubaia.

The little thief indicated the gliderboat overhead. 'Yes, it is understood, lords. But will you permit me to return to the craft so that I can attempt the rescue of Aru and any of her allies when the assault begins?'

'It would be better for you to remain with your friends, here among us,' said Ondrabal, looking for and indicating Fomond. His distrust was no longer masked.

Jubaia looked horrified by this suggestion, but Azrand stepped forward. 'With respect, sire, I suggest you permit the little one to take to the skies once more. When the storms begin, he and the strange craft will have to seek safety among us.'

Ondrabal looked as if he might argue, but Vittargattus gave him a nod which surprisingly satisfied him. The two warriors had clearly grown to trust each other on the long march from their lands.

The gliderboat drifted down, again amazing the warriors in the valley, until it was very close to Jubaia on the rock. Lithely he leapt upwards on to the prow, turning to wave as if he had just stepped into a simple boat. Before anyone could say anything further, the craft swung away, faster than any arrow could have and in moments had become a speck among the upper peaks of the pass.

'They'll not betray us,' said Fomond.

Vittargattus merely nodded. But inwardly he was thinking of the incident of the Dhumvald, where he had lost many warriors. His entire army would have perished had it not been for Ussemitus. But that aerial craft was, as Ondrabal kept pointing out, a *machine*. Such things had always been held evil. Well, in the coming storms, who could say what might happen to it?

Aru found it easy to slip into the old ways, ducking and hiding, weaving through the streets by night. It brought back a flood of chilling memories, of her friends who had been betrayed in this city, cut down by Zellorian's henchmen. And her father, so cruelly used, destroyed. The pain brought by the memories spurred her. She slipped into a narrow lane that led between high walls towards the streets of the city, the inns where she knew some of her knights would once have roistered. It was unlikely that there would be any Casruels

30

in those inns now. But there would be someone she knew. Who could she trust?

She had to assume that Pyramors was dead, or at best, stranded beyond Innasmorn, incapable of returning. No matter what powers Ussemitus had tapped, he could never hope to move between world cycles. She was alone now. And somehow she knew that there would be little mercy from the Innasmornian armies waiting to bring this city down.

Sheathing her sword, she waited in an alleyway opposite one of the inns. She listened to the sounds of carousing. It was late and most of the people using the inn would have gone to bed by now. That left a few, some of whom would be too drunk to talk to, but others who would be gambling, a few more womanising.

Gradually the men began leaving the inn; she had been right in her guesses. Most of them lurched out, bawling at each other, staggering out of sight, some in drunken song. Others came out, arms about the women who plied their trade here, leading them away with false laughter. A few came out arguing with one another, furious at their foolishness in losing so much money. It looked as if a brawl might start, but other men broke it up.

At last Aru saw a man she remembered. He was a soldier, a youth who had served the knights, not yet experienced enough himself to become one. He was drunk, but not so bad he could not walk back to his barracks. Aru thought him a poor choice because of his youth and the drink in him, but there were no others. She followed him.

He had no idea he was being followed until she called to him. They were in a dark street, not far from the barracks.

'I told them back there,' he called. 'Don't want a woman for the night.'

Aru grinned in spite of her misgivings and came up beside him. She gripped his arm. 'You're Petric. Assigned to the old Casruel barracks, aren't you?'

'Look, woman,' he belched, 'I'm late as it is. Gladimyr will kick my arse, but that's all. But if I leave it another hour, I'll spend the day cleaning out the latrines tomorrow. You're no doubt very beautiful, but I've had it — '

She swung him round into another entry, easily manipulating him. Her fingers went up to his neck, her hand pinning his head back. His eyes goggled in amazement. He was unable to break the woman's grip.

'Shut up and listen, Petric,' she snapped, her eyes surprisingly cold. He couldn't move his mouth. 'I need your help. A lot of people will do. I know Gladimyr. He's a tough old bastard, but he's a good knight. Didn't he serve Consul Gannatyne once?'

Petric nodded, afraid to deny it. Was this one of Zellorian's assassins? But. . .didn't he know this woman?

'Who does he serve now?'

She released his mouth and let him blurt a reply. 'Consul Pyramors. But he's not here – '

'I know.'

'Aren't you a Casruel?'

'I am. How close are you to Gladimyr and the friends of Pyramors? If I know you, Petric, you are in their trust. As a Casruel, I share that trust.'

'My masters have enemies – '

'I bring death to their enemies, Petric.' She showed him her blade and again his eyes started. 'If Pyramors is not here, to whom has your master been assigned?'

'To Consul Gratello.'

Aru hissed softly. 'Gratello? That prevaricating old fool? He's Zellorian's puppet.' But Petric shook his head. 'Gladimyr said as much. But no longer. Word has come secretly that Gratello and his close friend, Tremazon, have spoken to other friends of Pyramors. They are tired of the tyrant.'

'They have found the stomach for rebellion?' she said, surprised by this news.

Petric nodded furiously. 'There are still many of us who would leave the city and search out Jorissimal and the rebels. Even though Consul Pyramors forbade it before he was lost. We would still free Gannatyne if we could. But there is a new curfew. And no one leaves the city, under pain of death. The Imperator decreed it, though it is Zellorian's doing.'

Aru grunted. 'We must get all of you out. All those who oppose Zellorian and that imbecile of an Imperator.' She released him and he massaged his mouth, surprised at the strength and tenacity of this woman.

'May I ask who you are?'

'Aru Casruel. Daughter of Mannaston. Our house and that of Consul Pyramors are very close. But we were not so close to Consul Gratello. Can he be trusted?'

'It is only fear of Zellorian that has kept him from an alliance with Pyramors. But now that Pyramors has been removed by Zellorian's treachery – '

'What do you mean?'

He found her eyes boring into his and had to look away. If he had been drunk, he was sobering rapidly. 'We don't know. Only that he was taken one night up into the dark citadel of the Prime Consul.'

'You have no proof he is dead?'

'No. But we fear the worst. And it has, ironically, brought the likes of Gratello over to us.'

Aru considered this for a moment, but decided quickly. If she was to achieve anything in the city, it would have to be through the Consulate who were against Zellorian. Since Petric served under men now assigned to Gratello, and as time was short, she would have to begin with him. 'I must see Gratello tonight.'

Petric's eyes bulged. 'But at this hour he'll be asleep! If you try and get to him, his guards will hold you up until morning at least.'

'And your master, Gladimyr? Will he take me to Gratello?'

'He resents the Consul, having been loyal to Pyramors.'

'He will remember me.'

'If I take you to him – '

She grinned, and he realised that she was more beautiful than he had thought. But the warrior in her made him wary.

'Gladimyr will not be angry with you, Petric. Not on my account. He was a good friend to one of my knights, Denandys.'

'He was murdered – '

'I know that.'

Petric felt himself go cold. Here was an avenger if ever there was one. Perhaps it would be better if he did take her to Gladimyr. 'Come with me,' he told her, and together they wound through the streets, careful to avoid any guards, though the watch was careless.

Gladimyr sat alone in a guardhouse before the gates of the barracks, having sent two of his colleagues to bed. He himself was bored, sitting back on the leather seat, imagining scenes on the wall before him, a landscape of a world far from this gloomy place. It was a terrain he peopled mostly with ghosts, for like many men of this city, he had lost countless comrades in the bloody wars with the Csendook before he had come here. Often he wondered if he would have done better to remain behind.

A sound outside drew him off the chair, and he grinned to himself. One of the last stragglers, coming home to roost for the night. Should he duck the luckless soldier, or let him sleep off his drunk in peace? He leaned on the doorway, watching the small square beyond.

'Sir, it's Petric.'

'You're late, soldier,' Gladimyr growled, his pretence at anger strikingly realistic. He had a thick beard and eyes that blazed even in this poor light. His chest butted out like a stone wall, his arms banded with muscle.

'I bring another,' said Petric, stepping forward.

Gladimyr growled another curse, hand on the hilt of his sword. 'Are you drunk, boy? This is no place to be bringing *friends*, whatever sex they are.'

Aru stepped out into the light. 'Not even a Casruel knight?'

Gladimyr blinked, not sure whether he should be on the offence in this sudden exchange of words. 'I know you – '

'I am Aru Casruel.'

'Of course!' Gladimyr exclaimed, stepping forward. 'Am I dreaming? You fled the city – '

'My story must keep, Gladimyr. But can we talk on the move?'

He scowled. 'Move? Where do you want to go?'

Petric pointed across the roofs. 'To Gratello, sir. With urgent news.'

34

Aru grinned at the youth's serious expression. 'I should think it will be in order for you to retire for the night, soldier. Don't you agree, Gladimyr?'

The big warrior considered for a moment only, then dismissed the youth. 'Aye, be off with you lad. And duck your head in the cold tub before you take to your sheets. I can smell the drink on you from here.'

Petric bowed awkwardly and lurched off through the open gate as if he had suddenly again become as drunk as he had been earlier.

'What's this about seeing Gratello?'

'The city is in danger, Gladimyr. There will be a storm, beyond imagining. Don't ask me to explain it to you here. But we must get our people out. All those who, like you, would see the Imperator spitted, and that merciless bastard of a Prime Consul of his. Gratello must get any of the Consulate who can be trusted. Those who stay in this city will not survive. Innasmorn is preparing a deluge.'

'Can this not wait? In the morning I could see Consul Amasdar. He is far more reliable. Gratello is a recent convert, and weak.'

Aru shook her head. 'There is no time, believe me. The chaos we endured on Eannor was no worse than what is coming to this city.'

Gladimyr looked taken aback by her words. But Denandys had always spoken most highly of this girl, and he had served her with real devotion. Her father, on the other hand, had been a drunkard, a disgrace to the family name he bore.

'Come with me. But first let me rouse one of the others. Mind, they won't thank me for getting them out of bed again.'

Shortly afterwards, Gladimyr was leading Aru through further streets towards a higher part of the city where the private home of Consul Gratello was situated. There was a certain amount of argument about allowing the burly knight into the grounds, but at length the house guards relented and Aru found herself inside the house of the Consul.

'He won't thank any of us for this intrusion,' snorted the principal guard. 'He's not a young man and once he's in bed, he sleeps like one dead. This had better be urgent.'

'Rest assured, it is,' said Aru.

When they were finally ushered into an inner atrium where a number of small braziers had been lit, they found the Consul, wrapped in a thick robe, sitting on a divan, hair dishevelled, eyes bleary with sleep. He was too tired to be angry.

'Whatever is it?' he grunted as Gladimyr bowed before him. 'You look as though the cursed Csendook are about us.' He suddenly paled at his own words, his age almost doubling. 'It's not possible – '

'A similar disaster may yet befall the Sculpted City,' said Aru, cutting in. She told him about the storm, the gathered host of the Innasmornians. 'I've lived among them and I know what they can do. They'll let us take out our allies. But they want the Imperator and Zellorian, and all who serve them.'

Gratello gaped, wide awake at this news. 'An open rebellion! This is a little hasty. Even Pyramors was more cautious.'

'There are thousands of these warriors,' said Aru. 'Consul, they drive storms before them that they control at will. They will bring desolation to this city.'

'But what do you want me to do?' gasped Gratello.

'Tell all those among the Consulate who are loyal to Gannatyne and the rebels that they must get their families ready. We will take the gliderboat fleet and leave the city, as soon as we can. This very night.'

Gratello stared at her for a long moment, but rose unsteadily. He pointed to her and Gladimyr. 'Then the reports that Zellorian heard are not exaggerated! And you are in league with these abominations!'

A dozen guards drew their blades, ringing Aru and Gladimyr, waiting on Gratello's next command. They had clearly been prepared for this moment.

'Kill them both,' said the Consul, stepping back to the safety of his knights. 'Zellorian will reward us all well for their traitorous hides.'

4

TREMAZON

As Jannovar was taken up into the remoter peaks to the hidden stronghold of the rebels, further and further from Pyramors, she felt more than the loss of his presence, his sustaining determination. Although he had told her she was with his allies, men who had fought beside him in the past and who would guard her life with their own, she felt a loss of security, a sense of being apart from these people. Their leader, Crohalt, was sullen and said very little, but Jannovar took comfort from the fact that he paid attention to her needs and saw that she was made as comfortable as possible on the journey up into the mountains. She put the mood of these men down to the fact that they would have preferred to go with Pyramors and Jorissimal to the city and the fighting, rather than remain behind to keep an eye on the few women and children who were in the wilds.

The party consisted of eight warriors, most of them young men, though their skills in the field did them credit and they moved over the hilly terrain with the silence and ease of veterans. At the rear of the column, two of them were constant companions, Kelwars and Tennegar, a wiry, dark-haired man who could have been mistaken for the former's brother. Tennegar was the more silent of the two, but he nodded in agreement to most things Kelwars said to him.

Jannovar kept as far apart from these two as she could, particularly Kelwars, whose eyes studied her in a way she understood only too well. He was a man who would have no true ruler, only his own desires, and she had known such men in Rannor Tarul.

'Some of us have got to look after the camp,' Kelwars muttered, out of earshot of the rest of the group. 'No dispute there. But what do you make of the woman?'

Tennegar shrugged. 'If she's the wife of Consul Pyramors —'

'Wife!' hissed Kelwars through his teeth. 'She's no more his wife than she's mine. You know who it is, don't you?'

'Jannovar.'

'Don't you know the tales about her family, her husband?'

Tennegar shook his head. 'But you do, of course.' He knew Kelwars had always been an opportunist, one to make the most out of every scrap of gossip he could glean.

'I know this much, she's a Djorganist. She was the wife of Fromhal. He was supposed to have crossed from Eannor with his family. He was part of the fighting rearguard, but the Swarms got him before he made it through.'

'How do you know that?'

'I knew some of the Djorganist troops. In Rannor Tarul, before the fighting got really bad on Eannor, we used to get men from most of the Houses in the flesh pots and gambling houses. Talk was cheap. They said they were being taken to the front line while the Crossing got under way.'

'So Pyramors is protecting her?'

Kelwars snorted. 'Oh yeah? With Fromhal dead? You saw the way it was with her and him. They're lovers, or I'm a Csendook.'

Tennegar watched the woman discreetly. She was young, her body perfectly moulded, her skin smooth, lightly tanned by the constant exposure to the sun. What must it be like to hold such a woman?

'Nothing much has changed, has it?' said Kelwars, cutting into his thoughts.

'How do you mean?'

'Well, seems to me like it'll still be one law for them and one for us. Consulate, knights. Once the Imperator is kicked out and Gannatyne takes control, if he ever does, men like Pyramors will rule us. And women like Jannovar, a Djorganist, will have it easy. We'll still be in the front line, taking on whatever this world throws at us.'

'You have a grudge against the Djorganists?'

'Arrogant bastards, the lot of them. Think they're better

than other soldiers. But it didn't do them a lot of good, did it? Most of them must have been wiped out.'

'You'd better be careful what you say to the woman. If you insult her, you'll have the Consul to deal with.'

Kelwars grinned lasciviously. 'You've got me wrong, my friend. I wouldn't insult the lady. I'd be very careful with her. If I got my hands on her. Who knows? Maybe I will.'

Tennegar snorted, looking away, but he knew Kelwars well enough to understand his hot-headedness, the impulsiveness that had already brought him more than his share of the trouble. And this Jannovar, this golden haired beauty, would be a prize worth having.

'I heard she never made the Crossing,' said Kelwars.

'Then you must have heard wrong.'

'Yeah? So where did Pyramors go when he left the Sculpted City? How come the rebellion is so dead? Why no more escapes? They used to be regular. Why? Because the Consul called it off.'

'That's just a rumour – '

'Is it? Know what I think? I think Zellorian *bought* that bastard of a Consul. And that's the piece of flesh he used for coin!'

Tennegar scowled. 'You think Zellorian kept her in the city, as a prisoner?'

'Maybe. But I'm going to find out, I swear it.'

Jorissimal pointed down into the deep trough of night, the valley of the Sculpted City. Beside him Pyramors nodded. They were high above the city on a rock ledge, their warriors amassed along the ridge, some two hundred strong. By no means enough to seek a battle with the knights of Zellorian's stronghold, but enough, they hoped, to cause the confusion that would be their real weapon.

'How well do they watch the walls?' Jorissimal asked. 'I know you've not been in the city for some time, but – '

'I doubt that it's changed. In fact, Zellorian thinks that the rebellion in the city is over.'

Jorissimal frowned. 'Oh? Why should he think that?'

'I surrendered myself to him in exchange for an end to any persecutions.'

Jorissimal looked confused. Then the rumours were true! What was this Consul planning? None of this was at all clear. Jorissimal had listened to all that Pyramors had told him in the mountains with deep interest, but had always sensed there was far more to the Consul's story, facts he would rather not speak about.

'We've no time to go into detail here,' said Pyramors a little too sharply. 'But I doubt that the knights will be watching for an assault. They will, if anything, be looking out for anyone trying to get *out* of the city.'

'I trust you are right, sire. Otherwise we will lose the best of our warriors.'

'When I was brought back from Eannor by this being I told you of, this spectral, it told me that Aru Casruel was alive, a firm ally of the Innasmornians. If we could find her – '

'I've heard nothing. We've had no contact at all with the Innasmornians. If they come to these mountains, they are very discreet.'

Pyramors nodded. Again, there had been no time to search for potential allies. In just over three months, Auganzar would arrive, and there would be no second taste of mercy.

'We go down within the hour.'

'For the gliderboats?'

Pyramors nodded. 'They *will* be guarded, though no one will expect anyone to try and fly one by night. Not in these skies. We have enough Controllers to bring them out, and we'll capture a few more.'

'How many craft, sire?'

'We need at least fifty if we are to bring our families out.'

Jorissimal screwed up his face in anticipation of the raid. 'Fifty gliderboats.' He went over the plan in his mind for the hundredth time. It was typically daring of Pyramors. Snatch the gliderboats first. Hide for a day, then return the following night when the city would least expect it. And in the meantime enough warriors would be left in the city to prepare the families for the exodus. Stars, but they risked so much! The women and children that might die in this venture! And still there was this nagging doubt about Pyramors. Why had he called the rebellion off? To deceive Zellorian? That must be the reason.

Artificer Wyarne saluted stiffly as he entered the Prime Consul's chamber, deep in the heart of the mountain retreat. Though the engineer did not show it, he was staggered at the change in Zellorian. The Prime Consul looked emaciated, his face drawn, skin like old parchment, the eyes wide and staring as though he must either be in a fever or perpetually drugged. No one had seen him sleep for weeks, and he was always moving about this inner citadel, restless as a caged animal, incapable of rest. But his energy was unflagging, as though whatever drove him worked from within and fed on limitless power. He was obsessed with the completion of his designs, the perfection of the new gliderboats and the strange warriors that would crew them. Only the very best of Wyarne's servants had been retained, the others relieved of their duties, though confined to this citadel. Wyarne guessed they would never be allowed to see the open skies of Innasmorn.

'How soon will you be ready?' said Zellorian, the question he asked every day. Even his voice had changed, shaped and moulded by the dark powers that drove him.

'Very soon, Prime Consul. The best of the craft are almost ready. The others – '

'Leave them.' Zellorian's eyes narrowed in a forced smile, but Wyarne took no comfort from it. Zellorian could read the Artificer's fears, however. 'We go to search for greater powers on Innasmorn. We take the most developed tools we can, Wyarne. The city is well enough protected. The rebellion, such as it was, has sputtered out.'

'Of course, Prime Consul. But you told me you would have new pilots for my gliderboats. I must meet them, work with them, if I am to finalise arrangements for the flight.'

Zellorian's eyes gleamed. 'Ah, yes, the pilots. I, too, have been busy, Wyarne. Just as you develop a new breed of gliderboat, so I develop a new breed of warrior. Perhaps I should introduce you to one of them. Yes, I will.' Zellorian went soundlessly to a thick hanging at the far end of the chamber, drawing it aside. He whispered into the darkness beyond it and in a moment he was joined by another being.

Wyarne gasped as he saw it enter into the light. It may once have been a man, but it was no longer human. A darkness clung to it, the face distorted, strangely angled, the eyes disturbingly alien. As it moved, uncertainly, like a wounded man lately risen from his sick bed, there was a powerful stench of earth, of rotting vegetation. But this was no corpse. This thing was alive, fuelled by inhuman powers. Innasmorn? Was that it? Had Zellorian's art plumbed the outer reaches of this world, dredged up forces from the darkness beyond the city?

Wyarne shuddered as the thing stood close to him, and as it breathed, he thought he heard the distant sound of a storm, winds tearing across a bleak, broken terrain.

Aru and Gladimyr drew their swords swiftly, standing back to back without even giving the tactic a thought. They understood their position with absolute clarity. They had been betrayed by a spineless man who could not make up his mind who to support, but who had finally come down on the side of their enemies.

'You're being a fool!' Aru told Gratello. 'This is a chance to be rid of Zellorian – '

Gratello shook his head, wide awake now. 'Possibly. But unless you could be certain, I will not be coerced. I will pass on your news to the Prime Consul. My family, my knights and I will prosper by it. If we throw in with the rebels, it is a gamble. I've no desire to take risks.' He gestured to his guards and the first of them moved in on Aru and Gladimyr.

They parried the first attacks, the blades ringing in the night air, and they soon knew that Gratello had deliberately brought the best of his swordsmen to this meeting. These men fought in silence, assured and cool, and very fast. Even so, first blood went to Gladimyr, whose blade ripped along the arm of one of the knights, disarming him. Gladimyr would have followed up with a kill if he had not been outnumbered, but as it was had to be content with holding his position.

The fight continued, but Aru knew that it could not last. She knew her own abilities and Gladimyr would undoubtedly be excellent, but there could be only one outcome.

Although her attention was fixed firmly on the blades of her assailants, three of whom were now confronting her, there was a movement behind them which they had not noticed, or had chosen to ignore. Someone else had come into the atrium. Aru caught a glimpse of his face, his robes of office. It was Consul Tremazon, the close companion of Gratello.

'It is late for such activities,' observed the Consul as he walked around the outside of the circle of guards.

Gratello's face puckered in a frown. 'I was not expecting to see you at this hour — '

Tremazon walked to him casually, as though the fight before them was no more than an exercise. If he had seen the blood on the tiles, he paid it no heed. 'There is something I felt we should discuss.'

'Can't it wait?'

'No,' said Tremazon. With a speed that was totally unexpected, he threw back the folds of his robe and brought out a curved blade of his own. Before anyone was aware of it he had bent himself and swung it in an arc that made the air hiss. Gratello's head, eyes enormous with shock, sprung from his neck, thumping down on the tiles, spinning and leaving a greasy bloodstain. His body, fountaining blood, toppled.

Before anyone was able to react to the staggering execution, a group of archers appeared in the doorway that Tremazon had entered by, and they let loose their arrows with absolute precision. Aru and Gladimyr's opponents gasped as the arrows took them, toppling them alongside their decapitated master.

Tremazon used his blade to chop at the sword of one of the guards, breaking his defence and running him through with dazzling speed.

It was done with in moments, Aru running her own blade up under the ribs of the last knight, taking joy from his death.

Tremazon wiped his sword on the robe of the fallen Gratello. There was nothing in his face to indicate pleasure or disgust.

'Your timing, sire, is impeccable,' said Gladimyr.

'It was no accident. I've had Gratello watched for some weekks. Since I first put to him the suggestion that we turn away from the beast that rules us. In his heart, he loathed Zellorian and the Imperator Elect as we all do. But he was a coward. I should not be too critical of him for that. I, too, have been a coward.'

'You have your family to think of,' said Aru, still unsure of the Consul, who had never before hinted at sympathy for Pyramors or the rebels of Gannatyne.

'I do. And my knights. I had no wish to see them ground under the heel of the Prime Consul for rebellion. I remember Denandys and other Casruel knights. I had no wish to see my own knights murdered so ruthlessly. And I admit, that is what I feared. That rebellion was doomed to such an ignoble end.'

'Yet no longer,' said Aru.

Tremazon shook his head. 'Man did not come here to Innasmorn to rot. But under the Imperator Elect, that is what he will do. Or be fodder for the latest experiment that Zellorian dreams up in his madness. Come, we must get away from here quickly. Gratello's servants will rouse the entire barracks. There is somewhere we can hide for the night.'

Tremazon led them back out of the atrium. The way was strewn with the dead, for his own knights had cut down any of Gratello's knights they had met on entering the house, and had been utterly ruthless about the matter.

In the grounds of the house, more of Gratello's knights were waiting with horses. 'My men on watch saw you enter,' he told Aru and Gladimyr. 'I guessed at once you were from the rebels. My men knew you for a Casruel. I guessed, therefore, that you were from the rebels. Is Pyramors alive? Zellorian sent him back to Eannor. He spoke to his supporters before he went and told them to give up the rebellion. It was after some fifty of Pyramors's knights were killed in an attempt to flee the city.'

They mounted the horses and rode swiftly away from the home of the fallen Consul, leaving no evidence to show who it was that had been to him and cut him down with so many of his knights. Tremazon insisted that he would be the last man expected of such a crime.

'We cannot know if Pyramors is alive,' Aru told him. 'There are allies of mine who have been attempting to bring him back from Eannor.'

'Bring him back? How?' said Tremazon, amazed. 'Surely only Zellorian can tamper with the Paths?'

Aru could feel the eyes of both Tremazon and Gladimyr on her. Of course, they would be afraid of the Csendook, the possibility of them finding Innasmorn. 'There is a place on Innasmorn that I've visited. It is a source of great power, and one who focuses that power is able to send his servants through the Paths beyond worlds. But it is a limited power. One man could come through, but that is all that could be achieved. The Csendook would not be permitted through.'

'And you think Pyramors may be brought back?' said Gladimyr. 'But that would be marvellous. The rebellion would gather real strength.'

Tremazon nodded, though his face was severe. 'If he comes, yes. But is it really possible?'

They rode through the streets, too quickly for anyone to challenge them, all suitably covered so that they would not be recognised. Half an hour's ride brought them to Tremazon's own estate, and they entered it, the gates bolted behind them. Tremazon was evidently a Consul who took very few chances.

He offered Aru and Gladimyr rooms for the night, but Aru demurred. 'We have to act immediately,' she told him. 'I went to Gratello in the hope of stirring him to instant action. A mistake, but I would now press you just as keenly, Tremazon. Death hovers over this city in the clouds. Innasmorn is about to unleash chaos.' Again that night she explained the situation, telling her listeners about the armies who were about to begin an assault that would leave the Sculpted City in ruins, its people slaughtered.

'Men are not weak when it comes to war,' she ended. 'But when the storms come, they will fall, I promise you. This is Innasmorn. You have seen no other world like it. She is the Mother of Storms, and her wrath is uniquely powerful.'

'What do you want to do?' said Tremazon.

'How many of the Consulate can you trust?'

'Gannatyne's supporters? A dozen, though they may not trust me. My support is freshly given. They may not trust me.'

'Take me with you then, as proof. We must spread the news about the storms. We must begin the evacuation at once.'

Tremazon's frown deepened. 'But surely you understand how difficult it will be. To mobilise several thousand of our people, including women and children. How are we to do it without bringing the knights of Zellorian upon them?'

'We'll take them out by gliderboat. Use the fleet. Zellorian would never expect such a trick. But we must begin the operation *at once*. Otherwise it will be too late.'

Tremazon was silent for only a while. Then he got to his feet, calling to his knights. 'Very well. Aru, you come with me and we'll begin rousing the Consulate we can trust. Gladimyr. You see to the knights. Begin with these, and spread the word. Then the families. And the pens. There are three main gliderboat pens. We'll need all of them.'

As if in answer to their words, the sound of thunder rolled in from over the mountains, like the first salvo in the advance of an elemental army.

Vittargattus looked down at the valley. It was deep but wide, and even in the darkness he was amazed at the extent of the city. It seemed to reflect greater powers than even that of Amerandabad, and beside him, Ondrabal confirmed that none of his southern cities could match the Sculpted City for scale and splendour.

'These are dangerous foes,' he told the burly Vaza clan chief. 'We will do well to erase them. Are you sure we should spare any of them? Beings who use machines, Vittargattus?'

The Vaza clan chief tugged thoughtfully on his beard. Beyond him the Windmasters and Seers were preparing for their rituals that would unleash the storms on the still unsuspecting city. 'It seems to me, Ondrabal, that we have given these people, those who say they are our friends, time enough to put their houses in order. Can you imagine them escaping the deluge this night? Where are they? Where is the retreat? Since we arrived, we have seen none of them break free of the city. It is too late, eh?'

'We've honoured our part of the bargain. Release the storms, I say. Do it now.'

Vittargattus nodded. He strode back to where Fomond and Armestor waited in the shadows. Fomond looked grim, his face lined with anxiety. Armestor was apparently as petrified as he always was, and Vittargattus wondered how such as he could have been chosen to represent the Men who claimed to be allies.

'It's time,' Vittargattus told them. 'While we still have the cover of night. I will delay no longer.'

Fomond drew in his breath, nodding slowly. 'Aye.'

As Vittargattus went to the Windmasters, Fomond searched the skies a last time, but the darkness of the gathering clouds made it impossible to make anything out. 'Our allies are scattered! No word from Ussemitus, no sign of Jubaia and the gliderboat. And Aru is somewhere in the city.'

Angry lightning crackled overhead, mocking his words. Azrand had lifted his arms, as had his fellows, and the Seers of Ondrabal called out their own invocations. Never before had such a gathering of Innasmornian masters of the ancient lores been seen.

'They'll never get out in time,' said Armestor glumly, looking down into the dark valley. 'Never.'

5

THE CONSUMMATE ORDER

They emerged in darkness, but it was not an enclosing darkness, as Paths often generated, being somehow suggestive of a great space, open, possibly, to the sky, though Auganzar felt sure this remote realm must be sheltered from any outside world. This was the heart of the Openers' sanctuary, a place where even their creators, the Csendook rarely set foot. He had not been certain himself that agreement would be given for him to come here. But after many delays, it had, though only one other was permitted to come with him.

Beside him he could feel Gehennon, his own Opener, obscured by the pitch dark, but nevertheless obviously present, quivering with a tension that communicated itself as clearly as speech. The crossing from Eannor had tired him, but it was his nervousness in this place that weakened him most. Even so, word had been given that Gehennon, banned from the halls of the Consummate Order, would not be harmed during his visit.

Auganzar was not given to fear. It had been bred out of him, he sometimes thought, though this place made him uneasy. He was putting himself too much at risk. Enemies here would crush him far more easily than elsewhere. But there were things he must achieve, and not possible without the agreement of the Openers, who united under a very powerful body, in spite of their servitude to the Garazenda.

He heard soft footfalls, and then torches were set alight, the shadows leaping back. The cavern was indeed large, its high ceiling curved and remote, but Auganzar's attention fixed on the being before him. It was not itself an Opener, but instead was tall and seemingly emaciated, its face stark white, its tapered hands equally so. The eyes were dead, as if blind, and yet the creature studied the visitors with them.

It spoke, mechanically, but with power.

'Supreme Sanguinary,' it said, bowing. 'And the Opener, Gehennon, formerly of Tsalhuk.'

Gehennon's large bulk quivered. Nothing of his past would be hidden from the beings of this dreadful place. They did not forgive, or stop hating.

Auganzar returned the bow. 'Are the Order ready to receive me?'

'Master, they are. Will you follow?'

'Of course.'

The gangling being turned silently and walked back across the hall, its long robe flowing around it as if it hid little more than a skeleton.

'A filial,' hissed Gehennon beside his master. 'The higher orders use them. For their blood,' he added, as if he himself found the thought repulsive.

Auganzar's eyes alone indicated that he had heard. They followed in silence through other gloom-haunted halls, coming before a high portal that was guarded by a number of the filials. Whispered commands from the guide were followed by the opening of the door, which glided back to one side as if on air.

The chamber beyond was large, but not so vast as some of the others Auganzar had passed through. It was lit by a combination of blazing braziers and huge candles that were as thick around and as tall as trees, their trunks embossed with remarkable art, all of it of a kind totally alien to the Csendook. Auganzar wondered how a race like the Openers could have developed their own history and art, having been artificially created, but there was much evidence of this around him. The centre of the hall was circular, set several feet down in the stone, while opposite a bank of stone ledges rose steeply up towards the back ceiling. Gathered on these ledges were the masters of the Openers, their Consummate Order, whose word over their kind was said to overrule even that of the Csendook.

Auganzar took it as a compliment to himself that there were so many of them here. There were at least twenty of them, and on the lower steps a further fifty, though these

Openers were not of the Order itself, being its main servants, the Ultimates. Gehennon had been one of them, and although he had been forced to leave them, he still retained their level of powers. He looked about him uncomfortably, more so than Auganzar had ever known him to be. There were several dozen filials around the rim of the hall, up on the level of the braziers, their empty eyes gazing before them with the interest of the dead, or so it seemed.

The gathering was silent, the air as still as a tomb. Auganzar waited patiently, motionless. They hated him and all he stood for, he knew that. But they were bound by strange powers. He would not be harmed.

One of the central Openers among the Consummate Order rose, his bulk even more vast than that of Gehennon. All the Consummate Order were huge, great gloated beings, gorged on feasts that would make a Csendook shudder. But it was necessary for their arts, for their service.

'It is Gmargau, the Voice,' whispered Gehennon. 'All voices will be directed through him.'

Auganzar's eyes again flickered to show that he had heard. He was secretly amazed that such power could exist outside the ken of the Csendook, though he had known the Openers had their secret places and gatherings. Did the Garażenda realise how well organised, how powerful, these beings must now be?

'Supreme Sanguinary, you honour us with your presence,' boomed the voice of Gmargau, his thick lips wet by a tongue that gleamed in the firelight, a scarlet serpent. There was more than a hint of sarcasm in the statement.

'I realise I am going against your traditions in coming here,' said Auganzar, though he did not bow. These creatures were the slaves of the Csendook, whether they agreed with it or not. 'But it is no trivial matter that forces me upon you.'

'You command us, Supreme Sanguinary. You created us.'

Auganzar remained impassive, aware of the eyes that were fixed on him, the intense scrutiny of the Consummate Order. 'You serve other masters.'

If he had expected to cause a stir among them, he was disappointed, though his words must have struck home. Their secrets were not entirely inaccessible, and they must know that.

Gmargau's dark eyes widened, huge, black orbs. 'There are laws that govern the World Cycle, Supreme Sanguinary. Laws that we must all abide by, unless chaos is to overrun us.'

'Chaos? Curious that you mention it. It is what brings me here. It is what threatens us all.'

Gmargau's chins multiplied as he bent forward to study the Csendook more closely. 'Surely the many years of war with Mankind draw to a conclusion. Do we not look forward to a time of peace, of development within the Cycle?'

Auganzar paused for a moment, as though he might be angry. 'You refer to the great Cycle. The laws of the World Cycle. I know that there are more than this to creation. There are World Cycles and World Cycles.'

Again, the Openers did not react visibly. Auganzar knew they all understood the reality of the World Cycles. A reality they had never been prepared to share with the race who ruled them.

'What leads you to such a conclusion?' said Gmargau.

'I have proof.'

Gmargau's eyes lidded as he turned his massive neck to look down at Gehennon. 'And has this creature unlocked such truths?'

Auganzar shook his head. 'No. But another of your Order did so. My previous Opener was Ipsellin. An Ultimate, who died in pursuit of a Path beyond this cycle.'

'As all die who attempt such folly.'

'He may have died, but certain Csendook warriors went beyond. To a world in another World Cycle, Innasmorn.'

Gmargau scowled at the name, but he knew it, and his eyes proclaimed as much. He studied Auganzar for long moments then sat back. Since the Supreme Sanguinary knew the name, he must also know the truth. 'So, you have the name.'

'Others found this world before my warriors,' said Auganzar. 'I think you know to whom I refer.'

Gmargau looked about him. There were grimaces of concern. The Openers knew their dilemma well enough. Disobedience would bring mayhem upon them, for the Csendook were terrible in their anger.

'I spoke of the laws of the World Cycle,' said Gmargau after another long pause. 'Laws that govern other World Cycles.' He ignored the looks some of his colleagues gave him. Auganzar was no fool, and would not be turned. He *knew* certain truths.

'What about them?' said the Csendook.

'Do you know of the Conceptors?'

Auganzar nodded. 'A little. There are Conceptors at the heart of the Warhive, are there not? Beings who, some believe, created the Csendook, just as we created Openers.'

'They are the Oibarene,' said Gmargau, with a contemptuous sneer. 'Mutants, corrupted by their own abuse of powers, cast out by the Conceptors, slave now to another purpose, the driving of your Warhive. They are its captive heart, the engine that powers it. And they rely on it to power them. A fitting prison, when the very walls provide life blood.'

Gehennon had already imparted this knowledge to Auganzar, but the Csendook nodded as if mildly surprised by it.

'I speak of the Conceptors, the Grand Designers, who are known but not known. They are the ones who bind together the worlds, and the Cycles. They are responsible for stability. In our service to our masters, the Csendook, Supreme Sanguinary, we are obliged to recognise the laws of the Conceptors. This is not disloyalty to you, nor is it contrary to your command of us. It is for the safety of our worlds. Should any of us, any race, have disregard for the laws of the Conceptors, the consequences could be extreme.'

Auganzar knew that here was a challenge to the authority of the Csendook, no matter how diplomatically it had been phrased. It was interesting that Gmargau had actually thrown down the gauntlet. But Auganzar had not come here to criticise the order of things. He had no reason to take issue with the Conceptors, for all their claims. 'Stability is something I welcome. It is something I would strive for. It is why I am here now.'

'Supreme Sanguinary, what is it you wish of us?'

'You have spoken truthfully of the other World Cycles. It is in the interests of my people that such knowledge is sacred, imparted to few. I agree it is dangerous. But I am pleased that you have seen fit not to deny their existence to me. The rule of silence should, however, be applied.'

'It is pleasing to us, Supreme Sanguinary, that you are of this persuasion.'

'There are other truths which should also remain known to certain parties. For example, the truth that Innasmorn exists and houses certain Men, once hunted by the Garazenda.'

The Openers were riveted. Some of them were probably aware of the truth, Auganzar guessed, but most of them would not be.

'Some things are known,' said Gmargau. But he showed no sign of being eager to dismiss any of the gathering. If Auganzar wanted to reveal what he knew of Innasmorn, Gmargau was not about to try and stop him. 'The Imperator Elect survived the fall of Eannor,' said Auganzar, his eyes challenging them all. He saw mixed reaction, much of it surprise, but no amazement, as if such a thing was by no means impossible. 'That is bad enough,' Auganzar went on. 'But his Prime Consul also survived. Zellorian, who alone represents a true threat to our survival. He *must* be found and destroyed.'

'But if he has entered another Cycle of Worlds,' said Gmargau, 'then he is unreachable.'

'Ipsellin sent a number of my warriors through.'

'And how many died in order for this to happen?' replied Gmargau, his face grave. 'How many died so that a few might transverse that bloody gulf?'

Auganzar nodded. 'Oh yes, there was sacrifice. On a vast scale, as there had been when Zellorian went through. It must not happen again. Such a price is too high to pay for entry to Innasmorn.'

Gmargau glanced uneasily at his fellows. Auganzar had not come here to say that there were to be no more attempts to breach the World Cycle's boundaries. Gmargau drew in his breath, his great chest swelling as if his body would split. 'The Conceptors are most concerned at the Crossings to Innasmorn. They have given instructions to this Consummate Order that no more such Crossings are to be made. The World Cycles are to be sealed from themselves. There have been a great many disasters in the past through the linking of World Cycles. It must cease. If it does not, Supreme Sanguinary, the entire fabric of the cosmos will be torn apart. We face entropy.'

'I am sure. Which is why I proclaim my deep concern at the activities of Prime Consul Zellorian. He already possesses incalculable knowledge. He is party to lost powers that may well provide him with newer powers, powers that could bring him back to our World Cycle. If he unleashes such things upon us, what will be our fate? Who can say that we will triumph?

'I say, he must be destroyed. I do not ask for the genocide of Mankind. They are no longer our masters, nor will they ever be so again. But if Zellorian goes unchecked, as the Garazenda seem to prefer, he will undo us. Such wars as we have known will be nothing to the apocalypse he will bring.'

Gmargau nodded very slowly. 'This may be so, but do you know that Zellorian can do this?'

'He will devote his every waking hour to it. Just as he did to finding a way to escape us. In so doing, he unlocked doors that the Conceptors themselves must have closed.' It was a chilling argument, and one that the Order could not decry.

'You wish to follow Zellorian?'

Auganzar nodded. 'It must be done. But with Zellorian's passing, true order can be restored. The stability that the Conceptors strive for will be better assured.'

'You have discussed this with the Garazenda?'

Auganzar smiled grimly. 'I have not. I have acted beyond my brief on Eannor and elsewhere. The Garazenda, like the Conceptors, are not in favour of any breaching of the World Cycle. Such breaches, they feel, are what caused the ancient disasters. It is so.

'Also, the Garazenda, on the whole, would not believe that the Imperator Elect has survived. I have enemies among the

Marozul. In coming to you with my proposal, I am putting my very life at risk. Denounce me before them, and there would be an end of the matter. They would have me swiftly executed.'

Gmargau nodded. This was indeed the truth. Auganzar had taken a remarkable risk in exposing himself. Yet did he know that the Consummate Order passed no secrets to their masters unless a majority decision decreed it? But of course, Gehennon would have told him so. Support, then. If he gained it, all would be well for him. If not, he would fall. But without support, he would have no future as Supreme Sanguinary.

'I must take a strong force to Innasmorn,' said Auganzar. 'But know this, I am willing to have the Path sealed behind me. I will not return.'

Gmargau frowned deeply. 'You would sacrifice your position, your very life among the Csendook nations?'

'Yes, even that. The Path must be closed, just as the Conceptors wish. I will be the last to breach the walls. But if I go to Innasmorn, Zellorian and all his rabble will perish.'

'And this is to be done in secrecy? The Garazenda are not to be told?'

Auganzar nodded.

'How will you cover up your disappearance? It will cause concern, confusion. Others may start to pry where you have pried.'

'The word will be that I and my warriors have been destroyed. I will leave documented evidence to show that I have deliberately disobeyed my orders and attempted a Crossing. There will be enough to convince the Marozul that I died. No one must know the reality.'

'And on Innasmorn, when you have destroyed the enemy?'

Auganzar shrugged. 'The war will be over. Those of us who survive will have plenty of time to consider their future.'

'A future without conflict, for Csendook?'

Auganzar laughed sharply. 'Perhaps. That is not the issue here.'

Gmargau studied the huge warrior for long moments. He

knew the intensity of his hatred for Zellorian, the power behind the last of Mankind. To destroy him, Auganzar might well be prepared to sacrifice everything he had. Possibly he would not wish to be a principal power in a Csendook empire that had no more wars to fight.

'We will debate this,' said Gmargau. 'Give us a little time, Supreme Sanguinary.'

'Of course,' Auganzar bowed.

'Our servants will accompany you. We will speak again.'

'Decide quickly,' said Auganzar, turning. Gehennon walked with him to the doors of the hall, and a number of the filials drifted to them like ghosts, guiding them out.

They were escorted in silence to a small chamber, cut from stone, though it was warm, lit from somewhere in its low ceiling. Auganzar sat patiently, looking at the wall a few feet from him as though it were a map on which his future was penned for him to read.

Gehennon, on the other hand, was agitated, sitting restlessly on the bare seat, wiping his hands and face repeatedly.

'You think they'll reject me?' said Auganzar coldly.

'I don't know. If they do – '

'If they do, they will denounce me to the Garazenda. My enemies, Zuldamar, Horzumar and the rest, will have my head. Yours, too, probably, Gehennon. But I had to take the risk. We cannot get through without the help of the Consummate Order. We have certain keys, thanks to the Man, Pyramors. But I must arrive on Innasmorn with a Swarm, not just a handful of Zemoks. I would achieve nothing without a Swarm.'

It was two hours before word came.

They were again escorted into the presence of the Consummate Order. Gmargau sat, statuesque and solemn, his fellows no less severe, features inscrutable. Auganzar waited, ignoring the possibility of rejection, the decision he had already made should it be taken.

'Supreme Sanguinary,' said Gmargau at last, voice tolling like a bell at the funeral of an emperor, 'we have given tongue to our thoughts. We have listened to reports from our Ultimates who have brought further evidence to us that there has certainly been a breach between World Cycles. It must be sealed, with all speed. The Conceptors will have it no other way.

Then it is death, thought Auganzar. Nothing will change their decision

'But first, you must take your warriors through. You must pursue your goal, for the good of all the Cycles.'

No, not death after all. They have *agreed*.

'It will be as you asked. Behind you, the Path will be sealed. You will not come back.'

Auganzar was very still, but as it seemed Gmargau had finished speaking, he grunted his approval. 'I am pleased that the Order has seen my viewpoint.'

'There is a condition, beyond those already specified.'

Auganzar waited silently. There were always conditions.

'The Conceptors are concerned about a mutated being that has attached itself to the Paths that run between the World Cycles.'

'The Accrual,' said Auganzar softly, but there was not an Opener present who did not hear him. For once they evinced dread.

'Yes. You know of this abomination?'

'It feeds on the blood of those sacrificed to open Paths.'

'Is a parasite, a dangerous organism weakening the very Paths it treads. It was put there by the Conceptors, but has mutated into something beyond their control. It turns its hunger outwards from time to time, having already engorged itself on the countless dead of Eannor.'

And would have had my blood, too, thought Auganzar, had not Gehennon warned me of it. The Man, Pyramors, had also warned me of this thing. 'What of this Accrual?'

'It must be destroyed.' The statement was bald, left to hang.

'This is the price the Conceptors ask of me? The price of my passage to Innasmorn?'

'It is. For the sealing of the World Cycle to be effective, the Accrual must be destroyed.'

'What must be done? How many Zemoks?'

'You wish to take an entire Swarm through to Innasmorn. You can take no more than that. It is the limit permitted.'

Auganzar nodded. 'I could not engineer more. It would be too great a deceit. A Swarm I can organise. How many will I need to deal with the Accrual?'

Gmargau shook his head. 'The Accrual has never been engaged in open battle. It merely attaches itself to the walls of the Path and feeds, like a huge slug. But it is immense and powerful. It will not die easily, and it will invoke whatever powers it can. There are strange forces at large in the Paths between Cycles. We know little enough about them.'

I'll lose warriors, thought Auganzar. But how many? Is this merely a way of disposing of me? How powerful is this Accrual? But I will have tigerhounds, Zemaal. And the sword. Enough, perhaps. But there is no choice.

'I agree.'

'Then a Path will be opened. Nothing of our agreement will go beyond these walls. We will bring instructions to you, word of when we are ready. But it will be soon.'

'That is good, as I wish to leave soon. I have already begun to prepare for this.'

'The Garazenda will not hear of this. Even though there are Ultimates here who are loyal to the Garazenda, and even though there are others who could not come, they will not break the silence. The will of the Conceptors is fulfilled.'

For the first time in Auganzar's presence, the company of Openers spoke. 'The will of the Conceptors is fulfilled,' came the echoed response, the walls of the hall throbbing to the chant as if they were already in the curling tube that was a Path.

As he left, Auganzar heard the echoes of the chant again, recognising the awesome power that the nebulous gods of the Openers exercised.

BOOK TWO
ONSLAUGHT

6

ASPHOGOL

Auganzar had been sitting patiently and silently, listening to the affairs of the Garazenda, the reports, content to contribute an occasional comment when asked. His enemies, Zuldamar and Horzumar, sat with the Marozul at the head of the council chamber, and there could have been very few of the assembled Csendook who knew of the depth of the conflict between them and the Supreme Sanguinary.

The matters for discussion had gone swiftly, with no real debate. Since the cessation of war, the worlds of the Cycle were settling, reports of Human rebellion dwindling.

Xeltagar, the old war horse, stood up stiffly and bowed to the Supreme Sanguinary, inviting him to deliver his routine report. There was yet a gleam in the old warrior's eye as he looked at Auganzar, as if he was always ready to launch out again into some new crusade, more bloody conflict.

Auganzar rose, bowing slowly and deliberately. 'As advised by the Garazenda, I have maintained close vigil of the terrain of Eannor, and the area known to us as the zone of sacrifice is carefully monitored by night as well as day. My conclusions are that this area will always be dangerous. Whatever the Imperator Elect and his servants did there had an appalling effect on the world, though it is something that cannot be adequately measured or tested.

'I therefore propose that Eannor is used solely as a *moillum* world, and that no further development of it for Csendook use is considered.'

'You do not think,' said Horzumar, 'that it would be better to seal the world off altogether, forbid any use of it?'

'If the Garazenda were to do this, my fear would be that Eannor would develop an even greater mystique, attracting the curious, the more daring. There would be those who could not resist searching among the ruins for its lost secrets.'

Zuldamar listened attentively without commenting, but he was secretly amused by Auganzar's nerve.

'The Supreme Sanguinary has an excellent point,' said Xeltagar.

'Better, I think, to go on with the policing of Eannor,' said Auganzar. 'What I would also like to suggest to the Garazenda is that we remove all *moillum* from our worlds and house them on Eannor. There would then be no Men among our people, except for the last of the rebel worlds, which are now extremely few in number.'

'Would you have Eannor a prison world?' said Zuldamar.

'It would be much easier to control Men if they were confined to one world. Though, of course, we would still use them in our cleaning up of the World Cycle.'

'If there are any dangers on Eannor,' said Xeltagar, 'then let them be a problem to Men and not our people.'

'What of the *moillum* each of us controls?' said Kazramar, the youngest of the Marozul, a Csendook who was respected for his skill in debate as well as in the arena. 'You are proposing that we forfeit the right to own warhalls? Return all our *moillum* to Eannor? Under whom?'

'I merely suggest a transfer of the warhalls. Many of you already have warhalls on Eannor. I have always been a strong believer in the warhall system. It should continue. The rivalry between warhalls is to be encouraged. It produces such excellent combatants for the Testaments.' Auganzar looked at but through Zuldamar as he said this, but the Marozul merely inclined his head.

'I have to say,' cut in Vulkormar, 'that in my estimation it would be more sensible to coordinate the *moillum*. It is more expensive and more demanding on our own Zemoi to have warhalls on so many of our worlds. If there were ever to be a rebellion, it would be far more easy to contain on one world, such as Eannor. Provided we retain authority over our own warhalls, I would be pleased to adopt the Supreme Sanguinary's excellent suggestion.'

There was further debate, the balance of which swung towards Auganzar.

'In my own capacity as the Csendook responsible for bringing the last of the rebels to heel,' said Auganzar, 'I would find it far easier to monitor the *moillum* on one world, and to select the best of them for any fighting force that would be sent to deal with rebels.'

This proved to be the deciding factor, and shortly afterwards the Garazenda agreed in principle to the redeploying of all *moillum*. Most of them were glad to be able to remove from their own estates warhalls which they were glad to own, but which could now be operated at a distance.

'I spoke of a fighting force,' Auganzar continued, once the discussion had settled. 'I would like to gather such a force.'

'For what purpose?' said Horzumar suspiciously. His fellows had noticed his quickness to question the Supreme Sanguinary on most things. Zuldamar had warned him of this.

'I wish to make a major sweep of some of the worlds where rebels are known to be hiding. As you know, *moillum* have been used in a number of minor attacks, but I am ready to select a true fighting force. I am certain that such a force, which will also contain a large core of Zemoks, will have a demoralising effect on any rebels.'

Xeltagar cleared his throat noisily. 'Seems to me this is precisely why we set up the warhalls in the first place. I am fully in favour of this proposal.'

Again the Garazenda agreed, and Auganzar was given the directive to carry out his suggestion. The gathering would have broken up quickly after this, but Zuldamar stood up, asking for a last word.

'I am, as are we all, delighted that the Supreme Sanguinary has considered his strategy against the remaining rebels and will soon be ready to begin what will hopefully be the final sweeps to end all rebellion. His success in this venture will crown what I am sure you will agree has been a superb career.'

There were murmurs of approval, though a few of the Csendook looked a little puzzled. Auganzar himself remained inscrutable.

'We must endeavour to ensure,' went on Zuldamar, 'that the Supreme Sanguinary is served as well as he can be. To this end I would suggest that he should be provided with the very best materials available to him.'

'Could you be more explicit?' asked Vulkormar.

'I was thinking of the Openers,' nodded Zuldamar. 'A Swarm such as the Supreme Sanguinary proposes will need to move swiftly and effectively between worlds of the Cycle, and along their many Paths. Therefore he will need an Opener of the highest calibre.'

There were nods of assent: it was a good point.

'I think we should appoint a specific Opener to the Supreme Sanguinary, an Ultimate at least. And one of the most respected of his breed.'

Vulkormar nodded. 'I'm sure the Supreme Sanguinary would welcome such an Opener. One of the very best the Garazenda could provide.'

Auganzar nodded gently. He dare not argue for a personal Opener. They would be immediately suspicious of him. 'As always, it will be an honour to serve the Garazenda.'

'Who do you consider suitable?' said Xeltagar.

'I have no doubt that Asphogol is the finest Opener we have,' said Zuldamar.

Vulformar grunted approval at once. 'Yes, he is excellent. Not only at his work, but at organising and reporting to us. On such a matter as the Supreme Sanguinary's offensive, he would be an ideal choice.'

'His loyalty is unquestionable,' said Horzumar.

'Does the Supreme Sanguinary approve of Asphogol?' Zuldamar called, knowing that if Auganzar were to argue, he would have to have good grounds. He would be furious, of course, knowing that his every move would be reported back through Asphogol's excellent network, which was renowned among the worlds.

Auganzar did the only thing that he could do. 'It is an honour. Asphogol will be admirable.'

They sat quietly in the private gardens, lost for a while in their thoughts. The servants had gone, the air was very still.

Zuldamar watched the play of a small fountain, seemingly fascinated by the shapes that formed and reformed in the water. But he began to sense the impatience of his friend and turned to him. 'Well?'

'Does he have him or not?' said Horzumar.

'Of course. But so far it has been impossible to get word to him. And Pyramors is the most careful of Men. He will not get word to us until he knows it is safe. Even the women are cautious.'

'Is there no word from them about Jannovar?'

'She is somewhere deep in Auganzar's system, as Pyramors must be. Word has not come out.'

'Zuldamar, we cannot assume Pyramors will assassinate Auganzar if he has no escape route. He is depending on us to get him away. Without contact, no matter how tenuous – '

'Yes, I know,' grunted Zuldamar, for once in danger of losing his composure. The assassination plot had always been fraught with danger. It may already have failed.

'If Pyramors has been discovered in his treachery,' he said, 'we must assume that Auganzar will drag the truth from him. Probably by torturing Jannovar before his eyes.'

'But he would have denounced us by now.'

'Possibly. But if he is to bring us down, he will want to be very sure.'

'So many could betray us,' said Horzumar sullenly. 'The *moillum* from Skellunda, Cmizen, others.'

'I have another theory.'

'Oh?'

'Let us assume that Pyramors has been discovered. Perhaps he has already attempted to kill Auganzar. All his associates, our spies, have been killed, or kept in the dark. But Pyramors would be alive. Auganzar would know by now that Pyramors has been beyond our World Cycles. To the sanctuary of the Imperator Elect.'

'But if Auganzar knows that, why has he not used it against us? Coupled with the other deceptions we have wrought on the Garazenda, it would destroy us.'

'I have been pondering over it. Perhaps Pyramors is safe, the plot still running. We knew it would take time. But I don't like the absolute silence. We would have had some kind of report by now, even if it had been only a whisper. What does Auganzar want most of all?'

Horzumar snorted. 'Power. A place among the Marozul.'

'What would be his best means of attaining such a goal? In my view, he would think that by bringing to the Garazenda the head of the Imperator Elect and that of his Prime Consul, Zellorian, he would become the most esteemed Csendook of our times. He would have to be elevated to the Marozul.'

'He won't seek approval from the Garazenda to attempt to find a way beyond the Cycle of Worlds, and risk being refused, possibly disciplined.'

'But he'll search secretly. And if Pyramors has the key, Auganzar will use it.'

'And this Swarm, this sweep of rebel worlds?' said Horzumar.

'If, as I suspect, Pyramors has been discovered, this Swarm is intended not for the rebel worlds at all, but for Innasmorn.'

Horzumar grinned. 'Auganzar's duplicity will undo him. Instead of denouncing us, he risks everything on a successful pursuit of the Imperator Elect.'

'But we have the means to control Auganzar.'

'Asphogol.'

Zuldamar nodded. 'Auganzar will not be able to move his forces without using Asphogol. We will have full reports of everything.'

'Auganzar must know that Asphogol will not countermand orders from the Garazenda. Even if he taught Asphogol that there is a way to Innasmorn, the Opener would not attempt to find the way through. Not without reporting to the Garazenda.'

'Exactly.'

'Auganzar will not be content to have Asphogol for an Opener. But he would be foolish to arrange an accident.'

Again Zuldamar nodded. 'And we have Etrascu.'

Horzumar grimaced. 'A minor Opener. Very limited in what he can do.'

'He has the protection of the Garazenda, as does that idiot, Cmizen. But if anything untoward happens to Asphogol, we will be told. Again, we will have Auganzar in a compromising position. If he tries for Innasmorn, we will bring him down.'

Horzumar studied the fountain. 'The day does not, after all, seem quite so dark.'

The Opener stepped out of the cell into the huge chamber that was the Warhive's centre for the creation of Paths to the Cycle of Worlds. He was a large being, like most of his kind bloated, his limbs swollen, his neck thick, his head huge, glistening with perspiration as though he had been hurrying too fast. But his expression was composed, his thick lips turned down in a hint of scorn, as though the Csendook he passed were beneath him, not his masters.

A Zemok confronted him, eyes narrowing, his own expression one of faint distaste. The Openers were obese, incapable of much physical activity, and the warriors scorned their appearance.

The Opener ignored this, his eyes opening a fraction as if to question this affront to his dignity.

'What business do you have here?' snapped the Zemok.

'Business with your superiors,' said the Opener, stressing the last word. His contempt was not lost on the Zemok.

'This is a restricted area. You want – '

The Opener pulled back the folds of his thick gown, revealing a design on another layer of clothing beneath. The twin eyes, motif of Auganzar, were emblazoned there.

'You serve the Supreme Sanguinary?' said the Zemok, surprised. He had not been forewarned of this.

'I am assigned to his Swarm. He is expecting me.'

The Zemok did not argue. The Eyes of Auganzar were proof enough of the Opener's rights. Instead he turned and led the way into the Warhive. It was a complex journey through the citadel, but the Opener seemed to glide behind the Zemok without the usual effort of his kind. He entered the private grounds of the warhall where Auganzar was visiting his warriors without thanking his escort.

Auganzar was not to be found, but the Opener was taken to a room underground, a poorly lit place with little furnishings, that might once have been a cell. As he waited, he heard the coming of another Opener, recognising its laboured tread at once.

Framed in the doorway, almost as large as the visitor, stood Gehennon. He carried a torch, placing it slowly in the bracket in the wall by the door. By its glow, his face was smeared with perspiration, his eyes gleaming.

'Welcome, Asphogol,' he said.

Asphogol nodded cursorily.

'Sit down, please.' Gehennon had never been one to rush his words. He sat himself slowly, his huge arms resting on the table.

Asphogol saw no reason to remain standing and sat. 'You are Gehennon.' He said this as if pronouncing a sentence.

But Gehennon smiled mildly. 'Banished by the Order for my indiscretions. Yes, I am Gehennon.'

'I did not approve of what you did. I support the ruling of the Consummate Order. How is it you are here?'

'I have a new master now.'

'You serve him before the Order?'

Gehennon spread his hands. 'I am an Opener. My first duty should be to the Order. But they cast me out.'

'They were generous enough to spare your life.'

'They were. And with it I serve Auganzar.'

'Do you mean, the Garazenda, of whom he is the instrument?'

'Since the Garazenda are served by the Order, I am in a curious position. I no longer have the authority of the Order to serve the Garazenda.'

'You twist words – '

'No. On the contrary, I am most careful. One should know one's status, one's place in the scheme of things.'

'What are you implying?' said Asphogol, his face a cold mask, his fists bunched hugely before him.

'Unlike you, I am unable to serve the Order. My old vows have been removed from me. I am free to choose.

You are not. You are bound by the absolute laws of the Order.'

'I am perfectly aware of my obligations.'

'Then you serve the Order first, the Garazenda second?'

Asphogol sat back slowly, refusing to be disturbed by the banished Opener who studied him so calmly. Gehennon had had a fine reputation and had been an Opener of significant skill. Too ambitious for one of his kind, though, and such things led inevitably to disaster. He had, they said, walked a very dark path.

'All Openers serve the Order first. But since the Order was created to serve the Garazenda – '

'Ah, but I would dispute that statement. Openers were created by the Csendook. Yes. But the Consummate Order answers to higher beings than the Csendook, who are no better than Openers in the final analysis.'

'The Conceptors.'

'Why, yes. They control the balance of the many worlds, of the Five Cycles.'

Asphogol hissed through his lips. *You dare to speak of the Five in this place?*'

'We will not be heard.'

'Only the Openers know of the Five,' said Asphogol coldly. 'If you have spread this greatest of secrets – '

'I have not. I have not betrayed our race. For I do respect our race, Asphogol, whatever you might think of me. I use the Five only as an illustration, to remind you that your service is to the Conceptors.'

Asphogol's anger simmered, but he did not speak.

'Unless I am wrong, you have received two instructions. The Garazenda have sent you here, to be the assigned Opener to the Supreme Sanguinary. I see from those circles embroidered on your chest that you are now one of the Thousand.'

'Yes, the Garazenda have appointed me.'

'But you have a further instruction from the Order.'

'You think so?'

Gehennon leaned forward and the table protested under the weight. 'I do indeed. For I saw you among the other

71

Ultimates when Auganzar and I stood before the Consummate Order. You know well enough the agreements that were made.'

'What your master asked was contrary to the wishes of the Garazenda. A dangerous thing.'

'You are bound by those agreements. You serve the Order first. They want the Path opened.'

'And you, Gehennon, wish to walk that Path, is that it? To go to this forbidden world. You say you serve a new master now, but it is not so. You serve the same master that you have always served.'

Gehennon leaned back, smiling grimly.

'Yourself,' hissed Asphogol. 'No one else.'

Gehennon did not answer, though his amusement was evident.

'Why should you be part of this Crossing? Why should I need you? I am capable of serving Auganzar without your help. You assume you are important to me.'

Still Gehennon smiled. 'Perhaps I am not. The Order will provide Auganzar with the key to cross to Innasmorn. But he will take me. I was not questioned when we stood before the Order.'

'It was assumed at that time that you would be used. The Order have approved my appointment only since the intervention of the Garazenda in Auganzar's decision to send a Swarm out against the rebel worlds. The Garazenda do not know the true purpose of the Order, naturally. But since I am here, you are not needed.'

'Ah, but if you take me across, Asphogol, there will be no way back for me. I'd be less dangerous to you and the Order in another Cycle than I am here, wouldn't you say?'

Asphogol stood up slowly. 'I know this: you have no interest in the fate of the Imperator Elect, nor of his Consulate. In my eyes, you are a threat to any expedition. These are views I shall express to Auganzar.'

Gehennon nodded politely. 'As you wish. I will, naturally, abide by his decision.'

FULVULUS

Auganzar studied the warriors before him. They stood in their neat ranks, like Zemoks ready for inspection, though these were his Zolutars and his Zemaal, his crack commanders, the cream of his so-called Thousand. He knew their loyalty to him. None of them would be capable of defection, and none of them would be won over by Zuldamar and Horzumar, or any of their agents. And they would die before betraying Auganzar. In them, Csendook traditions were ingrained, part of their blood, their dedication to the cause, Auganzar's cause, unwavering.

'I have called you here to tell you that we are almost ready to begin the last drive of our Crusade against the enemies of the Csendook race.'

They were silent, but he could feel their tension, the air of excitement. This was a day for which they had all been eagerly waiting.

'It is, as you know, a Crusade which officially ended some time ago. The Garazenda decreed it, and appointed me to tidy up the rebellions, to bring the last Men to heel, as *moillum*. They were certain that the Imperator Elect had perished.

'I have positive knowledge that he is alive. Zellorian guided him on a perilous Crossing to another world, a world beyond the Cycle.' Auganzar paused, letting this sink in, knowing many of them had guessed this truth.

They murmured softly, but remained to attention, waiting eagerly for his decision.

'A world that has a name. Innasmorn. Remember it, but do not speak it. It is a secret known only to my most loyal followers. The Path to this world has, in the past, been locked, but it was opened. Ipsellin, a former Opener, found a way, though many died in the Crossing. Much sacrifice may be needed. Countless lives were lost, just as they were when Zellorian took his master through. You have all seen the zone of sacrifice on Eannor, the heaped bones. Many more died beyond the portal. Csendook died, as well as Men, and, when Ipsellin opened the gate, *moillum* also.

'I had intended to gather a large force of *moillum*, to use them as fodder for the horrors beyond the portal. A shield for our passing. But I have given my word not to do this. I have had aid from a strange quarter. A Man.'

Again he let them consider this. Some of them had seen him in discussion with Pyramors at the zone of sacrifice on Eannor, where they had tracked him after a long hunt. Zuarzol, master of the tigerhounds, had been there, and was still baffled by his master's decision to let the Man and girl, Jannovar, go.

'The Imperator has many enemies. No one hates him more than his own kind. There are many Men, many survivors of the wars, who would see him brought down, together with his Prime Consul. One such Man, Pyramors, was here. You saw him rise to glory at the Testament. He would have killed me, but I offered him a greater prize, as he saw it. The Imperator.

'Now he waits on Innasmorn. He has given me the key to that other World Cycle. And the Consummate Order of Openers has given me further power. I do not need to sacrifice thousands of lives to breach the dividing wall.

'But the Garazenda are in ignorance of this. They have been told that I am about to embark on the sweeps that will clear our own World Cycle of rebels. They have appointed their most powerful Opener, Asphogol, to guide us. He, however, serves his Order first, and thus serves me before he serves the Garazenda. He will lead us to our true goal.'

This time there were cheers, and in a moment the entire company was saluting the Supreme Sanguinary. He held up his hand for silence after a while, and within minutes his troops were waiting quietly.

'Even though we will not have to face the terrible chaos that met Ipsellin and Zellorian before him, there will still be bloodshed. There is a creature, a parasite. I know very little about it, but it guards the way, and is capable of terrible fury. It is part of the agreement that we destroy it.'

Zuarzol raised his mailed fist, eyes gleaming. 'I say, let us welcome this conflict, Zaru! Let us be the first to meet this creature. We'll show it our teeth, and those of the tigerhounds!'

Auganzar smiled patiently, waiting for the cries of enthusiasm to die down again. 'I'm sure, with the force at our disposal, we can discharge this duty to the Consummate Order. But there is another, more disturbing condition.

'This opening of gates between World Cycles has done a certain amount of damage to the very fabric of the worlds. It may even be a reflection of the ancient disasters that unquestionably rent the Cycles. This must be addressed. The Consummate Order fears for the safety of all worlds, and they have deep knowledge of such things, knowledge which I would not question. Our Crusade to Innasmorn is twofold. First, we seek and destroy the Imperator and Zellorian. Before they uncover more of the lost arts and do further harm to the many worlds.

'Secondly, we must seal up the breach that has been opened. It is like a wound, in danger of turning to poison. The Path to Innasmorn must be sealed. So – we will not return. We will be locked out of our Cycle of Worlds. We will not return to the Warhive or any other Csendook world again. I will, therefore, not order you to follow. Those who wish to stay may do so without shame.' They would have unanimously shouted out their desire to follow him, but he put up an arresting hand.

'There is something else first. Many of you have families, children. We go to war, and as with all wars, we do not take our families. They remain here. We will not return to them.'

For a moment it seemed that there must be an outcry of protest. Auganzar knew that many of his finest warriors had young children that they were already schooling as potential warriors for the years to come. Bonds among them were stronger than they had been at the height of the Crusade, when a warrior might die at any time. This ruling was going to hit them hard. He saw them stiffen, waiting for the protests, however polite.

'What of your own family, Zaru?' someone called, and he wondered if this was how they would test him. If they must make sacrifices, so must he.

'They must come with us, under our protection,' another warrior called out. 'If we cannot honour the Supreme Sanguinary, there is no honour.'

Many voices were raised to agree with this, but Auganzar forced silence upon them before an argument could break out.

He shook his head. 'No. I will not take them.'

The warriors were absolutely still, silent. No one moved for a long moment, until at last one of the Zolutars stepped forward and put his swords together on the floor before Auganzar. He said nothing, but his meaning was clear. Auganzar took up the swords and returned them to the Zolutar, who bowed.

'Our cause transcends all other duties,' Auganzar said. 'None of you is commanded to follow me. But if you do, it must be on my terms, whatever personal grief it causes.'

After that, every warrior present confirmed his action. They would not desert the Supreme Sanguinary. Their pride would not let them do otherwise.

The two *moillum* circled each other warily. One, the larger of them, wore light mail and carried a long sword, an unwieldy weapon, but one which he seemed strong enough to handle well. He had almost caught his wirier opponent across the midriff more than once. The other, shorter gladiator, shifted from side to side. He carried a round shield and an elongated metal club. He seemed to concentrate on a defensive strategy, content to back-off and deflect any blows.

The battle was fought in a ring, under the baking sun of the Warhive, and a score of other *moillum* watched, cheering on their particular favourite. They had all been training, the sweat dripping from them, as it did from the two combatants. They were so absorbed by the battle that they did not hear the coming of the two Csendook behind them. They, too, watched the conflict.

It was quickly over. The smaller man turned aside the big blade with his shield, opening up the defence of the taller figure. He used his club like a whiplash, cracking it down on the shoulder of his opponent, who gasped in pain and dropped to his knees. Before he could recover, the man with the club stepped on his sword and rammed the hard edge of the shield into his mask, toppling him.

Turning, raising his club, the victor pulled off his own face mask. His face was scarred, where a sword had once sliced his flesh.

'Easy, Fulvulus, you'll kill him,' someone protested.

Fulvulus spat, noticing the two Csendook. He knew they would not interfere. 'He'll live,' he growled. 'But he'll have to quicken up if he wants to last. The women are quicker than he is.'

There may have been an argument, but the *moillum* realised they were no longer alone. They all stood, saluting the Csendook, who came down the slope to the edge of the sand arena. One of them, they saw with some surprise, was a Zolutar, the twin circles on his breast proclaiming him to be one of Auganzar's principal warriors. It was unusual for one of such rank to enter the *moillum* areas.

The Zolutar inclined his head at Fulvulus, though the Csendook was masked. 'You fight well,' he said.

Fulvulus tossed down the shield and rested the club on his shoulder. 'Well enough against these poxy dogs. I could do with a real contest.'

The eyes of the Csendook Zolutar gleamed within his helm. 'It may be possible to arrange such a contest.'

Fulvulus grunted. 'You looking for me?'

'A private word,' said the Zolutar.

Fulvulus nodded at the men, and at once they picked up their weapons, preparing to dismiss. Two of them went to the dazed victim of Fulvulus's attack and helped him to his feet, mopping at the blood that streamed from his split lips.

The Zolutar waited until the men were out of earshot. Only the lone Zemok watched from beside the arena. Fulvulus could see that this particular conversation was for his ears alone.

The Zolutar did not remove his helm, walking slowly to the centre of the arena, which was some thirty yards across. 'I am Vandarzol, and I have been sent to you by the Supreme Sanguinary himself.'

Fulvulus grunted, though the news was in itself interesting. As one of the principal *moillum* in Auganzar's elite corps, he knew that at some point he would be called upon to report to the Csendook warlord. Perhaps this was, at last, news that the *moillum* were to be used as an active unit. The endless days of training and exercising were becoming progressively more tedious. He should not have beaten Hammur so badly just now. A month ago he would have spared him the broken shoulder and the ruined mouth.

'I have direct orders from Auganzar,' said Vandarzol.

'I'm all ears.'

Vandarzol ignored the Man's attitude. He knew his worth. 'No doubt you and your *moillum* find the monotonous rituals of the Warhive tedious.'

'We're the best fighting *moillum* anywnere,' Fulvulus snorted. 'Send us out, dammit! Give us something to do with our skills. You want us to round up the rebels? Okay, let us loose. Or doesn't your lord and master trust us?'

If the Zolutar smiled, the helm hid it. 'A Swarm is being prepared.'

Fulvulus frowned. 'A Csendook force?'

'It will be serviced by *moillum*. Your *moillum*. The best, as you say. Auganzar wants you to prepare them for war.'

'The rebels?'

'More than that.'

Fulvulus screwed up his features suspiciously. Then he grinned. 'Don't tell me Auganzar is thinking about a coup? He wants to overthrow the Garazenda, is that it?' He laughed. 'Well, that comes as no surprise.'

But Vandarzol shook his head. 'No, we hunt rebels. Certain, special rebels.'

'Like who?'

'The Imperator Elect is not dead.'

Fulvulus's mouth opened, then closed again. 'I'd heard a whisper. Where in the stars is he, though?'

'In another Cycle. With the Prime Consul.'

Fulvulus's eyes gleamed. 'Is he indeed? There is proof?'

Vandarzol nodded. 'You will be needed for the hunt. But it is not sanctioned by the Garazenda. They persist in denying the existence of these other worlds, and insist also that the Imperator Elect is dead. Auganzar has proof that he lives. And he has the key to the world where his enemies have taken sanctuary.'

'Where is this world?'

'You will be told.'

'And to get to it, we transfer to...where? Eannor, by any chance?'

Vandarzol's eyes gave nothing away. 'Perhaps. But Auganzar acts in secrecy. The Swarm, and the *moillum* who serve it, will not have the sanction of the Garazenda. It will be prepared on the understanding that it is going out to the worlds of this Cycle where there are rebel forces in hiding. The Garazenda have already given approval to this action. They have appointed an Opener, Asphogol, to open Paths for the Swarm.'

'But in reality we are going *outside* the World Cycle?'

'That is so.'

Fulvulus looked away at the open fields beyond the arena. There had been a lot of speculation about the fate of the Imperator. It was mostly accepted that he had perished in a disastrous attempt to perform rituals on Eannor that had cost the lives of thousands. Rumours about a whole region of skulls, littered with bones, were rife among the warhalls.

'Auganzar would not have taken *moillum* on the expedition through the gate between Cycles. But he has to.'

Fulvulus turned. He did not know this Zolutar, could not tell how truthful he would be. His dealings had always been with Zemoks, warriors he would never love, but who were fair with him and whose word he had no reason to doubt. But this Zolutar had been sent to him because he was Auganzar's own, and here, he was the very voice of the Supreme Sanguinary. He had no choice but to trust him.

'If Auganzar's Swarm takes war to the rebels,' Vandarzol went on, 'the Garazenda would expect *moillum* to be present. After all, the very reason for your existence is to build you into a force that can go out and bring to heel your own kind. No Swarm can hunt rebels without its force of *moillum*.'

'That's pretty logical. But if you're going to try to cross between Cycles, you'll need ballast. Is that it? Sacrifices? Better to get rid of the human rabble instead of the Csendook, eh?'

Vandarzol was impressed by the nerve of this warrior. He was vulnerable, in no position to make demands, or hurl insults, and yet he was clearly not afraid of Vandarzol. Auganzar had said that he was a superb leader of *moillum*. There could be no doubt of that.

'You will not be sacrificed. Not wasted. But the Crossing will not be easy, for any of us. There will be conflict. But the Swarm will go through.'

'And then we hunt down that bastard, the Imperator?'

'That is our mission.'

'So what do we tell the Garazenda when we bring back his head? Or will they just eat humble pie and shower even more favours on Auganzar? What will it make him, one of the Marozul?'

Vandarzol made no comment for a moment, allowing the Man his humour. 'We will not be coming back to this Cycle. Any of us. The way will be sealed behind us.'

Fulvulus snorted with derision, but then began to chuckle. 'Wait a moment. I see this more clearly. A *new* World Cycle? Then Auganzar can take control of all of it. Seal it off. He has no need of the Garazenda, the Warhive, or any of this Cycle. *That* sounds more like the Supreme Sanguinary I know about.'

'No one can say what will happen after we have destroyed the Imperator Elect and the last of his vermin.'

'Okay, let's leave that to our imagination. But it sounds good to me.'

'You must make it sound attractive to your *moillum*.'

'Yes, I see that,' Fulvulus laughed.

'You must tell only your commanders that we are going in search of the Imperator. The rest of the *moillum* must believe that the Swarm is doing the bidding of the Garazenda, that is, going out into this World Cycle in search of rebels.'

'That's what they've been training for.'

'On no account must the truth escape and be heard by the agents of the Garazenda. The reprisals will be dire if that happens.'

Fulvulus understood Csendook threats. They were never idle. 'I need tell only a few of my men.'

'It will not be necessary for all the *moillum* to be taken. Auganzar has expressed a will to have no more than two thousand with the Swarm.'

Fulvulus scowled. 'Two thousand? But there are almost that many in his own warhall. What about the other warhalls? I expected to muster ten thousand at least.'

'The Garazenda have not yet stipulated that they want their own *moillum* used. In principal it would be difficult, as they have already agreed that Auganzar should create the spearhead of the *moillum* from the best of his own, the elite. But the Garazenda may yet wish to include some of their own in this new venture.'

'Still, if we're going beyond the reach of the Garazenda, we can soon deal with them, eh?'

For once the Zolutar laughed, a soft, deep sound. 'I am sure you could find a way of solving this problem, should it arise.'

'Two thousand. They'll be good, very good.'

Vandarzol's tone changed once more. 'Bear in mind that they will not come back to this World Cycle.'

'They'll live with that – '

'They have mates. Wives?'

Fulvulus again looked away. Of course! Stupid of him not to think for the men. The Csendook had given them as much freedom as they dared, and Auganzar himself had insisted that all his *moillum* should have the opportunity to mate, for life if they desired. Many of the *moillum* now lived almost as they would have on their own worlds. They were slaves, but at times they almost forgot it, they had so much freedom.

'Only warriors will go on this hunt,' said Vandarzol. 'To take women would be unthinkable. It would be obvious to the Garazenda that something was amiss.'

'If I were to select my best two thousand warriors,' said Fulvulus, 'most of them would have partners. Some may be willing to sacrifice them for this new freedom you speak of. But not all.'

'There are many Csendook who serve the Swarm who have families. You are not permitted access to the children you breed. But the Csendook raise their children as family units.'

Fulvulus could have retorted, but this was hardly the place to bring up old bones of contention. There was much bitter resentment of the Csendook laws about *moillum* children. The mothers reared them, but the fathers never saw them.

'We will not see our families again, those of us who go,' said Vandarzol. He looked away, though Fulvulus could not tell if this was through dignity or through personal anguish.

'And Auganzar?'

'He has a wife, and several children. He also has mistresses, other children by some. None of them will be taken. As always, the Supreme Sanguinary leads by example. He is beyond criticism. Such a ruler can give difficult commands, but he stands by them, always.'

Fulvulus could see the extent of the power Auganzar must have over these people. Yet they did not hate him for it. There was the difference between their races.

'I may not be able to force my men to go,' he said.

'You are to take only willing *moillum*. Those who wish to remain must do so. But you must find two thousand who will go and who leave everything behind them. They will have no past. Just as the Csendook of this Swarm will have no past.'

'Killing the Imperator is that important, eh?'

'It is everything.'

Fulvulus grunted. 'What if I want to stay?'

'You have a mate?'

'Perhaps. But maybe I like it here.'

'You may not enjoy the Warhive so much if you were to be absorbed into another warhall. You would likely be demoted.'

'Whereas by going to this new Cycle, I could become the supreme *moillum*, is that it? Or even the new Imperator!' he laughed.

But the Csendook did not respond with laughter. 'Find your warriors. And do it soon.'

Throcastor pushed aside the empty mug, wiping his lips. He missed the ale houses of the troops, but at least the Csendook kept the *moillum* supplied with good beer, wine, too, if you wanted it. Throcastor glanced across at Fulvulus, who had himself drunk more than was usual for him, though he had a remarkable capacity for one so fit.

'Who's to say what'll happen once we break free of this World Cycle, then?' said Throcastor, though he kept his voice very low. Fulvulus had not spread the word far. Only to say that a Swarm left for battle on rebel worlds. Throcastor was one of the few men Fulvulus had trusted with the truth.

'Aye,' nodded Fulvulus. 'Those of us who survive the hunting of the Imperator may get a fine chance to cut and run.'

Throcastor leaned forward. 'And I daresay slit a few Csendook gizzards into the bargain, eh?'

'You sound like a man with scores to settle.'

'I've licked arse long enough, Fulvulus. So have you. Okay, so it's done us proud here. Better off than we were under the Imperial fornicator. But I'd welcome a change. True freedom.'

Fulvulus put a hand on Throcastor's bronzed arm. He gripped until the man winced. 'That's fine by me. But not until I give the word. Until I say otherwise, we serve Auganzar. Got it?'

Throcastor grinned. 'Sure. You call it, Fulvulus. Only don't wait too long.'

8

DEATH SENTENCE

Ussemitus opened his eyes, but the darkness bathed him as surely as though he had been immersed in a fathomless pool. His body knew no sensations, no pain. Am I dead? he asked himself.

No, Ussemitus, came a whispered reply from all around him, the voice of the utter dark. The will of the Mother, amplified by the powers of the World Splinter. *Soon it will be time for you to go from here and become part of the great conflict that I have prepared. For millennia I have drawn these many threads together. My tapestry is almost woven. You are my needle, Ussemitus.*

What must I do? his mind cried.

In you will be the power. You must bind the forces. You have already spoken to the people of this world. You speak and the Windmasters listen. Vittargattus listens. Man's rebels listen.

The armies bear down on the Sculpted City. Many of Aru's people will die –

Your love for this Human girl is not an evil thing, Ussemitus, though you must not permit your heart to rule your head, the powers I will give you.

She knows that I have chosen service –

So she does. I feel her bitterness towards me for that. But your love cannot be, Ussemitus.

I have accepted that! Please, do not torment me with it.

I will not torment you. But I tell you these things for good reason. Judgements must be made, Ussemitus. I did not bring the people of the Imperator Elect to this world so that they could conquer my children. The best of them, like Aru Casruel, will become my children, too. Man and Innasmornian will interbreed. It is an important part of the future. Just as it was an important part of the past. I brought Man here before, in this fragment of another world. It was no accident. You yourself are descended from the cross-breedings.

But the bad seed must wither. The Imperator Elect and his blight. My storms will serve Vittargattus and Ondrabal well.

And after that? Once Zellorian is destroyed?

I am not yet ready to destroy Zellorian. I guided him here, and I need his power, no matter how corrupt it may be. I will use him, and he will not know, as he has never suspected the way I have used him in the past.

To what end?

Man will change, as Innasmornian will change. A new being, capable of facing the real threat to our world, and all the worlds of our Cycle. The Csendook. Up until now they have used their superior speed and strength to lay waste all before them. Man has lost his Empire to them. The destruction will cease. My new children will reverse that. The Csendook are as a plague. I have brought their warriors here, and studied them. They will be stamped out.

More are coming. The proudest of them, their greatest leader.

Auganzar!

Yes. He prepares. Let him come. You must unleash my children's power upon him that they may understand them. My will. Teach them that the time will soon come when they will no longer need to hide away.

Ussemitus mentally gasped. A holy war! The Mother meant to reverse the terrible flow of destruction that swept the Csendook through countless worlds.

This must not be! he told her.

The surrounding whispers were silent for a while. But they spoke again, a harshness in the words. *It has to be, child. If the Csendook are not destroyed, they will end all other life.*

But Auganzar will not bring war upon your children! He seeks only his enemies, the evil that is in Zellorian and his Imperator.

You are naive, Ussemitus. You have not watched the histories unfold as I have. You cannot imagine the destruction, the carnage.

If you do not oppose Zellorian soon, he may use other powers, developing them, unlocking older, far more terrible things. Have you not felt the stirring of the Malefics?

Zellorian is flesh. His mind, its powers, are infinitesimally small. I have chained the Malefics. Oh yes, I hear them stir, and groan in their agonies. They may rant. But that is all. Our war is long over. You hear its echoes, no more than that.

Ussemitus was appalled. Mother, you have been deceived in this. Zellorian seeks ways to wake them, and they hunger for him. For any vessel. They will use the Csendook, feed on them. And grow strong.

If that were possible, Ussemitus, then it would strengthen my argument for the destruction of the Csendook.

But we will need Auganzar if we are to subdue Zellorian! Just as Man must forget his feuds with the Innasmornians, so we must put aside our dispute with the Csendook. To allow Zellorian power to defeat the Csendook would be a mistake, a disaster –

I admire your spirit. You have been chosen well. But I will not tolerate disobedience.

I wish only to serve you. Have I not shown you that?

In giving up the Human girl? Perhaps you have. But there may be other sacrifices, Ussemitus.

I will obey you in all things. But let me go back. Let me shape these forces that will clash. Let me show you the darkness that rises.

Silence followed his plea; he thought he had been abandoned, that his words had caused only fury, scorn. He would become like all those other beings who had journeyed here only to be judged wanting. But the whispers began again. *I read your heart, Ussemitus. There is goodness there. I see what you believe, the dangers you perceive. Very well, I will allow you to go back. And I will watch through your eyes. Be careful how you exercise my powers. They are not bestowed lightly.*

Ussemitus closed his eyes, his strength failing him, and again the utter darkness of the pool took him and his consciousness. There were no dreams, only the emptiness.

Asphogol sat very still in the shadows of the chamber. It was cold and gloomy, but Asphogol paid no attention to such things, closing his mind to them, his body seemingly unaffected. It sharpened his thoughts, and he mulled over his situation here on Eannor. He had not been here before, but as he had been told by other Openers, it was not the dead world that it had once been proclaimed. That had been a sham to cover up the realities. Certainly there had been much death here: the stench of slaughter clung yet to the area known as the zone of sacrifice beyond the walls of this fortress, the Bone Watch.

In order to achieve the goal of the Consummate Order, Asphogol knew that certain things had to be done. This place reeked not only of death, but also of subterfuge, of intrigue, of treachery. He would have to add to that chaos.

He considered Etrascu, the Opener assigned to the Keeper of this grim hold. Etrascu was a low bred Opener, ambitious but lacking in the true skills of the higher orders. He would be useful as a player in the game, but no more than that. And of course, he could not be trusted. The information fed to Etrascu was, therefore, carefully doctored. It went directly to Zuldamar.

Asphogol's dual role meant that he had to design his own plans with extreme care. The Garazenda, and in particular, Zuldamar, assumed that Asphogol was working exclusively for them, and Zuldamar expected regular reports. In the past he had always received such reports from Cmizen, through Etrascu. Asphogol had chosen to continue with this system, using Etrascu as his exclusive messenger. But he had not yet brought Etrascu into his confidence. How far did his apparent loyalty to Zuldamar stretch?

There was a knock on the door.

'Come in,' said Asphogol lazily.

As he had assumed, it was the object of his thoughts, Etrascu, whom he had summoned earlier.

Etrascu closed the door behind him, bowed, and sat in the wide chair that Asphogol indicated. Eannor's Opener was gross, though not so large as Asphogol, who in spite of his size maintained a certain dignity, that Etrascu could never hope to acquire.

'How may I serve you, master?' said Etrascu, correctly addressing the Ultimate.

'I think we should have a private talk, Etrascu. Let us do away with some of the formalities for a moment. Agreed?'

Etrascu sweated profusely, wiping his chin, but nodded. He had known this meeting would come, that he would be questioned. 'Of course.'

'Good. You have passed on the latest information to the Garazenda?'

'I have.'

'Tell me, do you deliver this information to a particular member of the Garazenda?'

'To Zuldamar. I have always been under his control. As is my master, Cmizen.'

'He has always taken a great interest in Eannor, has he not?'

'Yes. He has certain concerns about its dangers.'

'Laudable. And your loyalty is also laudable.'

'If I may say so, the loyalty of an Opener is his life blood. The two things are the same.'

Asphogol nodded, his eyes lidded as if he were on the point of dropping off to sleep. He is giving me a path to discussion, he told himself. How much can he be turned? 'A prime rule for our kind. Loyalty. Of course, loyalties become confused sometimes.'

'Oh?'

'Where the chain of command is complicated by political issues, or on matters of military strategy, for example. In fact, we have a complex chain of command ringing us now, Etrascu. Don't you sometimes find it confusing?'

'In what way?'

He's very cautious. But then, he's survived a long time in this cauldron. 'Take this world. Eannor. You must know how the Garazenda have argued among themselves about its fate. They are far from united, even now. And I can tell you, the Consummate Order have their own views.'

'That is fascinating. But, as you know, Asphogol, I do not have the ear of the Order. My contact is, necessarily, very indirect.'

'Whereas my own is by direct attendance on the Order.'

'I envy you that, though I am unworthy – '

'But your loyalty is, I am sure, as fierce as my own.'

'Naturally, the Order come before everything.'

Asphogol yawned, but Etrascu was not fooled. He had not been brought here for amusement. Asphogol served Auganzar, he was sure of it, possibly even before the Order, which was incredible. Zuldamar had *chosen* Asphogol himself.

'The Order moves strangely,' said Etrascu. 'Possibly the complexity of the Garazenda makes this necessary.'

'It does. And the Order place the safety of the worlds first. That is our only real purpose. Balance. It is difficult, is it not, to accept this sometimes? To do the will of the Order when it must seem contrary to the will of our other masters? On such a controversial world as Eannor, it must sometimes seem particularly perverse.'

Etrascu smiled. He serves Auganzar first. I am sure of it! But will he reveal this? 'At such times, one clings to one's loyalty.'

'Inevitably one questions it. But one should be most careful. As you say, the Order moves strangely. Would you say that I serve the Order well?'

The question surprised Etrascu with its directness. He felt himself going cold. He could sense death in the air. If Asphogol had been corrupted by Auganzar, then Etrascu would be in grave danger, having always favoured Zuldamar.

'I'm sure you must. It is not for me to question – '

'No? Then you are quite content for the reports that I have given you to go back to Zuldamar? Reports that show developments here on Eannor, the preparations the Supreme Sanguinary is making for taking his Swarm to the rebel worlds? You find these preparations perfectly natural?'

Etrascu swallowed. 'I have passed on all information just as it has been given to me, master.'

'This is an informal talk, remember?' Asphogol smiled, his mouth glistening in the dim light. 'You have added no reports of your own to Zuldamar?'

'I have not.'

'You think I serve the Supreme Sanguinary?'

'You are assigned to him – '

'Yes, but you think I serve him as Gehennon does. That my loyalty is to Auganzar before any other. You think that. I know you think it.'

'Before the Order?'

'Is that what you think?'

Etrascu knew that the moment of choice had come. Asphogol would open to him, but should he make one wrong step, he was doomed. 'Yes. I know that the Supreme Sanguinary has one desire, and one desire only. To find the way through the barrier to the other World Cycle, the Cycle where the Imperator Elect and his survivors are hiding.'

'You know such a world exists? That the Imperator Elect did survive the Crossing?'

Etrascu nodded. 'The information I have given to Zuldamar on your behalf I have not changed. Even though I have had my suspicions about the troop movements here, and about the preparations. Auganzar is not preparing to go to the rebel worlds.'

'You have not spoken of your suspicions to Zuldamar?'

'I have not.'

'Why not?' said Asphogol coldly, the words a challenge.

Etrascu could not avoid their thrust. 'You serve the Order, master.'

'You said you think I serve Auganzar.'

'Yes. I – '

'Then what do you conclude? That I have betrayed the Order?'

Etrascu felt the sweat running down his neck, soaking into the material of his clothing, chilling him in the air of this bare chamber. 'Surely not – '

'Do you think it possible that the Supreme Sanguinary serves the Consummate Order? That his purpose is *their* purpose? Or is that too much for you to grasp?'

Etrascu drew in his breath, the idea a shock to him. He could not imagine Auganzar serving anything but his own ambitions.

Asphogol sat back with another yawn. 'No, I see you had not considered it. But it is so. Auganzar has his desires, yes, but he will not pursue them at the expense of his loyalty to our masters.'

'Then you do serve Auganzar, but sanctioned by the Order?'

'Yes. However, the Order have had to go over the Garazenda in this matter. They do not know. Nor must they. You understand? Zuldamar works for the downfall of Auganzar, and carries more and more of the Garazenda with him in his thinking. So you, Etrascu, are in a very powerful position.'

'I could deliver Auganzar into Zuldamar's hands.'

'You could. But if you did, you would betray the Order.'

Etrascu said nothing for a moment. He could not look at the calm face of his tormentor, for Asphogol had said everything with a rigid calmness, a lack of discernible emotion. But the hand of the executioner was raised, unseen but ready to fall.

'Master, how is it that the Order approve the intentions of the Supreme Sanguinary?'

'To open a gate? The truth is simply this, that they, too, want Zellorian destroyed. He and his lost arts are a threat to the very fabric of the World Cycles. Auganzar must be allowed to pursue and destroy him. Only then can the Cycles be properly sealed.' Asphogol calmly watched the reactions of the lesser Opener. What an odious creature Etrascu was. Greedy, scheming, and quite dangerous. Of course, he could not be trusted, and must be eliminated as soon as possible. But Zuldamar must have his reports, from someone he trusted. And those reports must contain nothing prejudicial to Auganzar's course.

'Then,' said Etrascu, attempting calmness but not fooling Asphogol, 'I can only state my own loyalty. I serve Cmizen, the Keeper, and Zuldamar of the Garazenda. But as an Opener my prime loyalty lies with the Consummate Order.'

'I am very pleased that we begin to understand one another. In view of the delicacy of the situation.'

'Naturally I will do whatever is needed – '

Asphogol cleared his throat, his huge hands resting across his stomach as he seemed to study the darkness overhead, listening, perhaps, to the numerous movements in the fortress. 'Tell me something, Etrascu,' he said lazily. 'Your immediate master, Cmizen. What of him? He seems a poor specimen of a Csendook to me. Weak, nervous, probably never been in an arena in his life. A puppet.'

'Chosen because of it, master. He serves Zuldamar, but is afraid to go against him.'

'Terrified to make a move of any kind, I would suspect.'

'Yes. If he could flee Eannor and be sure of never being found again, he would do so.'

'He enjoys Zuldamar's protection, though. As you do, Etrascu. No one would be so foolish as to arrange for Cmizen's death, nor yours, I think.'

Etrascu nodded very slowly. 'Zuldamar would capitalise on such killings.'

'It is interesting, though, that recent events on Eannor could seriously embarrass Zuldamar. The Consul, Pyramors, who fought as a *moillum* in the Testament.'

Etrascu felt his insides constricting, the onset of terror very close. They knew everything! Just as he feared. He was not free of this trap yet.

'Should the incident be made known to the Garazenda, Marozul Zuldamar would be discredited. All those known to be involved in the incident, the secret assistance given to the Man Pyramors, would, in my estimation, be publicly executed.'

'But if Auganzar knows, why hasn't he exposed Zuldamar?'

'He has his reasons.'

'Does Zuldamar know that Auganzar is aware?'

Asphogol nodded. 'Naturally. Which puts all Zuldamar's conspirators on somewhat uneasy ground. Cmizen, for example. And, of course, yourself.'

'Then Zuldamar will want to silence the conspirators. You think he will arrange for their removal?'

'It's not for me to say. I have no idea how ruthless Zuldamar is. But if I were one of his conspirators, I would consider my position carefully.'

92

Etrascu leaned forward, face gleaming. 'If I might ask, master, what advice would you give to me?'

Asphogol studied his hands thoughtfully. 'You have stated your loyalty to the Order. Cmizen, however, can have no such loyalty. It is not in his blood as it is in the blood of an Opener. I think there is a way in which certain matters can be resolved.'

Etrascu waited, knowing that Asphogol had summoned him with this very purpose in mind, and would have prepared it, the detail of it, long before. But survival depended upon serving Asphogol. The balance of power on Eannor was unquestionably in his hands.

'As I see it,' said the huge Opener, 'Cmizen is a threat to Auganzar. He serves Zuldamar and will not be turned from that. He must be eliminated.'

'An accident?'

Asphogol shrugged, his great bulk quivering. 'It does not matter how you do it.'

Again Etrascu felt a wave of fear. So that was it. They wanted him to perform their sacrifice. But if he did this, would they then betray him for it? They would have the perfect excuse for executing him.

'Zuldamar will have you killed,' Asphogol said suddenly. 'Rest assured. So show me your loyalty. Destroy Cmizen.'

Etrascu breathed as evenly as he could, though he felt the blood racing through his veins. 'When must it be done?'

'At the last possible moment before we cross.'

'And what about me?'

'We'll need considerable power to create an opening to this other cycle. I have Gehennon.'

'He is loyal?'

'To himself. But dedicated to finding this Path. You, Etrascu, will also come. I will give you the task of monitoring Gehennon. Watch his movements carefully. He may yet harm us in some way. When this affair is over, you will account to the Consummate Order. They will weigh your deeds and no doubt consider your rank.'

'Serving them is enough, master.'

'I am pleased to know that you see this.' Though you lie as

93

easily as one of Man's common whores. 'We will speak again of these things.'

Etrascu bowed, rising. The interview was ended.

'Your views?' said Auganzar, turning from the narrow window that overlooked the zone of sacrifice.

Asphogol sat on the couch, ignoring the wine that had been placed on the table by one of the Supreme Sanguinary's servants. Auganzar knew the Opener never drank wine.

'He is untrustworthy, better dead, Supreme Sanguinary. His talents are small. He slips easily into the role of petty assassin.'

'But I have been careful not to destroy him, nor his master,' replied Auganzar.

'He has agreed to arrange the elimination of Cmizen. But he must realise you will kill him as soon as it is done.'

Auganzar shook his head. 'No. He's too afraid of Zuldamar. I think he'll kill Cmizen to please me, and the Order. What do you think he wants for himself?'

Asphogol snorted. 'He's an Opener. Advancement.'

'Then he'll serve us to get it.'

'He has no talent.'

Auganzar turned to the far end of the chamber. Another large figure sat there, motionless, as though it had heard nothing. But Gehennon had been listening with interest.

'And you, Gehennon? What is your view of Etrascu?'

'I agree with Asphogol. He is dangerous, a liability. But let him eliminate Cmizen. That is an excellent plan. Of course, we should kill Etrascu. But take him with us. Use him during the Crossing. On Innasmorn, there will be no constraints.'

Asphogol's face softened. 'Perhaps, Gehennon, you'd consider watching him while we prepare? Monitoring his movements?'

Gehennon smiled. 'As long as you don't expect me to go with him to the Warhive when he reports to the Garazenda.'

Asphogol also smiled. 'Of course not. But otherwise, a close watch.'

'Gladly.'

'See that he doesn't renege on his assignment.'

Gehennon nodded. 'Cmizen is marked.'

Auganzar turned back to the window. 'In that case, it needn't be long before we begin the real work.'

9

UMUS UTMAR

Zellorian studied the faces of the gathering. Little more than two hundred men stood before him. From the steps he looked down like a god on his servants. Many of them feared him as much as any god. He needed that fear, that goad, if they were to follow him now. He had removed anyone who he could not trust absolutely.

The chamber was huge, scooped out of the heart of the mountain under the Sculpted City, but its weird distances were obscured by the shifting smoke that rose from the numerous bowls of glowing fuel. Twin pillars rose up behind Zellorian at the top of the wide stairs, hinting at a gateway, but to where? The men below were restless: they knew that tonight meant something new, some fresh undertaking by the Prime Consul. Perhaps he had stumbled across further lost powers. He never ceased in his search for them, spared himself no pain to attain his secret goals.

Artificer Wyarne was at the forefront of the ranks, his face blank, his eyes fixed firmly on the space between the huge pillars as though expecting something to coalesce there. Many of his technicians were with him: he had selected the very best of them. Others had been left down in the deep pens, working on oblivious to the developments above them. It was the same with the soldiers. Zellorian had chosen only those he knew would obey him completely and without question, fanatics who would kill a Consul if the order was given to them.

As for the Consulate, Zellorian had brought only five, preferring to leave the rest to their fate in the city. There should have been six, but that fool Gratello had not appeared by the specified time. No doubt he was grovelling outside the huge, locked doors at this very moment. But it was too late. No one would break those doors down, not in a month. But even a few days would be too late, if what the Malefic had said was true. Doom already rushed down upon the Sculpted City. Zellorian had heard its shrieking voice, the voice of the slaughtering storm, the wrath of Innasmorn.

Zellorian drew himself up. He had until recently looked drawn, exhausted, but somehow tonight he had restored something of his old fire, his energy, as though inspired by whatever it was that he intended. He waited briefly while the gathering settled.

'Tonight,' he called, his voice harsh and shrill, infected with this new zeal, 'we are leaving this rock. We are going to a place far from here where we will taste true powers. Man must move onward if he is to survive. Behind us we will leave the husks that he has become. They will rot away and end their lines here in these mountain wastes. But we will go on, growing to new powers that none of our ancestors ever knew. And with them we will rise to question the powers of all other species. *All other species.* There will be none that we need fear.'

He swung round, facing Wyarne, who stood beside the sweating Onando. 'Are the craft ready?'

Wyarne bowed, his face betraying a hint of pride. 'Sire, the gliderboats have reached a new degree of perfection. They are ready to receive their Controllers.'

'Have them brought through,' nodded Zellorian.

Wyarne bowed again, then gestured to a team of his engineers. They went to the edge of the chamber and opened a curved door, which slid upwards into the ceiling. Beyond it was a cavern of darkness, but from this emerged more engineers. They wheeled in flat trucks on which were stretched out the new gliderboats. They came in in pairs, but rows of them stretched back into the dark cave.

They were sleek machines, more streamlined than their predecessors, with intricate steel wings that had been furled up to their sides. Under their shining bellies there were curled claws, closed up tightly for the moment, while behind them, rising up like a huge sting was a tail, thin as a whiplash. Black steel, yet somehow pulsing with life, as though the human blood that coursed through them sang aloud.

'They are ready, sire,' said Wyarne once more.

Zellorian turned to the void behind him, climbing to the last step. He called out words that no one below him understood, but at once there was movement in the smoke. A shape began to nose forward, a large craft, or so it seemed. But the men below gasped as they saw for the first time the true nature of the being that their master had summoned.

It was the servant of the Malefic. Part gliderboat, it seemed to hover in the air over the stairs, its prow formed into a bizarre visage, with twin globes, scarlet eyes. There was a mouth of sorts below this, but it was huge, sagging, as though deformed, distorted by some terrible plague. Behind it in the smoke, its own wings rose up in a steady beat, silent and awesome, maintaining its balance. One was as intricate as the wing of any of Wyarne's masterpieces, the other was a travesty, a massive, claw-like thing, sharp with teeth, oozing with a secretion that looked deadly. It did not speak, but gazed with unfeigned hunger on the people below it.

Zellorian watched for a hint of rebellion in his followers. He saw none. But their terror was like a current of air.

'Let the first of you embark,' he told them, indicating the leading pair of gliderboats.

Silently, under the baleful gaze of the thing that the Prime Consul had summoned, the men obeyed, and in a moment the craft were ready for flight. Zellorian spoke to the thing beyond him. It drew in its breath, then released it in a roar, like a sudden gale rushing through a high mountain gorge. Something flashed in that hideous breath, green and cold.

The gliderboats shuddered, like great beasts suddenly stricken by deep-reaching barbs. They shook, and the men within them felt them pulse to life, like engines. Moments later they were hovering above the floor, drifting towards the stairs.

'The first Controllers are in place,' said Zellorian.

Wyarne gaped. Zellorian had given control of the craft to – what? An alien? The monstrous creation behind him was essentially a gliderboat, but what else? Something of this world resided in it, a questionable power. Yet Zellorian had obviously put his entire trust in it.

Zellorian ordered the next men aboard the second pair of gliderboats. They obeyed, watching the gliderboat beyond their master carefully. Again it released whatever powers it used to bring life to the gliderboats. The first pair of craft rose up and passed along each side of the creature, slowly going beyond it and into the smoke of the void.

Wyarne, in the second pair of craft, wondered where it was they were going. Surely not back through the gate of worlds. But he dared not ask. Like everyone among the company, his fear of Zellorian's awesome powers kept him silent.

In all twenty gliderboats loaded up with Zellorian's followers, powered by the being that the Prime Consul had summoned. Steadily they glided past it and on into the void, where the shadows clung to them, wreathing them. Their occupants felt something steal over them, a darkness, lethargy, so that they were like men drugged. No one cried out. It was a simple submission, an obeisance to the powers of the night.

Zellorian turned as the last of the craft diisappeared. The chamber was empty. Its seals would not be broken from without, and if they ever were, it would be no matter. Any fortunate enough to survive the horrors that were about to fall upon the Sculpted City would find no solace in this cavern, only emptiness. Zellorian climbed into the waiting master craft. He felt the throb of its own powers, exulted in his mental link with this monstrous deity.

It swung round lazily, in supreme control, and Zellorian could sense the eagerness within its vitals. Whatever twisted beings had beenn absorbed into its shell, they no longer had identity. Vymark, Vorenzar, the others, they were distant echoes of pain. This was Innasmorn, raw and elemental. Zellorian gloated as he felt it surge into his own veins, as though he, too, would become part of its structure.

The journey through the shadows began, swiftly, the gliderboats gathering speed as their controlling force lifted them through the ether at tremendous speed, so that they became one with the night and its storms. Somewhere below them the landscape of Innasmorn flickered by, and the voice of the world, its mounting storms, was smothered by the roar of flight, the swift journey away from the mountains, the Sculpted City and all that man had been.

None of them, even Zellorian, would remember much about the flight. It flickered at the edge of knowledge like a dream.

Waking in near dark again, they were aware that everything was still, the gliderboats quiescent. Darkness clamped them, but slowly it began to recede as light flared. They could not see what it was that lit this new realm, no torches being visible. But yellow and scarlet lights surrounded them. The winds had died. They could have been in yet another cavern, deep underground. The air was still, free of dust.

Hovering near the edge of their vision they saw Zellorian in the prow of the strange gliderboat. He stepped down from it on to yet another stone dais. In the growing light, the travellers could see that they were in a sort of circular arena, with tiered steps going up to high walls beyond. The tops of the walls were broken, in places badly, and in the gaps buildings could be seen, though these were also in varying stages of decay. This place was old, crumbling, a mausoleum of a city. Overhead the night sky was clear, stars blinking.

Zellorian waited while his dazed followers climbed out of the gliderboats. He could feel the power surging through himself, eager to impart itself, but he delayed, watching the gliderboats drift away, through dark tunnels down into this ancient city. Only when his followers were alone, gathered in the centre of the arena, did he speak.

'Already you see the nature of the powers we commune with! We have come half way around the world to reach this haven. We are in a derelict city, once a proud Innasmornian fortress. Its name is Umus Utmar, and while we continue our work, no one will disturb us. Even the agents of the Mother of Storms herself will not pass the guardians.'

Onando felt himself shudder. It was a nightmare region, housing as it did the spirits of a past age, the ghosts of another time, other races. What were these monstrous forces that Zellorian had tapped? They had used him so easily.

Wyarne also felt concern. How simply the winds had snatched at the gliderboats. It should be men who controlled them. But Innasmorn? This was too dangerous a game. How could Zellorian hope to control it?

For answer, Zellorian walked towards Wyarne, as though he had read every thought, every fear in his head.

'The Malefics await us. Imprisoned deep in the heart of this world. They are the weapons that we will bring to bear on all our enemies. We are ready to begin, I think? Is there anyone among us who would return to the Sculpted City? Who will not taste true godhood?'

Wyarne kept himself rigid, knowing that Zellorian had at last slipped over into the realm of fanaticism that itself bordered on madness.

Zellorian gazed at him, eyes blazing with a strange intensity, almost an inner fire, the fire of a man possessed. Did a Malefic look through his eyes? Wyarne wondered.

'Artificer Wyarne,' came Zellorian's voice, rich with power, a terrible depth to it. 'You doubt the cause. Let me put my hands upon you, that you may know the gods you question. Feel them. Understand their will, their infallibility. Trust them.'

'Sire, I do.' .

Zellorian smiled horribly, reaching out with both hands and placing them on each of Wyarne's shoulders. 'Good,' he said, but the voice was no longer his own.

Wyarne felt the fingers digging into him, and winced with agony as the grip tightened. Zellorian began to compress his hands, forcing Wyarne to his knees, squeezing with immense, impossible force. Blood spurted through his fingers as the hands gripped bone, the pressure growing further until the bones ground, snapping. Wyarne screamed, but he could not break free. He felt himself being crushed, his chest constricting until the ribs snapped and closed up. Still the merciless release of power went on, Wyarne unable to cry out as blood seeped thickly from his mouth and ears.

No one in the company dared to interfere. Zellorian exerted fresh power, squeezing the deformed flesh, compacting it as though between the immense wheels of a stone mill. The ruined flesh and bone before him toppled as he released it, the blood flowing from a score of ruptured arteries, the corpse no bigger than a child's.

Zellorian lifted his bloody hands. 'This is how you die, those who would betray us now. Look down on this bloody wreckage. The dark is hungry for such sacrifices, but we have enemies enough to sate it.'

Onando stepped forward, his face as white as that of a corpse, his eyes filled with terror. 'We are yours! Give us the strength to drive on to our destiny.'

Zellorian looked witheringly at him, but only for a moment. Then he smiled again, the cold, merciless smile of the dark. 'Your destiny. Of course. We need not delay. You shall have it. All of you.'

He turned and climbed quickly up the steps behind him. The dark form of the gliderboat creature was silent, as if dormant, its eyes closed. But as Zellorian spoke to it, the eyes opened, again scarlet, lamps burning with hellish light. Above it, on the rim of the arena, more shapes gathered. They ringed the arena, slowly coming downwards, some of them large, some far smaller, and in the glow of the light they were like elemental things, things fused from the earth, or from stone, partly flesh.

None of the men moved, eyes riveted on these bizarre creatures, the servants of the Malefic. As they reached the foot of the steps, hundreds of them, they began to move in a circular dance, linking arms and shuffling clumsily across the stones. But they made no sound, as though all were mute.

At last, overcome by the eeriness of the scene, someone broke ranks and rushed from the body of men towards the shambling creatures. Half way across the paved stones, the man suddenly screamed, his back arching. He writhed as if he had been caught on an invisible fence, swinging this way and that, face contorted. Light speared into him from a dozen unseen sources, lifting him, spinning him, rolling him. But at the end of it he stood, grinning strangely. Then he balled his fists and shook them at the skies. He turned his eyes on his fellow men, and they were the eyes of a mad beast, yellow as the light that now blazed from his hands.

'He was the first,' said Zellorian. 'Who will be next to receive the blessing of the dark?'

As the silent dancers continued to prowl around the edge of the arena, the men waited, but whatever powers the Malefic was putting forth could not be avoided. Here a man fell, twisting and screaming, there another, until, one by one, the entire company was infected. Zellorian watched avidly as his followers were suffused with power, drawn into the Malefic's web.

The dance of silence ended. The creatures that the Malefic had dredged up from their secret lairs stood still. Their alien faces were blank, their powers lulled. And in the centre of the arena, the men had ceased their own jerky movements. One by one they formed into ranks. Already their compositions had reformed. They were bipeds, vaguely human, but with an animal alertness, a wildness, like killer hounds waiting for a word of command.

'Go to your places in the city,' Zellorian told them.

They had no need of questions, their minds bulging with fresh visions. Zellorian watched them troop off with the other creatures. In the shadows they fused well.

Behind him, Zellorian heard the voice of the Malefic, speaking through its servant. 'Simple powers,' its voice grated. 'Transformations such as these are nothing. And your followers are so eager to drink. They will serve us well in the coming confrontations.'

Zellorian nodded. 'No man could withstand them, not with the new powers they have.'

'They have barely begun to change. Soon they will experience deeper alterations to their structures, to their nervous systems. The naked elements of Innasmorn will drive them, and I will give them other gifts. The Mother is powerless to prevent me. She has no control over alien bodies.'

'And the gliderboats?'

'They, too, will change. Your followers will become as the dhumhagga and as the urmurels and as the other furies of the earth and wind. And when they make their first kill for us, then we shall have what we need to give birth to a new creation. The gliderboats will take on real powers, as I have. They will be prepared for what is to come.'

'The Malefics?'

'I have seen the doorway beyond this world cycle. Your science, Zellorian, has opened this door. It is a thing of wonder. There have been wars on Innasmorn between the Mother and the Malefics for unimaginable eons. But never have the wars been taken beyond our World Cycle. Innasmorn chains the dark. Denies it these forbidden paths. Yet you, Prime Consul, are a man of immense power, a worthy ally. I watched as you breached the wall to the next World Cycle. You sent a single Man through that gate.'

'To his doom. To the Csendook, who will have destroyed him and the last of my race that lingered beyond this World Cycle.'

'Your lust for vengeance is a strong fountain of power. Yet the Csendook are strong. I have tasted the minds of the ones built into me. They will make superb warriors, these aliens. You want their downfall, and shall see it. Their funeral pyre will be the energy that awakens the Malefics. You will have what you seek.'

'And after?'

'The Mother will bow to new masters. She has reigned for untold centuries. But after this time, she will be slave to the Malefics. They will bring the glory of true darkness to the World Cycles. And you, Prime Consul, who knows what powers you will share? In your wildest dreams of revenge, you could not have imagined what will await you.'

Crohalt's party camped high up in the mountains. He was leading them to one of the settlements, far from the communication lines between the Sculpted City and Starhanger fortress, but they would have to cross the only road first.

Jannovar, the lone woman in the company, sat apart from the others, wrapped in the thick pelts that had been given to her. The mountains were far colder than what she had been used to on the Warhive, and the night was chill; without Pyramors she felt doubly vulnerable.

'Worried about the crossing?'

The voice came thickly from the shadows. She drew in her breath, then saw the satisfaction in the man's eyes. Kelwars was enjoying her discomfort.

She shook her head.

'We cross tomorrow night. It's unlikely we'll be seen. There aren't likely to be any of the Imperator's scum on the road at night. They'll be in their beds in Starhanger.'

She looked beyond the shadow he had become, the light from the fire some distance behind him. It seemed somehow far away. 'I wasn't thinking of our safety.'

'No, I suppose not,' said Kelwars, shuffling forward. 'There's a storm brewing south west of us. It'll help our rebels. Pyramors is a capable man – '

'You can be sure of that,' she said coldly. Should she call Crohalt? But Kelwars had done nothing. None of the men thought much of her, she could sense that. She did not want to offend them. Better to humour them if she must.

'You must have had it rough in the Sculpted City,' he said, changing the subject abruptly.

'The Sculpted City? No, I was – ' But she stopped.

'Treated all right? As a what – servant? Of Zellorian, or the Imperator himself?'

'What are you talking about?' she snapped.

'Why did Pyramors call off the rebellion?' he said, coming closer, eyes fixed on her. 'So that he could pry you free of them? Was that it? Now that you're free of them, the rebellion starts anew. Isn't that right, my lady?' He said this last with cold contempt.

'I was never their prisoner, you fool! I was left behind on Eannor. It was the Csendook who held me – ' She stopped, turning from his gaze, suddenly realising she had probably said too much.

'Then he's been *back*? To fetch you. And how in the stars did he get back? Who sent him?'

But she would not look at him and said nothing.

'It could only have been Zellorian! A bargain, was that it?'

'This is fool's talk! Leave me. I want to rest. You're an idiot to taunt me with this. Pyramors will – '

'What? What will he do, if he ever finds us again? If he ever comes back! You're quick to call men idiots, but it seems to me, my lady, that there's none so foolish as those who think they can breach the walls of the Sculpted City with no more than a handful of warriors.'

'You don't know him,' she said tersely.

He smiled evilly. 'And what if he doesn't come back, eh? What then? You'll need another to shelter you.'

She faced him, eyes filled with scorn. 'And *you* think you're man enough for that? I'd rather be back on the Warhive – '

He drew back slowly. 'The Warhive, was it? The Warhive. That's very interesting. Well, maybe you're right,' he added slyly. 'Maybe you'd be safer than you would be here.'

'Pyramors will be back. If I were you, I'd be far away when he comes.'

He snorted, but began to move away. She watched him uneasily, cursing herself for having spoken to him at all. These men were no lovers of the Consul. He may have had their respect once, but not now. How close were they to treachery?

Kelwars made his way down to the fire and looked for Tennegar, finding him sitting astride a boulder, gazing into the flames.

'Been chancing your arm with the fair damsel?' he grinned. 'Take a knife to you, did she?'

Kelwars looked angry, but only fleetingly. His face changed and he smiled lasciviously. 'We'll see about that.' He slumped down next to his companion. 'But I did learn something interesting.'

'Not to mess about with a Consul's woman?'

Kelwars swore. 'Consul? They're all the bloody same. You know where he got her from? Where she was before he got her here?'

'The City?'

'Crap. It was the Warhive. And he went back there for her. I *told* you it was a deal. Zellorian. He's the only one who could have done it. I tell you, Tennegar, something stinks in this. That bastard will sell us off yet. It wouldn't surprise me if he hasn't set Jorissimal and the rest of us up. A trap.'

Tennegar gasped. 'But he did so much to get us out of the City in the first place! Most of the rebels owe their freedom to Pyramors. He's the only real champion Gannatyne has.'

'So you say. But she's a pretty wench. Worth going back to the *Warhive* for.'

'You can't be sure of that – '

'No? She let it slip. I believed her.'

Tennegar nodded to where Crohalt was prodding the fire. 'You going to tell him?'

'Crohalt? Not yet. But I'll tell you this. I'll watch my back. And that girl had better look out for hers. This is a wide open world. Plenty of room for a man to go off and find a new life beyond all this. With a good woman.'

Tennegar snorted. 'You think you could live like that?'

'A man could do a lot worse. A lot worse.'

10

STORM FURY

Forked tongues of brilliant lightning crackled down from the skies, and with a tremendous detonation struck at an isolated tower above the Sculpted City. The top of the tower burst as if it had been smashed by the fist of a gigantic god of the skies, bursting in a shower of flames and debris, raining down on the streets below. Elsewhere in the city, lightning licked downwards, blows from a celestial hammer, and with it came the rains, torrential and violent. The wind whipped it into lashes, tearing at roofs, ripping up tiles, exposing beams, finding any tiny flaw in the architecture of the city. And in the skies, the elementals screamed and shrieked like demons, intent on creating utter chaos below.

As the storm burst, most of the streets had been empty. A few guards marked key places, and there were the usual revellers on the way to their beds. Those who saw the sudden destruction of the tower quickly ran for cover, slamming doors behind them as more tongues of vivid light reached down.

Near the tower, in the confusion, men tried to organise themselves into a team that could begin clearing up the rubble, but as they began work, the wind tore down at them, buffeting them. Several men were plucked up like straw dolls and tossed into the darkness, smashed by the ferocity of the storm. Other buildings were groaning under the onslaught, and an entire wall near the central citadel toppled over, burying a score of knights. The rain flooded in, the streets instantly awash in some places as the drains, blocked by earthfalls, spewed up fresh torrents, diverted by rubble, causing more disaster as they flooded houses and stores alike.

Aru and Tremazon had been racing through the streets as discreetly as they could, searching out those that the Consul knew would be allies. Their families were jostled from their beds, warned to dress and get to the nearest of the gliderboat pens as soon as they could.

Very quickly the streets became a scene of utter chaos all over the city. The majority of the population locked themselves in their homes, going as deep underground as they could, knowing that parts of the city were collapsing, as though an earthquake had struck, or the advance forces of a Csendook Swarm. The destruction seemed to be no less terrible. It soon became evident to the city guards that there was nothing they could do while the storm raged. It was a bizarre event, for unlike other storms they had known, this one seemed maliciously intent on seeking them out and plucking them up. It was an enemy they could not fight.

The central gliderboat pens were not far from the palace, ringed in by a wall that was thirty feet high. The gatehouse was secured, with a dozen guards on duty, huddled inside the building, watching the skies where madness had broken loose. Thunder boomed incessantly, and the skies lit up as bolt after bolt of lightning crackled down. They, too, wondered if this was some alien attack, rather than a mere storm, so colossal were the powers being hurled on the Sculpted City. They saw with horror another tower topple over, smashing into buildings as it fell, ruining them. Fires had broken out in a number of parts of the city: they raged, tall and furious. Even the stones seemed ablaze.

Aru and two score of Gladimyr's knights reached the gate house to the pens. A steel portcullis had been locked into place, barring entry. Gladimyr banged his sword haft on the steel.

'Hoy, you fellows! The buildings are falling down around us. Let us in before we're flattened!'

He had to repeat his call twice before a face appeared in the inner door. A hand waved him away, but he insisted.

A guard came out, bent over in the gale, and stood beyond the portcullis, his hair plastered to his head in the rain. The wind screamed around him as he shouted. 'You'll have to find shelter elsewhere – '

'We're cut off!' Gladimyr yelled, pointing with his blade. 'There's fire that way and the other end is blocked, and the drains are filling. The water's risen. For pity's sake, man, let us in!'

Reluctantly the guard dragged out his keys, his fingers working slowly in the cold. But he unlocked the portcullis and went back to the gate house. After a moment the steel rose enough to admit Gladimyr and the knights. Aru followed them in.

There were a dozen guards here, no more, and all looked shaken by the scale of the storm. Even the gate house, a solid enough block, seemed to shake every time the thunder roared.

'This is no ordinary storm!' one of them gasped. 'What's happening out in the mountains?'

'Don't close the portcullis,' warned Gladimyr as one of the guards was about to work the equipment that would again drop it into place.

'Why not?' said the guard suspiciously. But Gladimyr's men quickly took the initiative, disarming the guards before they realised.

'You'll be unhurt if you do as I say,' Gladimyr told them. 'In a while we will be bringing more people in here, to the pens.'

'The pens?' the guard frowned. 'Surely you don't mean to attempt *flight*. The craft are terrified. You'd have no chance of getting them into the air, not in this.'

Gladimyr turned to Aru. 'I have to say, Aru, that I think he's right. Did you realise what the skies would be like? No gliderboat could hope to lift in this. Surely it would be better to wait out the storm – '

She shook her head. 'We have to try. We'll have help. Believe me, the storm will not attack the gliderboats.' But already she could feel the combined terror of the gliderboats beyond the building in the yards. They were under thin cover, but they could sense the monstrous storm, its threat of annihilation. To get them up into it would be extremely difficult. They could sense only their death in the screaming heavens.

The gate house guards were in no mood to argue with anyone, concerned as they were for their own safety and the chaos in the streets. They were confused by Gladimyr's actions, but the storm absorbed all their attention. This was no time for any kind of dispute.

Not long afterwards, the first of the families began to arrive. Beyond the gate house, inside the huge walls, there was an open area, and on the other side of it, the pens. There were too many people gathered now to crowd under cover: they spilled out into the lashing rain, the children protesting. Aru tried to calm them, but the noise of the storm made it almost impossible. Gladimyr was in conversation with two of the Consulate who had arrived, bemused as the children, and Aru could see him gesticulating and talking quickly in an attempt to explain to them what had to be done.

Aru went to the gliderboats and opened up the sheeting that secured them. She could hear their unified mental anguish, but she spoke to them, trying to calm them. Overhead the wind mocked her efforts, the rain continuing to pour from the skies, slanting into the pens, creating fresh terror.

'Unless you take to the skies and fly through the eye of the storm, you'll perish here with the rest of the city,' she shouted at them, and although they understood her, their fears were not calmed. She would need Circu to goad them.

Standing in the centre of the court, rain ripping into her as if it would tear her off her feet, she sent out a mental call to the gliderboat and Jubaia, knowing that they would be somewhere above in that whirling maelstrom. She was answered by peals of thunder, more sizzling trails of lightning, and she thought then that it was over. Without contact, this exodus was doomed. Neither the gliderboat nor the little thief answered her.

Pyramors gritted his teeth against the onslaught of the wind. It had seemed like a stroke of luck when the storms broke, but their extraordinary violence was something he had not been prepared for. He had heard that the storms on Innasmorn could be abnormally powerful, but these storms were unlike anything he had ever witnessed before. They were more than elemental forces at work, fused as they were into a destructive machine. They were more like the engines of an army. And had someone said that the shamen of the Innasmornians controlled these storms? It was as if a number of them had raced in from varying directions, swirling together into one great release of energy, focused over the Sculpted City.

Beside him, huddled down among the rocks beyond the city walls, Jorissimal grunted. 'This is lunacy! The storms will rip the city apart. We should take cover under the earth. There are caves in the mountains. But exposed as we are – '

Pyramors was shaking his head. 'This is an opportunity we won't get again. Did you see the towers fall? There'll be utter chaos in the streets. I doubt if many of the citizens will be outside in this. Even the guards would be foolish. They'll wait until this is over.'

'You want to go in?'

'We must.'

'But, Pyramors, the gliderboats!' said Jorissimal. 'They could never fly in this!'

'Maybe not, but if we can win the pens, control them, get our people into them, and wait. We could hold off a siege in those pens until the storm breaks.'

Jorissimal grunted. There was an almost frightening determination in the Consul. 'Maybe.'

'Get your men ready.'

The burly warrior nodded, passing back the word. In a while the company moved forward, lashed by the wind and rain. By the time they got to the walls, they felt exhausted, buffeted and punched as if they had already been in a long battle. But Pyramors and Jorissimal cajoled them, voices almost hoarse as they shouted in the teeth of the gales.

They had intended to get into the city by the new drains that were under construction, but the flooding prevented that, the huge pipes filled to capacity as water gushed out in foaming torrents, the force of its passage incredibly fast. No one could possibly swim against such a tide.

'We'll have to chance going over,' said Pyramors, but one of the scouts came struggling through the mud towards him, trying to shout something.

He had to put his mouth close to Pyramors's ear to be heard against the howling winds. 'Part of the outer wall's been washed away. Gaping hole. We can get in.'

It was enough. Pyramors diverted his men and they fought their way through the dangerous mud slides along the outer wall until they came to the gap. Huge lengths of wall had crumbled, water spewing out over ramparts, pulling more stonework to pieces. Beyond there were whole lines of buildings that had been flattened, reduced to sludge, and although the rain continued to pelt down, there were numerous fires.

'Stars above,' murmured Jorissimal to himself. 'The city is being ripped up, destroyed. This is no natural storm.' He had no time to contemplate further.

Pyramors led them in. They picked their way over the treacherous rubble towards the area where Pyramors knew the first of the gliderboat pens would be. At first the streets seemed empty. The citizens were sensible enough to know they could not halt this catastrophe while it raged. Doors were locked and sealed. A few guards were seen, running to and fro on whatever hopeless errands they had been given. But no one attempted to halt the party's progress. They had to be careful of more flooding, and walls that fell, roofs that tore free and catapulted through the streets, smashing into more buildings, adding to the ruin.

But they found the pens at last. A circular wall enclosed them, and at the gatehouse there was no sign of life. If the guards had been here, they had deserted their post for safer housing, no doubt under the city. The doors of the pens were wide, one of them ripped free of its hinges.

'But how do we gather our people together?' Jorissimal shouted against the wind.

'We wait until after the storm,' Pyramors told him. 'We must secure these pens.' He rushed over the compound to the low houses where the gliderboats were kept. He was not himself a Controller, nor was Jorissimal. They would have to take Controllers from the city. The gliderboats looked utterly lifeless under their shelter. It was impossible to say if they would be capable of flight, even after the storm had subsided.

Jorissimal had deployed his men as best he could. They were in command of these pens, but for now there was no one to dispute this command. He shook his head. They had trapped themselves in here. Once the knights in the city got organised, the return to freedom would be no easy path.

'We'll have to leave the other pens,' Pyramors called beside him. 'But there are enough craft here for our needs.'

'I don't think we should wait for this storm to clear,' said Jorissimal. 'Some of us will have to go into the city now. We must bring people here before we are discovered. We can only hold this for so long.'

'I agree,' said Pyramors. 'You must hold this position. I'll take Lascor and two others and go on. I'll get word back to you before dawn. If you hear nothing, take the men back out to the mountains.'

Jorissimal scowled, but he could see the sense in it. No point them all dying. He nodded slowly.

Minutes later Pyramors and the three rebels were moving on into the city. They all knew who they were looking for, the friends they could trust, the families they must contact. Pyramors separated from them, each taking his own path.

For an hour Pyramors wound through streets that threatened to collapse on him. He saw very few of the citizens, and those that he did ignored him, too busy about the business of survival to take any notice, assuming him to be another victim of the storm. He was in a narrow street, near the heart of the city, when he almost walked into the party of armed knights. He was about to turn and make a rush for safety, when he decided it would be better not to draw attention to himself.

'How is it at the citadel?' he cried above the wind, which had not dropped and still screamed overhead.

The men eyed him suspiciously and at once he realised

he had made a mistake. He should have run. But they were on to him and wouldn't let him run now. He knew it would be fatal to try.

One of them raised his naked blade, stepping forward. Was it to be a fight? But beside the knight, a slightly shorter figure put a hand on his arm. The figure came forward, a flicker of lightning throwing its face into momentary sharp relief.

Pyramors gasped. 'Aru! Aru Casruel.'.

They gaped at each other stupidly, unable to credit the evidence of their eyes, then she came to him, smiling, sudden tears welling in her eyes. 'Pyramors? How could it be?'

He laughed at her look of utter amazement, throwing his arms about her, hugging her. 'I could ask the same of you. I could ask a hundred questions, but there simply isn't time now. Listen, I have taken the southern pens – '

She grinned, still amazed at meeting him here under these circumstances. 'What? But we were on our way there. We have the central yards secured. Our people are gathering there now.'

'For flight?'

'Yes. Soon.'

'In this storm? Are you mad? They'll be torn from the skies – '

'Never mind how. But they'll fly, Pyramors. Where are your own men?'

He explained briefly about the attempt to steal craft from the southern yards, his men waiting there.

'Send word back to them. One of the guards will go for you. Tell all your men to come to the central pens. Any families that are found, any allies, they must all come to the central pens. Between us we'll hold them against any assaults from within the city. And we'll begin the airlift soon.' She looked upwards as she said this last. Where was Jubaia?

Amazed by her apparent confidence and her undoubted organisation, Pyramors agreed to let his men be summoned. Lascor made off quickly for Jorissimal in the southern pens, while he accompanied Aru back to the central area.

115

'We were coming to the other pens,' she told him. 'We'll need all the city's gliderboats. No one in the city thinks the gliderboats will be used in this weather. But they will be, I promise you. They'll fly and survive!'

Jubaia circled over the city, swept along by the maniacal howlings of the storms. But Circu would not be cowered by them, even though her fear shone like a beacon. Jubaia spoke to her constantly, and true to their words, the Innasmornian Windmasters did nothing to harm the gliderboat. Jubaia coaxed her in lower sweeps over the city, slipping between the fingers of lightning that persistently groped down, tearing great chunks out of the masonry below.

'Can you sense her at all?' Jubaia asked, leaning over the prow of the craft, rain soaking into him, the way ahead a screen of water through which he peered as if into a murky lake.

I'm trying, was the slightly impatient retort. *But I've never known conditions like these. Except for the storm we encountered in the Dhumvald.*

Jubaia snorted. 'Evil storm. This is drawn from the Mother, and not the terrors of the storm-of-the-dark.'

Some might say the work of this storm is evil work.

'Better not to voice your thoughts, Circu.'

Many will die tonight. Mankind will suffer great losses.

'So let's hurry up and help our allies to freedom! Keep searching for. . .what was that? Did you feel something? Like a sudden stab of light below us somewhere.'

Jubaia felt the gliderboat shudder. Yes, she, too, had felt contact. Aru! She was alive.

I have found her.

'Go down. You must. Quickly.'

The gliderboat used the wild currents as best she could, but she knew that the winds were essentially against her, even though their masters controlled them. But she dropped ever lower, skimming the upper towers as close as she dared.

Aru, I hear you.

Down in the streets, Pyramors felt the girl beside him suddenly stiffen. She looked upwards as if expecting something to fall, and he automatically put an arm out to shield her.

'It's all right,' she told him. 'It's the gliderboat! Jubaia will come to our aid.' She ignored his look of bewilderment.

How far are you from the gliderboat pens? came the question to her mind. It was rare that the gliderboat spoke directly to anyone other than Jubaia, but it had obviously become essential.

Pyramors watched as Aru mouthed words to something above, as if talking to the storm. But he did not interfere. 'Close. I have Pyramors with me. His rebels are in the city, at the other pens. Can you make the other craft fly? Already we've started gathering the families.'

I'll go there. Come quickly.

Aru turned to Pyramors, her face gleaming.

'Whatever is it?' he said.

'No time for explanations. Jubaia is above us. He's an exceptional Innasmornian. He is controlling a gliderboat that will communicate with the others.'

'A gliderboat is up in this?'

'Yes. Come on. There's work for us at the pens.'

Pyramors allowed himself to be rushed along the streets. There was more chaos and confusion. They saw a number of people crushed under fallen masonry and there was evidence that part of the northern city was blazing in a raging fire. There was no cessation above: the storms, if anything, were intensifying.

At the pens, Aru's allies waited. Pyramors recognised some of the men at once. Gladimyr stood forward, bowing. And behind him came Consul Tremazon. Pyramors nodded to him, but at once he felt uneasy. He had never been sure of this taciturn man. Was he to be trusted?

'I have thrown my lot in with your cause, Pyramors,' said the Consul. He took out his sword and held it out for Pyramors. 'I am yours to command now.'

'You realise,' said Pyramors, 'that the penalty for flight from this city is death? Zellorian has marked us all as rebels.'

'For which I spit upon him,' said Tremazon. 'I have brought my family here, together with as many of the families of your rebels as can be found. The blood of your enemies is on my sword.'

'It's true, sire,' said Gladimyr. 'Consul Tremazon's knights have worked tirelessly this night to help us.'

Pyramors nodded soberly. 'Then put away your sword, Tremazon. We'll discuss politics later. My own men are coming from the southern pens. They secured them, but Aru says they'd be better here.'

'The gliderboats will be summoned,' said Aru with confidence. 'Jubaia will bring them to us. And also those in the north eastern pens. Though that fire looks bad over there.'

'All the more reason for them to fly,' said Gladimyr.

Pyramors's attention was snared by something overhead. They all turned to see what it was. Out of the swirling rain, a dark shape drifted down, hovering as though by sorcery above the compound. It was a single gliderboat, black and sleek, and in its prow sat a lone figure.

'Jubaia!' called Aru.

'Are the first families ready?' he called to her, the words almost torn away by a fresh blast of air.

Aru nodded, quickly ushering people aboard the uncovered gliderboats, though everyone there was in a state of complete panic. Like Pyramors, they found it almost impossible to believe that they would be going up into this dreadful storm.

'It's either that or a swift death on the swords of the Imperator's knights,' Aru told them. 'Once they know we're here, they'll be out in force, and they'll cut down every one of us without a second look. So move!'

Gladimyr and Tremazon were busy then, ushering the people into the craft.

Circu had already begun to link her mind with that of the gliderboats in the pens. Their terror was plain enough, but no Controller had ever spoken to them as this new voice did, no Controller had ever plumbed as deep into their minds. Slowly, rationally, Circu began convincing the craft that the skies would not harm them, that allies waited beyond the mountains. The storm had been sent for the enemies of Innasmorn, the servants of the mad Imperator, and his corrupt Consulate.

During the next two hours, Pyramors's rebels arrived under Jorissimal, dubious at first, but relieved to see their leader and the exodus beginning in the pens. Several hundred people from the city had been brought here, including many rebel families who had not seen their men for months, and though the storms continued to hammer the city, there were many happy reunions.

The gliderboats from the southern pens were finally persuaded to leave them and fly to this central zone, guided by Jubaia and Circu. But in the city, word had gone about that there were rebels abroad. Other craft from the last of the pens had also arrived, telling Circu of the fire that had almost engulfed them. Gradually the fleet, some fifty strong, filled with people, and the airlift started.

But beyond the gates of the pens, the knights had drawn up their lines. Pyramors and Aru could see that a battle was inevitable. The question was whether or not the gliderboats could lift everyone to safety in time to avoid it. There would need to be a number of trips.

Pyramors gripped his sword, standing by the closed portcullis. He hailed the Imperator's guards beyond. 'Go back to the city and look to your own families! There's work enough for you there.'

'Open these gates,' snarled the warrior in charge of the knights, a huge figure in armour, helmet obscuring his face. 'The Imperator himself has decreed that you be executed if you resist. We have others of your rebels out here. If you want to see them live, open the gates and throw down your arms.'

Pyramors knew that a small number of rebels and their families had not been able to get to the pens quickly enough. But it was too late to save them. They could not be snatched from the knights, who must outnumber the rebels by ten to one. A sacrifice, then. He gritted his teeth, turning back.

Tremazon stood close to him, his face a cold mask. But he nodded. 'We have no choice,' he said, and although the words were stolen by the wind, Pyramors understood him.

'Tell the Imperator that if he survives this night, we will return for his head.' Pyramors swung away from the knights beyond the gate. But the last thing he heard as he prepared to rally his defenders was the call to arms, and the clash of steel as the first wave assaulted the portcullis. It would only hold for so long.

BOOK THREE

THE SCATTERING

11

DELUGE

Vittargattus watched the shamen very closely, not daring to disturb their communion with the raging elements. The storms swirled about them all, enveloping the entire army, yet none of the Innasmornians was affected by it. The warriors waited calmly, as did the small steeds they rode. Ondrabal, too, watched in calm silence. Below them, in the city, the darkness churned like the waters of a huge whirlpool, the lightning stabbing down into it from over the mountains, the winds screaming, a fusion of banshee and elemental forces, nightmare unleashed. The clan chief of the Vaza looked on grimly, but knew that this was necessary work. The invader must be halted here, otherwise, like a plague, he would sweep out over all Innasmorn. Already he had been allowed far too much time to settle. The city had been far more sophisticated than Vittargattus had expected, and he had been stunned by its architecture. Its inhabitants were not savages. How many of the forbidden arts did they have control over?

He heard a murmur from below, and several heads turned to look beyond the city into the clouds. Vittargattus could discern something moving there, a number of dark shapes, like huge bats fleeing from a cave. These must be the promised craft, the things the woman had spoken of. But Vittargattus had given his word: they must be spared. Ondrabal glanced at him. He had also seen the shapes in the distance. He was disturbed by them, but for the moment had not challenged the decision of the Vaza clan chief. Yet Vittargattus knew his patience could not last.

'Let us waste no more time,' Vittargattus called. 'The city is in turmoil. We go down.'

Ondrabal nodded curtly, swinging his steed around, calling to his commanders. The army had already planned its movements for the assault. Now, with speed and precision, it began the descent into the valley. The Windmasters protected the army, the skies above it filled with dancing lights as the wind creatures they commanded swept over it, shrieking with glee in anticipation of the battle that would soon begin.

Among the ranks, close behind the two great leaders, Fomond and Armestor also rode. Both had unslung their bows, and had short swords in their belts, though neither enjoyed the prospect of battle. They could feel the tension in the warriors around them, Innasmornians who had been readying for this conflict for months, their nerves pulled taut as bowstrings. It could not possibly be something to enjoy, this conflict, and yet there was an eagerness about the warriors now, a need to begin the onslaught.

'If the city is in such disorder,' said Armestor, 'the Men in it won't welcome a battle.'

'Too much killing would be bad,' agreed Fomond. 'If there's to be any kind of peace and stability afterwards, this siege ought not to be a cruel one. But you've seen Vittargattus. He's still very bitter about the loss of his warriors in the Dhumvald. In a way, he blames the Men of this city for that. I don't know how merciful he's prepared to be.'

They had no time to discuss it further. The march had become a swift ride down through a narrow defile, beyond which were the walls of the Sculpted City. Rain hammered down, the visibility poor, but even through the sheets of water, the warriors could see that parts of the outer wall had been breached by the elements. The wind elementals tore at the bare stone, rocks being flung this way and that, so that anyone within the walls was in danger of being crushed by them.

But Fomond could see Men of the city on the ramparts. A few of them had braved the chaos to watch the land beyond the walls. They saw the coming of the invasion. But those who opposed its apex were powerless to stop it. Through the first of the rubble the Innasmornians poured, smashing aside all opposition as they arrowed into the city.

Already the streets immediately beyond the wall were

choked with debris, and there were numerous corpses strewn about, victims of the storm. Vittargattus and Ondrabal split up, taking two wedges of their warriors into the city, cutting down anyone that opposed them. Most of the citizens had locked themselves underground, away from the claws of the storm. Knights from the watch, who had been busy trying to stem the spread of fire, or clear rubble from the main streets so that they could get to the worst of the flooding, were forced to turn and meet this sudden wave of fighting fury.

Already the spirit of the knights was wavering. There was so much disaster around them: they held their ground uncertainly as the winds tore down at them, lifting them like dolls, destroying whole streets with contemptuous ease. They had recognised in these storms some uncanny element, a living force, knowing that whatever wild rumours they had heard about Innasmorn were somehow grounded in truth. The storm was a living thing.

The arrival of the Innasmornians, warriors whom they would normally have cut down easily with their superior force and weaponry, was the final cut, the last killing blow to their morale and their cohesive defence. If the storm did not smash the knights down, these leaping warriors would do so. And they were not afraid of the storm, nor were they in any way harmed by it. In fact, some of the knights realised in horror, the leaders of the invasion actually seemed to *command* the elements, as though the things that swept down from the storm were themselves warriors in this intruding army. The overwhelming combination was too much for the knights, and all along their defensive lines they were flung back, impotent against the fury of this suddenly hostile world.

Fomond and Armestor were less enthusiastic than the warriors around them about the destruction of the city. It must have been a proud place, for all its youth, but already it was being reduced to a sprawling region of chaos. If this went on, all that would remain would be a shell, with little life crawling in its remains.

Fomond saw Azrand the Blue Hair near to the warriors on his left as they picked their way through more rubble.

The Windmaster was gazing up into the storm, as though receiving instructions from the gods. Fomond swung his steed around and forced through the pack of warriors to the Blue Hair's side.

Azrand turned, recognising the young woodsman. He nodded, but his face was stern, his manner suggesting no compromise.

'There's no need for further slaughter!' Fomond called above the perpetual din of the storm. 'This city is on its knees, Azrand. The Men will surrender. Give them that chance.'

Azrand nodded. 'Word is being sent to their ruler, the Imperator Elect, as he calls himself. We will not put everyone to death. I agree, that would be a mistake.'

Beside him, another figure coalesced in the rain. Its face was pale, its eyes narrow, though in them a strange power seemed to glow. Fomond recognised the being as a Seer, one of Ondrabal's shamen. Like Azrand, he had the gift of power that the Mother sometimes bestowed on her servants.

The Seer, Freghai, studied Fomond for a moment. 'You have much sympathy for the invaders. I have heard you speak out against their destruction.'

'I welcome the death of the worst of them,' said Fomond, refusing to be cowed by the imperious gaze. 'But that is all.'

Freghai nodded. 'Ondrabal may not share those views.'

Fomond would have asked him to explain, regardless of his high status, but there was a fresh surge from the warriors, and he was carried away from the shamen. He caught sight of Armestor, near him in the crush, and worked his way back to his side.

'Word's come that the defenders have given in to us already!' Armestor shouted. 'There are a few knots of them, driven into corners. And the Imperator and his closest defenders are shut away in the citadel. Otherwise the Sculpted City is ours.'

Fomond nodded thankfully. 'Then there's no need for this lunacy to go on.'

Armestor's face clouded. 'But there is something else. I saw Kuraal once more. He has been watching us.'

Fomond looked around, but he could not see the Blue Hair in the press of bodies. 'Why should we fear him?'

'Whatever protection Vittargattus has given us, even if Azrand himself favours us, Kuraal is our enemy. He will seek ways to capitalise on this invasion. So watch your back, Fomond.'

Fomond grinned. 'Perhaps, in such a closely confined space, a knife in *his* back would not be noticed, eh?'

Armestor gasped. 'Don't joke. The wind hears you.'

Fomond snorted, but he knew how sensible Armestor's advice was. Kuraal was unquestionably a very real threat to their mission.

Pyramors looked back over his shoulder anxiously. He could see another gliderboat rising slowly into the sheeting rain, a dozen or so occupants clinging precariously to its sides. Above it, hovering like a black ghost, was the gliderboat that Aru had summoned, its strange Controller sitting in its prow, seemingly organising the lifting of the families single-handedly. This world of Innasmorn is rich in mysteries, and here was the strangest he had yet encountered. A creature linked to the craft by the power of its mind: an unexpected fusion of cultures.

But Pyramors had no time to watch the flight. Before him the gates were about to crash inward as the knights beyond amassed and began their determined attempt to prevent the exodus from the city.

Lines of warriors were prepared to defend the pens, including Jorissimal and his rebels, who had found their way across the city with Lascor as their guide. The last of the gliderboats had come from beyond the towers, pulled by the power of the gliderboat controlled by the Innasmornian pilot. But Pyramors knew that the knights of the Imperator now concentrated their efforts on this compound. They had no intention of letting the rebels lift their families out from under their noses, storm or no storm, although they fought with an almost blind instinct.

Aru was no longer beside the knights, sword ready with theirs to fight to the death to hold this line of defence. She was with the families, the children, trying to soothe them, calm them in the teeth of the gales, the stinging rain. Overhead the wild elementals still soared and swooped, though they did not attack the people in the pens. The sound of the storm was deafening.

With a groan of protest that pierced even the noise of the storm, the gates were wrenched aside, the knights beyond them rushing in, trampling over them. There was no call for surrender. The terms of this battle had already been settled. The Imperator's knights had been given explicit instructions to cut down anyone they found, and the chaos of the storm infused them with a new kind of mindless, killing fury.

Tremazon and other rebel members of the Consulate stood shoulder to shoulder in defence of their families, and the arch under the gateway became the focus for a terrible conflict as swords clashed. It was too constricted an area for any tactical manoeuvres, and soon the crush of bodies from outside the compound made it impossible for even close quarter fighting. Pyramors and his followers found themselves being physically heaved backwards, unable to stem the sheer weight of the attackers. Hundreds of knights had been brought in to deal with the rebels. The storm and all it had brought to the city was forgotten. Somewhere above the snarling fury of the mob, Pyramors imagined he could see the face of Zellorian, gloating over the despair he had brought to the rebels.

The line of defenders held, though some of them fell and were trampled by the knights. Behind the rebels the next gliderboat rose up. Aru knew that she could have had several of the craft manned with warriors who could have harassed the knights, but there was so little time to effect the exodus. The craft had to concentrate on getting the families to safety.

'Tell the warriors to hold their ranks!' Jubaia shouted down to her, hovering close. 'Vittargattus is in the city. A column of his warriors is coming this way. I will direct them.'

Aru could not call out an answer. The gliderboat swung away like a leaf, Jubaia talking to it constantly.

Tremazon, meanwhile, looked to Pyramors, his face mapping his deep concern. His expression said, we cannot hold them. But Pyramors gritted his teeth, thrusting at the knight before him. Both groups were locked tightly, swearing and cursing in the storm, frustrated, tired, unable to do anything but push and heave, an actual contest of arms impossible in the packed ranks. In a moment, Pyramors knew, another combined thrust would force his defenders back deep into the compound, so that the last of the families would be threatened, crushed.

Beyond the ranks of the knights, from one of the narrow streets, other warriors joined the affray, but these were not the armoured knights of the Imperator. Spurred on by the strange craft above them, as though it were the voice of the storm, the Innasmornian van burst into the courtyard outside the walls of the pens. Without delay, they tore into the knights, rocking them back with the unexpected ferocity of their assault.

Above this mayhem, Jubaia looked down on a nightmare scene. The Windmasters poured fire down from the storm, bolts of light ripping into the knights, destroying scores of them, and in their utter confusion, the Innasmornians cut down even more.

Pyramors was abruptly aware of a lessening of the pressure from the knights before him, and Tremazon realised they were no longer trying to carry all before them. At once the defenders of the pens rallied and thrust back at the knights, bit by bit making room so that they could engage in combat. As soon as they did this, they struck down a number of the knights, who were bewildered by what must be happening behind them. Events moved on extraordinarily quickly after that. Those of the knights who were able, fled from this new scene of destruction, filing back down a narrow alleyway towards the heart of the city, where any remaining knights had gone. They did not stop until they came to the walls of the inner citadel, but there they found the gates locked tightly against them. The Imperator, in his terror, had decided on his stand.

At the pens, the last of the killings took place, both defenders and Innasmornians cutting down the trapped knights who were unfortunate enough not to be able to get away from the sudden turn in fortune.

Pyramors found himself facing warriors from this world of storms, beings far smaller than he was, but who were evidently no less effective in combat. For a moment he wondered if the battle would go on, but Aru forced herself through the ranks of the rebels, sword in hand. Without waiting for explanations, she stood directly in front of the Innasmornians.

'Who commands this unit?' she shouted above yet another blast of air.

One of the Innasmornians in the front rank was quick to lift his sword. It was a metal weapon, something that was not common among his warriors, denoting his rank. 'I do.'

Pyramors wondered if the warriors behind this swordsman, and they were numerous, would urge him to continue the offensive, but the Innasmornian lowered his blade.

'You are Aru, whom Vittargattus has marked. Are these the people you have been permitted to spare?'

'They are,' nodded Aru. 'Your enemies rally around the Imperator.' She pointed to the citadel, which loomed from the clouds of falling rain.

'For a while longer only,' said the warrior. He gestured to his followers, urging them on down the street, watching them as they raced by.

'They'll find the citadel closed off,' said Pyramors.

The Innasmornian nodded. 'Aye, but the Windmasters and the Seers will bring it down in ruin. This entire city will be levelled before another dawn breaks.' He glanced back into the pens, where the gliderboats were still hastily getting the families airborne. 'Better take your own people to safety quickly. This storm will not break for many hours.'

He nodded abruptly to Aru, then joined the warriors as they moved ever inward towards the citadel.

Pyramors gazed about him at the devastation. Hundreds of knights had been killed, and a good many of the rebels. He saw fallen friends among the debris, but mercifully the women and children had been spared.

Tremazon stood beside him, wiping his bloody blade. 'This is surely a day of madness. Man killing man. Like rats fighting for a raft in a flooded sewer. Our days are numbered, I think.'

'If we are to have any future,' said Pyramors, watching the storm, 'it lies in the hands of the Innasmornians. Once we would have taken such a world as this effortlessly. Perhaps that was our mistake, to be tyrants. Somewhere along that path, we forfeited our rights.'

Aru broke into his gloomy thoughts. 'The clan chief approaches. And the king of the southern lands. Be careful what you tell them.' Her face was deeply concerned, so much so that Pyramors grinned in spite of himself.

He put his arm around her shoulders. 'The Casruels were, as I recall, always a commanding force. If you are, as you seem to think, the last of them, Aru, you are a tribute to their traditions.'

She would have smiled with him, but exhaustion took her and she began to shudder. He folded his arms about her, talking softly to her, steadying her. 'It's almost over for now,' he whispered. 'Help me with these Innasmornians. After that, we all must rest. And count the cost of this storm.'

She nodded, composing herself.

Tremazon had organised the last of the defenders into lines, their swords put away. He nodded to Pyramors, and together with Aru they waited under the gate to the pens.

A short while later, they watched as Vittargattus and Ondrabal, riding side by side, entered the now deserted plaza before the pens. The knights were stunned at the savage appearance of these conquerors, although it was not their build, smaller than that of Man, that was so surprising. They wore thick furs, adorned with wooden ornaments, their bare arms marked with tattoos. Something in the eyes of both rulers mirrored the wildness, the harnessed anger of the storm, and it was this that gave them the essence of their power. For power it was: these were not primitive barbarians.

They ignored the litter of corpses. Beside them rode Azrand, Freghai and a number of Windmasters and Seers, and beyond that the ranks of yet more of their countless warriors. Overhead there was a lull in the storm, although in other parts of the city it yet appeared to rage.

Aru again walked out into the open plaza, facing the clan chief apparently without fear, though Pyramors felt uneasy. There were far too many archers here for comfort: one well placed arrow would bring the girl down before anyone could act to prevent it. But treachery seemed unlikely, in view of the sweeping victory the Innasmornians had won.

Vittargattus pointed to Pyramors and Tremazon. 'Are these the Men you spoke of?' he said in his own tongue.

Aru nodded. 'The blood they have shed is that of your enemies. The Imperator is the enemy of us both.'

'Have they removed their families as you said they would?'

Aru pointed to the hovering gliderboats. 'It is almost done.'

'In this city, Men are surrendering to our armies,' Ondrabal cut in. 'If we spare their lives, what should we do with them? Imprison them? Execute them?'

'Let me speak to them,' said Aru. 'When the Imperator falls, they will have a choice. Serve another master, or perish.'

'Another master?' said Ondrabal, giving Pyramors a critical glance. 'Who would this be?'

'We must discuss this. The future of Man on Innasmorn.'

'Will Man desire another ruler, one of his own kind?' said Ondrabal. 'Will he build another city?'

Pyramors could not understand the conversation, but he could see that Aru was uncomfortable, troubled by the words of the haughty Innasmornian from the south.

'When the Imperator falls,' she said, 'we must all come together and discuss these things. It is not for me to make demands now. None of us would do that. But we are united in our cause.'

'Very well,' said Vittargattus, realising there would be matters of considerable weight to resolve after the siege.

In some ways it had created far more problems than it had solved. 'We will pursue our enemies. Those of your warriors who wish to aid us in this are welcome to do so.'

He nodded to his followers, and the long cavalcade began to wind its way onward into the city, towards the citadel and its last defenders.

As it passed, watched by the rebels, someone rode from the ranks, hailing Aru. Two of the Innasmornians trotted their horses across the plaza and dismounted before Aru. She smiled warmly at both of them, and to Pyramors's surprise hugged them. One of them grinned hugely, the other seemingly much embarrassed.

'You survived this nightmare!' Aru laughed. 'Come and meet Pyramors and the others.'

She introduced Fomond and Armestor to Pyramors and Tremazon, explaining that they did not know Man's language. They both appeared shy, uncertain of themselves. Pyramors was staggered at how frail they seemed, never having been so close to these people before. And yet their warriors had just reduced the Sculpted City to rubble.

'Gannatyne told me,' said Pyramors, 'that Man's destiny was in their hands. More than ever before, I see that is true.'

'If we are to win the trust of Vittargattus and Ondrabal,' said Aru gravely, 'we will need every kind word these two can give us. And where is Jubaia?' She explained to Fomond and Armestor that the little thief had successfully masterminded the flight of the gliderboats. The news evidently cheered them.

Pyramors hid his innermost thoughts. All allies were welcome in these dark times. But he could not help but wonder how these Innasmornians would fare against the might of the Csendook. The time would come, all too soon, when that testing would be upon them.

Crohalt's shadow waved to the grouped men in the rocks above him. Jannovar was with them, uncomfortable and cold in the night. They would cross the road soon, exposed briefly to the unusual glare of Innasmorn's moonlight. The girl could sense Kelwars not far from her shoulder, feel his eyes upon her, his hungry gaze no less offensive than it had been through the day's trek through the mountains.

Below them, beyond the figure of Crohalt, the narrow gorge threaded its tortuous way up to the northern masses and on to the fortress of Starhanger. Dug from the side of the gorge, a precarious ledge was the road that led from the fortress back to the Sculpted City. Crohalt's party would have to slide down the crumbling scree of this side of the gorge to the lone span that served as the only makeshift bridge for miles. A scout had already crossed it earlier in the evening, and he had been up and down the road to see that it was clear. His word had come back to Crohalt that it was safe to cross. Once over, they would climb up and away to the peaks beyond the eyes of the Imperator's knights.

Slowly Jannovar and her guards went down to the gorge. The rocks were silent, the air very still. There were no clouds above, although throughout the day they had heard the distant sounds of thunder, the storm that Kelwars had said would come to the southern parts of the range, where the Sculpted City lay. Light flashed in the skies there, as though a conflict of powers raged, but Jannovar tried not to think of what it might mean.

She and the men saw Crohalt lithely cross the stone span and merge with the shadows beyond at the edge of the crude road. In a moment Tennegar was urging her to cross with him, Kelwars and the others at her back. She heard the rush of water far below and shut out the thought of the drop, which must have been substantial, though it was thankfully screened in the darkness. Then they were on the road, pausing only briefly before crossing it.

They found Crohalt and he ushered them all into the cover of a rockfall that had almost spilled out over the road, the boulders huge.

'Where's Hadrus?' Tennegar asked softly.

Crohalt motioned for absolute silence. 'He heard someone on the road to the south. He's gone to look. We may have to wait while they pass on up to Starhanger. Keep well down. We've not been seen.'

To Jannovar, crouched down among the rocks with the men pressed close to her, the minutes dragged away. Again she saw Kelwars, his teeth flashing in a crude smile, but she was powerless to say anything to him.

At last they heard a soft call. It was Hadrus. Crohalt slipped from cover and went to him, returning in a moment.

'Refugees from the City,' he explained, whispering. 'A handful of them, fleeing from a great battle. Some are wounded. They know there are rebels in the mountains.'

'Then they're heading the wrong way,' snorted Kelwars, 'if they keep to this road.'

'Hadrus says we should guide them up into our retreat.'

'Does he know them?'

'No,' said Crohalt. 'But they say that the Sculpted City has suffered terrible losses. A storm struck, and from it, an invading army. Innasmornians. The Imperator may be dead.'

'Then let's welcome these runaways!' said Tennegar. 'Surely they don't support him now.'

'They say not,' said Crohalt. He slipped away on to the road, and soon after called to the hidden party. Tennegar led it out from the shadows. They stood uneasily on the road.

Coming up from the south, a small party of knights trotted their horses in the moonlight. There were barely a dozen, and they all had the look of beaten men about them, the weariness and exhaustion plain. And their arms and chests were bloodied.

Hadrus joined Crohalt. 'They'll not make the settlement tonight, Crohalt. They're far too –' But he never finished his sentence, gagging as the arrow took him cleanly between the shoulderblades, its point rupturing a lung. Bubbling blood, Hadrus collapsed into Crohalt's arms.

'Bastards!' gasped the warrior. 'It's a trap! Get back into the rocks.'

Tennegar turned, trying to shelter Jannovar, and an arrow took him in the arm. Another of the men went down, an arrow in his neck, and Jannovar dropped to the ground, scurrying up into the cover. Kelwars followed her, and the other men drew their swords. Chaos broke loose as the riders from the City urged their horses forward, bearing down on the rebels, their own weapons swinging.

Jannovar pressed herself into the rocks, her heart thundering. It was hopeless thinking of flight, the sides of the gorge were too steep for climbing swiftly. She heard Kelwars curse as he drew his own weapon no more than feet from her. He swung round to face the onslaught.

Steel rang in the night, and men swore as they cut at one another. But there were more men on the road, coming up from the south. Hadrus had been deceived.

It was a swift affair. Crohalt was cut down mercilessly, blood seeping over the rocks, mingling with that of the fallen Hadrus, and beside them, others were chopped down. In a short while, only Tennegar, Kelwars and one other, Dulvars, stood shoulder to shoulder, surrounded by knights.

'We guessed we'd meet some of you vermin on this road to Starhanger,' grimaced one of the knights. 'Though we thought maybe there'd be a bigger pack than this.' He dabbed at the blood on his arms. It was not his own, part of the deceit.

Behind him, Tennegar could see another, much larger party, coming up the road. The Imperator Elect's standard fluttered in the moonlight. The City must have been partially evacuated.

'What has happened?' said Tennegar.

'Never mind that,' snapped the knight.

'Sir!' called a harsh voice, almost beside Jannovar's ear. She jerked, finding herself gazing up at the blade of another warrior who had discovered her hiding place. He bent down and gripped her arm, dragging her to her feet. She tried to reach his eyes with her nails but he caught her a stinging blow across the cheek with the flat of his blade.

'Bring out anyone you find,' called the leading knight.

Jannovar was thrust forward, standing once more beside Kelwars.

'A woman?' said the knight. 'What sort of party is this?'

'Say nothing,' muttered Dulvars under his breath.

'If you want to avoid a lingering death,' said the knight, leaning forward in his saddle, 'you'll not waste our time.'

As he spoke, one of the leading knights from the approaching party galloped up to his side, the eyes of his horse staring wildly. 'Is is safe to pass on?' snapped the knight, his face masked by a war helm. 'We cannot afford to dally out in this wilderness. It's a good ride yet to Starhanger.'

'Is this all of you?' the first knight snapped at Tennegar.

'Yes,' the latter nodded.

'Where's your camp?'

'Say nothing,' said Dulvars.

At once the knight gestured men forward, and they spitted Dulvars where he stood. Neither Kelwars nor Tennegar dared move. They looked askance at each other.

'Tell them,' said Kelwars.

Tennegar hesitated, trying not to look at the twitching form of Dulvars, the bloody corpses of Crohalt and the others.

'You will tell us,' said the knight. 'You know that.'

12

IN THE PALACE

'Will they be safe?' Pyramors asked, shielding his eyes from the driving rain as he looked skywards beyond the city to where the mountains were hidden by the storm.

Aru nodded. 'Jubaia has found a plateau up among the peaks. The gliderboats can shelter and Vittargattus has already promised that no one will be harmed.'

'If they're high in the mountains, how could his forces attack them?' said Tremazon.

'You don't realise how much power the Innasmornians have over these storms,' Aru told him. 'They *control* them, I promise you. And they could strike the gliderboats from the sky as easily as we would swat flies.'

'Then the Innasmornians really did allow the fleet to escape under sufferance?' said Pyramors.

Again Aru nodded. 'It is a measure of the respect in which Ussemitus is held. Vittargattus and the Windmasters know he has the ears of their gods. They respect such power and won't won't go against him. But I do wish he was here now.'

Pyramors and Tremazon said nothing, but from what Aru had been telling them about Ussemitus, they were also eager to meet him. Pyramors wondered if the girl had been exaggerating his so-called powers. He also detected within her an emotional tie with the man that she could not disguise. Could she perhaps be in love with him? But he preferred to say nothing about his suspicions.

The warriors had reorganised themselves now that the last of the gliderboats had gone out of the city. Every woman and child that had been found had been rescued and lifted away, even a few families who were not part of the original plan, for the storm had created so much confusion that people were desperate to flee to whatever haven they could find.

Even flight up into the storm was preferable to the terrible dangers in the city, which toppled, burning around their ears. Someone had remarked that it was as though the Csendook had come again.

As Pyramors and Tremazon prepared to take the troops into the heart of the city, they were met by scouts. One of these rushed up to Tremazon, bowing.

'Sire, news from the citadel. All resistance outside it has ended. Many men have died, but the rest have thrown down their arms. The Innasmornians are about to go into the citadel in search of the Imperator and Zellorian.'

'If they find them,' said Aru, 'they'll think they can tear them limb from limb. But Zellorian is dangerous – '

'They can't know how dangerous,' agreed Pyramors. 'We must get to them quickly. Before their victory is turned around.'

At once the warriors moved on into the city, threading through its ruins, Fomond and Armestor keeping beside Aru, who hurriedly translated all that was said for them.

The Innasmornian forces had concentrated around the tall gates of the inner citadel, but already the Windmasters had directed energies at them that were threatening to blast them aside. Pyramors was stunned by the forces that the Innasmornians were able to bring to bear on their enemies. Azrand and others of his order were actually calling upon lightning, using it to rip into the gates, and the wind had itself coalesced into a stream of beings, creatures that combined their own powers to add might to this invading army.

The huge gates collapsed, crushing whatever opposition waited behind them, and the inner citadel was breached. Fires burned there and few men could be seen. Pyramors and his rebels went in through the gates behind the Innasmornian van. They met no opposition. The knights who had defended the outer gates had already thrown down their arms. They were guarded by a small party of the invaders, but they looked disconsolate, exhausted. Pyramors understood their position very clearly. This was indeed a repetition of the fall of Rannor Tarul, the grim acceptance of defeat. Perhaps if the Csendook had not so mercilessly crushed the defences on Eannor, the spirit of these men would have stood a little more bombardment. But it could not. Yet it was for the best, Pyramors reflected. The Innasmornians were deceptively powerful. Only time would show if they had it in them to be more compassionate than the Csendook.

They came at last to the gates of the palace. These were wide open. There was no sign of movement: not even a hound raised its head from the ruins. Vittargattus sent word for Aru to join him. She took Fomond, Armestor, Pyramors and Tremazon with her and they met the clan chief and Ondrabal at the very gates of the inner palace.

Vittargattus pointed ominously at the buildings, most of which were as yet intact. 'I will raze them,' he said, Aru translating for the men. 'I will leave no one alive, not even the children. This is the heart of your city. Your Imperator is there. If you are indeed allies to my people, show me the way to these enemies.'

'Gladly,' said Aru. 'But I must warn you again, Vittargattus, that there will be danger. The Prime Consul uses dark powers. We suspect him of trying to use such forces as he used in the Dhumvald.'

'The storm-of-the-dark,' muttered Azrand, but his voice was heard over a lull in the storm. 'He cannot have mastered the calling of such a thing.'

'Perhaps he has,' said Aru. 'So we'll go in with care.'

'You will lead us in?' said Ondrabal.

Aru nodded.

She was surprised to find Fomond at her side. 'And I will. With my companion.' He indicated Armestor, who tried not to look appalled.

Azrand was also nodding at the suggestion. 'Shoulder to shoulder. Freghai and I will form part of the spear that must strike at the heart of this evil.'

Vittargattus and Ondrabal glanced at one another. Throughout their invasion their respect for one another had grown, and there were times now when they did not have to speak to know what was in each other's mind. Both nodded.

They led the first wave, guiding their nervous steeds

slowly forward through the open gates. There were gardens beyond and courts, all deserted. Some of the buildings had been smitten by the bolts from above, but most of the palace was intact, as if it had been untouched by the storm. The skies had become quieter, though still dark, as if at any moment they would again unleash their devastating powers. The rain had become a steady drizzle, the wind falling away, though it was as if the skies were filled with hidden eyes.

Pyramors and Tremazon knew the palace best, though neither of them had ever been wont to visit it often. As they guided the company forward, through yet more gardens and then into the main structure itself, they felt sure that it had been abandoned. There was evidence of that: weapons strewn about, uniforms cast aside. But no people. All had fled. Pyramors knew that under the palace there would be innumerable passages and tunnels, bolt-holes. The Innasmornians were remorseless enough to find them, he guessed.

At length, unopposed, they reached the principal chambers, where they would have expected the Imperator Elect to have been concealed. The two lavish doors, carved intricately and set with gold inlay, caused the Innasmornians to gasp in wonder. The opulence of the palace had not gone unnoticed, though they had kept their thoughts to themselves. Somewhere outside the storm held its breath. A deep silence had clamped down, as though the warriors had slipped through a portal into another realm.

Azrand turned to Aru. 'Are these doors locked, or must we force them?'

Aru considered, but asked Pyramors, 'Could Zellorian have set some kind of trap for us?'

'I can't say. But it may be dangerous for the Windmasters to try and unleash power in here.'

Aru passed this message on, and Vittargattus looked suspiciously at Pyramors, as though contemplating whether or not this could be a trap.

Pyramors pushed forward, to the doors. He gave a twist to the huge ring set on the right hand one. The door opened silently. Behind him, Pyramors felt the Innasmornians tense, a score of bows trained on his back. But he stepped over the threshold.

The vast chamber within was silent, dimly lit from the windows in its domed ceiling. But it was empty. The Imperator had long since fled.

Pyramors threw open both doors. 'They've gone,' he said.

Vittargattus motioned some of his warriors in and they checked the chamber at once. But Pyramors was correct in his assumption. The inner chambers were as void as those outside.

'Where are they hiding?' Azrand asked Aru. 'They must be within the city. If they had tried to flee its boundaries, our forces would have seen them. Word would have come to us by now.'

'What do you think?' Aru asked Pyramors and Tremazon.

'There are inner sanctums, of course,' said the latter. 'You must know how careful the Prime Consul was.'

'He must be here,' said Pyramors. 'But where are the knights? Where are the technicians, the monitors? We'll have to search the entire palace.'

Aru again explained the difficulties to Azrand. It was agreed that every stone would be overturned if need be. But both Vittargattus and Ondrabal were determined to handle the situation with extreme caution. They conversed privately.

'This may be a trap,' said Ondrabal. 'If we bring our armies into the citadel and camp here, we court disaster, for all our powers.'

'I agree. Let us draw up our armies outside the palace. Should we both continue the search ourselves?'

Ondrabal, usually severe, laughed gently. 'I think so, my friend. If one of us were to perish, there would be a degree of confusion as to who should command. Our partnership alone has held our armies together, I think.'

Vittargattus also permitted himself a wry smile. 'A good point. But what of these others? And the prisoners?'

Ondrabal grimaced. 'And those who have gone up into the mountains in those craft. What is their future to be? Will our nations be safe while any of these invaders live?'

'I confess their presence makes me uneasy, though they have shown themselves most worthy in this affair. They certainly hold their ruler in the utmost contempt.'

'Then let us defer a decision on their future. Clearly we have the balance of power, the power to decide their fate.'

'Very well.'

Ondrabal turned back to the warriors and issued them with instructions. 'Azrand, Freghai, you remain with us, but let most of your shamen go back with the armies to the outer walls of the palace. You will be summoned if needed.'

'What is their plan?' Pyramors asked Aru.

'They suspect a trap. Not from you, I think. But from Zellorian. They won't commit their entire army to this search, not in here.'

'They're good commanders,' observed Tremazon. 'I'd have done the same.'

'They can call on the Windmasters and the Seers to focus their powers, wherever they are,' said Aru.

The search began afresh, hours passing as the company looked throughout the many layers and levels of the palace. But they knew in the end that the Imperator was not here, nor was his Prime Consul. Whatever staff they had kept close to them, they had taken with them. Knights who had been on duty in the outer palace was brought in and interrogated, but they knew nothing. They had been locked out, that was all they could say.

'Then they have either shut themselves up in a region we have not been able to find,' said Azrand in conclusion, 'or else have fled by some other route.'

'We will set our elementals to search,' said Freghai.

Vittargattus and Ondrabal nodded grimly. They were both growing increasingly frustrated at the lack of success of the company, and more than once had come close to issuing the order to have the entire palace brought crashing down in flames.

Azrand and Freghai sent messages back to their fellows beyond the walls and they began the new search, using the power of the elements to scour the realms of Innasmorn beyond the city, and in the mountains and under them.

It was Pyramors who discovered the passageway that led down to an area with which he was unfamiliar. It seemed at first to be no more than a way down to an area for housing a company of guards, like many others in the inner palace. But it lacked some of the basic characteristics of such a passage, having a gradual incline and a steady curve. It was unusually long, whereas most such passages led to a brief flight of steps down to a small guard chamber. Many of these had been concealed in the palace so that the knights and guards would not be intrusive when not on duty.

'What has he found?' said Vittargattus as Pyramors came back up into the main chamber above the passage where the company had temporarily come to an exasperated halt.

'It's narrow,' Pyramors told Aru, who quickly translated his comments. 'And long. We are in an area that would have been under the direct control of Zellorian. I think we should go down.'

He agreed to lead, and the company filed into the tunnel in complete silence. Pyramors held aloft a lighted brand, for there was no light down here. The air was warm, however, and stank of something metallic. A hundred yards down the now steepening passage it opened out to a narrow balcony. Steps led down from this to a small chamber. There were unlit torches in it, and Pyramors used the last of his brand to ignite them.

In their glow they could see that this was merely an antechamber to a bigger one. The door to it may once have been guarded, for there were spears and shields lying discarded, as in the upper palace. The door itself, cast in thick metal, hung open. Silence waited beyond.

Even Azrand looked dubious about going on.

'This must be Zellorian's lair!' gasped Pyramors.

'Could it be the place of the Path?' said Tremazon, close by his shoulder. They stood at the brink of the doorway to the utter darkness.

'What are they saying?' Vittargattus asked Aru impatiently.

'They think that this might be the very place where our people emerged after crossing to Innasmorn from our own Cycle of Worlds.'

'Then our enemies have retraced their steps? Gone back to their own world of origin?' said Azrand.

Pyramors turned to Aru. 'I have been here,' he said thickly, for some reason she couldn't understand his voice dropping to an emotional whisper, as if there were memories in this place that disturbed him very deeply.

'Can we enter safely?' she asked him.

'Bring torches,' he said, before anyone could reply, and stepped through the door. Tremazon was close behind him, and in a moment the entire company followed, bearing a dozen torches between them.

The smell of death met them, as though they had come into a region where many battles had been fought, and where many warriors must have fallen. But there were no bones here, no sign of a corpse. Nothing moved: already the dust was thickening like a carpet. It was a huge place, shadows fleeing from the firebrands' glow, and massive columns held up the ceiling, its arches lost in the darkness overhead.

Azrand shook his head in amazement. It was as though the company had stepped outside space into some otherwhere. Magic and power clung to this place, sorcery dancing round every stone.

'Yes,' Pyramors was nodding. 'I was here. Zellorian sent me back to Eannor.' He pointed to the two largest of the columns, which former a kind of gateway to a deeper darkness, a well that could have been space itself.

'Is that where they have gone?' Ondrabal was asking.

'Dare we follow?' said Vittargattus.

Aru answered him with a shake of the head. 'It has been sealed. And it would be sheer madness to attempt to reopen it. If Zellorian has fled down that avenue, then Innasmorn is well rid of him.'

Pyramors sagged, dropping to his knees. His exhaustion hit him now. 'He used the blood of my men to send me through,' he murmured. 'There was no limit to his cruelty.'

'You say this. . .gate, leads to other worlds?' said Ondrabal, stepping a little closer to the columns.

'It must remain closed,' said Aru. 'There are things beyond it that must never be aroused.'

'If our enemies left so easily,' Ondrabal went on, mounting the first of the wide steps, 'could they not return as easily? If they have sealed it, may they not open it again when it suits them? Perhaps we should pursue them after all.'

Aru appealed to Azrand. 'That's insane,' she hissed. 'You must make him understand.'

They were all too fascinated by Ondrabal's steady climb up the steps to speak for a moment, as if words would break the brittle air, the spell that seemed to hang there.

In the darkness beside the left column, something moved, subtle as a ghost. Ondrabal swung round to face it, teeth barred like those of a wolf, his weapon held out protectively.

'Are you all so eager to meet your doom?' said a voice that could have come from anywhere in the huge chamber. The ghost moved into the light, taking on more substantial form.

Aru recognised the figure, gasping. It was Ussemitus, clothed now in a white robe, his face serene, though his eyes were troubled as he looked down at her and the others.

'Ussemitus?' said Azrand, stepping forward. He was stunned at how much the youth had changed. When he had first seen him, he was a forester, a young man from the eastern woodlands who had little more than his spirit to lift him from the common track of his fellows. But now he seemed to exude power, as if he had only to lift his hand to summon a gale, or to cast stars through the air. And, strangely, there was something in his eyes that suggested a much greater age, a deeper wisdom. That wisdom seemed to have been bought at a high cost.

Vittargattus also recognised the youth, himself surprised at the transformation.

'Why are you here?' said Ussemitus. 'Have you no concept of the dangers?'

Ondrabal glared at him, though he was unconsciously backing off, recognising the awesome power in this figure. 'Where is the Imperator? Do you know?'

Ussemitus turned to him, eyes unblinking. 'Far from this place of death, Ondrabal. With all his minions. Gathering up the forces of nightmare. Readying to do untold harm to the Mother.'

'You know these things?' said Vittargattus.

Ussemitus began the descent of the stair. At first the company had thought him to be an illusion, a projection. Pyramors and Tremazon held back, uncertain. On Innasmorn they had seen so much that contradicted their understanding of things that this new marvel was almost acceptable. But Aru had said Ussemitus was thousands of miles from here, in the far west. Had the youth used some kind of gate? But how was it done?

'The Mother has taught me much,' said Ussemitus.

'Where are they?' said Vittargattus, holding his anger in check.

'Zellorian is in the lost city of Umus Utmar. He and his followers are not as they were. They have become slaves to the Malefics. And they will raise them from the deep wells that were their prison. They have that power.'

'The *Malefics*!' cried Freghai. 'That is impossible – '

Ussemitus shook his head. 'No. Already Zellorian has begun the workings. Umus Utmar shudders to them.'

'And the Imperator? Where is he, his craven followers?' said Vittargattus.

'Less far. What is left of his army he has taken with him through the passages under this city out into the mountains to the fortress in the north east.'

'Where Gannatyne is imprisoned?' said Aru.

Ussemitus nodded. 'Yes. Gannatyne is there. The last of the Imperator's troops guard him closely. It is all they have left to bargain with for their lives.'

He had spoken in his own tongue, but Pyramors had heard Gannatyne's name. 'What is he saying?' he asked Aru urgently.

She explained and Pyramors and Tremazon shook their heads in frustration and fury.

'We must free Gannatyne,' said Pyramors. But he looked about him at the gathered Innasmornians. Where would their priorities lie in these matters?

'You will need to be strong,' said Ussemitus, again winning the attention of all of them. 'Already you have fought side by side in this city. You must continue to do so.'

'A formal alliance?' said Ondrabal.

'How are the people of this city to be treated?' said Vittargattus. 'They have fought each other in this war. There are many prisoners. Who rules them now?'

'Who would they accept as ruler?' said Ussemitus.

Vittargattus grunted. 'These two warriors have shown themselves to be equal to the situation. Let them decide.'

Aru had been translating this as swiftly as she could to the men, but at this point Pyramors shook his head. 'Tell them that the only man who could properly weld us now is Gannatyne. We have to free him.'

Aru nodded, repeating this for the benefit of the others.

'Men will be fine allies,' Ussemitus told Vittargattus and Ondrabal. 'If you are to defeat Zellorian and the things he serves, you will need such allies.'

'Will this Gannatyne serve us?' said Vittargattus.

Ussemitus smiled. 'No. But he will be your friend.'

'Is he to be their new Imperator?' said Ondrabal, making no attempt to conceal his contempt.

Pyramors answered, once Aru had translated. 'Tell them that there will be no more Imperators. There will be a new Consulate. Possibly not even. that. But a controlling body. Some sort of council. Do you agree, Tremazon?'

'I do. Power should not be vested in one ruler. Those days must end.'

'The Empire truly ends here,' said Pyramors.

'Umus Utmar and all it holds must be overthrown,' said Ussemitus. 'You must be strong, your power absolute, if you are to cast down that black city.'

'You speak for the Mother?' said Ondrabal.

Ussemitus paused for only a moment before he answered, his mouth drawn into a tight line, the strain in his eyes never clearer. 'She speaks to you through me.'

Vittargattus nodded very slowly. Alliances. The north east. Men as allies. There was so much to consider, and so little time.

Aru turned her eyes from the figure in white. She had already known that they could not share their love. But now, seeing him garbed in his new power, godlike, hearing him speak with the voice of a world, she knew that she had indeed lost him, and all hope of ever winning back what they had once shared as they travelled across Innasmorn, not knowing then that it would be to separate destinies.

Tennegar was on his knees, holding his bloody arm, the arrow's point gleaming in the moonlight. Two of the knights stood over him, both holding their swords as though eager to despatch him. Jannovar watched them in wide-eyed horror, trying not to look at the other corpses.

The mounted knight looked over his shoulder as the men on the road trotted past. There were several score of them, knights from the Sculpted City, fleeing its destruction, making for Starhanger. There were three carriages with them, drawn by teams of eight steeds, and Jannovar guessed that some of the Consulate must have got away from the battle.

'Well?' snapped the knight, turning to glare at Kelwars.

'What do you want to know?'

Tennegar made no attempt to prevent Kelwars from speaking, gritting his teeth on his pain.

'I'd rather die than tell you anything!' said Jannovar, but she knew she could not endure the tortures these men would inflict on her.

'You're Jorissimal's scum,' said the knight. 'So where's his base? Be quick about your answer, or that one dies next.' He indicated Tennegar.

'I can lead you to it,' said Kelwars, looking away from Jannovar.

'How many are there? Is the place well defended? How many warriors should I take?'

'Only a handful of men. Mostly wounded or unsuitable for the battle down in the City.'

'And who is this woman? Is she the only one you have? Perhaps she serves your entire army?'

Jannovar glared up at him, her face flushed with fury. Pyramors would rip his heart out for that if only. . .but it was pointless to say it. She realised it would be better for her if she kept silent. They must not know who she was.

'She belongs to one of the leaders,' said Kelwars.

'Jorissimal?'

Kelwars shook his head slowly.

'Don't waste my time. Tell me where this base is, and who the woman belongs to. You'll be spared. Hurry, I haven't time to hang about on this accursed road!'

'You'll spare me?' said Kelwars, his eyes narrowing.

'It's of no importance to me, so save yourself.'

'She's the wife of Fromhal Djorganist. The mistress of the Consul, Pyramors.'

The knight gasped. 'They say that bastard was with the forces that attacked the City. Is this true?' He addressed this to Jannovar.

She lifted her head contemptuously. 'Yes, it's true! And he's put your own vermin to flight, that's plain to see!'

The knight's eyes blazed as though he would have her cut down where she stood. But he leaned back, nodding thoughtfully. 'The Djorganist woman, eh? Then you're a valuable prize after all.' He lifted his blade, indicating Kelwars. 'Your name?'

'Kelwars, sir.'

'Well, Kelwars, you've earned your life. If you want to earn your future, you'd better finish the bargain. I want that base.'

'Kelwars!' hissed Tennegar. 'Don't be a fool! They'll kill you – '

One of the knights beside him lifted his sword and the mounted knight nodded. Tennegar tried to fling himself aside, but the edge of the sword bit into his side. He toppled among the rocks, the knight straddling him, about to plunge the blade down into him. But the mounted knight called him off.

'Leave him here. Let him crawl back down the road to anyone that is following. He can carry the news to them. You hear me, soldier? Tell your commanders that the only welcome they'll get in their base is from the ghosts.'

'No!' protested Jannovar, but another of the knights pulled her back, gripping her arms.

The knight dismounted. Behind him, the knights still rode past and up the road. He studied Jannovar from close up, smiling cruelly. 'A pretty wench. But then, your type were bred for it. The Imperator would welcome you among his harlots. But such a waste, when he has so many.' He turned away from her scathing gaze and came over to Kelwars.

'You were wise to speak,' he said, lowering his voice. 'And if you do as I tell you, you'll survive this slaughter.'

'Whatever you say, sir,' replied Kelwars, barely above a whisper.

'There's no need for anyone other than my men and me to know who this girl is. If anyone else finds out, I'll have you disembowelled. But do as you're told and forget about these shit-eating rebels – '

Kelwars smiled. 'As you wish, sir. It will be a pleasure to know her detestable pride will be curbed.'

'Rest assured, Kelwars, it will be.'

13

MOUNTAIN ROAD

Across the skies, the storms faded as swiftly as they had come. Darkness swallowed the land, and only in the city where the fires bloomed could much be seen. Pyramors and his followers marvelled at the skills of the shamen, recognising that somehow they were able to control the elements. As dawn arrived, the armies gathered together, still wary of each other, but the Innasmornian leaders had given out orders that there was to be no more killing. They began the march out from the city and up into the first slopes of the mountains to the north east.

Pyramors and Tremazon had spoken to the prisoners, explaining that if they did not throw themselves on the mercy of the new regime and instead sought freedom out in the wastes of Innasmorn, their chances of survival were minimal. Vittargattus and Ondrabal had made it quite clear that Men who were not prepared to come under a new banner would be hunted down without pity and destroyed. But there was no resistance: the survivors were dumbfounded by the extent of the damage, the totality of their defeat. The Sculpted City was an utter ruin, most of its buildings reduced to rubble, its streets collapsed. There was no spirit of resistance left in the people, and they willingly accepted the terms given to them by Pyramors and Tremazon. The Innasmornians insisted that they should not be given arms, and that Pyramors would be responsible for them.

Aru did her best to soothe the mounting anger of Pyramors and Tremazon. 'Be thankful that they're prepared to help you bring Gannatyne out of the mountains.'

'If it weren't for Ussemitus, we would not have been spared,' said Tremazon. 'There are a good many of these people who would have us removed from their world altogether.'

Aru managed a wry grin. 'Then you'd better learn their language. Fomond and I will teach you as we travel.'

Pyramors nodded moodily, looking back at the ruins spread below them. The fires were burning out, but there was little left for them to eat into. None of the proud towers stood, and the palace at the heart of the citadel was devastated. If there were survivors huddling down amongst the ruins, their existence from now on would be an unhappy one. They would be better taking to the mountains, although it seemed likely they would be more prone to the vengeance of the Innasmornians there.

'Speaking of Ussemitus,' said Tremazon, 'where is he?'

'Searching for Jubaia and the gliderboats.'

'If we are to besiege the fortress, we'll need the craft.'

'Perhaps. But word will come.'

Tremazon had noticed the girl's mood. The strain of the night's events had left her almost completely exhausted, more than a hint of depression behind her eyes. He assumed it must be sadness at the sight of the abrupt demise of the city, the ease with which the Innasmornians had brought it down. Pyramors, too, was brooding, almost sullen. Something chafed at him, though Tremazon could only imagine it must be the anxiety of command, the uncertainty of the future. Innasmorn had been man's haven, his hope, an unexpected escape from the wrath of the Csendook. But now it might, after all, become his grave.

Will you sleep all day? The words sounded as clearly as bells in Jubaia's mind, probing the murky shallows of his dream. He rubbed at his eyes and sat up, hands immediately going out to steady himself on the sides of the gliderboat as though the craft would still be swooping through the turbulent air currents of another storm. But the early morning was calm. The storms had gone. Dawn began to spread thinly over the high peaks.

'Is it over?' he said sleepily. The events of the night had completely worn him out. He stretched himself now, his muscles stiff and protesting.

If you mean the storm, the destruction, said Circu.

'Did I detect a little facetiousness in your tone?' Jubaia chuckled. But he sobered as he detected the melancholy in the gliderboat. It had been a terrifying night, the air filled with the writhing terror of the families they had brought out of the city. Events had left their mark on the gliderboat.

Even so, she softened. *I'm sorry. I feel as though I've been turned inside out.*

Jubaia nodded, looking around him. They had come to rest on a narrow plateau, high up in the mountains to the west of the city. There were in all some fifty gliderboats, and they had brought out several hundred survivors from the Sculpted City, the women and children mostly, though there were men with them: the older ones and a number of wounded soldiers who would have died had they been left. At the end, no one had bothered to think about who was in support of who: they had just brought out whoever they could. There would be no disputes here. It would be a long time before these bewildered people would be able to do anything other than lick their wounds. They had managed to bring food and some supplies with them, and all around the plateau now the women were beginning to organise the day's first meal and tending to the wounded.

Jubaia grunted to himself, pleased.

Did you think they would be any less practical than your own people in a situation like this? said Circu.

Again he chuckled. 'No, no. I am relieved that they are able to put last night out of their thoughts.'

They may seem to have closed it from their minds. But their pain is deep, Jubaia. Many of them know their men are lost to them.

Jubaia again detected the sorrow within Circu. Perhaps, he thought privately, she feels her own particular tragedy more deeply having been brought among the women of her kind once more. He would have speculated on this further, but his attention was caught by a cry from the rocks above, where guards had been stationed to watch for any sign of pursuit.

He was amazed to see the familiar figure coming down the rough path, escorted by two of the older boys. Both of them looked a little bewildered by the arrival of the white-robed being with them, but they offered it no aggression.

Jubaia skipped over the rocks and halted before the trio.

'He doesn't seem like an enemy,' the older of the boys said sheepishly, as if he might have failed in his duty by allowing the stranger to come here.

'No, he's no enemy,' said Jubaia, going to Ussemitus and unexpectedly putting his arms about him.

Ussemitus laughed gently. 'Well, little thief, last night you pulled off one of your better acts, lifting these people to safety. Theft on the grand scale, I should say.'

'And you?' said Jubaia anxiously. 'When did you come? How?'

'The Mother uses me now,' Ussemitus replied, but his smile thinned, as though he, too, was troubled by something.

'The city?'

'Destroyed. The storms were thorough. Aru has brought Pyramors and another of the Consulate, Tremazon, to the clan chief and his allies. There is an uneasy truce, and I have persuaded them all that they must go into the far mountains and free Gannatyne. The Imperator is there. Once he is taken, the pursuit of Zellorian will begin. All are aware of how dangerous he has become. The threat of his power is what will unite our people and those of Aru.'

'Who will rule Man?'

'They want it to be Gannatyne.'

'Aru always spoke of him with deep respect.'

'They will need the gliderboats if they are to storm the fortress. Will they be able to fly?'

'They'll need Controllers. We have a few here. I was able to help last night. But it was a dangerous flight. The craft need particular attention. For the flight you envisage, we would need Controllers. There must be survivors among the Men Pyramors has.'

'I'll attend to it.' Ussemitus surveyed the plateau, satisfied that there was nothing he could do here. The people seemed able to gather their wits to them. 'This will be as good a place as any for a base for these people,' he told Jubaia.

'How long must I stay with them?'

Ussemitus smiled. 'Be patient. When we need the glider-boats, we'll come for them. As you know, Vittargattus and Ondrabal still have reservations about them.' Just as the Mother does, he thought, but he did not say it, knowing how it would hurt both his friend and the craft.

Jubaia snorted. But he knew Ussemitus was right. Perhaps he would be better up here, out of the way of the clan chief and the shamen after all.

Later that day, as the armies wove their way up into the mountains, their front lines were alerted by scouts that Men had been found in the passes ahead. Aru and Pyramors were summoned by Vittargattus.

Aru listened to the excited report of the scout who had come scurrying down the scree banks to their left, bringing word from the Innasmornians who watched the road ahead.

'What is it?' said Pyramors. 'We're still a long march from the fortress.'

'They've found men. Some dead, some wounded.'

'Fleeing from the city?'

Aru shook her head. 'No. They've come out of the mountains.'

Vittargattus nudged his horse up beside them. 'I'll have one of these Men brought to us. Will you know them?' He addressed Aru, but she knew that the question was really for Pyramors.

Aru nodded. They waited as the scout raced off back up the slope. A short while later a party of three Innasmornian scouts came down from the mountains, leading a horse. Bent over it, badly wounded, was one of the rebels. Pyramors did not know the man's name, but he immediately recognised him as being one of Jorrisimal's warriors who had been left to watch over the camps while the raid on the Sculpted City took place. Jannovar! his mind cried. What of her? She might have been with this man's group.

Water was brought to the stricken man, whose chest was caked in blood. He had received a deep cut in his side, and his arm had been bandaged up by the warriors who had found him: his face was white with shock and pain. They made a shelter for him and Vittargattus watched grimly as Aru sponged his face. Azrand and Freghai were also close by. The entire army seemed to hold its breath, waiting for any news the stricken warrior might have. For once the skies were clear, the air very still.

'My name is Tennegar,' he said with difficulty.

Pyramors sensed a shadow behind him. It was Jorissimal himself, his face grave as he saw the fallen warrior. 'I think he was one of the guards we left at your base.'

Jorissimal nodded, bending down beside Aru. 'Tennegar, what happened? Who has done this? Innasmornians?'

Tennegar shook his head. 'No. We were crossing the road to Starhanger, heading for one of our eeries up in the central mass, when Hadrus, our scout, told us there were men coming. We thought they were escaping from the city, men that you had freed. At first we were cautious, but Hadrus said these men seemed, like us, enemies of the Imperator. They asked for guidance, saying they were looking for you, Jorissimal. Some of them appeared to be wounded.' He coughed, blood dribbling down over his ragged beard.

Jorissimal glanced up at Pyramors. He could see that the Consul had come to the same conclusion he had: Tennegar would not live for very much longer.

But the warrior went on. 'They told Hadrus they had been hoping to find us as they were indeed fleeing the city, as were many others. There was a battle raging. The Imperator, they said, was dead, the Consulate overthrown. Perhaps we were not cautious enough, but we were taken in. We agreed to take them with us. It was a trap. They were not alone. There were others, and when they knew how many we were, they quickly overwhelmed us, coming in greater numbers. They acted without mercy. They killed all of us except for me, Kelwars, and the girl.'

157

Pyramors glared down at the man as if he would take a sword to him. 'They *killed* their own kind? Rather than take them prisoner?'

'Aye, and laughed about it. The Imperator was not dead. He was with their main body, making his way up to the fortress. I was wounded and left as an example to. . .those of you who would return.'

Pyramors bent down beside Jorissimal, his eyes cold, his mouth a taut, hard line. 'What of Jannovar?' he said so quietly that the wounded man almost missed it.

But his eyes flickered with recognition. 'Yes, she lives, Consul. But it would have been better for her if she had died. They took her with them up into the mountains, with Kelwars.'

'For what reason?' said Jorissimal.

'Kelwars betrayed us! He will lead the knights to our base. And he used the girl as the price of his freedom. They know who she is.'

Pyramors stood up very slowly. He turned, face alive with suppressed fury, to meet the steady gaze of Vittargattus.

'What is wrong?' said the clan chief.

He spoke in Innasmornian, but Pyramors understood him perfectly. 'They have my woman,' he said, using the same tongue, his words not perfect, but Aru had taught him the rudiments of the language well.

Vittargattus understood and nodded. He called Aru to him, and she explained in more detail what had happened.

'Then they have a hostage,' said Ondrabal, listening. 'A dangerous hold over you and these Men,' he told Aru.

She nodded.

Tennegar raised himself and gripped Jorissimal by the arm. 'They know about the girl. Kelwars spoke privately to their leader. He will know she is the woman of Consul Pyramors. The wife of Fromhal Djorganist.' He slumped back.

Pyramors had turned away, but he had heard.

Aru put her hand lightly on his arm, but for the moment she could think of nothing to console him.

Tremazon was less sensitive. 'We must consider our plan

of attack very carefully in view of this, Pyramors. If they see us preparing to begin a siege, they will hold up the girl as a hostage. We should let the Innasmornians take the initiative.'

Pyramors looked at him sharply. 'I have made a fool of myself too often over the woman,' he said. 'There are greater things at stake here.'

'Sire,' said Jorissimal beside him, 'we must think of Gannatyne. We must not jeopardise his safety.'

'What do they propose?' Vittargattus said to Aru.

'They should leave the matter to us,' said Ondrabal impatiently. 'We will do to this fortress what we did to the city.'

'And risk the lives of their friends?' cut in Azrand softly. 'They seem to think this Gannatyne is crucial to our alliance.'

Vittargattus scowled deeply, but then shrugged. 'I say we march onward. We will have to discuss the matter more fully before we reach the fortress. By then we must have a definite strategy. Either we bring these invaders down, or we ride away and allow them to fester here like a disease.'

'When we get there,' said Aru, trying to control her own anger, 'we'll have a plan. Even if it means making sacrifices. The Imperator will fall, I swear it.'

She went back to Tennegar, but his eyes had closed, his breathing becoming irregular, more blood dribbling from his mouth. There was nothing more to be done. He would be dead within the hour. Two men were left with him to ease his passing.

The company broke up into groups, each of them discussing the possible paths they could follow. Aru listened as Tremazon and Jorissimal talked to their commanders about the position, Pyramors having fallen very silent and having nothing more to say at the moment. There was a darkness in him she had never known before, something that Gannatyne would not have approved of, but she understood how Eannor and the Warhive must have changed him, have hardened him.

She sought some comfort in the company of Fomond and Armestor. The latter was no more optimistic than she would have expected, but Fomond tried not to allow the news, which was spreading rapidly throughout the entire company, to unnerve him.

'It may be an impossible situation,' he said seriously. 'At least the defenders must know that if they harm the girl in any way, they'll open themselves to attack. And the fortress will fall eventually. If I were the Imperator, I'd be looking for terms. The girl would be my only hope of getting out alive.'

'Yes, you're right,' said Aru. 'We have to think of them first. But I doubt if Vittargattus and Ondrabal will see it that way. Even Azrand, who is the most sympathetic of them, has doubts about this. There'll be no peace until Zellorian and the Imperator are dead.'

'Let's hope Ussemitus gets back soon,' Fomond added. 'He's the one person who can sway my people.'

While they spoke, Pyramors studied the mountain peaks about them. He could see disaster racing towards this world, a tide that could not be reversed, that must sweep them up on its flow.

'It is grave news,' said Jorissimal, who had left the discussion to join him. 'I fear that Tremazon may press for a siege. He does not seem to me to want to wait too long. You know him better than I. Is he ambitious?'

Pyramors tugged away from his thoughts, watching the other Consul as he talked to his warriors. He shook his head. 'He never has been. He was always one of the quiet ones. It took him a long time to decide he had had enough of the Imperator. I did not know he was with our cause until we met in the city.'

'You trust him?'

'As far as it is possible to trust anyone. Yes, we have to share trust. But if he is eager to expedite the siege, I think he may be right.'

Jorissimal looked surprised. 'You favour an early confrontation? It would put Gannatyne at risk.'

'I know. But there is another factor to consider. Time is something we cannot ignore. Soon there will be others here. I told you of my bargain with Auganzar. When he enters Innasmorn, it will be on a tide of blood. There will

160

be no more discussion, no more delays. He will unleash his forces upon the Imperator, regardless of who survives and who dies. And I doubt if he will bend to the wishes of these people, nor their terrible storms. Auganzar has powers of his own, believe me.'

The sun died on another day, another long march up into the mountains. Among the various components of the army there was little talk in the day, but at night, around the fires, everyone talked softly of what might happen when they reached their goal.

At one such fire, set apart from the Innasmornian ranks, a number of the shamen had settled. These were Blue Hairs and Seers, the lesser ranks who did not share the fire of Azrand, Freghai and other senior members of their brotherhoods. But they, too, had their own thoughts on how the coming conflict should be resolved.

Hunched by the fire, eyes glittering in its flames, one of the Blue Hairs turned the thin stake on which he was roasting a slice of meat. 'How readily we trust these Men,' he said softly.

Others craned forward. It was no accident that they were all like-minded. The one who had spoken, Kuraal, was known among them to be particularly critical of Men, even those who would be allies.

'The Ipsissimus has woven a spell over our masters,' said Duchaal, another of the Windmasters. 'Though he must have great power.'

Kuraal's eyes narrowed. 'I saw him in his forest village. Before the Mother blessed him with her power, as he tells us. A mere youth. His alliance with the intruders was fixed in him then. The girl is the key. She is bewitching, is she not?'

Kuraal looked about him, not expecting them to agree openly. But they understood his meaning well enough.

'Why else could a simple forester risk everything to gain power? Oh, Ussemitus has power now. He tapped something in the forbidden lands. But he is as anxious to bestow it upon Men as he is on us. He does not use it to smite our enemies. Does he speak for the Mother in this, or does he speak for himself? For the sake of the girl?'

'You think she has that power, Kuraal?'

'You saw the flying machines. She speaks to them. To that creature of the air that uses them. The wretched thief. Oh yes, the girl has power.'

'What is it she wants?'

'Control. What else? She wants to free this rebel, this Gannatyne. The Imperator will die, and with him all his support. The girl will then have all the control she wants of her people.'

'They will make her their ruler?' someone whispered.

'She may be more subtle than that. She will control us through Ussemitus, as she already does. And no doubt she will wed herself to one of the Consulate, Pyramors possibly. Whichever of them triumphs after the siege.'

'And if she does?'

'We are not all blind,' said Kuraal, delicately biting into the soft, cooked meat. He chewed slowly. 'Since we can see the future, it would not be so hard to alter its structure.'

'Kill her? But our masters – '

'Azrand has already fallen under her spell. Have you not marked that well? You hear how he urges Vittargattus to compassion. But there will be a battle. Many will fall. Who can be sure of surviving such a conflict? Even a warrior like this girl could not be sure of surviving.'

Jannovar slumped on the bed. It was the first comfortable bed she had seen since coming to this world of Innasmorn, but she could not sleep on it, in spite of how tired she was. The room was warm, heated by the system of the fortress that compared well enough with the heating in the cities she was used to on Eannor and the Warhive. And the room, her prison, was carpeted, reasonably furnished. Yet despair gnawed at her.

Kelwars had betrayed his companions. He had led the knights under the command of the cruel warrior Ancastron to the hidden base of Jorissimal's rebels. There were few men there. None of them had been spared. The butchery was, mercifully, swift.

On the ride back to Starhanger, Kelwars had actually joked with Ancastron. They neither of them intended to tell their superiors who Jannovar was. Ancastron had promised her a comfortable existence in Starhanger if she obeyed him. She had refused, but he had put her in this chamber anyway, telling her that she would bend to him.

The days passed slowly, and although she ate very little of the food that the knight brought to her at first, her hunger got the better of her in time, so that she did begin to eat. The food was excellent, and she ate her fill, telling herself that she would maintain her strength, find some way to thwart Ancastron's intentions. Several times he tried to force himself upon her, and she bit and kicked until he desisted. But he laughed, saying she could not resist for ever.

There was never any word of the rebels. She saw no one but Ancastron. He told her nothing, only that he would make her his own. No one of any importance, he said, knew she was alive.

She did learn to sleep again, but the nights were filled with terrible dreams, the horrors of Rannor Tarul coming back to haunt her, mingling with the recent events of her life. Often she woke up in the total darkness of the night, her heart thundering. It was one such night that she woke to the sound of the door being opened. She was up at once, fists bunching. Ancastron had not come this late before, but this must be a new approach. Perhaps he thought she would be too weak to resist him at this late hour.

But as the door swung in and the faint light of a candle wavered beyond it, she knew it was not her usual tormentor who stood there. To her horror, she saw that it was Kelwars.

He shuffled in, his face a white mask, eyes staring as if in madness. As he lifted the candle, she saw that his hand

and wrist were slick with blood. She gaped, for his mouth also dripped blood. He stood shakily by the end of the bed, and it was only then that she realised that he was not alone. Something had entered the chamber with him.

Sounds beyond the door caught her attention: screams, shouting, the clash of steel. The rebels! Had they broken into Starhanger? There was a sudden gust of wind that smacked the door against stonework, a roar from below as though a storm had sprung up within the walls of the very castle. More screams, terrifying sounds.

'What is happening?' Jannovar cried.

But Kelwars could not speak. The shape behind him, all shadow, swung into view, thrusting Kelwars aside. The man fell, a thick blade plunged deep into his back. He had been held on his feet by the other intruder.

Jannovar felt a scream rushing up from deep within her, but the shock of seeing this creature prevented it from filling the room. Was it a man? It seemed to have partially human features, but the face was blurred, as if half-finished. It wore no clothes, coated in mud and filth, as if it had been dredged up from a mire.

Beyond it, in the corridor, other things shuffled by, shapes more horrible than this thing, and there were even more piercing shrieks in the halls of Starhanger. Were these the allies of the Innasmornians? Their weapons? Jannovar was too terrified of this monster to speak. She felt herself weakening, but drew in air in deep gulps.

The semi-human creature slumped towards her, a mis-shapen arm reaching out. Its purpose was clear. It had come to fetch her. But for whom?

14

THE FACE OF FEAR

Etrascu calmed himself, using the stillness of the night, its darkness. In his chamber, nothing stirred, not even the dust. He had thought over his plan many times, once he had resolved to follow the lead given to him by Asphogol. How afraid he was of the huge Opener! A being who could inspire real fear, even more so than Auganzar. The Bone Watch had become a place of many terrors since they had come. But soon it would be empty, the Swarm would leave, bound for that forbidden realm beyond the World Cycle that was its true goal. Auganzar, Asphogol, Gehennon. And he, Etrascu, must go with them. Would the Consummate Order truly elevate him for his part in all this? He had to believe it. If not, if he betrayed Asphogol, it was possible that Zuldamar would fall.

I have always known Auganzar to be the stronger. Time and time I have hinted at this to Cmizen, but the Keeper has never had the courage to risk a change of loyalty. Well, he has had his opportunity. I am resolved. Yes, I am truly resolved. I will do it now. This very night. Gehennon has prepared a way for me.

He rose sluggishly, pulling his thick robes about him. The door to the stairs opened and he listened at it. Would Gehennon, or even Asphogol, be listening to each sound in the night? Would they know each step he took? He must assume they did.

The stairway was narrow, winding up privately to the rear of Cmizen's apartments. But Etrascu knew the Keeper would not be asleep. If he were, it would be only fitfully. Since the arrival of Auganzar, Cmizen had been almost deranged with fear. He had been living on raw nerves for a long time.

Etrascu reached the door to the rooms, unlocking it with a key that had been hidden behind a loose brick. He entered the room. A few candles sputtered; Cmizen hated the dark, did not trust even the shadows. His form was slumped over the central table.

To Etrascu's surprise, the Keeper jerked up, hearing even the softest of footfalls. Etrascu had been gliding over the stone floor, himself capable of absolute stealth.

Cmizen swung round. His face was extraordinarily haggard for a Csendook, the skin pinched, jowls loose, as if he suffered from some dreadful, terminal illness. The eyes were shrunk back into deep sockets, ringed with darkness, the lips drained of colour.

'Oh, it's you, Etrascu.'

'Still awake, Cmizen? It is long past the middle of the night. You should rest. The Swarm will be moving on very soon. It may even be tomorrow.'

'Have they told you so?' said Cmizen, stiffening. He could not rise, but straightened in the chair. 'They are so secretive, Etrascu. Damn them! What do they think I am!'

'If you want my true feelings on the matter, I do not think they trust us.'

'Because we send word to the Garazenda? Are they plotting against them still? Asphogol? You think *he* plots against the Garazenda? It's not possible. He is their premier Ultimate. I can't believe even he has been suborned by the Supreme Sanguinary – '

Cmizen was beginning to babble, the sweat running from his face, his eyes widening. Etrascu stood before him as calmly as he could.

'I am sure Asphogol will never allow himself to be compromised by any situation. He is far too intelligent. But there are other things you should know.'

Cmizen's hands, also deplorably thin, reached out and gripped Etrascu. He was repulsed by their touch, but did not let it show. 'Gehennon speaks to me a little more openly than Asphogol. He is his own master, as much as he can be. Only his loyalty to Auganzar has saved him from the full wrath of the Order, I think.'

'What has he said? What do you know?'

Etrascu gently removed the hands and sat down opposite

Cmizen. Oddly, now that the moment had come to act, he felt himself calm, the trepidations of earlier fading before the arrant terror of his master.

'Zuldamar knows about the failure of the assassination plot. He also knows that the Man Pyramors has abandoned the plot and has entered into some sort of bargain with the Supreme Sanguinary. He is assuming, quite rightly, that Pyramors will show Auganzar how to find the path through to the world where the Imperator Elect is hiding.'

Cmizen shuddered, sinking back, his tired body almost seeming to reduce in size. He hung his head, shaking it hopelessly. 'As we feared, as we feared!'

Etrascu leaned forward. It would be easy to have this pathetic creature destroyed. There could be no shame in such an act. 'Cmizen, we must consider our own position very carefully.'

Cmizen's head snapped up, his eyes flaring. 'Yes. Yes, we must! What has happened?'

'Zuldamar's position is threatened. Since Auganzar knows of the assassination plot, he is in a position to embarrass Zuldamar and his allies. Therefore Zuldamar is making every effort to remove all trace of the plot. Already he has recalled Uldenzar and Vulporzol, key agents in the affair. The official line is that they have been removed to worlds where Auganzar's agents are not likely to find them.'

'But – '

Etrascu shrugged. 'Zuldamar is as humane as any of your race. But we can hardly assume that he would allow Uldenzar and Vulporzol to live, can we? No, Zuldamar clearly has only one course open to him. Eliminate as many of the conspirators as he can before Auganzar decides to move against him.'

'Why is Auganzar waiting?'

Etrascu grunted. 'He has the upper hand. His prime desire is to find the Imperator. And he will.'

'Then. . .we are to be summoned? Executed? Is that our reward?'

'Zuldamar will not protect us. We know far too much. I. . .have heard something that makes me think we will soon be summoned to the Warhive. Some pretext. But in fact it will mean incarceration. That is the best we can hope for.'

'What have you heard? From whom?' Again Cmizen's terror flared up, his entire body shaking uncontrollably as though he had been exposed to a sudden, chilling wind.

'I have no special regard for Gehennon, but he has no reason to hate me. He is indifferent to my plight. So from time to time he passes on to me things he hears. He travels to the strangest of places. One of the reasons why he has fallen foul of his masters, I would guess.'

'*What has he said!*'

'That Zuldamar will recall us and eliminate us, along with others on Eannor. You recall your visit to Skellunda?'

Cmizen's eyes widened further. 'What of it?'

'None of the prisoners are alive. And the Csendook who guarded them are either dead or dispersed. Our turn is coming.'

'Then we must. . .talk to Auganzar. Or maybe Gehennon. You have his ear. Will he help us?'

'We don't matter to him, but he has no reason to hate us.'

Cmizen struggled to his feet and Etrascu wondered if he had been drinking. It was unusual for the Csendook. But there were no signs of drink in the chamber. Perhaps it was exhaustion.

'We must act now. Tonight!' Cmizen gasped. 'We cannot delay. Fetch Gehennon.'

Etrascu rose slowly. 'I think we should be careful. You are in no condition, sir, to discuss anything. You should sleep first – '

'Sleep! With death hovering over me! How can you talk of sleep – '

'The only thing left for us is flight.'

Cmizen turned an agonised stare at the Opener. There were traces of fear in Etrascu's face, but he did not appear as distressed as he should have been. How could he be so calm? Were the Openers so capable of cutting off their emotions?

'Flight?' echoed Cmizen. 'To where? What world could possibly shelter us when we are the enemies of the Garazenda?'

'Gehennon once hid from the Garazenda, from the Consummate Order, the rulers of the Openers. They have far reaching power. Yet he eluded them.'

'How? Where did he hide?' Cmizen was becoming more desperate, pacing about like a trapped animal.

'Strangely enough, he hid on the Warhive itself. Where no one thought to look.'

'How do you know this? Why should he confide in you?'

'He told me of it casually. As I said, he is indifferent to me. It was no great secret he was bestowing. And he has no need to keep it to himself. He has done with that retreat. His own future is secure with Auganzar, as he supposes.'

'Then he told you of a place? On the Warhive?'

Etrascu nodded.

'Where? I cannot believe it could be safe – '

'It is beneath the city. Csendook never go there. They have no conception of what lies beneath them.'

'It's a trap!' said Cmizen suddenly. 'This is how they will rid themselves of us.'

Etrascu controlled his frustration. He must not let Cmizen slip through his grasp now. If he failed with him, Asphogol would come down very hard upon him. There would be no promotion, no future at all. 'Cmizen, if we cannot trust Gehennon, we are at the mercy of Zuldamar. You have seen the tigerhounds that Auganzar uses. Zuldamar will use such measures in hunting us down. No world will be safe. But under the Warhive, we have a chance.'

Cmizen sat at the table, wiping at the sheen of sweat on his face. In the dim glow of the torch he looked like a living corpse.

'We must decide quickly,' said Etrascu, leaning on the table, face close to the Keeper's. 'Tonight. I have already decided.'

Cmizen reacted as if he had been stabbed, eyes staring up into the moon-like face. 'You are going?'

Etrascu nodded. 'It's folly to remain. Death rings us in. No one wants us alive. You can come with me, or perish here. But I promise you, you'll not see many more mornings on Eannor. Zuldamar will send for us very soon.'

Cmizen seemed to be on the point of tears, of collapse. 'What. . .must we do? How do we..?'

'Gehennon has told me how to open a path through to the place where we can shelter. He has given me a name, someone who will help us.'

Cmizen looked confused. 'Help? Who? Who do they serve?'

'There are numerous renegades under the Warhive. A community. They have their own laws. We will learn them. But first we must get there.'

'What must we pay them?'

'You need pay nothing for a while. But I am an Opener. From time to time these people need paths opening for them. Gehennon has trafficked with them for some time, he tells me. He found it a lucrative pursuit. Now that Gehennon has left them, they would be glad of another Opener. My services will amply pay for our keep.'

Cmizen blinked away the sweat, trying to envisage the place Etrascu had described. 'Yes, yes, I see,' he muttered. 'They would be glad of that.'

'Again I must prompt you to a quick decision. I will not stay longer than this night.'

'You can open a path to this place now?'

Etrascu nodded. 'Is this chamber sealed?' He knew that all the doors and windows would be bolted and barred. Cmizen never shut himself away without taking every precaution.

'Yes, all. Save the one through which you entered.'

Etrascu went to the low door to the stairs, pulling out the key he had left in it. He pulled it closed and locked it, pocketing the key. 'I am ready.'

Cmizen stared about him, though the room was bare. There was nothing to gather, no riches, no weapons. The tower was his home, its stones his only possessions, that and his rank. He had amassed no personal treasures, had no family. In going he would take nothing with him, merely the clothes he wore.

Etrascu understood his thoughts. 'Cmizen, you take with you one very valuable prize. Your life.' He slipped something from his sleeve, something that gleamed in the torchlight.

Cmizen recognised the steel instrument. Already Etrascu was pushing back his sleeve, preparing for the letting of a little blood, the art of the Opener. They would go, then. Now, without another word. They would risk everything on the say of a rebel Opener, one who did not care one way or the other about them. But perhaps in Gehennon's indifference there was the only ray of hope they could hope for. Everyone else in this scenario of terror was their undoubted enemy.

Etrascu placed the sharp edge of the steel to his wrist. He looked at Cmizen. 'Do we go?'

Cmizen nodded, turning away, unable to watch the incision, the blood that would be spilled.

Ungertel sniffed the air like a rodent. Above him the huge girders angled this way and that like black pillars holding up an even blacker sky, deep under the surface of the Warhive. There were several of the Girder Folk with him. They enjoyed hunting with him, for he carried the long weapon, the pike that he had been given by Gehennon, former lord of their Hive. Ungertel's fingers tightened around the haft of the well-crafted weapon. Each time he took it out to hunt, he recalled the Man who had first brought it down to the levels of the Girder Folk. The Man Pyramors. A powerful gladiator, a *moillum* from above, fleeing from the cold justice of the Csendook, whom he had offended. And the woman, Jannovar, the incredibly lovely woman, the like of whom none of the Girder Folk had imagined.

It was good that Gehennon had helped Pyramors and his beautiful woman to a safer world. These realms were not for them. This was a place of ghosts, a place of misery. One lived as one could, hunting the huge rats and the spider-things and other monsters that crawled and hopped about the gigantic girders of the construction. For Ungertel and the Girder Folk these realms were home. But Men, true Men, should be free. Free to walk on the surface, under a true sky, and hunt the beasts that roamed such plains.

Ungertel deployed his hunters. They were after something they had seen earlier, a dark, slithering something that was slipping downwards towards a junction of girders. Other hunters were closing in. There would be a fight, some of them might even perish. But they would have food at the end of it. If Gehennon had remained here among them, he would have been much pleased.

'There is something else approaching,' a voice whispered close to Ungertel.

He cursed inwardly. Rival hunters from another Hive? It was always a danger. There were constant skirmishes. Food was sometimes difficult to come by.

'There!'

Ungertel peered into the gloom. On a smaller girder running parallel to the one he was on, he could discern figures. But he knew at once they were no danger. Both looked injured, or exhausted. More fleeing rebels?

'See to the hunt,' he told the one beside him. 'I'll cross over.' He slipped on ahead, taking another spoke of metal that swung him out precariously over the utter blackness that was the drop down into the very heart of the Warhive. Already he had forgotten the hunt: here all fugitives were a priority. It was the code of the Girder Folk. There could never be enough of them, and strength stemmed from numbers.

Ungertel stepped lightly on to the girder where the two figures moved. The light was poor, filtering down from torches high above where another party was engaged in a hunt. Ungertel had deliberately told his own hunters to work without other light as they did not want to frighten off the thing they were hunting. Light often caused them to lose possible kills.

Edging along the girder, Ungertel saw to his amazement that one of the figures was an Opener. He thought at once of Gehennon, but this was not his former master. It was smaller, though far bigger than any of the Girder Folk, who were themselves diminutive beside the Openers. With the Opener was a cloaked being that Ungertel first took to be a man, but as he watched more closely he

172

realised it was a Csendook. A Csendook down here! His instant reaction was one of horror. The creature must be killed -

But the thought dissipated as quickly as it had formed. Gehennon had left word that these would come: an Opener to replace him, and a Csendook. Ungertel moved very close to the figures.

The Opener seemed to be in some way distressed. It must be the condition of the Csendook, which had almost collapsed, clinging to the girder, in danger of tumbling from it to a death far down in darkness. But the Opener gripped the cloak of its ward.

'Etrascu?' called Ungertel.

The Opener swung round, face bloated, glistening with the sweat of its unaccustomed exertions. 'Yes. Quickly. Help me before this fool drags us both into oblivion!'

Ungertel moved forward with caution, nimble as a spider on the steel girder, but he could see he had nothing to fear. He used the pike to snare the cloak of the Csendook, and with the Opener's help they dragged the creature to safety, letting it fall on the girder. The Csendook rasped with effort, eyes closed, chest heaving.

'Is it wounded?' asked Ungertel.

'How did you know my name?' hissed Etrascu.

'I am Ungertel. Gehennon told me you would come. Since he left us he has returned only once, and that only briefly. He told me you would be coming, with the Csendook, Cmizen.'

Etrascu nodded slowly. Then Gehennon had prepared the way even more carefully than he had said. 'Yes, this is Cmizen.'

'Is the Csendook wounded?' repeated Ungertel. He would never harbour anything but hatred for the Csendook race, but since Gehennon had a hand in this, he would do as he had been told.

Etrascu shook his head. 'He is ill. Food will revive him. And knowing that he is safe will help. Certain of his own kind are hunting him.'

'Usually Csendook who came here would die.'

Etrascu looked coldly at the wizened figure. This had once been a Man? Was this how they mutated, down here in this hellish realm? He would be fitting company for Cmizen. 'This one must live.'

'And you? Gehennon said you would replace him among us. What crimes have you committed against the Csendook?'

'I'll talk of that another time. I must go back – '

Ungertel looked deeply suspicious. 'Back? Your place is here now. We need an Opener – '

Etrascu covered his sudden fear. Was this the reward Gehennon had planned for him? To *serve* this garbage? 'There are a few things I must bring. After that, my place will indeed be here. Take Cmizen to a place of safety. I will come to you soon.'

'Usually Csendook would be killed. It is only because you are allies of Pyramors that this one will be spared.'

Again Etrascu felt a stab of alarm. What had Gehennon told these people! 'Pyramors. Yes, we are not his enemies.'

'He was a fine warrior,' said Ungertel. 'But his destiny was not here. Is he well? Have you seen him?'

Etrascu felt the gaze probing him, nodding. 'Yes, Pyramors is well. In safe hands. You need have no fear for him.'

Ungertel grunted, and Etrascu could not tell if he was pleased or not. He pointed to Cmizen, who was stirring. 'See to him. I must leave quickly.'

Ungertel nodded, going to Cmizen and standing over him, pike raised in case the Csendook should prove treacherous. He could never bring himself to trust such a being. And he could not take him to the Hive. No matter what Gehennon had said, it would be far too dangerous a place to conceal a Csendook. The Girder Folk would want its execution, and having killed it would likely eat it, though even they might blanch at that.

Etrascu slipped away along the girder, eager to perform the brief ritual that would open the path for him back to Eannor. Surely Asphogol would be pleased at the outcome. Cmizen would live, but for how long? And there was no possibility of his surviving in this place. It was a fitting end for him. At first Etrascu had been surprised that

Asphogol had not simply wanted him killed. But this way was far better.

'Let Cmizen suffer before he finally dies. Let him understand what it is to be punished for the endless deceits he has practised,' Asphogol had said. 'Yes, I like Gehennon's suggestion. Let the Girder Folk have Cmizen. And we can tell Zuldamar, quite legitimately, that he fled.'

Etrascu let the blood flow gently, just enough to open the way. His work in this grim region was over almost as soon as it was begun. He had discharged a debt. Now Asphogol must know that he was committed to his own cause. At last, Etrascu told himself. At last I will have the opportunity I have dreamed of, and with this next step back to Eannor I walk on a greater path, the way to real service.

Cmizen opened his eyes. His throat was raw, his skin dry, as though he suffered from a fever. His clothes were like hair, his skin irritated by them. Above him there was a low ceiling, like leather, or pelts of some kind. Skins, perhaps. The smell of the place hit him, its warmth, its pungency. Turning, he saw a strange being watching him, squatting down, leaning on a long pike. A Csendook weapon, it seemed.

'Who are you?' Cmizen croaked.

The figure reached out and handed him a cracked cup. The water inside it was dirty and lukewarm, but Cmizen gulped it down. Where was Etrascu?

'You are with the Girder Folk.' said the grotesque being, its face a disapproving mask. 'If you want food, say so.'

'No. I want sleep.'

'You have slept long. Eat. Or die.'

'Is this the Warhive?'

The creature nodded, pointing up with the pike. 'High up there. Your people.'

Cmizen shook his head. 'No. I cannot go there. Where is Etrascu?'

'The Opener? He has gone back for a while – '

Cmizen sat up, his head throbbing. 'Back! To Eannor? Why?'

'He returns soon.'

Cmizen looked vacantly at the walls of his tiny room, a hovel constructed of more pelts and skins. The truth closed around him like a serpent. *He has deserted me.*

15

BREAKTHROUGH

Now it begins.

Auganzar steadied the huge xillatraal, easing its tension with a muttered word, though in his mind the one sentence repeated itself. His Swarm was at last ready, after careful months of preparation. It would be a little earlier than he had promised Pyramors, but there was no time to delay at this stage: Zuldamar must be more than a little suspicious. That was inevitable, but the Marozul could prove nothing. Auganzar and his agents had worked with extreme care and diplomacy.

Yes, they are ready.

He raised himself up in the saddle, gazing about him at the gathered forces. His finest Csendook warriors were arrayed on either side and behind him, an armoured wedge of fighting machine. Beyond them were Fulvulus and the chosen *moillum*, who knew the true destiny of this Swarm, the forbidden destination for which it was bound. And they were ready, as eager as the Zemoks to begin the ultimate hunt.

In the front ranks of the Csendook, the tigerhounds strained to be released, sensing the quest, all fifty of them programmed with the scents of the prey. They snarled in frustration at being checked, snapping at the xillatraal, but the Zemaal controlling the tigerhounds used their leashes to bring them to heel, dark thoughts calming them, readying them.

Auganzar's right hand fell to the haft of the strange weapon belted to his side, the sword crafted by the skills of his master technicians. It was the only one of its kind: he had made sure that no other like it had been cast. The powers within it were unique to it, and he could feel them tremble, themselves like the ferocious tigerhounds, waiting to be unleashed, to ravage the enemy. He did not understand them, but he knew they could be used and were too valuable to reject.

Asphogol had gone on across the wide plaza, now cleared of its heaped bones and skulls, the terrible evidence of the carnage that had once occurred here on Eannor. It was called the zone of sacrifice, this place, and there was no denying the chill atmosphere that still clung to it, the sense of spilled blood, of life ripped out from countless victims, Human and Csendook alike. The huge Opener mounted the steps to the area where the Path would be opened. Following him were Gehennon and Etrascu, the former apparently calm, his face betraying little emotion, as though this was no different a ritual to any other he had performed. Etrascu, on the other hand, was terrified, and it was evident. The beasts smelled his fear and it irritated them: one huge tigerhound had almost caught him with its claws as he passed it.

Up on the dais, Asphogol began the ritual. He had been given instructions by the Consummate Order, and also a strange series of commands by Auganzar, who had received them from the Man, Pyramors. The summons that would bring the Accrual, eager for blood. Asphogol knew the dangers inherent in this quest, but his own qualms were, like Gehennon's, well masked. He turned, facing the Swarm. It was, unquestionably, a magnificent force, doubtless the most potent of its kind ever assembled. Even the *moillum* were gifted with exceptional fighting skills, and Asphogol doubted that Men had ever before been trained to such a degree of perfection for war.

Auganzar looked up, edging his xillatraal forward. He nodded to Asphogol, dropping his war helm. Asphogol spoke once to Gehennon and Etrascu. Both of them prepared to make the blood sacrifice. The Openers began their work.

Beyond them, watched in silence by the Swarm, the air seethed, as if a storm had quickly sprung up from nothing, coiling about itself. Something crackled across the wide plaza, light blazing up and dying as quickly as it had come. The wind gusted, then tore across the broken slabs, wrapping the entire zone in its embrace, a colossal aerial whirlpool. Already the air beyond the dais was darkening, like a huge wall, a column of shadows reaching up to the heavens. It seethed like the waters of an ocean, heaving and tossing, though nothing could be glimpsed beyond it. It threatened only chaos.

The xillatraal and tigerhounds reacted violently, trying to slip their leashes, but their masters held them. Auganzar mounted the steps on his beast, waiting for the moment when Asphogol would confirm that a way had been opened.

Behind the ranks of Csendook, Fulvulus and his gladiators watched, smothering their dismay. They knew what had happened here, how the Imperator's followers had been used in their thousands to create a bloody path to another realm. In spite of all the promises, was this the reason they had been brought? Fodder for whatever it was that guarded the way beyond? Fulvulus looked about him, seeing the doubts in his fellows. To a man they had drawn their blades, ready to begin the grim business of their kind, watching both the darkness ahead and their leader. A word from him and they would rebel, even though such a rebellion could only end in slaughter.

At his right side, Throcaster glared at him. 'Too late to go back now, eh? Into the maelstrom, Fulvulus. Still think we'll come out of this laughing?' He had to raise his voice to be heard above the anger of the winds.

Fulvulus spat. 'Auganzar hasn't come here to waste his Zemoks. These are his crack troops.'

'Just make sure you keep the bastards in front of us.' The words were almost crushed as the wind thundered over the plaza. Up on the dais, the Openers had found the key to the way beyond. A huge rift of darkness, like a jagged black fork of night, split the sky in a vertical line, rising from the dais to a point far overhead. The rift widened, fresh winds tearing from it as if a host of demonic powers had been released on the world. The noise became deafening, thunder rumbling through the skies, and the darkness bled down over the host.

The gate was opening, its sides like the walls of a black ocean, somehow contained instead of collapsing and smashing all below them in a ferocious tide. Asphogol, arms raised, streaming blood, screamed out whatever incantations were required, and beside him Gehennon, also daubbed in blood, chanted fervently to the unknownn powers of the beyond. Etrascu had fallen to his knees, face white with terror, gabbling the words he hhad been told to say, his nerve at breaking point. But he clung on to the chant, shutting out the madness that threatened to overwhelm him.

Asphogol turned, facing Auganzar, whose xillatraal reared up in terror. But the massive Csendook gripped it with his knees, dragging its head round on a tight rein to face the madness beyond. Asphogol called the warrior on, and the exodus from Eannor began.

Auganzar raised his sword, keeping Hozermaak's weapon sheathed, scarlet light dancing from it as though it had already bathed in blood, and waved his Swarm forward. A tunnel of swirling darkness had opened up, and Asphogol went into it. Hundreds of feet high, its sides defying the eyes with their churning fury, it ran off into a remote distance, like a bridge across the stars, unfathomable and endless. Gehennon struggled to keep up with Asphogol, and behind him Etrascu stumbled. But he heard the snarl of Auganzar's xillatraal at his side and leapt away from it, knowing its teeth would rip him limb from limb if he did not move on. Shivering with terror, he lurched on into the Path, following the two obese figures of the Openers.

Behind the Supreme Sanguinary the Swarm moved forward, closing ranks. Csendook and *moillum* were locked now, committed to the course that their leader had set for them. They would seek out this new Cycle of Worlds, whatever the cost. They would take their chances, pay the toll.

Fulvulus and Throcaster glanced at each a last time as they crossed over the threshold on the dais to whatever realm it was that linked worlds, feeling the ground beneath them sag like flesh, the darkness swarming with untold powers, hellish furies. But they nodded. It was done. They had begun. Let the storm break. There were no favourites here.

Gradually the Way settled, though the noise of the winds did not abate. The Csendook had to dismount their xillatraal,

180

and the tigerhounds were not easy to control, wanting to race at the walls of the Path as if they would rip from them whatever unseen powers hid behind them. The Swarm followed the Openers: behind it the walls of the Way closed, the light of Eannor shutting off. In the plaza, all was again silent. Not even a breeze stirred the dust. And there was no one to see the departure, no lookout at the edge of that region of the dead.

In the Bone Watch, a few Csendook Zemoks listened, seated in a chamber below the walls. The sounds of thunder they had heard, the rushing of winds, had died.

A Zemok lifted the jar of beer that they had been passing round. Apart from his colleagues, the Bone Watch was deserted. 'A last toast to a fine Swarm.'

The others nodded, offering their mugs for refilling. Soon it would be over and they would go back to the Warhive, to their kin.

'Perhaps we should have gone with them after all,' grunted one of them. 'Who knows what they'll find.'

'We've served him well enough by staying on. The Garazenda will send searchers here. They'll want explanations when they know the Supreme Sanguinary is not on any world of this Cycle.'

'Yes, you're right, Varuzem.'

Varuzem paused as he poured out the beers, as if he had heard something in the distance. He scowled for a moment, but then shook his head. 'A toast. To those we shall not see again.'

'It comes,' said Asphogol.

Auganzar tightened his grip on the reins of his xillatraal. The beast could smell something in the huge tunnel beyond them. The Openers, too, could sense the arrival of some grim power. Gehennon stepped back, for once his composure deserting him, and Etrascu had again dropped to his knees.

Auganzar shouted out a command to his Zemoks and the

first rank stepped forward, blocking the tunnel, weapons raised, ready to advance against whatever it was that was coming. Auganzar had told them about the Accrual. But no one had described it.

When it emerged from a branch of the tunnel, the warriors were stunned by the sight of it. Monstrous, its immense bulk squeezing out into the main tunnel like a vast maggot, it writhed and shuddered, its scarlet flesh folded over on itself, its head merging with its body, the mouth hanging slack and wet as if it had just fed on the very walls of the tunnel. It dragged itself into the tunnel and towards the Swarm, using misshapen limbs, rolling with effort.

At last you come, said its voice, simultaneously heard by Auganzar, Asphogol and the others, a rasp in their minds, a jolt of power that staggered them. *I have been waiting too long. The Man Pyramors promised you to me. I thought he had deceived me. But I heard you, Openers. I heard the words you used. Do you know me?*

Asphogol stood in the centre of the tunnel, lifting his thick arms to point at the horrific creature. 'Accrual,' he said. 'You are known to the Consummate Order. By their decree, you are outlawed.'

Auganzar was shaken by the crude sounds of laughter that suddenly rang through his mind. The Accrual mocked any suggestion of power invading its bloody domain.

And have you brought an army to seek me out? Or do you seek other victims? The skulking remnants of humanity on Innasmorn?

'The Consummate Order have passed judgement on you,' said Asphogol. 'You have sinned in creating Paths for your own ends. Paths that have critically damaged the balance of the World Cycles.'

Ah, then you have brought the instrument of my punishment with you. Well, I have tasted the rich blood of Csendook before. Not often enough in such quantity! Then there is nothing to discuss!

Asphogol's composure was remarkable, Auganzar thought. Not only could the words of the Accrual be heard, but also its emotions, its hatred, its anger, and worst of all, its appalling *hunger.* Its desire for blood pulsed in waves.

The Opener turned to Auganzar. 'We must destroy it if we are to survive.'

Auganzar nodded. 'Then stand aside. My Csendook are prepared.'

The Opener did as bidden, and Gehennon was relieved to join Asphogol. Etrascu scrambled back along the walls of the tunnel, hand over his face, afraid to look at the thing that waited.

The Accrual slithered back slowly until it had passed the entrance to the side tunnel from which it had emerged. There were passages to the right and left of it, and from out of these there now emerged other creatures. Hopping, slithering, they dropped down into the main tunnel, a hundred beings, slick with the blood of the tunnels, their heads little more than amorphous scarlet blobs, their arms elongated and clawed. Their legs were inversely jointed at the knee so that they were capable of great leaps. And they were at the command of the Accrual, like a plague of insects or huge fleas. As they hopped forward towards the waiting Csendook, their bulbous, empty heads split to reveal mouths that had no teeth, but which could fasten on their prey, draining it of its blood.

Whatever disgust or nausea the Csendook felt at being confronted by these creatures they put aside. Here was a duty they could understand. A dozen of the tigerhounds were unleashed, and they sprang forward, ahead of the Zemoks. Within moments they were among the first ranks of the hideous children of the Accrual, ripping and tearing at them. These beings were fragile, for all their ferocious looks, and the tigerhounds used their claws and teeth to devastating effect, ripping and tearing, reducing scores of the creatures to bleeding meat. The Zemoks followed up the staggering impact of the tigerhound attack, themselves chopping into the creatures with their curved blades. Scores more of them began to appear from the side tunnels, and from out of the walls of the main tunnel other monstrosities began to emerge, some of them larger than the flea-like beings, spider-like, others like bloated worms.

It was not a contest, but butchery, as the tigerhounds and the Csendook thrust forward, ripping to pieces the opposition. The armour of the Zemoks protected them, just as the metal hides of the tigerhounds deflected the claws of their assailants. Beyond the awful mêlée of the battle, the Accrual withdrew slowly, knowing that its servants would be annihilated in the face of such an onslaught.

Auganzar marshalled his forces, splitting his front line of Zemoks so that they could deal with the assault, while he took a central core of warriors forward to meet the Accrual. He had every intention of engaging it, in spite of its size, its unquestionable power.

As the creatures fell, the floor of the tunnel absorbed them, sucking them down into it like some huge, carnivorous plant. The Zemoks were careful not to get caught in the many openings that were now appearing, steadily cutting into the flea creatures, reducing their flow. Behind them the *moillum* also found themselves under attack as the Accrual summoned more of its grotesque servants to beset the far ranks of the Swarm. But the gladiators were equally as able to hold back the waves of attack as the Csendook, using their blades to stunning effect.

Auganzar broke through the ranks of the defenders of the Accrual, facing it with a knot of some twenty Zemoks.

Throw down your arms and succumb to me, the creature whispered into his mind. *I'll give you a warm death, a joy you cannot imagine. You'll join with me, feel true power, Auganzar. You and all your worthy Csendook. Here is power eternal. Blood goes on, from body to body. In mine it never ceases. Taste it, taste ecstasy undreamed of. No worlds will be a barrier to you.*

Auganzar was staggered by the power of the voice, knowing that it would seduce him if he listened to it for too long. There was a deep subtlety in it, tapping powers unheard of, the very roots of being, yearnings that even he had not been aware of. But he closed it all out, casting a javelin up into the face of the monster. Others followed and he could feel the pain as the metal bit into thick flesh.

A dozen Zemoks leapt forward, swords cutting down, biting into the limbs of the creature. It dragged itself

184

backwards, shocked by the ferocity of the warriors, trying to prepare itself for its own onslaught. But it was unused to battle. It was used to an easier life than this. It had never been hunted before. Its prey had always come easily to it, caught in the madness of the Path, confused and bewildered. But these warriors were organised, protected by the Openers. sanctioned by the Consummate Order! They had given power to this warlord and his warriors.

You cannot destroy me! cried the mind of the Accrual. *If you try, you will be lost here in these tunnels, between World Cycles. You will never get away, not even to the worlds you have left.*

Auganzar roared to his Zemoks to ignore everything they heard. There was only one course open to them now, to destroy it.

The Accrual read his purpose, his ferocious determination to end its rule here in the bloody tunnels where it had enjoyed its rogue freedom for so long. And it read, too, the reasoning behind Auganzar's crusade, his will to find the path to his enemy. No sacrifice was too great for him to make. Nothing would turn him from that course. And in that knowledge, the Accrual knew despair, understood its own destiny.

It felt the shafts of the Zemoks tearing into it, their battle fury. Beyond the first ranks of its tormentors, the Accrual saw the slaughtered remnants of the beings it had sent in waves against them. There would be no blood feast, no triumph. An empire was toppling in these slick tunnels, and a new kind of darkness was coming.

Incensed, releasing the last vestiges of its fury, the Accrual lashed out, limbs crushing Zemoks, mouth dipping down obscenely to lap up and swallow wholesale a trio of the warriors, pulping them in its maw, savouring their deaths inside it. But there were too many of them to contain. They drove forward, releasing more of the tigerhounds, the monsters that knew no pain, no terror. Their teeth were steel, tearing, always tearing, and the vast body of the Accrual was opened up, whole areas of it exposed, weeping blood and organs onto the Path.

But it lived, the powers of the ages stored within it, the damage wreaked upon it—hardly subduing that demented life force. Auganzar watched in horror as it thrashed about, squashing yet more of his Zemoks, engulfing others, even pulling apart the tigerhounds where it could get at them. They may end the life of this monster, but in so doing ran the risk of reducing themselves to a mere handful.

Auganzar drew out the sword that had been fashioned uniquely for him. As he did so, he felt it sing, as if imbued with its own life. There were things about the sword that baffled him, mysteries that even its creators could not explain. And as he held it before him, advancing on the Accrual, he felt its hunger, akin to the hunger of the monstrous shape. Equally, he felt the blind terror of the Accrual. It sensed in the sword a power more dreadful than its own.

No, Auganzar! You cannot know what you possess. But how has the power of that place got into this thing?

'What power?' called the Supreme Sanguinary. 'What place?'

Innasmorn. The Malefics. They have tainted it. But the Accrual's attention was wrenched away, smothered by the waves of pain. The tigerhounds were ripping into its soft underbelly, tearing remorselessly at its vitals.

Auganzar could not understand the words of the Accrual, and there was no time to debate with it. It feared the weapon, its dread a palpable thing. Waiting for an opportunity, Auganzar ran up and sank the blade up to the hilt in the quivering bulk. The effect was instantaneous. Shuddering, tearing at itself, the Accrual swung this way and that, the weight of its movements flinging Auganzar to one side, breaking his grip on the sword haft so that he could not pull it free. The Accrual's agony was eclipsed only by its terror, as it sensed something immense and nightmarish reaching out from the darkness of its own mind.

The Zemoks were forced to pull back from the rolling, juddering body, and even the tigerhounds withdrew for a moment, gazing with scarlet orbs at the madness before them. The Accrual's mental screams rocked every living thing in the tunnel of death, many of the *moillum* and Csendook falling back, hands over their ears.

Auganzar caught a glimpse of the sword haft and reached up for it, gripping it fiercely, holding on as the Accrual rolled. The metal was cold, chilling to the bone, but he would not relinquish it. But as he held it, he felt the forces at play within it, and almost let go. Something intensely evil seemed to be working in the very metal, but it must be the Accrual, the untold centuries of its malign reign here. Suppressing his mounting revulsion, Auganzar held on.

The Accrual sagged at last, life draining away. The sword came free and Auganzar stared at the dripping steel. But it gave up none of its secrets. They drifted back into oblivion. Beyond them the corpse of the Accrual gave a last shudder. Blood seeped out of it thickly.

Auganzar turned to see Asphogol, his own face stricken with horror, as though he had glimpsed beyond the darkness within these walls and seen things which he could not put a name to. Auganzar instinctively sheathed the sword.

In the tunnel, the fighting was over. If any of the creatures had survived, they had fled. The rest were a bloody carpet of bone and sinew, thick with blood, seeping back into the ever-hungry walls.

'How are our losses?' said Auganzar, steadying himself as though he had been dealt a dozen crushing blows.

But the news revived him at once. A handful of Zemoks and *moillum* only had been lost. And the tigerhounds and xillatraal were unscathed. From the ranks of blood-bespattered Zemoks, Gehennon pushed his way forward. He pointed up ahead, beyond the already shrivelling mass of the Accrual.

'Our way is open to us. Whatever evils sought to bar the way have dispersed. It will not be for us as it was for others.'

'Apart from Zellorian,' growled Auganzar. 'He went down that Path to Innasmorn. We shall follow him.'

Asphogol nodded. 'The Consummate Order have sanctioned this. We must go ahead swiftly. There are other powers in these tunnels beyond our understanding. The Accrual was a parasitic being. Now that it is—dead, other entities may seek to feed upon it, and whatever life they may find near it.'

Auganzar mounted his xillatraal. The floor of the tunnel had settled. It was little different to the floor of a normal world Path, and the roar of the air, the gusting of the winds had abated.

'Swiftly then. Asphogol, Gehennon! Do what you must. Take us on to Innasmorn.'

Asphogol directed the warlord, and at once he rallied his Swarm. The Openers brought up the rear of the company, Gehennon relieved at the demise of the Accrual, Etrascu shivering as if his terrors would never loose him.

'We've work yet for the Order,' said Asphogol to him impatiently. 'The Way must be closed. The Conceptors themselves have granted the Order power through us. It was part of the pact. The Supreme Sanguinary goes beyond the world cycle, never to return. Are you ready?'

Gehennon bowed. 'I anticipate the new worlds eagerly. I am yours to command, Asphogol.'

'Etrascu?'

'What will become of us?'

'There will be no way back. But we are disciples of the Order now. Doubtless they will have work for us.'

Etrascu shuddered. 'No way back? To the Order?'

Asphogol scowled at him in annoyance. 'Our own petty desires are not important. If you think that, you are worthy only of contempt. Look to your loyalty when we close this portal. There is always a place for the worthy.'

In silence they followed the Swarm, until at last they were at a point along the vast tunnel system where Asphogol called for a halt. Again he began the ritual, the blood sacrifice, and Gehennon joined with him in the bizarre communion that opened the final door out to another World Cycle. Etrascu played his part, but in his heart there was only fear, in his mind a crawling terror of doubt and misery. He heard the coming of a fresh storm, the voices of another world.

'Innasmorn calls to us,' Asphogol shouted to Auganzar. 'She is eager to welcome us.'

Auganzar nodded, tempted to lift his sorcerous blade in salute. But as it shivered in his grip, he felt something within it surge, power that hungered, as he did, for release in this promised world, this promised Mother of Storms. He let it remain in its blood-oiled scabbard.

BOOK FOUR

THE GATHERING

16

HUNAR GADREEV

Vulporzol sat uneasily in the chair indicated by the servant. The atrium was still, a reliable place to sit and discuss confidential matters, the only sound the gentle murmur of the fountain. Zuldamar was usually here to greet his agent, and Vulporzol had become used to their meetings, the exchange of reports that would have had the Garazenda growling with alarm had they known the content of most of them. Vulporzol was left to his thoughts and his unease grew. Something had gone drastically amiss; there was a real danger that in the private war between Zuldamar and Auganzar, the Supreme Sanguinary had stolen the edge, possibly a winning edge. But Vulporzol pushed back such dark thoughts.

When Zuldamar entered, he had Horzumar with him. Vulporzol rose and bowed, knowing he could trust each of the Marozul. They were extremely close in their methods of governing. Vulporzol knew that if Zuldamar should ever fall from power, Horzumar would fall with him.

'Sit down, please,' said Zuldamar. Vulporzol could see the strain in his face, hear the edge in his voice. He, of all Csendook, had always been the calm one, the controller. This was not the time to give way.

Vulporzol sat, waiting for the Marozul to seat themselves opposite him. Horzumar's face was clouded, as though he expected nothing but bad news. But Vulporzol knew he lacked the subtle diplomacy of Zuldamar.

'You've returned from Eannor?' said the latter.

Vulporzol nodded. 'I have, Marozul.'

'The Openers?' cut in Horzumar.

'Gone, Marozul.'

Horzumar hissed through his teeth, but Zuldamar put a restraining hand on his arm. 'Give us your report, Vulporzol.

Do as you always do, and spare us nothing. We need to understand the position very clearly.'

'Marozul, I went to Eannor a day after we had the news that the Supreme Sanguinary and his Swarm had left. Thus I was little more than a day behind them.'

Zuldamar nodded for him to go on. He himself had sent Vulporzol to Eannor, alarmed by the fact that Auganzar and the Swarm had left it and no message had come from Asphogol about the move. Asphogol, who was supposed to be supplying the Garazenda with detailed information about all developments on Eannor. Word about the exodus had not come through the expected channels: Zuldamar considered himself fortunate to have found out quickly and been able to send Vulporzol to investigate.

'I went to the Bone Watch, announcing myself as envoy to the Garazenda. I was admitted without hesitation, but noticed at once that something was amiss. There were no more than a dozen Zemoks in the entire fortress. Their leader was himself a Zemok, Varuzem, and he explained that the Swarm had left for Troigannor, to begin the first expedition against known rebel forces.'

'Who took the Swarm?'

'According to Varuzem, Asphogol opened the way, as was the command of the Garazenda. I asked about Gehennon, the other Opener that was known to be with Auganzar, and although the Zemoks pretended to know nothing about him, I guessed that he, too, had accompanied Auganzar.'

'What about Cmizen, and his own Opener, Etrascu? There's been no word from them for weeks,' said Horzumar.

'The Zemoks were reluctant to speak about Cmizen for a while, but I warned them that if they did not, it would go badly for them. Varuzem asked for a private audience and led me to one side, pretending to take me into his confidence, though it seemed to me he was playing a role. His talents had not equipped him well for the part, and I saw through it. He told me that Cmizen fled in fear of his life.'

'From Auganzar?' said Zuldamar.

'From you, Marozul. Because the assassination plot with

Pyramors had failed. Cmizen knew that he would be eliminated for his part in the failed plot.'

'Failed?' said Horzumar, his anger barely under control.

'Auganzar knew what Pyramors intended. I was told that he was killed.'

'Did you believe it?' said Zuldamar.

'No, Marozul. I fear that Pyramors may yet be alive.'

'Where? With the Swarm?'

'Marozul, there is no doubt in my mind that Auganzar has attempted a Crossing to Innasmorn. He probably used Pyramors, just as he used Asphogol, Gehennon, and probably Etrascu. There was no word of Cmizen's Opener, though Varuzem assured me he worked with Asphogol and had not left when Cmizen fled.'

'Where did Cmizen go?' said Horzumar. 'Surely there would have been nowhere on Eannor that he could have felt safe from Auganzar.'

'I pressed that question a number of times. But the answer was always the same. Auganzar had no interest in Cmizen. He did not fear him, nor see him as a threat. I suspect that he was murdered and that his body will never be found. I would suggest, Marozul, that it would be a waste of time to seek him out.'

Zuldamar smiled thinly. 'Yes, I'm sure you're right.'

'Varuzem and his Zemoks did their best to convince me that nothing was wrong, and that the Crossing to Troigannor was perfectly legitimate. Was this not what the Garazenda were expecting? they asked me. I left them to their empty watch, insisting that I go, unaccompanied, to the zone of sacrifice. I did so, but found nothing there to help my search for information. The place had been cleared of much of the debris of bones that once littered it, and there was evidence that the Crossing lately made by Auganzar had been commenced there. But no blood had been spilled, no sacrifices given. In fact, all the evidence pointed quite reasonably to a proper Crossing. Zemoks, xillatraal, tigerhounds, which Auganzar uses without restriction, and *moillum*.'

'He took *moillum*?' said Horzumar. 'But that's strange. If he had been going to Troigannor, he would have taken and used his best *moillum* to unleash on the rebels. Why would he take *moillum* to Innasmorn? They might rebel.'

'I suspect, Marozul, that this was merely a blind. Auganzar could not know how closely his operations on Eannor were being watched. Thus he took the *moillum* to make it seem as though he were readying for a legitimate assault on a rebel world.'

Horzumar grunted. 'You are right, of course.'

'These questions are all questions that the assembled Marozul would ask,' said Zuldamar. 'Auganzar has tried to make it look as though nothing is wrong. Except that he has not appeared on Troigannor. I suspect his plan is to make the Garazenda think that something has gone wrong with a simple Crossing between worlds of our Cycle, and that, tragically, an entire Swarm has been lost. Precedents do exist for such things, though it has been a considerable time since something like that happened.'

'I went further afield in my investigations,' Vulporzol added, and the Marozul nodded for him to continue. 'As you know, there are several large warhalls on Eannor, serving a number of the Garazenda. Obviously Auganzar was very careful in choosing his own Zemoks, Zemaal and their commanders. But I wondered about the *moillum*.'

'What do you mean?' said Horzumar.

'As you know, Marozul, Auganzar has been able to develop his own private army of *moillum*, thanks to the system of the Testaments. But I wondered if, as an incentive to some of the more uncontrollable Men, as Pyramors had been, Auganzar had offered them a chance to fight against the Imperator. If they had refused, he may have had them killed. Something he could have had done, even in the warhalls of other Marozul, as he had access to them all.'

'What did your theory uncover?' said Zuldamar.

'I visited three warhalls, and a pattern emerged. None of the *moillum* had been approached, none of them considered at all for the Crossing. Officially Auganzar had already singled out the *moillum* he wanted and selected them for his own warhall. It was the only other place left for me to visit, and I confess when I reached it, it was with little hope left of learning anything useful. However, I did find something odd. Those in command of the warhall were uneasy, unsure of themselves. They were excellent warriors, but it surprised me that Auganzar had not left other, more capable warriors in charge of the *moillum* he had left behind. These had not been deserted, but they did not expect to see their Supreme Sanguinary again. It was as though they were waiting for fresh instructions, as though the warhall would be abandoned, its warriors and *moillum* transferred.

'But I have better evidence than that, Marozul. I visited the *moillum*. As you know, Auganzar took particular care of his Human warriors. They were not slaves, the best of them integrating into his Swarm very well. Men cannot be Zemoks, of course, but Auganzar's *moillum* were as close to our own kind as Man could expect to be. And respected by our own. They enjoyed every privilege, in return for which they gave themselves to Auganzar's cause.'

'The genocide of their own rebels?' said Horzumar, with a snort of contempt.

'No, Marozul. The elimination of the Imperator Elect. That was the real bait, I am sure of it. Auganzar's obsession, the search for the Imperator.'

Zuldamar smiled. 'You are perfectly correct.'

'Auganzar had taken the very best of the *moillum* with him when he left Eannor. There was Fulvulus, the finest of them, and Throcastor, second only to Fulvulus. Hundreds of others, superb Human warriors. They had earned their keep well, and many had been rewarded. Some had wives, children. It is an important thing to them, as one would expect.'

Horzumar leaned forward. 'They took them? Is that it? Took them, knowing that if they had left them, they'd never see them again?' His eyes widened as he saw a flaw in Auganzar's careful plans.

Vulporzol shook his head. 'No, Marozul. Again he was clever. He avoided the *moillum* with families. As he did with many of his Csendook. But I sought out the families of some of the *moillum* who had gone.'

'And?'

'Their sorrow was, for the most part, evident. They knew they would not see their Men again. They had not gone searching for rebels on Troigannor. The women knew that, though they would not tell me the truth. I had no need to press them.'

Vulporzol straightened, his report over.

Horzumar looked away, eyes narrowing, as he tried to master the fury he felt. There was so little they could use in the presence of the full Garazenda, so little to show that Auganzar must be discredited. No real proof.

Zuldamar rose and left them for a moment. When he returned, he carried with him a single sheet of paper. 'What Vulporzol has told us about the families is interesting.' He handed the sheet to Horzumar. 'Read it, aloud.'

Horzumar took the sheet. 'It is from Hunar Gadreev, wife of Auganzar. You had this when?'

'Early this morning.'

'It says:

To Marozul Zuldamar, with respect and obedience, Hunar Gadreev, Household of the Zaru, Auganzar, Supreme Sanguinary of the Csendook nations.

Honourable Marozul,
There is a matter about which I must speak to you urgently. It concerns my husband. My household is open to you and it is my express wish that you visit me privately here as soon as you are able. I would urge you to treat this communication in the utmost confidence.

It has been signed by Hunar Gadreev, and bears the seal of Auganzar.'

Zuldamar took the sheet and showed it to Vulporzol, who could see that it was authentic.

'Surely this is not a trap,' murmured Horzumar. 'Can it be that Auganzar taunts you? You'll not go, of course.'

'I feel I must,' said Zuldamar. 'I am protected by my position. Entering Auganzar's home will not be dangerous. Quite the reverse.'

'My friend,' said Horzumar patiently. 'You should spurn this. My guess is that Auganzar is using his wife to pave the way for the obvious request. If he succeeds in his outrageous hunt for the Imperator Elect, he will demand a place on the Marozul.'

'We shall see,' smiled Zuldamar. 'But I will go today. And I will go alone. It is the only way that I can be sure she will speak openly. And, as I say, I will not be in danger. But keep that letter, Horzumar. We may need it later.'

Zuldamar was expected. He arrived, as he had said he would, alone at the gates of the magnificent estate of the Supreme Sanguinary, where several Zemoks stood to attention, statuesque and forbidding. Zuldamar sat astride a xillus, a smaller, less ferocious relative of the xillatraal, and he gently eased it through the steel gates as the Zemoks bowed to let him pass. A rider was sent on ahead to the buildings that housed the home and family of Auganzar.

As Zuldamar rode along the curving drive, under a cloudless sky, with little more than the droning of bees to disturb him, he thought of the coming meeting yet again. He had not said so, but he was sure that Hunar Gadreev had been given the duty of delivering some grim message to him, a portent of disaster for his own cause. It was why he had chosen to come alone.

To his left, over the brow of the curving green lawns, a dark column of smoke rose, incongruous in such pleasant surroundings, its plumes thick and oily. Puzzled, Zuldamar urged his steed on more quickly. Not everything was as it should be here.

He heard a sudden outcry up on the brow of the slope and saw a figure running through the trees there. It was dressed in the robes of a technician: Zuldamar could see that the Janok was frightened of something, looking back over his shoulder as though he were the victim of a hunt. The Marozul turned his xillus and nudged it forward up the slope towards the fleeing figure. He came into the trees some way ahead of the Janok. His xillus showed its teeth in a snarl, uneasy, as if it had smelled blood.

Beyond the ridge, Zuldamar could see the buildings that must be part of Auganzar's laboratories. A number of Zemoks were waiting there, swords drawn as if about to do battle. But here? In such a private place? What could have disturbed them? Zuldamar had no spies here: it would have been pointless trying to get one in.

Abruptly the fleeing figure burst through some bushes before him and his xillus reared up. Taken completely unawares, the Janok fell back, rolling a few feet down the slope. The Zemoks below saw him and immediately rushed up towards him.

'Zaru!' called the Janok, not knowing who it was he addressed. 'Call them off! They mean to kill me. I've done nothing – '

Zuldamar turned to the Zemoks. They were soon up with the Janok, and though they glanced at him, they did not let his intrusion interfere with their intentions. Zuldamar said nothing, holding the xillus still, though it was agitated by the hunt.

There were no explanations, no exchanges of words. The Zemoks merely cut the Janok down, three of them plunging their steel into him. He shrieked in pain, but fell back, kicking.

Zuldamar urged his xillus forward slowly. 'Who is this Janok?'

The Zemoks recognised Zuldamar's insignia, though they could not have known who he was. They bowed, puzzled at seeing a Csendook of such high rank, wondering if he would admonish them for the swift execution.

'Auganzar has discovered a number of them, Marozul,' said the spokesman stiffly. 'Tampering with forbidden arts. They know the penalty for betraying trust.'

Zuldamar merely nodded, but his attention was caught now by another figure moving through the trees. It was older, more stooped than the fallen Janok, though it moved quickly in its flight. The Zemoks crested the rise and saw the figure as it made for the gates.

'Hozermaak,' said one of them, a cruel smile on his features.

Zuldamar frowned. This was the name of one of the most noted scientists among all Csendook. He was about to comment, when something else burst from the trees beyond. A black shape, crouched low to the ground, huge and hound-like, with ears that were flat to its elongated head, and eyes that were twin scarlet orbs. A tigerhound. It had been unleashed. As it tore across the lawns after Hozermaak, its Zemaal stepped out of the trees, holding the leash, watching.

It was too late to prevent what occurred next. The tigerhound caught up with Hozermaak very swiftly, leaping on to the figure and crashing it to the ground. The head dipped, metal teeth sank into the neck and shoulders and with one vicious twist the beast ended the life of the scientist. It swung round in one flowing movement, dragging the bloody corpse back up the hill to the Zemaal, dropping it at his feet.

'We are sorry that you have had to witness these executions, Marozul,' said the Zemok who had addressed him earlier.

'Who instructed you to kill them?'

'The Supreme Sanguinary, Marozul.'

'What arts were they practising?'

'Weaponry, Marozul.'

Zuldamar nodded slowly. 'I see. Very well. Do what you must. I am expected at your master's house.' He steadied his snapping xillus and trotted back down to the path, conscious of the smouldering eyes of the tigerhound upon him. What arts had they tapped? And what secret discoveries had they taken with them into the darkness of oblivion? Clearly Auganzar had not wanted these secrets shared. But he would know them. Oh, yes, he would know.

Hunar Gadreev's personal guard greeted him on the steps to the great house, their swords sheathed at their sides, the twin circles on their breastplates, scarlet and imposing.

'You are expected and most welcome, Marozul,' said the first of the Zemoks. 'Please will you come with me.'

Zuldamar was taken through the splendour of the house, which was no less opulent than he had expected. It was his first visit, and he enjoyed the extravagances he saw about him, as all his Csendook colleagues would have done.

He was escorted to a wide room, at the far end of which was a magnificent panoramic view of the best of the gardens. The room itself was filled with plants, the colours dazzling, and Zuldamar found himself detained for long moments, enjoying them. Auganzar had superlative taste, as one might expect.

Hunar Gadreev was waiting for him at a fountain and pool near to the curving window. She stood, tall and proud, her face very calm. It was the first time Zuldamar had ever seen her. She was very beautiful, but he hid his reaction. She had light hair, flowing midway down her back, and her eyes were a deep brown, her teeth perfect. Larger than a Human female, she had unusually elegant hands for a Csendook, with none of the common roughness. They even looked soft, almost Human. Csendook skin was generally much coarser than that of Men, and one of the reasons that Csendook so admired Human women was the delightful softness of their skin, its pallor. Yes, Zuldamar reflected, Hunar Gadreev was exceptional.

She spoke with a clear voice, precisely and with an elegance that echoed the elegance and regality of her bearing. How clever of him! Zuldamar laughed inwardly to himself. He has brought me here, shown me the quality of his matchless home, and now makes me doubly vulnerable by using this perfect creature as his voice. He is a genius, and I admire him for it. How tragic that we are such bitter enemies beneath the polite masks we wear.

'I am greatly honoured, Marozul,' Hunar Gadreev said. 'Please be seated. Anything that you wish will be provided. You have only to mention it. My husband was most insistent that you were made as comfortable as possible.'

Zuldamar inclined his head. 'Thank you,' he said, sitting beside the pool. 'But a conversation with you will be perfectly adequate.'

'I will not waste your time, Marozul. Auganzar asked me to give you a message from him. It is for you alone, so I am grateful that you have seen fit to visit me without an escort. You would, naturally, have been permitted to come with a company of Zemoks. All this estate is at the disposal of the Garazenda, at any time. Auganzar knew that. He would not have denied it.'

Zuldamar did not understand why she had said this, but he merely nodded gently.

'I can only ask you to hear the message and not repeat it. You are one of the Warhive's most respected Marozul. You may pass this message on to others. It is your prerogative. But I ask that you do not.'

'I must judge that when I have heard,' said Zuldamar.

'Very well. Auganzar wishes you to know this. He has left the World Cycle of the Warhive. Gone not to another of its worlds, but to an entirely different World Cycle.' She paused, as though to let him reflect on this.

Zuldamar's face did not change, though she had fully expected him to control his reactions. Her husband had told her he was the best, the strongest of them all. He nodded for her to go on.

'He has always known that the Imperator Elect and his Prime Consul, Zellorian, escaped the wrath of the Csendook and found sanctuary beyond our worlds. My husband has incontrovertible proof of this, and he believes you are also in possession of such proof. You chose to hide this from the Garazenda. My husband understood why. He respected that decision. But he was in possession of other facts, facts which neither you nor any other living Csendook are aware of. I am not to divulge these things, nor can I, for he did not tell them to me.

'But there are secret matters, keys to ancient powers, lost knowledge, that Zellorian has. In some matters he is ignorant, but if he lives, the nature of his research, his fanatic will to destroy our species, will lead him to uncover these things. He must be stopped. And the secrets must die with him.

'Auganzar has followed him to his retreat.'

'How?'

'A way was opened for him. I have not been told how. But now that he has passed through it, it has been sealed by the great powers that overshadow our World Cycle. There is no way back for my husband. We have seen him for the last time. My children will not see their father again.' She kept her voice level, her eyes fixed on Zuldamar. But he read her sorrow, the unquestionable pain.

He turned away from her royal gaze, studying instead the beautiful gardens, imagining the tall figure of the Supreme Sanguinary walking there, his children running along beside him. 'He knew that he could not return?'

'Yes. But his quest is for Zellorian, and for the ultimate safety of our species. The old mysteries must remain shrouded in darkness.'

Zuldamar saw again the black smoke, billowing now from buildings beyond the gardens. 'What is that smoke?' he asked casually.

'Certain things had to be removed. There were Janoks here, working on projects for my husband. Land reclamation on damaged worlds. That will go on, elsewhere. And some other work has been terminated. I know almost nothing about that.'

Work connected with the Crossing? Zuldamar wondered. How many more executions had there been? Auganzar had always been thorough, clinical.

'My husband asks that you take no action against the Csendook and *moillum* who he has left behind. They have been told that they will be transferred to new masters.' She stood up and walked to the window, as though she, too, relived memories of the events that must once have transpired there.

'It is over, Marozul. The gate is truly sealed. This time it will never reopen.'

Zuldamar knew this was no act. She believed what she had said implicitly. He could even hear her husband saying these things to her, see her tears as he spoke. But had Auganzar given up everything here? A chance of becoming a Marozul, of controlling the Csendook nations? Of returning in triumph? But he had always been a fanatic where Man was concerned, burning with a zeal to destroy the Imperator that was second to none: no, not him, but Zellorian. There was the key. Zellorian. Always the danger. The sorcerer, some said, the wielder of dark powers. He must be stopped. It was Auganzar's banner.

So he had carried it beyond. Never to return.

'Madam, I grieve for you in your loss.'

'We are at your mercy, Marozul. My children and I, my family. The Csendook once commanded by my husband. Yours to dispose of.'

'There will be no recriminations. No one will die.'

'Not here, Marozul. Not here.'

17

THE SWARM

Daylight gleamed brightly, spreading out from a central core, filling the eyes of the Csendook, dazzling them for a few moments. They stood bemused, as did the *moillum* with them. Beneath their feet was no longer the uneven, slippery surface of the Path between World Cycles. Instead there was earth, grass.

They were through. Was this the promised Innasmorn?

Auganzar shook off the last effects of dizziness and gazed about him. Once his eyes had become accustomed to the glare, he saw that he and his Swarm had emerged in a landscape that was not unlike that of parts of Eannor. They were on a narrow coastal strip, with low hills rising inland, and beyond them a valley between two ranges of mountains that soared upwards to white peaks, partially hidden in cloud. The land itself was deserted, an open plain, dotted with shrubs and copses. Behind the Swarm, the grey waters of a sea churned, buffeting the coast, eating into it with a steady, inexorable determination, carrying it away to the east to spread it in a wide expanse of sand.

Auganzar's xillatraal had survived the Crossing intact, as had the other beasts. The tigerhounds, too, seemed unaffected, crouching down at their Zemaals' feet, waiting for fresh commands. Asphogol stood at the front of the company, with Gehennon. The two Openers turned to Auganzar.

'This is Innasmorn,' said Asphogol, with conviction. 'We have entered another Cycle of Worlds.'

'Where is Etrascu?' said Auganzar, looking about him for the third Opener. But there was no immediate sign of him. Asphogol frowned, but Gehennon gave a grunt and went off to look for him, watched by the Csendook.

Auganzar began an inspection of the Swarm. It had quickly organised itself into battle lines as though there would be an instant conflict on this world, but there was no suggestion of life locally other than themselves. The Csendook were none the worse for the strange journey. A few had been lost in the battle with the Accrual, but otherwise there was a full compliment present. Auganzar rode up and down the ranks slowly, pleased with the discipline, the nerve of his warriors. His finest were with him: Zuarzol, commander of the tigerhounds, nodded grimly. A Zolutar who would, like his master, stop at nothing to achieve the goal of this particular crusade; Guntrazol, his fellow master handler of the tigerhounds, also an excellent warrior; Immarzol, Quenzol, young warriors who showed the promise of such veterans as Vorenzar, the Zaru who had first opened the way to Innasmorn for his master.

The ranks of the *moillum* were as regimented and calm as the Csendook, and Auganzar studied them as he rode up and down their lines. Fulvulus waited for him at the head of their ranks.

'I promised you and your warriors their freedom, Fulvulus,' the Supreme Sanguinary told him.

Fulvulus bowed, and beside him Throcastor also bowed. He, too, was a superb gladiator, and between them, these two Men would ensure that the *moillum* played their part in the coming hunt.

'He's here,' said Auganzar. 'You former Imperator. Help me find him and the remainder of his verminous Consulate, and you shall have that freedom.'

Fulvulus nodded. 'It is an honour, Zaru.'

Auganzar had been told that these *moillum* were completely trustworthy, eager to remove the hated Imperator. But Auganzar knew the ways of Men. No matter how well they adopted to Csendook discipline, they remained Men. When this was over, they would have to be released.

'We go inland. We'll set up a base there.'

'As you command, Zaru,' said Fulvulus.

As he watched Auganzar ride away, he felt Throcastor beside him. 'Have you thought over what I said?'

Fulvulus grunted. 'Seems a good idea to me. Auganzar has no intention of slaughtering all the runaways. He just wants the Imperator and the Prime Consul, and a few other bastards. The rest he'll free, like us.'

'You're sure?'

'He's no ordinary Csendook. He'll keep his word.'

'So when we're released, we'll bring the renegades to heel. And their women. You'll make a fine Imperator, Fulvulus.'

Fulvulus smiled grimly. 'Maybe.'

At the front of his Csendook ranks, Auganzar singled out Torzaru, a huge warrior who had served for many years under the ferocious warlord, Xeltagar.

'Take a dozen trackers, Torzaru. Guntrazol will lead the tigerhound pack for you. Go up into those mountains and begin the search for life.'

'Man, Zaru?'

'Yes, but we may find Innasmornian natives first. Whatever you can find. We need eyes ahead of us, and you'll be them. We come here blind. The Swarm will travel up the valley between those ranges: keep me well informed.'

Torzaru nodded, wheeling his xillatraal away at once, pleased to be able to begin without delay.

Zuarzol joined Auganzar moments later. 'You do not wish me to go ahead of you, Zaru?'

'I want you with me, Zuarzol. You and that magnificent tigerhound of yours.'

Zuarzol glanced down at the huge beast. Its eyes blazed as it took in the new scenery, eager to begin the hunt. 'Raal never disappoints, Zaru.'

Auganzar heard the pride in Zuarzol's voice. Raal was the only thing alive that seemed to inspire anything like love in the cold warrior. 'I'm sure he won't fail us here.'

Gehennon appeared once more, his face a sheen of sweat, his eyes tired. 'Etrascu may not have survived,' he said. 'He was weak – '

'I cannot think that it matters. If he's here, he'll never outrun us. But perhaps Raal would enjoy some early exercise, Zuarzol? Why not give him Etrascu's scent and let him loose?'

Zuarzol smiled grimly. 'As you wish, Zaru.' He bent down and undid the leash that connected him to the tigerhound's collar, whispering something as he did so. The tigerhound lifted its head, exposing the terrifying fangs, roared once, then leapt away into the scrub.

Gehennon maintained his outer calm with an effort. Clearly the beast had already been programmed with Etrascu's scent. Had his? Asphogol's? Auganzar was a Csendook who left nothing to chance. There would be no betrayals here.

Auganzar turned his gaze once more to the mountains. *I am here, Zellorian. You may even hear me on this alien world. Know this: I will find you. And you will need all your dark arts, all the powers of this realm to hold me back. Open whatever dark hell you have found and let its demons out. They'll find me ready.*

He motioned the Swarm forward, and they began the gallop across the plain to the mountains.

Pyramors had been almost asleep, another day's march behind him and the advancing army. The warrior who tugged at his arm, Gladimyr, put his finger to his lips; Pyramors nodded. Gladimyr indicated that Pyramors should go up into the rocks above the resting army. It was where Jorissimal had set his watch, above the road they had left for the night.

Up in the broken stone, Pyramors found Jorissimal and other men waiting for him. 'What is it?' he asked them, aware that the very air here seemed to listen in. Vittargattus and Ondrabal had set their own scouts and watches about the army, and there was considerable tension.

Jorissimal indicated one of the men, who looked exhausted, his tunic thick with dust, his hair unkempt. He had evidently been travelling, and very fast. 'This is Mendarkis. He has been in the mountains to the north of Starhanger, along with other spies of mine. Tell Pyramors what you told me.'

Mendarkis took a careful swig of water before beginning. 'Sire, I was watching for any movements of troops away from the fortress through the northern passes. There have been none. But something else has happened. I could hardly believe what I saw. Not here, not on Innasmorn.' His eyes held a momentary gleam of terror.

Pyramors understood him at once. 'I think I can guess what you saw. Csendook?'

Mendarkis gaped. 'Sire, how could – '

'I knew they would come.'

'A hunting party, sire. Six Zemoks, no more. But they had two creatures with them, the like of which I've never seen before. Huge beasts – '

Again Pyramors interrupted. 'Tigerhounds.'

'What does it mean?' said Jorissimal.

'It means,' said Pyramors, 'that Auganzar is already here. Sooner than I thought. But it is not us he hunts. His prey is our prey. The Imperator, and Zellorian. Well, Mendarkis, what else? Were you seen?'

'I was alone, and the hound creatures seemed to be locked in to another scent. They were not distracted by me, though I was high above them. I followed them, though I tell you, sire, I was terrified. They. . .found the fortress. Oh, they were careful, and they hid themselves so well, fused with the terrain so perfectly, that no guards would have see them. They circled the entire fortress, studying every detail, and were not seen. Those hounds are uncanny.'

Pyramors nodded. 'Yes, Auganzar is well equipped for this hunt. Where did the Csendook go?'

'Back to the north, sire. I followed them as far as I dared.'

'And?'

'There is an encampment. Again, well hidden. But it is not a small affair. A Swarm, I would say.'

Jorissimal looked at Pyramors with renewed concern. 'You said they would come. Do you still insist we should not fear them, sire? *Auganzar?*'

'We must not let the Innasmornians know,' said Pyramors, ignoring Jorissimal's question. 'They will assume betrayal.'

'But their own spy networks are excellent. They may already know of the arrival of the Csendook.'

'If they did,' said Pyramors, 'they would have confronted

210

us.'

'Then what will you do, sire?'

Pyramors replied without hesitation. 'I have to go to Auganzar.'

The others looked stunned, none of them able to speak.

'How long would it take us?' Pyramors asked Mendarkis.

'Maybe a week – '

'It's too long. If Auganzar begins an early assault on Starhanger, he'll lay it to waste, and kill everyone in it, no matter who they are.' He turned to Gladimyr. 'Fetch Aru Casruel. Tell her I must speak to her urgently.'

Gladimyr slipped away into the shadows at once.

'I'll go by gliderboat,' Pyramors told the others. 'We'll have to risk bringing one.'

Jorissimal nodded. 'I'll have this outcrop watched. We must not let the Innasmornians know or see. Their trust is already wearing thin.'

Soon afterwards, Aru appeared. Pyramors swiftly explained what had happened.

'I have to get to him as soon as I can, before he begins the slaughter,' he whispered. 'This time he will not wait. I need a gliderboat. Will you pilot it?'

'This is dangerous, Pyramors. Vittargattus and Ondrabal are full of mistrust. Machines, they call them. To them they are part of an ancient curse, a threat to them and their people. If we are seen – '

'I understand. But I must get to Auganzar, or Gannatyne and the others with him will die.'

Aru studied the night sky as if she could see something up there watching her. 'Jubaia will have to help us,' she muttered. 'If I can summon him.' She was never sure now of her relationship with the little thief, and the gliderboat he loved so deeply. Would he hear her if she called to him?

She opened her mind to the skies, whispering, focusing her thoughts on the little thief. Once it would have been the gliderboat that she spoke to, but she knew that if she was to have any success here, it would be through the Innasmornian. For a moment she sensed something fluttering in the dark, an elusive shadow, and Pyramors watched her shudder as though her thoughts had glanced off something unpleasant. Instinctively he looked to the skies, but they were impenetrable.

I hear you, Aru, came a voice in her mind.

'Jubaia!' she breathed. 'You can hear me.'

Faintly. He sounded just like the inner voice of the gliderboat, but there was no hint of its presence. Aru knew it must be near. Jubaia was never far from it.

'We need you here. With the craft.'

Ussemitus has asked us to watch over the families and the fleet.

'Where is he?'

He is linked to the World Splinter. I do not think he can be away from it for long. There is a conflict there, though I can't tell what it is. Ussemitus seems to me to be troubled by something. It is the Mother.

'Surely the gliderboats and the families are safe? You must come. Pyramors needs to travel quickly to the north.'

Very well. I will ask Circu.

The night became silent again, and it was only after a long delay that Jubaia's distant voice came again. *We must be careful. The night skies are filled with strange things. The destruction at the Sculpted City has attracted evil forces like moths to a flame.*

'Will you come?'

Yes. We leave now.

'Don't be seen,' she warned him, but he was already gone from her mind. She turned back to Pyramors. 'He's coming.'

'You spoke to him? This is a remarkable place,' he commented, shaking his head gently. 'Can all the Innasmornians do this?'

'Only a few of them. Like our own Controllers, though they have developed the skill far more deeply. We are children to them!' she smiled.

'You have a special rapport with them, that's evident.'

She looked away, but he realised he had somehow touched a nerve. He recognised in her the same melancholy that he was still subject to occasionally, when he thought of Jannovar, whom he had lost on Eannor. But he closed his mind to that, thinking instead of the new Jannovar, her imprisonment in the fortress. Angry that he had let his fears for her suddenly catch him unawares, he turned away from Aru.

'They are unique,' she was saying. 'Jubaia is extraordinary, even by their standards. One day, perhaps, he will tell you his story.' She swung back to him, face taut. 'I will go with you in the craft.'

But he shook his head. 'No. I must see Auganzar alone. It will be extremely dangerous. He is a Csendook of honour. But the agreement we made has been fulfilled. This time he may simply kill me. No one else must be risked, least of all you, Aru. You may have to lead our people.'

'If your life is to be at risk, you are taking too great a risk in going – '

He shook his head. 'Auganzar will speak to me, and no one else. I am sure of that. If Gannatyne and the others are to be saved, I am the only one to prevent it.'

'Are you doing this for Gannatyne, or for the Djorganist woman?'

'What do you mean?' he said, his cheeks flushing.

'You know exactly what I mean.' Her voice had hardened. She was no longer the sad girl, but the warrior, the victim of the wars, hardened and embittered. By him?

'You had better speak your mind now,' he said, his own voice cutting the air. 'If there are things to be said, then say them! What do you imply?'

'I've heard the men talking. You left the Sculpted City, told their leaders that the rebellion was hopeless. Enough had died. Zellorian would win in the end. Resistance was useless.'

He drew in his breath. 'It was true. I despaired. I had seen another attempt to smuggle men out of the city fail, and men had died. Zellorian told me that if I agreed to prevent more rebellion, he would see that there were as little deaths as need be.'

'That's not all he gave you,' she said coldly.

Their eyes met, locked in unspoken anger for a moment. 'What else do the men say?'

'That you traded their freedom for the Djorganist woman. That it's her you want to free, and not Gannatyne.'

Again he felt himself colouring. 'Of course I want to free her. But Gannatyne takes precedence. He is the hope of us all.'

'If you are to go to Auganzar, perhaps I should go with you.'

'I see,' he said coldly. 'You do not trust me, is that it? You think I am to make some deal with him, some arrangement whereby I can free Jannovar. You think I would sacrifice so much for her? You believe that of me!'

She shook her head. 'The men might. You do not have the respect you should have. Only Jorissimal is able to keep the dissenters quiet.'

She thought his fury would get the better of him for a moment, but he gritted his teeth against it, turning his back. 'Very well. Come with me. But be warned. Auganzar is set on his purpose. He wants the Imperator and Zellorian far more than we do. If he sees you as a threat in any way, he'll have you ripped apart by those tigerhounds of his.'

'I'll take that chance.' She may have said more, but looked up instead. The clouds had gathered in the pitch cauldron of the night, but he guessed that something else moved among them, very close, invisible.

'He's here,' Aru said softly, but Pyramors heard.

'Bring the craft down quickly. We'll go at once.' He said nothing more about their discussion, as though he had forgotten it, but Aru knew it chafed at him. How far had he let the woman infatuate him? But was that fair? What right had she to accuse him of that?

Jubaia brought the gliderboat down so smoothly and silently that it slipped from the dark as though cloaked in invisibility. Pyramors half expected to hear shouts from below, or on other rock outcrops, where he knew the Innasmornians would be watching. But there was only the impenetrable silence of the night. Pyramors and Aru embarked.

Jubaia glanced at Aru, as though he had not expected her to be joining them, but he did not speak.

'The warrior said north,' said Pyramors gruffly, seating himself as comfortably as he could.

Aru nodded at Pyramors. 'There are Csendook here. We must find them.'

The gliderboat took to the skies with great ease, moving very swiftly, but Pyramors was aware of the tension in its two occupants.

'Csendook,' said Jubaia, the horror in his voice evident. He felt the gliderboat shudder beneath him and spoke softly to her.

Aru was trying to scan the lands below them, to see if there was any danger that they might have been seen, but they had swung away so quickly that it seemed unlikely. She turned back to Jubaia, to meet with his appalled gaze. 'What is it?' she asked him.

'She is afraid. She has not forgotten Csendook.'

'What does he say?' cut in Pyramors. Jubaia had been speaking in his own tongue.

'It is the gliderboat,' Jubaia told him, as fluent in the language of men. 'She has not forgotten the terrors of the Csendook.'

'You're the Controller,' said Pyramors, though he still found it remarkable that an Innasmornian should be piloting a gliderboat. 'Can you not soothe such things?'

Aru laughed gently. 'Ah, but this is no ordinary gliderboat, Pyramors. No mere machine. She thinks and feels for herself, as we do.'

Jubaia shot an unexpected glance at her, as though pleading for silence. What were they hiding? Pyramors wondered.

'As long as the craft gets me to the north quickly, that's fine.' He turned away, still a little annoyed.

Aru would have spoken to Jubaia further, but he seemed to be in one of his sulky moods, as he was from time to time. Perhaps it was the strain of the last few weeks, the responsibility. Although something troubled him. And as usual, the gliderboat was not open to her. It could have been dull metal, mindless and inanimate for all she knew. She gazed ahead into the night, frustrated, unable to think ahead past the blind alleys that awaited them all.

Jubaia sat in the prow, ignoring his passengers. What was wrong with Circu? Why would she not speak to him? Three times he had tried to contact her, but she had clammed up. There was fear in her, no doubt of that. The Csendook? They were terrible creatures, he knew that from his first skirmish with them. But Circu was acting strangely. Pyramors? Was she embarrassed by his presence? Afraid to let him think she could converse with, and share the emotions of an Innasmornian? What was that to him? But then again, he was the Man most likely to emerge from this affair as ruler of Mankind, or what was left of it.

The little thief let it be, concentrating instead on the dark lands below.

They met alone on a hillock, overlooking the encampment of the Swarm. The gliderboat dropped Pyramors and Aru on the knoll, and they waited in silence as the solitary xillatraal and its rider came quietly up the incline, limned by the first rays of the dawn.

Aru shuddered as the huge Csendook dismounted, speaking to the xillatraal calmly, dropping its reins. It walked away, amazingly patient for such a ferocious beast, and for a moment Aru wondered if even the Csendook species had developed some kind of mental link with the creatures they controlled.

The Csendook warlord came closer to them, taking off the dark helm and holding it at his side. Pyramors knew him at once, and inclined his head respectfully. Aru had seen Csendook, fought them, but this one was immense, towering over them, his entire being a monument to power, battle strength. Even Pyramors, as muscular a warrior as any other man, was dwarfed by the Csendook Zaru. Strangely though, there was not the killing hatred in Auganzar's face that Aru had expected: there was a degree of mirth, compassion even. But she would not be fooled. He was unquestionably the single most powerful being in any World Cycle.

The gliderboat had made a single pass of the camp, creating momentary chaos, but Pyramors had called down his demands in perfect Csendook. Aru could speak the language, too, though she had never expected to hear it again.

'Thank you for agreeing to this meeting,' said Pyramors now.

'Not one I expected,' said Auganzar, his voice rolling deeply up from his chest, menacing but controlled. 'And you have a woman with you, as before.'

'She commands knights in the armies,' Pyramors said quickly.

Auganzar smiled, his teeth gleaming, and Aru felt her blood chilling. If these creatures saw fit to begin a war here, there was no hope for Man, and little for the Innasmornians, for all their strange talents.

'You have come to chastise me for being a little premature, I take it?' said Auganzar. 'I told you six months.'

'It was our bargain.'

Auganzar nodded. 'It was. But circumstances forced me to leave Eannor quickly.'

'Your – enemies?'

Aru was amazed at the easy way the two warriors spoke to each other. What else had they planned together? Was this, after all, some trap?

Auganzar smiled, and there was no terror in his expression. He was genuinely amused. 'Yes, Zuldamar and Horzumar were beginning to get a little edgy. I think they guessed their assassination attempt had misfired. They would like to have found you. But they will never find you now. Nor will they find me and the Swarm I have brought. The way back is closed, Pyramors. The World Cycle of the Warhive is no longer attainable.'

Pyramors did not smile. 'It is as I would have hoped.'

'Who is the girl?' said Auganzar.

'She is Aru Casruel.'

'I know the house. I know all the principal houses of your people. But why is she with you here? Is our business not private?'

'It seems my people do not trust me. They think that you and I, Auganzar, scheme privately to our personal mutual benefit.'

'Interesting. You are treated as I was, then. I have some sympathy for you! What do you suspect us of plotting, Aru Casruel?'

'If it is only the death of the Imperator Elect, then I am more than content,' said the girl.

But Auganzar shook his huge head. 'No, that would not content me. It is Zellorian I seek. He is in that fortress in the mountains. He and the last of his diseased crew. I will be there by sunset. I hope you have not come in the hope of deflecting my wrath?'

Pyramors pulled Aru gently back. 'No. We have the same aim, as I told you on Eannor. But there are a few of our people trapped in the fortress. Zellorian has them. If you begin the siege now, they'll be killed.'

Auganzar looked down at the two people without a sign of emotion. When he finally spoke, there was a trace of impatience in his voice. 'I warned you, Pyramors, what I would do. There would be no compromise.'

'Three days,' said Pyramors, cutting in. 'Give me three days.'

'What can you achieve in three days that you have not achieved in almost twice as many months?'

'Three days,' repeated Pyramors. 'After that, the fortress is yours.'

Auganzar looked back at the encampment below him. As dawn began to pick out its details, the size of it was more noticeable. And the Swarm was preparing for war. There could be no denying the sounds, the atmosphere of impending aggression.

'And while I delay the siege, the fortress empties and my enemies take flight. Is that it?'

'Have it watched. You have already had the place circled by your tigerhounds and their Zemaal.'

Auganzar looked at him, his eyes again betraying amusement. 'Your own watches are well informed. But yes, I will have the fortress studied very closely.'

218

'If Zellorian does attempt to break out, he'll find another host waiting for him. My own forces, and the armies of the Innasmornians.'

'It would be a pity if you were to deny me the pleasure of taking Zellorian myself. But that does not matter.'

Aru was puzzled. Auganzar really did not seem to object to the idea of someone else killing Zellorian. As long as the Prime Consul died, it would fulfil his ambition, or so it seemed.

'But if you have friends trapped in the fortress, hostages no doubt, how do you intend to save them?'

'I'll tell you that in three days.'

Auganzar grunted. He lifted his war helm. Aru knew that she could bring the gliderboat down swiftly, but if this huge Csendook attacked them, they would have no time to escape him.

'Three days? Very well. But I will move my Swarm closer. And I will indeed have Zemoks close at hand. At dawn on the fourth day, I will begin. And, Consul, I warn you. I will cut down every living thing in my path. Man, woman, child, Innasmornian. Take your people far from here. Only that way will they be safe. You understand me?'

'Perfectly.'

Auganzar nodded, calling to his xillatraal. It came to him and he mounted it in one flowing movement, wheeling it and riding away quickly. From above, the gliderboat swooped down.

18

STARHANGER

As the gliderboat drifted silently downwards towards the rock outcrops above the armies, Jubaia could see movement among the troops. He turned back to Aru and Pyramors, who had been sitting in silence for most of the return journey through the mountains. Jubaia sensed that Aru's faith in Pyramors had at some point been questioned. He would have asked Circu about the matter, but she remained almost totally closed to him. The atmosphere of gloom had clamped down like a sickness over them all.

'What is it?' said Aru, knowing instinctively that something had caught the little thief's attention.

'The camps are awake. Readying to move. Something must have stirred them up. We may not be able to land as discreetly as we would have liked.'

'Never mind,' grunted Pyramors. 'Land anyway.'

'Do you want me to go back to the gliderboat fleet?' Jubaia asked, directing the question at Aru.

She could see that he had no desire to go, even though both he and the gliderboat were uneasy in the presence of the Innasmornian armies. 'Keep close to us,' she told him.

'We'll be at the fortress soon,' said Pyramors. 'And we'll need those other craft.'

Jubaia took the gliderboat down to an outcrop and watched as Aru and Pyramors disembarked and slipped into the shadowed rocks. As he lifted the craft heavenwards, he was again aware of its strange mood.

'What troubles you, Circu?' he whispered to it.

But there was no answer, and he would not probe the coldness locked into the craft.

Below him, Aru and Pyramors were met by Jorissimal and two of Vittargattus's warriors. They could see from the latter's faces that something had happened in their brief absence.

'Starhanger,' said Jorissimal. 'The Innasmornians have been watching its walls closely.'

'There's been no movement for a day and night,' said one of the Innasmornians. 'Vittargattus is moving us forward at once, to surround the place. He wants to speak to you.'

Pyramors nodded tiredly. Aru followed him and the Innasmornians down the steep path, through the camp of the survivors of the Sculpted City and on down into the canyon where the main forces of the Innasmornians were already preparing to move on up the road into the higher mountains.

Vittargattus and Ondrabal were waiting, their armour strapped on, their Windmasters and Seers ready to begin the march anew.

'Where have you been?' said Vittargattus gruffly.

'There are other dangers abroad,' said Pyramors bluntly. He knew this was not the time to describe the threat of the Csendook.

But Ondrabal studied him suspiciously. 'You used the machine? You flew into the mountains?'

'It was necessary.'

'We move up at once.'

'I agree,' said a voice in the shadows, and the figure of Tremazon emerged. 'We must decide very soon, Pyramors.'

Pyramors tried to read his expression, but could not. Tremazon had learned Innasmornian quickly, he realised. Had he discussed the situation with Vittargattus and the others? Was he more inclined to an assault? Did he, after all, support Gannatyne, or had he other plans?

'I'll see that our men are mobilised at once,' said Pyramors, turning away as the light of dawn began to spread.

Aru watched him for a brief moment, then spoke to Vittargattus. 'Your men told us the fortress is silent.'

'Something is wrong,' cut in Ondrabal. 'Possibly a trap.'

'It can't be very well fortified. Not enough of the Imperator's forces survived.'

'We'll soon know,' said Vittargattus.

'They may want to talk,' said Aru. 'The hostages –'

'We'll see,' nodded Ondrabal, though Aru began to feel all hope of a solution slipping away. The darkness closed in. Where was Ussemitus? They needed him so badly.

'They're right,' breathed Pyramors, crouching down in the rocks. Beyond him, across the open gorge, the far walls rose up. Carved out of them was the fortress of Starhanger, its buildings and towers perched high among the crags, unassailable. The only access to them was across the open gorge where the river cut its way steeply downwards and in through the huge stone portal that led up into the heart of the fortress.

'Something is wrong,' Pyramors went on. He pointed to the jagged peaks that ringed the upper fortress. 'Look at the birds circling up there. I've seen that too many times.'

Aru gasped. 'Like over a battlefield – '

Pyramors grunted. 'Exactly. There's death in that place.'

Beside Aru, Armestor and Fomond studied the fortress across the gorge. Armestor was shaking his head in puzzlement. 'The doors are not closed,' he muttered.

'What?' said Aru. 'Can you see anyone?'

'The doors have been constructed to fit perfectly with the rock wall. But they are not flush. They are partly open.'

Aru had good reason to trust the remarkable eyesight of the woodsman. 'Open?'

'Could Gannatyne's supporters have rebelled?' said Fomond.

Pyramors understood the language enough to answer. 'Perhaps.'

Aru felt the air above her tremble. She looked up, expecting to see the gliderboat pass. But it was not to be seen. 'Jubaia,' she called, trying to form the familiar link with him. 'Can you see anything in the fortress?'

There was only a brief pause, then his voice answered. 'We dare not go too close, but there's blood, and nothing moves. It is very bad.'

Aru relayed this to her companions.

Pyramors's face was drawn. He wore a mantle of bitterness, suppressed fury. Turning to Jorissimal and Tremazon, he spat out instructions. 'I want a small unit. I'll take them to the gate.'

'Ondrabal was right. It may be a trap,' said Jorissimal. 'You can't risk – '

'The men? Then I'll go alone.'

Aru began to protest, but Pyramors shook his head.

'It has to be done. And we have no time.'

'I'll go with you,' said Aru.

But he shot her a fiery glance. *'You will not.* I will take a few picked men, that's all.'

She saw that he would not tolerate an argument. Already he was going down into the rocks, pointing out the warriors he wanted. When he was ready, he confronted the two Innasmornian leaders.

'You put yourself at risk?' said Vittargattus. 'If you must send your warriors in, and risk lives, why do you go with them?'

Pyramors listened to the words carefully. His command of Innasmornian was growing quickly, but he searched for the words to explain his actions. 'My woman is a prisoner in that place. Some of my people think that I value her above all other things.'

'And do you?' said Ondrabal.

Pyramors did not answer. 'I cannot ask my warriors to risk their lives for her sake. Not unless I lead them.'

'Is she more important to you than the safety of this Man you call Gannatyne?' asked Freghai.

'Some of my warriors think she is all that matters to me.'

'The gate is open,' said Vittargattus. 'Two of our scouts have seen it. It invites us in.'

Pyramors nodded. 'I will go at once.' He spun on his heel, calling out to the knights he had chosen. They obeyed him without question, mounting their horses, and his own horse was brought to him.

Aru felt the eyes of Fomond on her. 'Why does he do this?' asked the Innasmornian. 'For the woman?'

Guilt, she thought. It eats at him like a canker. But she did not answer.

Armestor gently pulled his companion away. 'Let him go, I say,' he whispered. 'Vittargattus and Ondrabal don't trust him.'

Fomond frowned. He could not believe Pyramors was anything but an ally, and yet there was something about his present mood that made Fomond uneasy. The harrowing experiences that Pyramors must have been through on Eannor had taken their toll, a cost the warrior as yet did not realise.

They rode across the narrow stone span, the waters boiling beneath them, the sound drowning out any others that might have filtered down from the heights beyond, where the fortress waited. But as they rode on slowly across the barren slope to the gates, the noise of the torrent subsided. Ahead of them the walls rose up, silent and forbidding, and high above them the black shapes still circled.

Pyramors could see the massive gate clearly now. It was, as Armestor had promised him, open, inviting. There were no guards. The battlements were too far overhead to see, carved into the naked rock, as were the windows and lower balustrades. The growing daylight picked out details, a ledge here, an edge of roof there. But no life. No cries echoed down to the riders.

At the very mouth of the portal Pyramors halted, his dozen followers waiting, swords drawn. Pyramors edged his steed through the door, into the cold shadow. They think I'm a fool, he said to himself. But even they can't know what will fall upon them when Auganzar arrives.

The horse snorted, tossing its head. It could smell the blood. There had been a contest here after all.

They found the first bodies on the lower stair. Knights of the Imperator, tossed aside as though something huge had smashed its way up the stair past them, a machine perhaps. Their limbs and necks were broken, their corpses torn, squashed like flies.

Pyramors tethered his horse in the open area beyond the main gate, motioning his men to do the same. No one spoke. They walked up the stair, through the horror of ruined knights. Blood smeared the walls. Rats scampered for safety as they heard the tread of the newcomers.

It was along climb up to the citadel. There were a few rooms along the way, store rooms, armouries, guard chambers, and the doors to all had been ripped off, smashed. It was as though a terrible storm had blasted its way through the very guts of the fortress. In every room, along each landing of the central stair, their were the bloody remains of the defenders. Many of them were only partly armed, and it was obvious they had tried to flee whatever nightmare had descended upon them.

The higher levels were the worst. There were women among the victims, and in other chambers, children. Pyramors drew off his helm, stifling within it. His face mirrored the utter horror he felt.

'Sire,' gasped one of the knights. 'Who could have done this? The Innasmornians? The storm that blasted our city – '

'Perhaps,' grunted Pyramors. He had to climb through a tangle of human remains, countless bodies that were heaped up outside one of the larger chambers. The smell was appalling.

Surely Auganzar did not lie to me. Surely he has not been here already.

But it did not look like the handiwork of Csendook. These people had not been cut to pieces with swords or with other Csendook weapons. They had been torn apart, ripped up like dolls. And Csendook did not kill women. They would have taken the women, protected them. Even the most bellicose of Auganzar's Zemoks would not have slaughtered women. And to do this to them – . No, it was unthinkable.

The knights stood inside the hall, shaking their heads in bewilderment, forcing back tears at what they saw. Had no one survived?

Pyramors said nothing, searching the hall, an audience chamber he guessed, for some kind of clue. He recognised the fallen. There were members of the Consulate here, those who had been loyal to the Imperator to the end. Members of the surviving Houses of the old Empire. Fighting men, officials.

'Sire,' called one of the knights.

Pyramors glared at him as if he had interrupted a sacred ritual.

'Shall we look for prisoners?'

Pyramors shuddered. He nodded.

The men broke up into small groups, none of them wanting to search this mausoleum alone. They left Pyramors to his dark thoughts.

'Zellorian,' Pyramors whispered, walking to the tall seat that must have served as the Imperator's makeshift thrown. It was empty, but one side was slick with the blood of some victim. Dead eyes gazed up at him from the corpses strewn about it. There had been no fight here, no battle. It had been a sudden, unexpected onslaught.

'Zellorian,' Pyramors whispered again. 'You have done this. You have dipped into the darkness of this accursed world. You've pulled out of its core this violence, this horror.'

He shook himself, his fury again impotent. Slowly he threaded through the carnage to one of the corridors. He walked its length in a daze, finding more death. It was becoming so common that he was getting numbed by it. It had lost its element of shock. Until he found the chamber.

It did not look like a cell, though it may have been used as a place of confinement. There were men who might have been guards at its threshold, but both had been crushed, as if a tonnage of stone had fallen on them, pulping them. Inside the room were the corpses of officials that Pyramors recognised, men who attended Gannatyne.

And there was a divan, its legs snapped from it, its cushions torn to shreds, soaked in blood. Beyond it, wrapped in robes that were deeply stained, was another corpse.

As Pyramors went to it, he knew what he would find, wanted to turn away, flee this place. But he moved forward.

It was Gannatyne. He, too, had suffered the fate of the defenders of the fortress. His dead eyes bulged, as if they had looked on some dire peril as he died; his body was crushed up, squeezed by unguessable forces, life pumped out of him.

Gently Pyramors lifted the body. It felt frail, like the body of an old, old man. He put it down oh the leaning divan, covering it with a fallen curtain, kneeling beside it. There were tears fighting for release, but still Pyramors choked them back. Gannatyne! Our best hope. Our noblest. What hope is there for us now?

He remained, kneeling over the fallen Consul, for a long time, eyes closed, despair his master. He did not hear the voice at the door.

One of the knights had found him. He came into the chamber, white faced, eyes haunted, the eyes of a man at the very brink of madness. Softly he touched the shoulder of the Consul. Slowly Pyramors tuned round, eyes almost as dead as the eyes of the countless victims.

'Sire. We've found something.'

Pyramors stood up. 'I, too.'

The knight gasped, looking down at the shape covered by the curtain. 'Is it the woman -?'

Pyramors felt a brief stab of anger. *They do think I place her first.* He shook his head, letting the anger ease back. This was no place for it. This was a time to be cold, to calculate, to act with precision. 'It is Consul Gannatyne.'

The knight sagged back. 'Ah, no. No, sire, surely – '

Pyramors gently led him from the room. 'There is no mistake.'

The knight put his hand over his eyes, lurching down the corridor as if he had been wounded, barely able to guide Pyramors to his companions. They went down a stairway to another series of chambers, and in one of them there were several more of the Consulate, each of them torn apart. Their deaths had been particularly terrible, some of the bodies unrecognisable. The other knights had gathered here, but there was no triumph in their faces, only a dull acceptance of what they saw.

Pyramors went to the centre of the room, a raised area on which there was a long seat. It had been broken, leaning to one side, and blood had run down over the steps, a thick carpet. Pyramors ignored it, going up the steps to the chair. Someone had been thrust into it, splinters of the wood puncturing the corpse in a dozen places, the arms and legs twisted at ludicrous angles, the head bent so far back on the neck that it looked as if it had been stretched, its bones jellied. It hung like the head of a chicken with its neck wrung.

But Pyramors knew who it must be. He reached down, gripping the soiled garments at the throat and tugged. The corpse came up easily, and he heard the soft movements of bone and organ grinding together within it. The head swung round, eyeless. But he would have known that face on a hundred worlds, a thousand bloody battlefields.

It was the Imperator Elect.

Pyramors let the body fall. He felt no emotion, no joy, no elation at having at last reached the goal. Only sickened. Disgusted at it all, the waste, the slaughter. He fought back the bile, looking at his men. They, too, were emotionally drained.

'I want this place burned.'

Putting on his helmet once more, Pyramors crossed the chamber and dragged more hangings from their pelmet. He chose a width of dark velvet and went back to the fallen Imperator. It was difficult tearing him free of his bizarre catafalque, but he did it and wrapped the body in the drapes, bundling it up, tossing it over his shoulder.

'For the others?' asked one of the men.

But Pyramors shook his head. 'For the Csendook.'

The knights followed him as he carried the corpse easily to the door to the chamber. He set it down for a moment.

'Will you ignite the fire yourself, sire?' one of the men asked him. They seemed bemused, unsure of themselves.

'Before we do,' he replied, his voice dropping, a terrible anger in it, 'I must be sure no one is left alive.'

'Sire, we have searched every room –'

'We will check.'

The knights glanced at one another, but none of them dared argue with the Consul.

As they were about to break up into groups again, they heard something in the chamber they had just left. Movement, as though a sack was being dragged across the floor. Pyramors whirled, framed in the doorway.

He gaped at the thing he saw rising from among the dead. It had once been human, but now, reshaped by some ghastly power, part flesh, part bone, it drew no more than a semblance of humanity about it, the dome of its malformed head gleaming in the light from above. It opened a wide gash that served as a mouth, toothless and scarlet like the mouth of something from beneath the sea. And it spoke in a voice that was strangled and alien. But they heard its words.

'Pyramors!' it gurgled, grotesque body weaving to and fro as if in an effort to maintain its substance. 'Hear me.'

'What are you?'

'The voice of your enemy. He is far away. But he leaves you this pitiful worm who was Imperator as a reward for your persistence.'

Pyramors stepped forward, ignoring the warnings of the knights. He raised his sword point to within inches of the gaping mouth. 'Where is she?' he hissed through his teeth.

'You seek your woman yet?'

'*Where is she?*'

'Not here. Not among the slaughtered. But alive. He has her. Far from here. Know this, Pyramors. Know it and despair!' The thing began to laugh, its bulk shivering.

Pyramors knew that it spoke the truth. He would not find the girl here. Zellorian, wherever he was, had taken her with him.

'Come to Umus Utmar,' the thing mocked. 'Bring all the powers you can find. Zellorian will welcome you.'

It laughed again, and for answer Pyramors drove his blade into its mouth, sinking deep into the reformed flesh. He drew out the blade and the creature sank down, its components flowing away from its torso, slick with fresh blood. Pyramors drew back. Whatever power had taken hold of it had left it.

He turned to his men, who gazed at the fallen monster in stupefaction. 'Bring torches. We'll start the fire here.'

'Sire, the search?'

But he did not answer. Instead he lifted the corpse of the Imperator and strode past them as though they did not exist. But in his eyes was the fire of intense hatred, the killing fury they had heard of. He would avenge the dead, they knew that. Wherever the Prime Consul had gone, wherever this Umus Utmar was, Pyramors would find it.

Vittargattus waited patiently while the solitary figure dismounted. Beside him, Ondrabal screwed up his face in suspicion, and with him were Freghai and others. Azrand and his Blue Hairs also waited. The knights had ridden back across the narrow bridge over the gorge. Behind them the fortress was still silent, except for the birds, which seemed to flock to it. The men had not spoken, merely shaken their heads as though too exhausted to speak.

From the rock walls, smoke was curling, and scouts shouted from their rocky perches that there were dark clouds of smoke up among the turrets. Fire had broken out.

Aru would have demanded explanations from the knights, as would Tremazon, but they both waited while Pyramors climbed down from his steed. He unslung from its back a strange bundle. He brought it before the host and tossed it to the ground, undoing the cords that bound it up.

'Have you put the fortress to the torch?' said Ondrabal, tired of waiting for an explanation.

Pyramors revealed the corpse of the Imperator. The knights recognised it for what it was at once, and drew back, as though amazed that after so long the tyrant had at last been brought to this.

'The Imperator Elect,' said Pyramors to the Innasmornians. 'He and every one of his followers are dead. Nothing lives in that citadel. It is a pyre.'

Vittargattus's eyes snapped up at the rock walls, the flames high among its towers. 'They fought themselves?'

'Zellorian has unleashed these dark powers he controls from afar. And he has killed all those he found in the citadel.'

'The dark powers?' said Ondrabal, guessing the truth.

Pyramors nodded. 'Zellorian is in the place Ussemitus told us of. Umus Utmar.'

Ondrabal and Vittargattus looked at one another, and then at the Windmasters and Seers. 'Is it possible?' said Ondrabal.

Azrand answered for them all. 'It is possible. If he has unleashed the Malefics.'

'Vittargattus,' said Pyramors. 'There are few of my people left. You see them all before you. These and our families up in the mountains, with the gliderboats. But we will carry this war to Umus Utmar, wherever it may be.'

Tremazon stepped forward. 'Before we decide on what is best for our people – ' he began, but Pyramors pointed at him.

'Zellorian is set on the destruction of this world. He has no respect for Man or Innasmornian. Until he is dead, nothing is safe. We must take the war to him without delay.'

Vittargattus nodded slowly. 'It is a difficult journey to so far a region as Umus Utmar. To take our armies – '

'We have other allies,' said Pyramors. He bent down and re-tied the knots that bound up the Imperator's corpse. 'This will be our security.'

'What other allies?' said Ondrabal, again bristling with suspicion.

'The Csendook,' said Pyramors, lifting his grisly trophy. 'They're here on Innasmorn. But they have come for Zellorian.'

The men gathered among the host were staggered by this news, just as Pyramors had guessed they would be.

'Csendook?' said Vittargattus. 'The race who sought to exterminate Man? They are *here*?'

'They will not take arms against us, nor your people. But if we are to carry the war to Umus Utmar, we will need the Csendook.'

'That's preposterous!' cried Tremazon. 'You cannot make an ally out of the Csendook! They are more of a danger to us than a dozen Zellorians!'

'Give me a few days,' said Pyramors. 'I will prove you wrong.'

'Where will you go?' said Vittargattus.

Pyramors shouldered the body. 'To the Csendook. This will convince them of our own intent.'

'How will you go to them?' said Ondrabal. 'In the machine?'

Pyramors looked at Aru. 'In the machine.'

Aru could not meet his gaze, but she nodded to the Innasmornians.

Vittargattus nodded slowly. 'Very well. Speak to these allies. But our armies have done with battle in these mountains. We ride south again, to cleanse ourselves, eh, Ondrabal?'

'Aye, let's get clear of these mountains. We'll camp in the foothills to the south. It will give us time to assess our position.'

Pyramors went to Aru, ignoring Jorissimal and Tremazon, both of whom seemed anxious to speak to him. He spoke to her in their own tongue. 'Bring the gliderboat. Quickly!'

'You think Auganzar will agree to an alliance? After what he said to us?'

'I will speak to him. Drop me before his camp. Alone this time.'

'No, I'll come – '

'There's no need! Do you think I'd betray you? For what? The last handful of Men left alive? Don't you think I want to give them some hope? Auganzar is the only hope they have!'

'You expect us to believe that!' snapped Tremazon. 'Have you lost your reason!'

Pyramors turned on him. 'Take the men with the Innasmornians. Strengthen this alliance, just as Ussemitus told you to. Without these people, we are doomed, Tremazon.'

'He's right, Tremazon,' said Aru.

'I'll trust the Innasmornians. But *Csendook*!'

'I'll face them alone,' said Pyramors. 'Get the gliderboat.'

Aru closed her eyes. Already the clan chief and the southern king were marshalling their armies, readying them for another long march. But they were glad there had been no battle here. They had seen the faces of the knights who had returned from the fortress.

Aru waited as Pyramors mounted his horse, and together they rode up into a cluster of boulders, threading through the rocks to a place above the flat bottom of the gorge. Jubaia had already brought the gliderboat down. It was the subject of great curiosity among the Innasmornians, but none of them had dared venture up here to see it, even the scouts.

Pyramors said nothing as he dropped the corpse of the Imperator into the bottom of the craft.

Jubaia felt Circu shudder at the contact.

'Take him back to the Csendook,' said Aru, her voice flat.

'And you mistress?' said Jubaia.

'I'm going with the armies. If Pyramors comes out of this alive, bring him to us. Now hurry!'

Jubaia was amazed at the sharpness of her tone, but she had wheeled her steed and began a dangerous gallop back down the path before he could comment further.

'Up, sweet one,' Jubaia whispered to the craft. She had heard him, and she obeyed. But the darkness still gripped her. It frightened him with its completeness, its impenetrable silences.

It did not take long for the aerial journey to bring them down through the peaks and into the pass where the Csendook rode in search of Starhanger. Jubaia took Circu over the Swarm in one careful pass before curving round in a tight arc to hover some distance from the van.

'Let me down, and then keep your distance,' Pyramors told him stiffly. 'If they kill me, go back to the armies with all speed and warn them.'

'Kill you!' gasped Jubaia. 'But you said – '

'I know! But these are Csendook. They will not have their hunting marred. I may not convince them.'

Jubaia had no alternative but to obey, and he guided the gliderboat lower. But Circu would not go close to the ground. He could feel her resistance. Was it fear of the Csendook? It must be. Something forced her back, but as she hid her emotions so well, he could not read if it was fear.

'Lower!' snapped Pyramors, his grip on the Imperator's corpse tightening.

'I can't! She won't respond.'

Pyramors could see a trio of Csendook warriors detaching themselves from the Swarm. They would soon be beneath him. But the gliderboat would go no lower.

Cursing, Pyramors slipped from the side of the craft, dropping twenty feet to the dirt below. He landed like a cat, rolling forward, sprawling. Moments later he gazed up through the cloud of dust. Three xillatraal snarled at him, heads dipping, teeth snapping. But they did not attack.

Pyramors turned. The velvet shroud had ripped, the Imperator's corpse spilling from it, a mangled doll. Overhead, the gliderboat made one brief dip towards the figures, but the Csendook ignored it.

One of them dismounted and went to the body. With its boot it turned the face to the light. The warrior, a Zolutar, strode over to Pyramors, who had risen slowly.

'A strange gift you bring us, Pyras.'

Pyramors frowned. He had not used his *moillum* alias for a long time.

The Zolutar raised its war helm. 'I am Immarzol. I saw your progress in the great Testament.'

'Then you know your master and I –'

'My master has finished discussion. He hunts.'

'Take the body to him. He'll recognise it.'

Immarzol frowned.

'It's the Imperator Elect.'

Immarzol swore, going at once to the hideous corpse, bending down to examine the torn face. He rose quickly, beckoning to one of the other warriors. 'Wrap the corpse.

234

Take it to the Supreme Sanguinary at once.' He swung round on Pyramors. 'Where is the Prime Consul?'

'That's what I want to discuss.'

Immarzol's eyes fixed him coldly, as though the Csendook would suddenly reach out and take hold of his neck in a death grip.

'I know where he is,' said Pyramors.

Immarzol let out a rush of air. 'You play a very dangerous game, Consul. A very dangerous game.'

19

FROM THE HISTORIES

'I gave you my word,' said Auganzar. 'I will not go back on it. You are free to take your people wherever you wish on Innasmorn. And I have no quarrel with the Innasmornians.'

He and Pyramors were not alone. The warriors who had found him stood close by. On the grass, crumpled like the corpse of a small child, the remains of the Imperator Elect lay between them.

'My search continues until the Prime Consul is brought to a similar pass. But what is it you want, Consul?'

'I want what you want,' said Pyramors coldly. 'My people have achieved an uneasy alliance with the Innasmornians and the powers they can control. Even that will not be enough to deal with Zellorian. And even your Swarm, on its own, may not bring him down.'

Auganzar scowled. 'You seek an alliance with me?'

Pyramors nodded. 'It may seem contemptible to you. But it's the only way. When you see the fortress, its carnage – '

'Meet me there, at its gates. Alone. Keep your people, your allies, well away. We'll discuss this matter then.'

Pyramors nodded, looking skywards for a sign of the gliderboat.

'Go to your craft,' said Auganzar, himself mounting his xillatraal. He called out to his warriors to bring the body of the Imperator. 'I will show this to my Swarm, and to the *moillum*.'

It was done as they had agreed.

Pyramors met Auganzar and his Zolutars at the gates of the fortress. Smoke still swirled in gusts from them, though the worst of the fires had died down. Vittargattus, Ondrabal and the Innasmornians had departed, riding back through the mountains towards their southern slopes, and the remainder of Pyramors's people had withdrawn a few miles to a rocky sanctuary where they had been told to wait. Neither Aru nor Tremazon liked the way Pyramors was handling the matter, but they had little alternative than to obey him.

Auganzar's Swarm camped in the gorge before the fortress, waiting while their leader and his Zolutars went up into the gutted place with Pyramors.

Auganzar said nothing as he studied the smouldering carnage. The fires had consumed most of the dead, but even they could not disguise the horrors that had befallen the defenders, the wholesale massacre that Zellorian had perpetrated.

High up on the broken parapets, Auganzar and Pyramors gazed out through a thin veil of smoke, their thoughts momentarily clogged with images of what they had seen below.

'It is as I feared,' said Auganzar. 'Zellorian has always sought arts that were once forbidden, forgotten. On this world, if what you tell me of it is true, Pyramors, he may well find the key to things that should not be disturbed. No price is too great to pay to stop him. Nothing else matters.'

Pyramors watched the Csendook grimly. This quest had driven him from the beginning. It was shrouded in secret knowledge, the past. But he would not ask for the details of whatever truths Auganzar masked. His hatred of Zellorian was enough. And he said nothing of Jannovar.

'No, nothing else matters,' he nodded.

'Zaru!' called one of the Zolutars sharply. He and his companions had stationed themselves along the parapet, always careful to cover their leader from the possibility of any attack.

Auganzar turned, but he saw at once what had drawn the attention of his warriors. Up on the next level of parapets, the highest, a strange light shone, and by its glow a figure could be seen. Auganzar glanced at Pyramors, but he could see at once that the Man was as puzzled as he was.

'Let us see who this survivor is,' said Auganzar, slipping one of his swords from its sheath. He motioned Pyramors to go before him. Together they led the party up a flight of stairs to the upper parapet.

There was a flat area at its summit, a lookout post that commanded a stunning view of the lands to the north and south. In the distance the tail of the Innasmornian retreat could be seen winding its way through the gorge.

But it was the solitary figure that drew the attention of the party. The Zolutars spread out in a semicircle around the parapet, partially ringing Auganzar and Pyramors. Facing them, a dozen yards across the flagstones, was a being dressed in white robes. Something hovered near its shoulder, the source of the light, though it could not be seen clearly, as though it might be a ghost or a spirit. There were other such things up in the rocks immediately beyond the parapet, silent as the stones through which they shimmered.

'Ussemitus,' said Pyramors.

'You know him? Innasmornian?' said Auganzar, guessing as much by the size of the figure.

Pyramors nodded. 'He has certain powers.'

Ussemitus's voice carried across the short distance with absolute clarity, and he spoke in perfect Csendook. 'Auganzar, Supreme Sanguinary, the Mother greets you. I am her Ipsissimus, her high servant, Ussemitus. We must talk, you and I. For the good of all our people, both here and on all other worlds, in all other World Cycles. You, above all other beings, understand this.'

Pyramors was staggered by the words. What was Ussemitus implying?

'I hear you,' said Auganzar, showing no surprise at the fluent use of his tongue. 'I am quite content to speak to you.'

'Our conversation will be private,' said Ussemitus. 'You and I alone.'

Pyramors growled in protest, and he could feel the Zolutars tensing, suspecting a trap. But Auganzar nodded.

'Watch me carefully,' he told his warriors. 'If there is any sign of treachery, destroy him.' He looked down at

Pyramors. 'You vouchsafe this creature? Mind how you answer me.'

Pyramors glared at Ussemitus, who nodded slowly. What else could he do but trust him? Aru swore that he was their strongest ally, though he knew that her emotions played more than a small part in her trust. 'Yes, you can trust him.'

'Your life on that,' said Auganzar, nodding at his Zolutars to see that they understood. He walked slowly over to where Ussemitus waited. Behind him there was a small raised area, the final lookout post, and Ussemitus led the huge Csendook up on to it, their privacy assured.

'What I must tell you,' said the Innasmornian, 'is knowledge that I have taken from the most secret places of this world. The Mother, whom I serve, would not thank me for imparting this knowledge. She may yet strike me down, but I am prepared to risk that.'

'I have been the enemy of your allies, Mankind. I have been the instrument of their annihilation. Why should you favour me with anything but your enmity?'

'Because I know the histories, the truths, the origins. And I suspect, Auganzar, you may be the only Csendook who also knows them, or much about them. Just as Zellorian is the only Man who knows them. It is why you hunt him so inexorably.'

Auganzar drew in his breath. This creature had struck to the very bone with his words.

Ussemitus could read it all in the Csendook's expression. The giant warrior towered over him, but he did not fear him.

Auganzar looked down at the Zolutars ringing the lookout. They could not hear this exchange, though they listened, trying to catch a stray word, their eyes fixed on the two contrasting figures.

'If we are to save Innasmorn and other worlds from the catastrophes that are about to be unleashed, we must bend our united wills to the death of Zellorian. I will tell you why. If, in the telling of the histories, I am mistaken, correct me.'

Auganzar nodded, gazing out over the peaks that lifted to the heart of the range, where snow gleamed. The voice of Ussemitus was low, soft, but clear, invoking the ages, their deeps of history.

'Innasmorn belongs to one of the Five Cycles, the five great World Circles.'

Auganzar did not turn, nor otherwise show that he had heard.

'Once they were independent of each other, the worlds of each Cycle having their own laws, their own relationships. The balance is preserved by the Conceptors, entities that move along the great circles of each Cycle, guardians of their bounds, the only beings capable of travelling between them. Like gods, the Conceptors are unseen, unknowable, powers beyond mortal understanding, greater even than the gods of Innasmorn, even of the Mother. The equilibrium of the Five Cycles has always rested in the hands of the Conceptors.

'Although the Five Cycles are independent, one world in each circle is common to all Five Cycles, though only the power of the Conceptors could once allow movement from one Cycle to another. In what was once Man's circle of worlds, Eannor is the common world, just as in the Innasmornian Cycle, Innasmorn is the common world. The other three worlds are Quendai, Ternannoc, and Islar-Namuth. These five worlds are the same, but not the same.'

'I understand,' said Auganzar softly, as though he saw the worlds before him and not the jagged peaks.

'On one of the worlds, countless ages ago, there was a catastrophe. Not a natural disaster, but one induced by the inhabitants of the world, Ternannoc. Terrible destruction spread as a result of the disaster, a manipulation of power that went out of control. It upset the unique balance of the World Circle in which Ternannoc belonged, unleashing forces that threatened to overwhelm the entire Cycle for millennia. Ternannoc, the key world, was destroyed.

'The other Cycles were also disturbed by the repercussions, some only mildly effected, but others severely. The Innasmornian Cycle did not suffer greatly, nor did that of

Man. But in Islar-Namuth there was great chaos, the extent of which is still unknown. And in Quendai there was also much destruction, on many of its sister worlds in its chain.

'Because of the immense scale of the forces unleashed in the catastrophe, there was also damage done to the Conceptors themselves. None of them died, but some of them mutated into lesser beings. They have become known as Accruals, and are now rogue Conceptors, who roam the borders and Paths of the Cycles, feeding on the worst effects of the catastrophe, sucking up its ills, gradually reducing them, in their blind way restoring equilibrium.'

'Such things are known to me,' said Auganzar. 'They are capable of opening Paths between Cycles.'

'They are,' said Ussemitus. 'Though they demand a grim toll in blood.'

'Eannor has known much of this. But that is ended. The Accrual that fed on the Path between worlds is destroyed.'

'Many Accruals have died since their hybrid birth. Man used them long before Zellorian, as he discovered when he pillaged the secrets of the lost sciences.

'After the great catastrophe on Ternannoc, the Men in the Cycle of Eannor realised that the chaos in the Cycle of Quendai would likely spread and damage their own Cycle. They needed to prevent this, and sought the aid of the Conceptors. Themselves anxious to restore equilibrium, the Conceptors imparted to these Men certain arts, enabling them to engineer their own servants, a breed of genetically enhanced beings who could enter the Cycle of Quendai and begin the restoration. Beings who were impervious to so-called sorcery, magic, and psychic influence, powers that Man had begun to toy with.'

Auganzar turned to him, his look cold, dangerous. His voice fell to little more than a whisper. 'Who shares this knowledge?'

'The Mother gave it to me. I have spoken to no one else.'

The Csendook looked for a moment as though some inner fury would rise, blotting reason, crushing this alien, this harbinger of nightmare. But he turned his gaze once more to the mountains.

'You, too, know this. How did you learn?' said Ussemitus.

Auganzar kept his voice low as he dipped into the icy pool of memory. 'During the Crusade, on one of the remote worlds in Eannor's Cycle. My Swarm had all but destroyed the last of Man's defences there. There were installations that we were determined to destroy, places where much of Man's science had been perfected. We were ruthless, many of our Zemoks sacrificing themselves. We broke into the heart of the complex and cut down every living thing we found. I led the final thrust into the inner sanctum of that nest of dark arts. I found the Man responsible for it, broken and dying like all the others we had cut to pieces. But he took pleasure in gasping out a last curse.

'I hear him yet. He told me the truth of the Csendook genesis. How we were engineered, *created* by the species we sought to eradicate. And how we could be destroyed, too. Man made us, and Man could unlock the doors to our destruction. There were weaknesses in us that could be exploited, technical subtleties. We could wipe away everything, he told me, but the sciences would be rediscovered by someone else. Man would walk that path again.'

'You never imparted this knowledge to anyone?'

Again Auganzar turned a cold stare upon him. He shook his head. 'My people must not be told.'

Ussemitus nodded.

'Go on with your history.'

'The first Csendook were sent to Quendai. At first as slaves, but as they began to restore the worlds of its Cycle, as settlers. They grew into a powerful race, at last becoming independent of Man and the other four Cycles. Contact was lost, no longer needed. Quendai became the centre of Csendook civilisation.'

'It should have ended there, then. The door should have closed on all this chaos.'

'Yes.'

'Why did it begin again?'

'Greed, avarice.'

'Man,' said Auganzar through his teeth. 'The star predator, the ceaseless hunter.'

'Man's scientists had tasted new powers. They knew of the other Cycles. They knew of the Conceptors, the Accruals. They were not content with the huge Empire they had built among the numerous, prosperous worlds of the Cycle of Eannor. They had new arts, sorceries, and with them weapons. By chance they stumbled again into the world circle of Quendai, centuries after they had sent the last of the Csendook warriors through, when they had forgotten their existence.

'War followed, and fresh disasters, escalating until Quendai itself was threatened. So dire was the conflict between Man and Csendook, that the Conceptors were forced to react to it, and Man fled back to his own Cycle, leaving countless numbers stranded on Quendai.

'Quendai was almost destroyed. It broke up, just as Ternannoc had, though it was not blown to dust as Ternannoc had been. Part of Quendai, tossed towards its own oblivion, was drawn through the walls of its own Cycle to that of Innasmorn. This World Splinter, as it has become known, lodged in the very surface of this world, Innasmorn. There were survivors of this awesome Crossing, but none of them were Csendook. Man had come to Innasmorn, in a fragment of a stolen world.'

'And in this fragment, this World Splinter, the secrets of the past are housed,' murmured Auganzar. 'Your goddess found them. Imparted them to you.'

Ussemitus nodded. 'Everything was there. In the Abyss of History.'

'I will visit this place.'

Ussemitus paused only briefly before going on. 'When Quendai broke up, other fragments of it changed. Part of it became the prison of mutated Conceptors, the Oibarene, trapped in the warping of powers. Now outcast, they were forced to rebuild the fragment as a shield for themselves.'

'The Warhive.'

'Yes, that is how it was born. And unlike the World Splinter, the Warhive was swarming with Csendook survivors. They grew strong quickly, fuelled by their desire for vengeance. And with the Oibarene acting as heart and engine of the Warhive, the Csendook took the Crusade through the fabric of the Cycles, to that of Eannor. The Thousand Year War began. Quendai was forgotten as the new Csendook grew stronger, pushing back the armies of Man. With each new victory, each new conquered world, the Csendook closed themselves off from their past.'

Auganzar shut his eyes. Such an immense vista. Worlds upon worlds. Powers beyond imagining, destruction beyond comprehension. And not over. His people were not safe yet. He looked up, searching for the disappearing Innasmornian army he had seen earlier, but it had been absorbed by the gorge, far away. 'And what of the Men who came here?'

'They were absorbed into the Innasmornian culture. Part of the Mother's plan.'

'Plan? For what?'

'The Mother brought the World Splinter here, when she could have let it disintegrate, destroying all those who clung to it for survival.'

'Why? Man was not native to Innasmorn. Or were there Men here?'

'No. The indigenous species were very unlike Mankind. The Innasmornians were elemental beings, except for a few races.'

'Then why should Innasmorn take pity on Man?'

'To use him. Shape him for her purpose.' Ussemitus had lowered his voice again, his eyes searching Auganzar as if he were afraid to say more, as though an even darker truth hovered between them.

Auganzar sensed the Innasmornian's fear, scowling at him. 'Tell me.'

'It will come hard – '

'Nevertheless, I will hear it.'

'The Mother brought the survivors here in order to design the destruction of the Csendook nations. To fuse Man's remnants with the races of Innasmorn. For centuries she has done that, until Innasmornians have become as you see them now. Like me, like those who have already left this place.'

Auganzar looked puzzled. 'You? You are to be the warriors who are to stand against *my* kind? When the best fighting forces of Mankind have been humbled by the Csendook Swarms?'

'You mock us – '

'I am mystified. What is it that you possess that you think can bring my race to heel?' There was a trace of a smile on his face, but no scorn in his voice.

'We have strange powers, we children of those long forgotten survivors. Some of us can call up the storms, raise the elements. And there are powers of the mind – '

'The ancient sorceries? The magic that Zellorian thought he could tap?'

'Yes, such things are possible here.'

To Ussemitus's surprise Auganzar did not scoff at his words, instead thinking about them carefully. 'Your goddess has prepared you, for centuries you say, for a war against my race? Is she, then, allied to Zellorian?'

Ussemitus sighed. 'No. But even a goddess, it seems, can become confused. I am her servant, but I have disobeyed her, even argued with her. I have not broken faith with her, but I believe a terrible darkness has risen to obscure her perception of the truth. I spoke of her manipulation of history.

'It was the Mother who aided Zellorian to come to this world. She used an Accrual, and other servants of hers, spectrals. You see them about me now, guardian spirits. Believe me, they are harmless. I am not your enemy. Much depends on my convincing you of that.'

'Go on,' said the Csendook, watching the lights that flickered deceptively among the rocks.

'Innasmorn brought Zellorian here, knowing that he would be a focal point for a fresh war against your race. Once he was here, the Mother used the spectrals to guide your own servant, Vorenzar, through.'

'Vorenzar! Is he safe?'

Ussemitus shuddered. 'He survived, but he is no longer what he was, nor are the Csendook who came with him. The Mother had not reckoned on other factors.'

Auganzar's face clouded with suspicion, and for long minutes Ussemitus explained to him about the ancient wars

245

of Innasmorn, of the chaining of the dark, of the Malefics.

'Once the Mother would have given such evil forces all
her attention, setting all other considerations aside. I have
tried to persuade her to do this now. I have warned her
that Zellorian has already been corrupted, may even have
been possessed by a Malefic. You have seen the destruction
he wrought here.'

'What does Innasmorn intend? The Mother you speak of.
What is her purpose now?'

'To fuse the refugees of Pyramors and Aru Casruel with
the people of Innasmorn, to create an invincible force. You
and your Swarm are to be the first victims of that force,
proof that the new race can carry the war back to the Cycle
of Eannor and exterminate the Csendook. For the safety of
the Five Cycles, for the keeping of the equilibrium.'

This time Auganzar laughed, but softly, a short bark. 'You
really think you can achieve this?'

Ussemitus shook his head, genuinely saddened at the
thought. 'It is madness. The Mother is not blind, but she
does not understand the dreadful dangers that threaten her
own safety. Zellorian is possessed of terrible powers. They
will grow. And he will find the one secret that you dread
most, Auganzar.'

Auganzar's eyes were like slits as he nodded. 'The key
I was told of. The ancient secret of our destruction. Just
as Man created Csendook, so there is a way to destroy us.
Zellorian will find it here.'

'I believe,' said Ussemitus, drawing himself up, 'that the
Mother is wrong to oppose your Swarm. I have told her
this, begged her to give me time to teach her the flaws
in her arguments. You must join my people, and those
of Pyramors and Aru. Between us we must destroy the
Malefics that have risen up, through Zellorian. The Path
between Cycles must not be reopened. It is what the Malefics
desire most, for once free of Innasmorn, they would rise
and rise in power, perhaps challenging even the Conceptors
themselves. Both Man and Csendook would be *insignificant*
in such a conflict.'

Auganzar nodded. 'I agree. The gate must not be opened. My own people know nothing of their true genesis. I, alone, understand that bitter truth.' And it is why I could never be open with Zuldamar and Horzumar, and all those others who thought me their enemy. How could I tell them, subject them to the *shame*?

'War gathers at Umus Utmar, Zellorian's new city,' said Ussemitus. 'We must gather, too.'

'Those who have come with me are sworn to my cause. Even the *moillum*, the gladiators of Mankind. If I command them to fight with your kind, they will do it. But they will not trust you, nor will your people trust me and mine.'

'Pyramors understands these things. His people think well of him. And of the girl, Aru. And there are gliderboats, adapted for flight through the Mother's skies.'

'I have Openers. Three of them. Or perhaps I should say two, as one of them cannot be found.' Ussemitus nodded, understanding the purpose of the servants of the Consummate Order. 'One has died?'

'I think not,' muttered Auganzar. 'He should be sought. His name is Etrascu, and he is loyal to no one but himself. Asphogol and Gehennon are loyal to the cause I follow. They, too, seek Zellorian's death.'

'Can we plan that together?'

Auganzar looked away, his inner conflict clear to Ussemitus. 'What you have told me, the things you have learned, are they to become common knowledge? My warriors are proud. If they knew what you have told me, about the birth of the Csendook, their anger would enflame them. Man here would not be safe from that anger.'

'Those truths were given only to me. I alone was permitted entry into the heart of the World Splinter, the Abyss of History. I stand before you, defenceless, Auganzar. Kill me now, and you could be sure of the secret. But if I live, I will not pass it on.'

'Kill you?' echoed Auganzar gently. 'Well, it would be easily done.'

'Call Pyramors to us. And your principal warriors. Tell them we are to form a new union.'

'And if this strange union you speak of destroys Zellorian and these forces that have corrupted him, what then? Will your goddess yet thirst for Csendook blood?'

'No. She is not possessed. The holy madness may be upon her, but she will come to understand. This war will open her mind to greater truths.'

Auganzar studied the tiny figure. Was it, too, possessed by madness? Standing, so utterly fearless, before him, so vulnerable, so small. But it had power, this frail being. Power enough to show outrage to his own goddess. He had survived that much.

'Then we had better begin quickly,' said the Csendook, waving to his Zolutars to bring Pyramors to him.

20

THE OIBARENE

Ungertel thrust aside the filthy hangings and entered, his hands curled around something he had killed out on the girders, some small creature that he had skinned and partly cooked. He snorted with contempt. The Csendook had eaten little for the first few days it had been here, but now its appetite grew as hunger prodded at it, and it was less particular. It would learn the laws of survival, just as the Girder Folk had had to.

But Ungertel was to be disappointed if he thought he could enjoy the humiliation of the Csendook as he watched it eat the rodent. Cmizen was not here. For the first time since being brought here, he had ventured outside. Ungertel sneered: the fool would not have gone far. Not if it had any sense. The Girder Folk would tear it to pieces, Csendook or not. Besides, it was weak for one of its kind. Ungertel could not understand why the Opener had brought it here, knowing the dangers.

He threw down the rodent and left the crude hut, going out on to the girders. His eyesight, like those of most of his people, was good. But he could see no sign of Cmizen. Should he follow him, or wait? But Cmizen could have gone nowhere. Exercising, possibly.

Ungertel sniffed, catching a trace of spoor, but ignored it. He had other things to do with his time. Snatching up his beloved pike, he crossed over to another tangle of girders and was soon one with the shadows.

Some distance below him, steeped in darkness, the object of his speculation clung to a narrow girder, listening to the sounds about him. Cmizen could hear the pounding of his own heart, like an engine down in the Hub of this bizarre world.

He had decided that he could not remain in the hut,

serviced by the uncouth Ungertel. The mutant had no love for him and it seemed unlikely that Etrascu would return. Either the Opener was dead, or he had betrayed him. He must have paid Ungertel something to look after him, for the mutant kept implying that the rest of his people, the Girder Folk, hated Csendook and would happily tear Cmizen limb from limb if they found him.

Consequently Cmizen had decided to seek a way out of here, though he had no idea how he could achieve his freedom. But there must be a way back to the surface. Ungertel had told him that there was a city directly above, and Cmizen assumed it was where the Garazenda were housed. He estimated that if he could travel far enough along the girders, which seemed to stretch on limitlessly, he could rise up somewhere outside the city, and find an exit to this vile lower world.

In the darkness he had seen a number of groups of the Girder Folk. They did not seem to hunt alone, with the rare exception of creatures like Ungertel. But in view of the dangers of this place, Cmizen was not surprised. He had a short sword with him, but he wondered what would happen if he was faced by a pack of the hybrid rodents and other similar denizens of these girders. Closing his mind to such nightmare thoughts, he moved on along his precarious perch.

Far below him he could hear strange sounds, the ebb and flow of what could have been machines. He had heard tales of how the Warhive was manufactured by the Csendook, though the truth of such matters was obscured by the passing of millennia. Something else caught his attention, a sound not far under him, to one side. Again he clung to the girder, peering into the darkness. He could feel the vibration of the steel, as if it were alive, though he knew it to be an illusion. But something powered the superstructure of this world.

Across the girders, a dark stain moved against the shadows. Three times Cmizen's size, it was humped, with tapering ends, a thick, black maggot-like creature. It was eyeless but one end rose up like a snout, scenting the stale air.

Cmizen bit back a strangled groan. The thing was hunting. Its snout pointed his way, fixing on him. Moments later it humped itself along the girder, crossing on to another. It seemed capable of moving very quickly.

Cmizen let himself slide down the leaning girder he was on, fetching up against another cross section. He did this a number of times, aware that he was playing a hazardous game, hanging above a bottomless abyss. One slip and he would be smashed to pieces on the webwork of girders far down below.

The hunting creature suddenly released the girder and swung out on a tacky thread, lowering itself with frightening speed. It dropped on to the girder a few yards above Cmizen, at once making for him. Backing up against another perpendicular girder, Cmizen drew his blade and prepared to defend himself. The huge mutant raised its snout once more, and Cmizen could see the beginning of its underbelly, glistening with the adhesive slime by which it attached itself so effectively to the steel. Cmizen drove forward with the sword, aiming for the soft chest of the monster, but with stunning rapidity, two pink arms shot out from the folds of flesh, claws unfolding, and gripped both his arms. He was dragged from his feet and held close to the flesh he had tried to pierce. The foul breath of the creature engulfed him and he shrieked as he thought it would ingest him there and then. But it held him to it and moved away.

The Csendook almost passed out in terror as the journey began. He was carried across a number of spans, or lowered dizzyingly on another thread, which the mutant produced as a spider might. There was no relaxing of the grip, the two pink arms enfolding him, affording him no opportunity to break free. Drained of strength, weakened by terror, Cmizen whimpered like a child.

Down they went, far down into yet more darkness, until at long last the monster ceased its journey, dropping Cmizen abruptly on to a wide girder that was slick with the oozings of its passing. He was too tired to move, his entire body aching. For a moment he considered rolling over the edge of the girder and letting oblivion take him, but he could not even do that: the secretions held him.

He watched the bulk of the mutant slipping away into the utter dark. Far up above him, through the intricate web of girders, there was a hint of light, of the world he had left. Again he struggled to move, but could not.

The girder shuddered, and he felt something pass through his body like a cold current. He cried out in horror: there had been something obscene about the caress. But he had no time to dwell on what it was. The mutant had returned. This time it seemed intent on devouring its prey, rearing up, opening a slit of a mouth beneath its snout.

As it dipped, preparing to suck the life from him, twin streaks of scarlet light struck at it from either side of its sightless head. Like miniature bolts of lightning, they flashed as they met. There was a sickening crash, and Cmizen felt gobbets of raw meat strike him as the head of the monster erupted. Through the haze, his eyes still reacting to the sudden flare, Cmizen saw the lower half of the creature writhing on the girder, contorting horribly in its death throes, its upper half completely blown away by the explosion. Giving a final twist, the remains of the mutant toppled from the girder and were lost to sight.

Cmizen turned his head, gagging.

He must have lost consciousness. When he came to, the air was still reeking with scorched flesh. But whoever had spared him from a grim death had not shown themselves.

Stand, hissed a voice. His head jerked around, but there was no one near him. Even so, he forced himself to a sitting position. The secretions no longer held him.

'Who are you?' murmured Cmizen. 'Show yourselves.'

You will know us soon enough.

He realised with a start that the voice was coming from inside his head, like a spoken thought. Was this sorcery of some kind? One of the lost arts rumoured to be hidden somewhere on the Warhive?

We will guide you down to us. It is a long and precarious journey, Cmizen. But you will make it. That or perish. We have heard other hunters. We will destroy them if they attack you, but you must hurry.

'Who are you?'

Come to us and learn.

He had no choice, he realised that. But if they had been responsible for the slaughter of the mutant, they must want him alive. He tried not to think what their reasons might be, though he sensed that they were in his mind, sifting it and every thought that flashed through it. Again he shuddered at the mental caress. But he listened to their instructions and began the difficult climb downwards.

A long time after he began the new descent, light filtered up to him, together with sounds the like of which he had never heard before. Engines, perhaps, though unlike normal machinery. The girders were not only warm, but they felt flesh-like, not steel at all, and more than once he was sure he could feel something pulsing through them. Surely it could not be blood. But he was going ever closer to the heart of the Warhive, the Hub. Yet it must be countless *miles* away: the diameter of the Warhive was unknown, but to traverse even its radius would take weeks.

In the event, it was only a day before he could go no further. The endless web of girders came to an abrupt end, though Cmizen sensed that it was replaced by something far more immense, as if somewhere near him in the darkness an incalculable steel construction, like the spoke of a cosmic wheel, plunged on down with others to the very Hub itself.

He came to rest on a thin girder, looking out into a darkness that was as vast as any ocean, or night sky. But it was starless, that vault, a wall without a mark. Even so, something stirred within it, something so vast as to beggar comprehension. Cmizen felt himself shrivelling before it, blind terror gluing him to the girder as firmly as the secretions of the mutant that had trapped him.

Light is not something we relish. Though we can use it, as you have seen, said the voice in his mind. It seemed as though the great darkness before him had directed it at him, and for a moment he expected to see something emerge, like a gigantic leviathan rising from the ocean deeps. But it did not break the surface, gliding just below it.

We are the Oibarene. Soon you will be a part of us, Cmizen. You are fortunate among lesser entities.

'I will do anything you ask of me,' Cmizen cried.

We know that. And you will.

'Anything you wish to know, I will gladly impart to you.'

That is why we have brought you.

Again Cmizen felt the soft mental touch of something, as though slim fingers had dipped into his very mind, touching the thoughts that were hidden there. Nothing was beyond the touch. All secrets were accessible. It was as if a dream had spread its blanket over him, and he sat transfixed, eyes locked on the dark before him. And as he sat, the Oibarene fed.

They fed on his mind, his knowledge. They saw everything that he had been, everything that he done. His plans, his hopes, his terrors. And his plotting, his deceit, his work for Zuldamar. They heard the conversations, the hidden thoughts, the betrayals, the uncertainty.

And they learned of all that had transpired on Eannor, from the first day Cmizen had stood there, to his untimely departure with Etrascu.

They emptied his mind, sucking it clean of every last vestige of thought. When they had done with him, he was no more than a vessel, waiting to be refilled. Satisfied that they had taken everything fromm him, they began pouring new knowledge into him, preparing him for a new purpose.

We have dwelt here at the Hub for untold centuries. Once we were Conceptors, enjoying the supreme freedom of the Five Cycles, maintaining the balance, the life stream that binds all worlds. But after the great catastrophe, three of us aided Man in his attempts to restore the Cycle of Quendai. We allowed Man to create the Csendook. But in so doing we imparted to Man many secret arts of our own. They were lost to Man after the Csendook went into the Cycle of Quendai. For many years the Csendook restored Quendai and its worlds, and Man forgot his creations. But in later years other Men discovered certain of the forbidden arts, thought to have been lost. Using them, they stumbled into the Cycle of Quendai.

There were more wars, more disasters, and the three of us who had aided Man initially were instructed by the Conceptors to restore

254

order out of the chaos. Quendai was almost destroyed, breaking up into fragments, some of which were lost forever in the void beyond the Cycles. One huge splinter lodged itself beyond the Cycle of Quendai, in that of Innasmorn. But the largest was the husk of Quendai itself. Our masters bound us to it, chaining us to it for our past.

It is a strange imprisonment, for we depend entirely on the body of Quendai for our nurture and survival. But we restored what we could of it, and made of it this Warhive. Ironically the Warhive now depends upon us, the Oibarene, which in the forgotten languages means, the corrupted ones.

We have added our curses to others who would bring Man to retribution, and we have given new strength to the children we helped to create, the Csendook. We took this Warhive from the diseased Cycle of Quendai into that of Eannor, and we have observed the fall of Man's Empire, the rise of the Csendook. But we tire of imprisonment, and long for the freedom we once knew as Conceptors. We dream of rebuilding lost Quendai. If we could restore the greater part of it, we could free ourselves to be what we were.

There are other great forces at work in the Five Cycles, not least of which are in the Innasmornian Cycle. There were ancient wars there, millennia before Man sent Csendook into the Cycle of Quendai. The darkness was overcome, chained just as we Oibarene have been chained. But it has eyes, just as we have.

Innasmorn has been linked to Eannor by many strange events, as it has to Quendai. The great World Splinter of Innasmorn is a part of Quendai. Innasmorn drew this fragment to herself, planning to use it as the beginning of a fresh war on the Csendook.

Zellorian, fleeing the wrath of the Csendook, fled to Innasmorn, unknowingly drawn there by its goddess. But the powers of the Malefics stir, awakened by him and by the Csendook who have followed Zellorian. And now the Malefics have turned their eyes upon this Cycle, seeing through the open portals that Eannor's Cycle beckons.

We have felt the power of these Malefics, and we have encouraged them. Through them we shall attain our freedom. The Warhive and the World Splinter shall be reunited, with Zellorian as the focal point of the union.

And when we break the chains that bind us, as the Malefics will break the chains that bind them, we shall use the life of Innasmorn,

*the Mother of Storms, and all her servants, god or beast, and begin
our own pogrom.*

The Conceptors who cast us out will shudder at our coming.

Cmizen opened his eyes. Still the great vault hung before
him, an empty cosmos. For a few seconds the knowledge
that had been poured into him threatened to overwhelm
him, ripping his sanity from its bed, but gradually he was
able to organise it, to concentrate.

He looked down at himself as though he was in an
different body. He no longer felt weak, tired. His shape
had changed. He was larger, more muscled, and his arms
were elongated, ending in tapering fingers unlike those of
a Csendook.

We are in you, came the voice in his mind.

He laughed, the sound rolling out over the abyss like
thunder. 'Yes! I am not as I was.'

*You are our envoy, and our host, Cmizen. You will be taken to
Zellorian on Innasmorn.*

'What am I to do?' But he had no need to ask. Dazzling
visions spread out before him, the engulfing of worlds,
the tides of warriors, Csendook, Human, quasi-Human,
breaking upon one another like clashing oceans. Worlds
floundering in the flood of the pogrom. And over it all,
rising like fresh gods from the carnage, the Oibarene, the
new rulers.

Your guide is coming.

Cmizen's mind teetered on the brink of new madness,
veering from it with an effort, controlled by other forces.
His terror was a trivial thing. He could pluck it from his
mind and hold it up before him like a helpless infant. He
laughed at the image.

Out of the dark vault, something swooped. Long-winged
and carved from shadows, it was a thing of nightmare, a
misshapen denizen of these depths, eyeless, but gifted like
a bat with the ability to steer itself. It dwelt in regions far
from the reality of world surfaces.

*We have created many things in the long centuries of our exile.
This is a servant that will reunite you with one who once professed
to serve you.*

Cmizen listened with interest, and questions formed in his mind, but they did not seem to matter. He found himself moving along the girders, as though his footsteps were pre-ordained, set out for him. He had no desire to resist. Instead a lethargy stole over him, a dream-like state of almost euphoric comfort. The Oibarene would shape his future, as they had promised.

Board this fine creature.

Cmizen waited while the bat-like shape hovered close to the girder's edge, then stepped on to its broad back, sitting easily. The thing drifted easily out into the darkness as though accustomed to carrying a burden. Upwards it soared, away from the Hub, the lure of its inestimable powers.

Close to the tight webbing of girders, the bat-thing allowed Cmizen to disembark, waiting for him as he peered into the maze of steel. Something else stirred in there, and for a moment he thought one of its many denizens would burst out upon him. But the figure who appeared was no mutant attacker. Dishevelled, covered in mud, blood and its own sweat, an Opener stood shakily clutching a vertical girder, face drawn, eyes bulging as if they would burst.

It was Etrascu.

'How have I come here?' he gasped, his fat lips quivering with emotion. Somewhere behind him a light glowed, as though a torch were burning among the girders. He stared open-mouthed at Cmizen, shaking his head as if to clear it of a haze. The former Keeper of Eannor had changed dramatically. Cmizen was taller, bulkier, his arms like two elongated claws.

But it was the Keeper's face that baffled Etrascu. Gone was the drawn look, the constant stare of fear, the etched terror. Now Cmizen smiled, and in that smile there was something of the lunatic, the careless grin of a creature who has passed beyond fear, or care.

'Etrascu! It is good to see you,' said Cmizen, but the voice was hollow, false. What had happened to him? Surely the Girder Folk had not abused him.

'I...I don't understand. I was on Innasmorn. The Path...the Accrual.'

They killed it, said the voice to Cmizen, and he nodded, picturing the savage death of the huge being, with Auganzar and his minions tearing into it with their many swords.

'As we reached Innasmorn, I performed a small ritual, a letting of my blood, to get me away from Asphogol and Gehennon. I read their loathing of me. My prize would have been death after all. But Innasmorn offered me freedom. I let my blood and fled. To some mountains, a bleak place.'

'And you tried again,' said Cmizen in his hollow way.

And as he opened his vein, so we brought him here. The Oibarene taught the Csendook to engineer the Openers. They, too, are a created race. They can be manipulated.

'The Oibarene brought you here,' said Cmizen coldly.

Etrascu was ashen, eyes searching the lower darkness. 'The. . .Oibarene? What do you mean?'

'I serve them now,' said Cmizen, holding out his grotesque arms. 'They have selected me. And they have selected you, Etrascu. We are fortunate.'

'No!' gasped the Opener, trying to back away, but he was weak, his legs threatening to collapse under him. 'I am not worthy, I – '

'Nonsense!' said Cmizen, but it was in a foreign voice, the harsh voice of control. Etrascu recognised its source and sank down to his knees.

'No, no, I implore you, lords! Not me. I am worthless. A mere novice among Openers – '

'Would you not be an Ultimate? Greater than that? A power beyond anything any Opener dreamed of, Etrascu?'

Etrascu felt the clutch of terror. This must not be, he must flee. But there was to be no escape.

'We need an envoy, Etrascu. A link with our allies on Eannor.'

'Allies? Who? Auganzar serves you?'

The Cmizen-voice laughed, mocking, cutting at Etrascu like the sharpness of a blade. 'No. There are more powerful forces there, waiting to obliterate that upstart. And all the Csendook vermin. We will swallow them.'

'What Csendook?'

'In our pogrom. Mankind is already expiring. The Csendook will be next. A new breed will rise and spread throughout the Five Cycles. You will be the first to taste their power, share in it.'

Still Etrascu could not shake off his terror. The voice spoke with the unease of madness. This was not Cmizen, and whatever gripped him had little reason of its own.

'Climb on to the servant,' said Cmizen, suddenly reaching out. His arm was too long to avoid: the claws locked on to Etrascu's fat wrist, dragging him to the edge of the drop. He could not prevent himself being flung towards the rising shape. He screamed in terror, but fell not into darkness, but on to the back of the bat-like monster that had suddenly materialised.

Cmizen watched as Etrascu seemed to be enfolded by the black flesh. The bat-thing lifted its wings, wrapping them around its burden. Its entire shape blurred as the shadows closed in, and Cmizen blinked as he tried to fathom what was happening.

It was a transmogrification, a bizarre fusion of the two beings before him. Darkness obscured it all for a long time, until at last, light from an unknown source filtered down on the appalling handiwork of the Oibärene. The change was complete.

The bat-thing still hovered, but now its head was changed, a long, ovoid shape, with distinct features. Something that was still Cmizen gaped in horror at those features, for they were recognisable as Etrascu's: the huge eyes, the stretched mouth. He had *become* the flying thing. The mouth opened, but all that came from it was a pitiful wail. Huge wings flapped, and the sagging belly of the creature heaved. But it hovered, unable to do anything but serve.

Go to Innasmorn, Cmizen. Seek out Umus Utmar, the citadel where Zellorian is summoning up the power that will release the Malefics. You have the means. Ride the Opener. We'll give it sacrifices enough to rip a way through to Innasmorn. We are the Oibärene. We have power, arts long forgotten by others. We scorn the restrictions of the Conceptors. We cannot die!

Go to Innasmorn. Help the Malefics. Quendai must be re-made. We long to be freed.

Cmizen smiled as though all the secrets of the Cycles were his. He leapt on to the back of the new creation, not seeing the utter despair in its immense eyes, the understanding that it could never again be free.

BOOK FIVE

THE UNLEASHING

21

DARK UNION

Umtareem and his small group of followers dismounted from their mountain ponies cautiously. The air was uncannily still, the sky grey but unthreatening. Around the party, the walls rose up, cracked and dusty, like vague and forgotten dreams, falling into disrepair. But the high city of Umus Utmar was no longer deserted, its dismal corridors paced only by shadows and nightmares. Life pulsed within these walls anew, albeit a very different kind of life to the proud race that must have once dwelt here, aeons in the past.

The Blue Hair nodded to his companions, other Wind-masters like himself, and they crossed the weed-infested courtyard within the main gates of the city. As promised by the winged messenger that had summoned them, the gates were open to them. Figures moved at the base of the cyclopean walls ahead of them, envoys of the being they had come to visit, this new prophet, this Zellorian.

Umtareem bowed briefly before the figures. They were only partly recognisable, faces distorted, eyes huge. But they had much of the old Innasmorn about them, an elemental essence that seemed to have taken over what must once have been the Human part of them. For they had been Men, Umtareem could see that much. They, too, bowed, and one of them stepped forward stiffly, as though movement was an effort for him. His robes had once been white, splendid, but now they were soiled and torn. His face, once flabby with rich living, was grey and lined, jowls sagging. The smile could have been painted on, the movements those of a machine. Those who had known him would not have recognised the obsequious Consul, Onando.

'Umus Utmar welcomes you,' intoned the voice, the eyes momentarily flashing. 'Zellorian will see you at once.'

Umtareem bowed again, nodding to his companions. They

263

looked up at the walls: this was not a fortress that would be broached easily. Untold centuries old, it had once housed forbidden powers, the remote seat of forces beyond the laws of Innasmorn, home some said, of those nameless priests who served the darker powers of the world, the Malefics. Black power seeped up from below: Umtareem could sense its grip even now. His lip curled in eager anticipation. Far above he could see the gathering of the winged beings up on the battlements, like a vast flock of huge crows.

The Blue Hairs were taken into the citadel, along huge corridors that had originally been designed for stranger forms than the Innasmornians, immense beings. The ceilings were high and angled, and the corridors that ran off in either direction were like huge tunnels, lit from above by spears of grey light. There were no stairs in this city, only ramps that sloped upwards, curling around central pillars to the higher reaches.

High up these wide ramps the party was led, the mechanical figures that led them silent and plodding, like the dead. But the Blue Hairs made no comment, looking down, seeing a dark gulf below, a suggestion that a shaft had been driven vertically into the very heart of the world.

They turned a sweeping curve of the ramp, and an arch led off it into the central block of the citadel. Lights burned, a hundred brands set inside another huge chamber where gods might have sat. Numerous pillars rose up to the sky, each of them vivid with designs, their paintwork as spectacularly bright as it must have been so long ago when it was first applied. Overhead the heavens opened up, and the sky lowered, clouds rolling by, twisting like sluggish beasts in a sea that heaved perpetually.

Umtareem's escort pointed to an area that overlooked the great chamber. The Blue Hair saw other figures there, the central one of which he guessed must be the being who had sent for him and his rebels.

As they came before these new masters of Umus Utmar, the Blue Hairs bowed.

Zellorian, dressed in a scarlet robe that flowed behind him in a long, ostentatious train, stood up. His hands were like claws, the nails talons, and his face was no longer the face of a Man, but of a beast, a wild creature of the earth. His eyes shrunken in their sockets, had a feral glow, as though they looked far beyond what was directly before them, sharing, perhaps, the vision of some dark god, some lord of the inner earth. On either side of him his immediate servants were gathered.

Umtareem was amazed by them. They may have been Human once, but no longer. Umus Utmar had changed them dramatically, as if it had remoulded them from its own earth, shaping them as though shaping Urmurels, or other elemental things of the wild places. And as the Windmaster looked beyond the figures to the outer edge of the chamber, he saw other shapes, huge things, like resting aerial denizens, their wings folded up over them, clawed and spectacular. They seemed neither machine nor beast, but he could sense the beating of their hearts, feel their senses on him.

Zellorian smiled at Umtareem's confusion. 'You are admiring my servants. Are they not beautiful?'

Umtareem bowed low. 'You are well prepared, master.'

'You were wise to come when I summoned you. Are these all the Blue Hair rebels? I expected more.' He looked at the Blue Hairs openly. They were smaller than his own creatures, their cloaks and robes wrapped about them, giving them the appearance of huge bat-like beings, their strange, flowing hair like an extension of their clothes. Umtareem had the sharp, chiselled face, his eyes filled with the greed for power that Zellorian so often used as bait for his minions.

'More may yet come, master. We are, after all, spread wide across Innasmorn. Hunted down, reviled by those who condemn our service to the old ways. But we have sent out the word to all our secret brethren. The call of Umus Utmar is strong.'

'Good. I promised you power if you came. You shall have it. And with it, we shall unlock many doors together. You understand what is imprisoned deep under this city, far from the thoughts of the Mother?'

'We do, master,' said Umtareem.

'They have read you. Your devotion is known to them. You have certain skills. As do all my servants. Now is the time to share them, to pour them into the unchaining.'

'With all haste, master.'

'You know also of the World Splinter?'

'We do, master.'

'When we have unlocked the primal powers, we will claim the World Splinter for our own. And beyond Innasmorn, others are waiting for us. Other great powers. All the powers must come together now. Soon. The gates will open. The Mother will shudder, then fall.'

Umtareem felt the strength of this creature's will, the faith. It was as he had been given to believe. Zellorian, the once Human prophet, the alien, had indeed come from the darkness to unbind the Malefics. Their voice was in him. It would be an ecstasy to serve him.

Jannovar opened her eyes slowly, afraid what they might reveal to her. Before, as the air had rushed past her like some fantastical storm, conjured up from nothing by forces she could not understand, her mind had shrank from the chaos around her, blacking her out. The stone fortress in which she had been kept a prisoner was under attack, but she had had no idea where the horrific assailants had come from. Surely they were not allies of Pyramors. She had heard the scream of the winds, the sudden gusts as they buffeted the walls of her chamber as she was dragged from it by the quasi-Human being that had cut Kelwars down. Darkness had closed in with the storm, and with it had come an elemental madness that she had never previously experienced.

Somewhere beyond the corridor, the knights of the citadel were under siege, and a terrible struggle was ensuing. It must have been raging somewhere below her for a long time, before the door to her room had been thrust open. Outside, the faces that had leered at her had not been human, nor had they been Csendook. Better if they had been, for these were horrific, malign, the faces of demons, things shaped from the chaos and ferocity of the storm.

Jannovar closed her eyes, trying to shut out the frightful memories. Slaughter, fire, torment. The citadel and its inhabitants had been torn apart by whatever had come upon them. Had these terrors been the inhabitants of Innasmorn, the allies that Pyramors had spoken of? Had they come to rip apart the defences of the Imperator, extracting a murderous revenge upon him for his perfidy on Innasmorn? Pyramors had spoken about elemental forces on this strange world. But nothing had prepared her for this.

She had passed out, the awful screams of the victims ringing out from the darkness about her. It had been as though the inside of the fortress had been exposed to a storm of staggering proportions, the wind ripping through chambers, destroying all in its wake.

Again she opened her eyes. Silence now. The storm had gone. How long ago had it been? Hours? Days? She forced it back into the recesses of her mind. Whoever had dragged her out of her chamber had put her in another. She looked about her. The room was small, the walls dirty, their stone flaking. The bed on which she had been put down was crude, the pelts that were the bedding worn and dusty. Cold and evil-smelling, it was undoubtedly a prison cell.

Who had brought here here? Why had she been isolated? For Pyramors? Perhaps this must be an Innasmornian retreat. But there must be others who had been spared in the fighting. And Gannatyne! Where was he? The Imperator? Was he a prisoner? Had Pyramors and Jorissimal succeeded in bringing him down?

She rose and tried the door, but it would not give. She shook it and it rattled in its frame as if it would break loose if she only had a little more strength. But it held. Locked.

A terrible thought began to take root in her mind. Perhaps the rebels had been defeated in the siege! Perhaps the Imperator's knights had won the day. Pyramors a prisoner?

Someone was outside. She drew back. Keys rattled. The door swung outward. She stifled a sound with her arm, waiting, wide-eyed.

Someone stood framed in the doorway, cowled and unrecognisable. 'Are you awake?' came its voice. She did not recognise it: it was not the voice of her former gaoler or his cronies. The creature spoke awkwardly, as if Human speech was difficult for it.

It came into the room. Tall, cloaked so that its body was difficult to see, it held its cowl across its lower face so that only the eyes showed. They were alien, wide and staring, unblinking. But it was larger than a man, and Pyramors had said the Innasmornians were much smaller than humans. Jannovar noticed its hands: they were like human hands, but oddly misshapen, the ends of the fingers metallic, as though the nails had grown unnaturally, or been grafted on.

The man saw her and inclined his head, letting the cowl slip a little. Jannovar saw the line of his nose, his mouth, with its tightly pursed lips. She knew him, but from where?

'Where is this place?' she snapped.

'You are in Umus Utmar, a city in the far south of Innasmorn.'

'*South*? But we were in the northern mountains – '

'The stormgliders brought you here.'

'Stormgliders? I don't understand.'

'They were once gliderboats. Now they have been changed. They serve other masters.'

Gliderboats? Jannovar's mind began to race. She thought back to the evil days in Rannor Tarul before the Crossing. The pens in which she had been forced to work. And one face came back to her. A face that had studied her and her fellow sufferers many times, devoid of compassion. Immediately she cowered back. But it could not be! This could not be the same man -

His eyes narrowed. 'Why do you stare at me, girl?'

'Who are you?' she said softly.

'It does not matter. Not now. The work begins. In Umus Utmar, we are one. Earth, wind – '

'Who are you!' she snarled, fingers curling like claws as though she would attack him.

'My name was Wyarne.'

She nodded slowly. Yes, she had known. Artificer Wyarne, the cold, inhuman creature that had been master of the pens, the principal instrument of so much human misery. The creator of the gliderboats, the surgeon whose skills mocked nature.

'Why am I here?'

Wyarne would have spoken, but something behind her caught his attention, at the window. He brushed past her, gripping the bars and staring out. She saw a glow beyond, a flicker of light against the perpetual gloom of the skies.

Wyarne turned back to her, eyes filled with anger. 'You belong to us now,' he said tersely.

A new dread filled her. What work did he do here? More research? These stormgliders – what could they be? Did he use people for them, as he had on Eannor?

'What about the attack, on Starhanger?' she whispered.

Whatever he had seen outside to cloud his face seemed to be forgotten. 'Ah, yes. The attack. It was a complete success.'

She shook her head, completely confused.

'Those who were not loyal to us perished. Every one of them. Some, like you, were brought back here.'

'The Innasmornians – '

Wyarne laughed coldly. 'They arrived far too late. We had gone by then. We left them the remains. The carcass of the Imperator, too. And your traitorous Consul, Gannatyne. All dead.'

'Zellorian – '

'Awaits you.'

She sagged back, the real horror of the situation sweeping toward her like a wave. 'Then he was responsible – '

Wyarne stood at the door, holding out his clawed hand. 'You will understand soon enough. Come along. Let the work be explained to you. I assure you, you will not be idle.'

They rode through the mountains, following the armies of Vittargattus and Ondrabal. It was an uneasy journey, the Csendook obedient to their master, but suspicious of every rock, as though Innasmorn would betray this strange pact that seemed to exist. Some distance ahead of the Swarm rode Pyramors and Ussemitus, now both mounted, Pyramors's warriors on either side, watching the gorge like hawks. Csendook Zemaal and tigerhounds were up in the higher rocks, while other Csendook scouts and tigerhounds were ahead of the Swarm, studying the lie of the land in every detail.

Pyramors glanced at Ussemitus, who had become something quite extraordinary in the scenario of Innasmorn's future. Next to the huge Auganzar, he was like a child, but his courage, his faith was equal to that of the huge Csendook. The little Innasmornian had promised Pyramors that he would unite him, the Csendook and the Innasmornian armies once they met down in the foothills. Pyramors was sceptical, having heard the doubts of the Innasmornians about forming an alliance with men.

Auganzar, amazingly, had been moved by Ussemitus's words up in the fortress. He was prepared to listen to reason. But it would be a miracle if Ussemitus could fuse these elements into one army. Pyramors heard the snarl of a tigerhound from above. Could the Innasmornians accept such a monster as an ally? And could the Zemaal control the beasts sufficiently to focus their attack only on Zellorian's forces? They were walking a dangerous path, with countless pitfalls gaping for them.

'This is sheer madness,' whispered Kuraal. His fellow Windmasters, those who clung to him, were close beside him now, waiting with the rest of the armies for the coming of the beings from the mountains.

The entire camp was stirring. Vittargattus and Ondrabal waited, armed for war, their principal Windmasters and Seers with them. And not far from where they waited, the Human envoys also waited, the Casruel woman, and the rebels from the mountains, under Jorissimal and Tremazon from the fallen Sculpted City.

'It must be a trap,' muttered Hubraak, another of the Blue Hairs. 'Vittargattus is a fool to listen to these intruders.'

'Azrand is too trusting,' said Kuraal. 'We must prepare ourselves carefully.'

'Azrand is not fit to lead the brotherhood,' nodded Hubraak meaningfully. 'We should select a more competent leader.'

Kuraal did not answer, but he was pleased with the words, knowing their implications well enough. He watched the hills above them, beyond which the skies had already become unduly grey, the wind already rising, though no one had summoned it.

'The air is filled with strange spirits,' said Hubraak. 'It is a time of dark omens.'

As he spoke, Azrand was studying the skies, some distance from them, his face creased in a deep frown. The Mother stirred, the air filled with uneasy winds, elements that shook themselves as restlessly as wild beasts. If there was a storm gathering, it would be a fell thing. Would it attack this company? But it could not be from the Mother.

Freghai glanced at him, also unsettled. 'What darkness is this that comes?'

Azrand shrugged. 'Hold your powers at hand, Freghai. Evil wakes, and the Mother stirs in her anger.'

Tremazon and Jorissimal saw movement above, the first signs of figures emerging from the higher mountains beyond.

'It's just as Jubaia said it would be,' Aru told them. The little thief, circling somewhere above them in the gliderboat, had seen the oncoming Csendook Swarm, its forerunners Ussemitus and Pyramors.

'Pyramors returns?' said Jorissimal.

Aru nodded.

Tremazon caught her sleeve gently, lowering his voice. 'Aru, in the name of survival, are you certain this is no trap? If these are truly Csendook, how can we be sure of any pact?'

'I've read the doubts in your face,' said Jorissimal to the girl. 'You're not sure of him.'

'Pyramors? No, how can I be? But I am sure of Ussemitus. He is the only one who can prevent a massacre.'

Tremazon growled something, turning to the knights. 'Take arms!' he called, and as one they obeyed, saluting him. He had assumed leadership, and Jorissimal did not seem to contradict it.

As the company watched, a group of figures came more clearly into view. Riders. There was a single pony, of the sort favoured by the Innasmornians, and a number of larger steeds. Behind them, rearing up in a line, were larger creatures, their teeth barred, visible even from this distance. Aru knew they were xillatraal.

'Csendook!' breathed Tremazon. 'Then it is true. He has brought them through!'

Above them, on the ridge, Ussemitus looked down, but his attention was snared suddenly by the skies. A darkness festered there, and he read its malice, the gathering menace. Somewhere half way across the world, colossal powers were uncoiling.

But something else moved in the clouds, too fast for a bird, using the shadows as cover. It was the gliderboat.

'Be careful, Jubaia,' Ussemitus mouthed, but his words were heard. 'Soon it begins. Keep closer to the earth. The sky is no sanctuary. Where are all the other craft?'

Near, was the reply. *I have brought them.*

'Did you speak?' said Pyramors, nudging his horse closer to that of the Innasmornian. He was becoming used to Ussemitus's strange ways, his apparent communion with the elements.

'Only to warn Jubaia of the dangers that are gathering.'

Pyramors grunted. He could not read the skies, but he could see the unnatural darkness, the glow to the south, beyond the lands of the forests.

'Tell Auganzar I will go down to my people,' said Ussemitus. He did not wait for an answer, but guided his pony through the rocks.

Pyramors watched him briefly, then swung his own horse back to where the ranks of the Csendook waited. As he trotted slowly to them, he could see the eagerness of the

Zemoks, the Zemaal holding back the tigerhounds, the faces of the *moillum*. They were all primed. A single word and they would have launched themselves down the hill, and the armies below would have been engulfed. But a single figure held them in check.

Auganzar waited on his huge xillatraal, fingers stroking its neck gently, soothing it. He waited patiently while Pyramors came to him.

'What is it to be?' said the Zaru.

'If they agree,' said Pyramors, 'we have to go swiftly to Umus Utmar, before Zellorian can unleash the powers he commands there.'

'If they agree?' echoed Auganzar. 'Do you doubt their priest's ability? He has gone against his goddess to bring us this close to one another without bloodshed.'

'We'll know soon enough.' Pyramors looked to his left: the two Openers were there, seemingly uncomfortable after their ride down from the mountains. There was only one way they could travel comfortably. Both of them were pale, faces slick with sweat. 'Will you use them?'

'If your allies will direct us to this southern stronghold,' nodded Auganzar.

'My own people will use the gliderboats.'

Auganzar looked up at the false twilight. 'In these skies you are welcome to them. But what of the Innasmornians? How will they travel so far as swiftly as we may?'

'We go together,' said Pyramors.

Auganzar would have smiled at his presumptuousness, but said nothing. Instead he watched the figure of Ussemitus as it reached the waiting armies.

Ussemitus rode up to Vittargattus and Ondrabal at the centre of the Innasmornian ranks.

'The Csendook have been persuaded to fight alongside us. Their leader has no desire to harm any but those he hunts, Zellorian and his servants. He has the means to go to Umus Utmar swiftly.'

'You trust them, Ussemitus?' said Ondrabal.

'Pyramors has been spared, as have his knights. It is not us they want.'

Aru had ridden up. 'They are willing?'

Ussemitus nodded. 'They have Openers. If we use their powers, and those of the Seers and the Windmasters, we can take these armies and the Swarm to the south at once.'

Tremazon had also joined the company, and had heard Ussemitus's last words. 'Openers? To open a way for us? A *Path*? You know what can happen when such things are done? *Do you?*' He glared at Ussemitus, his face contorted with horror.

'They do not intend to sacrifice us. The Openers will spill their own blood to open a way. It will not be difficult for them. They do not need any other sacrifices. If we don't travel swiftly, we will arrive too late at Umus Utmar.'

'What is happening there?' said Aru.

'Zellorian is preparing to unleash the Malefics. He is possessed. They use him already. By tonight they will all be freed. The Csendook are nothing compared to the Malefics.'

'I agree,' said Azrand, stepping forward. 'I can feel the Mother's outrage even now. We must decide at once.'

'Prepare our envoys,' said Vittargattus gruffly, and Ondrabal nodded. 'Go with them Ussemitus. Talk to these aliens. Tell them we carry war to the south in all haste. And if they seek to betray us, the Mother will take her own revenge upon them.'

Ussemitus bowed, but Aru felt less sure of the uneasy alliance. And she could feel the eyes of Tremazon on her, the ferocity of his own doubt.

'Jubaia, where are you?' whispered Aru. She waved Fomond and Armestor to her side, and they were quick to move to her, never far away among the ranks of their people.

An hour earlier the selected envoys of Vittargattus and Ondrabal had ridden up the slope, a dozen of them, towards the ridge where the Csendook waited, a motionless black line, like the promise of thunder.

'What is it?' breathed Fomond, aware that other eyes were on them.

'Jubaia was circling earlier. But he's gone. Can you reach him?'

'I can try, but I doubt it, if you can't.' Fomond looked up at the heavens, listening, but there was a vacuum, no hint of the little thief or his strange craft.

'Keep trying,' said Aru anxiously.

Auganzar watched the Innasmornian envoys coming slowly up the ridge. They were like children, so small. And yet they must be possessed of strange powers if they were like this Ussemitus.

'You interpret their words for me,' Auganzar told Ussemitus.

'And shall I interpret yours for them?' Ussemitus asked him.

Auganzar frowned briefly, glancing at Pyramors. 'Yes. Pyramors, why don't you wait beyond the ridge while I meet these remarkable people?'

Another test, thought Pyramors wearily. But he nodded, waving his knights to him. They rode with him out to a shoulder of the ridge that was away from the Csendook. One or two of the xillatraal snarled at them, restless at the delays, but they ignored them.

'Rest for a while,' said Pyramors, dismounting. He went down into a gully, away from his men, wanting the peace of isolation for a short time.

Pyramors, came the soft voice in his head. He almost fell from the rock in surprise.

'Who are – ?'

The pilot, came the inner reply. *Jubaia. Listen to me. I have seen the spectrals, the servants of Ussemitus. They have been to Umus Utmar. Your woman is there, just as you feared. I am afraid of these allies you call Csendook. And so is this craft.*

The gliderboat! thought Pyramors. Jubaia. He can speak to me with his mind –

I can hear you if you direct your words to me.

'What do you want?'

We cannot stay here. We are both afraid. But we will help you. Take you to the south. The others want too long to talk, to organise. There's no time. I've brought the fleet. The craft will respond to Aru and the other Controllers. I'm not essential.

'You'll take me?'

She is in danger. But the three of us might stand a chance of helping her. A faint hope, but –

'Where are you?'

Go down the gully. I can see you. When you are well beyond your men, I will come to you.

Pyramors nodded, quickly descending. His mind was a blur of doubt and confusion. He had to step away from the debates beyond the ridge. They would kill him for this. His own men would kill him. But he had done all he could to forge an alliance. If the Csendook would not agree to it now, they never would. Let Tremazon take the role he desired, let him command the knights. With the Casruel girl. They had no need of a man they could not trust.

And in the south, Zellorian would hardly be expecting a lone gliderboat to defy him.

22

AIR BATTLE

The half circle basin of rocks formed a wide, natural arena above the ridge that overlooked the camp of the Innasmornian armies. By mutual agreement, the leaders of the various forces gathered in this basin, one side lined with selected Innasmornian warriors and the combined survivors of the Sculpted City and of Jorissimal's rebels. They were faced directly by Zemoks chosen by Auganzar, though they had dismounted from their xillatraal and there were no Zemaal and tigerhounds with them. In the centre of the area, Auganzar and his Zolutars faced the Innasmornian rulers, their immediate guards, and the principal Windmasters and Seers. Aru and Tremazon were the only Humans permitted to the company. It was an unbearably tense situation, and the unease of the warriors on both sides of the basin could be felt. And it was not helped, Aru mused, by the fact that Pyramors had disappeared. Auganzar had not commented on this, but it must have caused him some concern.

Ironically, however, he seemed almost amused by events. He nodded to Ussemitus, the central figure. 'Our differences seem vast, little priest. But our goal is a common one.'

Ussemitus interpreted for the Innasmornians, and Vittargattus, awed by the size of the aliens, was first to answer. Ussemitus again translated. 'He accepts the terms you have suggested. A combined assault on Umus Utmar. As for afterwards – '

Auganzar smiled. 'You are concerned about our continued presence.' He glanced across at Immarzol, whose annoyance at any compromise was clear. 'Immarzol, we have nothing to fear from these people. Those of us who survive this war will have no need of new conflict. We will find a new way. I am sure Innasmorn must be large enough.'

Immarzol stiffened. 'Of course, Zaru. I did not mean to

imply – '

'My Zolutars find it difficult to understand how their warlord should be agreeing to terms, when in the past the Csendook have dictated terms to all other races,' Auganzar told Ussemitus. 'But they obey me, and I accept the terms. There will be, I suspect, many more councils after this war on Zellorian. Innasmorn will be the adopted home of more than one outsider.'

Aru nodded grimly. There was the fate of the *moillum* to consider. As servants of the Csendook, they were almost despised by the survivors of the Sculpted City. There was a potential conflict brewing there. It would take someone like Pyramors to take the sting out of it. Surely he knew that. But *where was he*?

'It is acknowledged,' Ussemitus said, translating this time for Ondrabal, who seemed unable to take his eyes off the huge Csendook, 'that our enemy is poised to strike, and that the Mother is in extreme peril. Our envoys that spoke to you told us that you have the means to travel quickly to Umus Utmar.'

Auganzar nodded. 'If you are willing, I will bring the Openers forward.'

Ussemitus said something to the Innasmornians, and each of them agreed, though their hands clutched at their weapons, their fear a palpable thing.

Auganzar summoned Asphogol and Gehennon. They had been waiting at the rear of the Zemoks, who parted to let them through. Again the Innasmornians were staggered by the sight of the aliens. There were not as tall as the Csendook, but they were bloated, heads and bodies swollen unnaturally, their skin pale, their hands huge. Both looked ill, unhappy in the open air, walking with some difficulty as though it did not come naturally to them.

'You understand what the Openers can do, Ussemitus,' said Auganzar. 'Have you told your people?'

'I have. They find it very difficult to understand.'

'They don't trust me,' Auganzar said bluntly, again with a faint smile.

Ussemitus marvelled at the patience of the warlord. There were others of his kind who would already have unleashed war, careless of any union. 'I have persuaded my people to let the Openers guide us all. But they have asked for proof of their skills.'

'A demonstration? Very well. Asphogol, what do you suggest?'

Asphogol maintained his dignity with a great effort. He was unused to the outdoors, and Innasmorn filled him with horror. There were things aloft in its turbulent skies that threatened his very reason. But he forced himself to gather his wits. The Consummate Order had given him clear directives on this mission. Whatever the cost, Zellorian was to be destroyed, his plans for Innasmorn crushed.

'Zaru, I can open a way to this city easily, as you know. I need only its coordinates. If you wish, I will take a small group close to there, where it will not be observed by the enemy and return them almost at once. They can report what I have done to their masters.'

Ussemitus explained this to the Innasmornians.

'Is it acceptable?' Auganzar asked Ussemitus.

'Yes, but they want it done their way,' he said with an awkward smile.

To his amazement, Auganzar laughed. 'Indeed? And what way is that?'

'One Opener, and with him a few chosen Innasmornians, one of the Windmasters, one Seer, and Aru Casruel as interpreter.' He turned to Aru as he said it, an apology to her in his eyes, but she nodded at once. Tremazon frowned, as though he would argue, but held back his doubts.

'I am sure,' said Auganzar to Asphogol, 'that this arrangement will be perfectly convenient.'

Asphogol bowed awkwardly. 'As you wish, Zaru.'

'Who is to go? Let them come forward,' said Auganzar.

Azrand offered himself, but Vittargattus would not have it. 'This is too dangerous,' he said softly to him. 'I will not put you at risk. Choose a reliable Blue Hair.'

Azrand did as bidden, while Ondrabal also chose one of his Seers, Grumhai. In a moment, eight Innasmornian warriors were ready, together with the Seer, and Azrand's choice, Kuraal. The latter spoke to Azrand, who turned to Ussemitus.

'One other should go.' The Windmaster pointed to the watching rows of warriors. 'Your companion from the forests, Fomond.'

Ussemitus did not react. 'Let him come forward.'

Auganzar seemed satisfied with the arrangements. 'Asphogol will do what is needed. He will bring them back within the hour.' It was an instruction, and Asphogol nodded.

A few moments later the Opener took the selected party across the rocks to an area that was open, free of stone. He called Aru to him. She understood his words as he asked for the coordinates of the southern city.

'Kuraal, he wishes to know the way to Umus Utmar.'

The Blue Hair, his eyes cold as stone, stood before them, but he gave the directions. Aru understood them well enough to translate for Asphogol, who had slipped something from the sleeves of his robe, something that gleamed in the fading sunlight.

'I begin,' said Asphogol, turning away.

Fomond stood beside Aru, knowing that Kuraal, Grumhai and the other Innasmornian warriors were poised to strike at them and the Opener at the slightest suggestion of treachery.

'We have to trust him,' Aru whispered to Fomond.

'Where is Pyramors?' he replied, equally as softly, and she was taken aback by the question. 'Doesn't he realise that the Men among us don't trust him? They suspect him of all manner of deceit. Even Jorissimal is unsure of him.'

'I..I don't know,' said Aru. But she closed her mind to the possibility of treachery, trying not to let him see her own doubts. 'But it's foolish to talk of deceit.'

'They say the woman has turned his mind – '

'Be silent!' she hissed.

Fomond was stung by the anger in her voice, but bit back a retort, watching the unexpected clot of darkness gathering before the group. Asphogol held up his arms, a suggestion of blood on the weapon he still wielded, and as he turned, there seemed to be a rent in the very air beyond him, a tunnel into it.

'The way is open. I will lead us. Keep close to me.'

Kuraal gaped, but quickly masked his amazement, as Grumhai did. Aru nudged Fomond and together they followed the Opener, with the rest of the Innasmornians behind them. In a moment they found themselves in a strange pool of clouds, which writhed about them.

'It is harmless,' Aru told the Innasmornians. 'It is how Man moved between worlds in his own Cycle, and how he moved quickly from place to place on each world.' Though we did not use these creatures to do it, she thought, appalled at the thought of the blood that Asphogol had shed to do this.

As they travelled down the featureless cloud tunnel, the Innasmornians lost their initial fears, murmuring among themselves. In a short time only, they saw the end of the tunnel, and with a sudden flurry of movement, the clouds were gone. But the party now stood on different terrain.

It was just as dusty as the bowl they had left, but here the ground was black, coated with grey dirt, the rocks beyond them falling away in shattered chunks. There was a gorge below them, and across its span could be seen another huge plateau, rising up, its peaks and pinnacles the carved towers of a city, though it was a city that seemed as dead and as lifeless as the blackened rocks about them, as though in ages gone by it had suffered some great catastrophe and been ruined. The skies of Innasmorn boiled around the towers, clouds twisting and contorting at tremendous speeds, resembling the turbulent waves of an ocean during a storm. Faces shaped themselves, wide mouths opening and closing in silent screams, while the wind whipped the dust into a frenzy, gusting and blowing so that he party had to duck down to avoid the worst of its buffetings.

'Umus Utmar,' said Grumhai, shaken by his view of the place.

'Already the darkness festers there,' said Fomond. He glanced over his shoulder at Kuraal. 'Has he begun?'

Kuraal understood the question. His eyes studied the writhing of the skies above the city, the gathering of darkness. But he shook his head, his hatred of the youth momentarily subdued.

'Are they satisfied?' shouted Asphogol to Aru.

'They know this place,' Fomond told Aru in answer to her question. 'The Opener can do as he promised. Let him take us back!'

Aru called to Asphogol.

'Wait,' said the Opener, showing an unexpected resilience, for the wind was strengthening and threatening to smash them all from the rocky heights. 'I need to locate somewhere that the armies can be brought. If they are to besiege the city, they will need to do it from a secure base.'

Aru agreed, and helped him to scan the rocky defiles.

She felt a presence behind her, turning to meet the cold gaze of the Blue Hair, Kuraal. She knew precisely how Fomond and Armestor felt about him, his loathing of them and Ussemitus.

'What is the fat one doing?' Kuraal said, irritated that the Human woman could understand his language so perfectly, as well as that of the aliens.

Aru explained. Neither Kuraal nor Grumhai seemed prepared to accept her explanation, but reluctantly they did not interfere with Asphogol. The Opener finally settled on an area across the gorge, a mile or more from the base of the city, which looked as though it could accommodate the combined forces of the alliance.

'I think there,' he said.

Aru nodded. There seemed to be little alternative.

'So you are the woman that has caused such a stir,' said Zellorian, leaning back in the huge, carved chair, a relic of days long gone, when this dismal city had boasted other inhabitants.

Jannovar stood before him, her wrists bound, two silent guards on either side of her. Wyarne had brought her to this huge chamber, and he stood before his monarch and bowed.

Jannovar was staggered at the change in Zellorian. She had seen the Prime Consul a number of times on Eannor, though only once from close up: she had been struck then by his coldness, the hint of cruelty about him, but even so the change in him was disturbing. He was far more altered than Wyarne, his face almost alien, drawn and white. Something inhuman looked through his eyes, as though a demon possessed him. Was this what Innasmorn had done to him? As he rose from his seat, he was like a huge, aerial creature, voluminous cape flapping out behind him, his arms long and extended, the fingers like those of a predator.

'You are beautiful, though no more so than a hundred others that served the Imperator in his pleasure gardens. Why should the redoubtable Pyramors select you among so many, eh? What magic did you wield over him, this paragon of a Consul?'

She bit her lip, stifling her fury. 'Why have you brought me here?'

'A whim, I suppose. Pyramors has been a nuisance to me. I thought I had disposed of him once, but he wasn't content to remain on Eannor once he'd found you. Now I gather he is back among the men of the Sculpted City, or what is left of them. I suspect that the Innasmornians will level the last of them and their pathetic rebels. No, I brought you here for amusement. I have left word for your lover. He knows where you are. If he and the last of his followers survive, they can try crossing the world to find you.' Zellorian laughed, a harsh, chilling sound. 'But by the time he arrives, there will be nothing here. There may be nothing left of Innasmorn soon, not as she is now.'

She looked away. It was pointless to speak to him, the powers that possessed him. If she could reach a weapon, she would gladly take her own life, but they were careful not to let her do that.

'Bring her!' Zellorian snapped to Wyarne, and the Artificer pulled at the girl's bonds so that she was forced to stagger after him.

Zellorian and his immediate guards, strange, deformed creatures that could once have been men but who now seemed more like machines, automatons, swept out of the chamber and up another of the city's many ramps. Wyarne and the girl followed. They emerged after a long climb on to a wide platform that overlooked a huge abyss at the heart of the citadel. Umus Utmar had been built round this colossal well, and up from its invisible deeps the winds of the earth roared, their voices the voices of the night, the voices not of despair, but of a wild, intoxicated glee.

'We begin!' shouted Zellorian, and all around the edge of the circular platform, scores of his servants emerged from their shadows, holding aloft their firebrands.

Jannovar shuddered as she felt the response of the earth, the shuddering of a beast, eager to be unleashed.

'How long will it take us?' Pyramors asked the little figure in the prow of the gliderboat. Both of them were tucked down against the flow of air, the craft moving incredibly fast through it, swerving and rising as it evaded the worst of the winds. To the south, darkness closed up tthe skies, shot through with flickering bolts of scarlet light. A dozen storms were amassing there, far worse than anything thattt had been seen at the Sculpted City.

'A few days,' replied Jubaia.

Pyramors shook his head, surprised. 'I have never seen a gliderboat perform this way. Where did this craft come from?'

'From your city,' said Jubaia. 'Aru stole it from the servants of Zellorian.'

'It is so swift! Does he have other craft like this? They would outmanoeuvre our own with ease.'

'There is no other craft like this,' said Jubaia, a note of pride in his voice.

Pyramors nodded. Perhaps it was simply that the Innasmornian, with his extraordinary mental powers, could pilot this craft in a way that no man could. But the *speed*!

Jubaia was not inclined to say anything more on the matter. He was wondering what it was that had so silenced Circu. She responded to him, but her mind was a dark pool, her thoughts almost secret, as they had been when he had first known her. But there was great sadness in her. Perhaps the tragedies that had befallen her people had taken their toll of her emotions.

Pyramors became thoughtful as the land sped by under them. The craft kept close to the surface, for there was always the danger that they might have to land in view of the raging of the elements: conditions in the skies worsened by the hour. Even so, the craft sped on, its efforts supreme.

'What we are doing,' said Jubaia, breaking into Pyramors's thoughts, 'may be hopeless. The girl will not be easy to find. And if we do find her – '

'I know,' said Pyramors. 'You must think me reckless,' he added, suddenly snorting at his own impetuousness.

Jubaia shrugged. 'I cannot criticise you. Not when I have done this myself.'

'What do you mean?'

'Oh, I put my life at risk not so long ago, for just such a reason as you do now.'

Pyramors smiled at the little being's expression. 'And were you successful?'

'Yes, but not in the way that I expected. I found something I did not know existed.' He touched the metal of his sleek craft with surprising tenderness. 'I understand myself better now.'

Pyramors did not question him on this, though he was unsure what the Innasmornian meant.

'You must love this girl deeply,' Jubaia said suddenly.

Pyramors looked away into the distance. He did love the girl, but if he was truthful, it was not why he was here. He was not sure why he had done this. A final stand, a final shout at the perfidy of Zellorian? But it was not purely for love, for the girl. If it had been Jannovar, the real Jannovar, he would not have hesitated. Was that it? The act, the illusion, had to be satisfied. If she is to replace Jannovar, then I must treat her as I would have –

'Of course!' he laughed suddenly. 'What else is there? A dozen worlds are crumbling before our very eyes, but she is my woman! Come, coax your craft to move even faster,'

Jubaia nodded, but he had not missed the note of despair in the warrior's voice, the empty humóur. This chase, this wild ride was the last desperate act of a man who had already tasted the fruit of defeat.

It was as Jubaia had promised. Three days later they reached the southern land mass, and soon after were in the mountains that housed the ancient city of Umus Utmar. The winds tore at them, clawed things, as though their very presence drove the elements to express their outrage so tempestuously. The gliderboat kept as low to the ground as was possible, twisting and turning to avoid the fangs of naked rock, while above the winds increased in velocity, the clouds almost blotting out the light completely.

Jubaia shook his head, eyes streaming at the coldness of the air. 'They know we are here. It is only a matter of time before they find us and drag us from the skies.'

'Let me down, as near to the city as you can. Will these elements, creatures, whatever they are, follow you?'

'Yes, but what can you achieve alone?'

No less than you did in Shung Nang, came Circu's voice, sharp as a bell.

Jubaia recoiled. She had not spoken to him so directly for days. She wanted Pyramors released into the city. She had made every effort to get him here for just that reason.

'This is not Shung Nang!' he replied.

It is no more dangerous. I will do as he says.

'Hurry,' shouted Pyramors above the roar of the winds through the canyons.

'We'll shelter somewhere close. If you call for us, we will hear you –' Jubaia began, but his words lacked conviction.

No. We've business elsewhere, said Circu.

'We can't abandon hiim –'

We will come back for him. But first we must go to Shung Nang.

Jubaia gasped. '*Shung Nang? It is instant death to go there –* '

We need the windriders here. And we must bring the other

286

gliderboats for Tremazon's people. Every power available to us must be used here if we are to overcome Zellorian and the things that are rising up through him.

Pyramors realised that the gliderboat was somehow communicating with the little figure. It amazed him to see such a depth of understanding. No Human Controller ever had such empathy with the machines. The craft seemed to be arguing with the Innasmornian. He wished that he could communicate with the craft, but knew that was impossible.

They broke through the sharp upper crags of another canyon, and Umus Utmar was directly below them. At once the air screamed, faces leering from it as the aerial defenders of the city battered at the gliderboat, threatening to spin it end over end and smash it on the rocks. But the craft responded amazingly, elusive as an eel in running water and the parapets of the citadel loomed closer.

'We will find you,' shouted Jubaia to Pyramors, but the noise around them was deafening.

Pyramors crouched in the prow of the craft, waiting for an opportunity to leap out into the madness. The craft edged closer to the parapet and the wind almost thumped it into the naked stone. Pyramors sprang, fingers clawing at the rock. At once the gliderboat swung back, dipping down, lost in shadow, followed by a host of shrieking shapes. Pyramors had no time to watch. Grimly he dragged himself on to the top of the parapet. It was more of a rock outcrop than a turret, Umus Utmar apparently hewn out of the rock rather than constructed.

He could feel the swirl of the wind as it began another attack, but rolled across the flat stone and up against another surface. Beyond it there were crudely cut steps and he followed them down to another small area, ducking as something swooped for his head, claws hissing through the air like scythes. There was a ramp curling around the tower and he made his way down at as fast as he could, coming close to slithering over its edge into the well beyond it several times.

The elements continued to rage, but he prayed that he would be too insignificant for them to focus upon, one single man in this unleashed chaos.

23

RITUALS

Jannovar stared in amazement at the heart of Umus Utmar. They had brought her across narrow spans from tower to tower, but now they had rounded a curve of stone, a last ramp, and were facing the innermost part of the city. It defied all attempts to comprehend it, as it was vast, a gaping hole in the very fabric of space itself, where the darkness below pulsed upwards, as though striving for the light. Overhead the clouds had lowered themselves, shot through with lightning like veins, and the winds continued to race in chaotic cross currents. Immense aerial faces leered, and swirls of cloud took on the form of huge, grasping arms, as if the company on the ledge below would be swept off their perch and into the waiting oblivion.

Around the rim of the huge orifice, disappearing in a curve to both her left and right, Jannovar could see the massed ranks of Umus Utmar's inhabitants. There were vestiges of humanity in them, glimpses of things they may once have been, but otherwise they had been transformed by the dark arts of the Prime Consul, the sculptors of this strange world. Other shapes flitted overhead in the winds, shadowed things that swooped down with terrifying cries, shrieks. They may have been gliderboats once but their resemblance to the aerial craft had become superficial. They were demonic, their minds a cry of pain. Only Zellorian could reach them and direct them.

He himself stood above the maw of the world, looking down into it as if he could read its unguessable depths. The storms rose up from it as if born deep down in the inner reaches of Innasmorn. Zellorian called to them, encouraging them, and the darkness above him whispered about him, caressing him, urging him on to whatever dire rituals he was set on performing.

A winged form hovered before him, its outline in part that of a gliderboat, but with a huge, leering face, a contorted, twisted thing, eyes blazing with elemental hunger. In its shifting expressions, Jannovar thought she saw a mixture of human, Csendook and Innasmornian, as though this world had fused them together in a parody of them all.

'Bring them forth!' screamed the monstrous craft, flapping wings that were part steel, part flesh. 'Unleash them!'

Zellorian suddenly snapped his head up, then turned, face dripping with sweat, picked out by the scarlet light that shafted down from another thunder-wracked cloud. He pointed to the outer city.

'They come, these doomed armies! And with them is the last of the keys.'

Beyond the city walls, from out of another darkness, a churning chaos of movement and bursting cloud, the Path erupted and spilled forth the first of the armies. The Openers, Gehennon and Asphogol, stood back at the portal, and behind them came the massed ranks of the allied assault. Auganzar rode his xillatraal on to the plain before the city, and behind him his Zemöks and *moillum* lined up, with their Zemaals and tigerhounds. Above them, riding the wind uneasily, the gliderboat fleet waited. Vittargattus and Ondrabal, still bemused by the enormity of the transformation, brought their own warriors through, with the Windmasters and Seers calling encouragement to them in the name of the Mother.

Ussemitus called them together. 'We must summon the Mother as one. Unleash her powers now, before the Malefics are fully awoken. Azrand! Let the winds break down the doors of the city.' He pointed to the titanic gates of Umus Utmar, closed against the host, and Azrand nodded.

'There are other powers we must waken,' said Freghai of the Seers. Both he and Azrand began the organising of their followers, the preparing of the rituals.

Ussemitus closed his eyes, focusing his attention on the

Mother, the powers that were housed in the distant World Splinter. 'Hear me now,' he said.

'Oh, I hear you perfectly, Ussemitus. You are never far from me, nor I from you.'

'The Csendook are with us. They are ready to use their own strength against these evils that Zellorian would raise up. I ask you now, give them of your strength! They are with us, not against us. Abandon your purpose.'

'I will watch them, Ussemitus. I will read their dark hearts.'

'You will see their purpose, then.'

'When the Malefics are again chained – '

'If they can be – '

'Yes, if they can be, I will see. But these steel warriors will spread like a tide throughout the Five Cycles and devour all powers if they are given an opportunity. It is dangerous to be swayed by their arguments.'

'I pray you, do not pass judgement on that until after this confrontation with Zellorian – '

'Ussemitus!' came a voice above the rising snarl of the winds. It was Vittargattus.

'What is it?' said the youth, dragged out of his mental conversation.

'The enemy dredges up the deep night in that city! There's no time to delay. Do your allies understand? We ride in as soon as the gates come down!'

'Let the Csendook lead the charge,' called a voice behind him. It was Auganzar, his visor down, his twin swords lifted above him. 'We'll cut a swathe through this filth for you, little warrior!'

Vittargattus's face was a ferocious mask, but suddenly his eyes gleamed. 'Aye, then do it, warlord. Take your hell-beasts through. We'll be behind you.'

'The winds come!' called another voice, and it was true, for over the peaks of the mountains that ringed them, a storm raced, the forerunning winds buffeting and howling, tearing down on Umus Utmar, sending great bolts of light at its walls. Chunks of stone rocked, blasted outward by the onslaught. Tremazon and his survivors from the Sculpted

City looked on it amazement as they saw again the aerial powers of this world unleashed. Up from the black city rose other winds, as a sister storm tore from its very walls to meet the onslaught from the mountains. Whipped on by the Windmasters, the storm, fostered by the Mother, clashed titanically with the dark clouds milling over the city. The sound of the heavenly fury was deafening, but the armies rolled forward, themselves like a tide of anger.

Bolt after bolt smote the huge gates, which shook and trembled in their beds. Up on the walls, the host of the enemy screamed in terror as the Seers began their own convocations, calling out of the air the demons and banshees, the devils which they communed with in their rituals.

Auganzar and his Zemoks swept forward, closing their minds to the nightmare events around them, the madness that the warriors of Innasmorn had brought into this strangest of conflicts. The tigerhounds ignored the confusion of sound. They howled at the gates, eager to rip through them and be at the enemy within.

Ussemitus and his companions stood together, weapons drawn, appalled at the scale of the battle, the chaos that boiled before them on the plain. Rain lashed down, and other things swarmed in the skies, whole legions of hellish beings from the night, thrust up from some inner realm by the madness of Zellorian and the many agents he used, the black Windmasters and other rebels of this world.

A colossal blast, showers of fire, heralded the collapse of the great doors and the Csendook went in like a raging torrent, their xillatraal squealing partly in fear, partly in excitement as they tore through, over the flaming debris. There were warriors beyond, but they were ripped to pieces by the attacking Swarm, and the tigerhounds, now let loose from their leashes, ran amok, ripping those they found to shreds.

The Innasmornians and the *moillum* went through the gates together, ignoring their differences as they drove forward into the defenders. There were thousands here inside Umus Utmar, warriors that Zellorian had culled from a hundred rebel camps, every refuge of darkness on

Innasmorn. But they were no match for the tremendous drive of the invaders. Auganzar and his Zemoks were like the hurricanes that grappled in the skies overhead, a violent fist of concentrated energy, beating its way deep into the city.

Up on the walls, squinting down through the sheets of rain, Zellorian's servants watched, passing the word on to their master that the enemy drew ever closer.

Jannovar heard the reports as they were brought to Zellorian. He smiled grimly, showing no anxiety, if anything, pleased at the word of the attack.

'Send word to the Oibarene,' he called out to his immediate priests, and they stood at the brink of the vast chasm before them.

Jannovar did not understand. The Oibarene? But hadn't she and Pyramors heard mention of them when they were inside the Warhive? But she had no time to deliberate, for there were strange developments out in the abyss.

Something rose up from its darkness, like huge, globular limbs, though they were shapeless things, like pillars of stone that had been melted by immense heat. Several of them jutted up from the darkness, towers across the wind-racked distance. From the sides of the pit, Jannovar watched as other things burst from the walls beyond, immensely thick coils, like those of serpents. They slithered down into the pit, dropping like endless loops of flesh into the dark. From their thick skins oozed filaments of white webbing, and these drifted on the winds, linking the coils to the humped towers beyond. The central tower was soon enmeshed in these long strands, and something began to pump through the strands, thick, dark fluid, like blood. The blood of the massive serpent-like creatures pulsed down through the web-like filaments to the central tower, and at once spread out inside it, turning it dark with its colouring.

Whatever these monstrous organisms were that hung over the sides of the huge pit, they were giving their life-blood to the thing out in the centre of the abyss. It glowed scarlet, light spreading as it, too began to pulse like some gigantic, obscene organ.

'Let union commence!' shouted Zellorian above the sound of the winds, which raced around and around the scene of the ritual, wild faces leering from them, talons clawing at the light.

Jannovar could sense the movements of something vast and immeasurable down in the abyss, rising slowly to answer the summons from above. Out across the pit, beyond the glowing tower, something else came into focus.

It was a huge, winged thing, like a giant gliderboat, with wings like steel claws, and a bloated head, the features twisted grotesquely. They were not human features, but there were two huge eyes, a squat nose and a mouth that contorted in a rictus of a grin. But something about the monstrous expression spoke of suffering, human suffering. The thing hovered, held aloft by its wings, its thick body almost too gross to be supported. Between its shoulders another being crouched, clinging to the thick folds of flesh for support.

'Welcome, Cmizen!' called Zellorian. 'Voice of the Oibarene!'

The rider tried to mouth words, its eyes bulging from their sockets as though this creature – was it part Csendook? Jannovar wondered – was gripped either by intense pain or madness. The storm mocked is efforts. Before it could intensify its lunatic efforts, the creature that carried it, flopped down on to the top of the pulsing tower. At once, thin limbs reached up, scores of them forming out of the scarlet substance of the tower, and wrapped themselves around the creature, holding it in place as a spider holds its prey before feasting upon it. The figure on the back of the creature rose up to its full height, waving its arms, but the strands that clung to the tower broke free and attached themselves instead to the figure. Blood pumped into it from a dozen of them, inflating it grotesquely so that Jannovar felt certain it must burst.

Neither Cmizen nor Etrascu were aware of anything beyond them. Now they could feel only the screaming agony of the things that held them, using them as a focus to open an unimaginable gate, to create a Path like none other before it. They were to be the fabric of it, the substance of it, and along this path the links would be strengthened. The Warhive itself would be anchored to Innasmorn, pulled through the very walls of the World Cycles. But the final element had to be dragged from its aeon-old bed first, the last link in the cosmic chain. The World Splinter.

'Do you hear me?' screamed the voice of Zellorian, amplified a hundred times by the walls of air that rushed to aid him, to focus his powers. Power pumped upwards from the Malefics in their bottomless prison as they sought to wrench themselves free.

'We hear you,' came a reply, the voice hurled down the vortex that was the Path between worlds. Etrascu and Cmizen shuddered as they felt the Oibarene using their re-shaped bodies, their essence, to perform the link. 'Show us the World Splinter. Let us use our energies upon it.'

Zellorian shouted out something to the winds and as one they twisted themselves into a cyclone of power and tore down into the abyss. Moments later light burst far down below as if another colossal storm was in progress half way across the world. Bolts of light shot skyward and Jannovar could make out a landscape somewhere beyond, as if Zellorian's power had ruptured the walls of space itself, opening a window into some other dimension. It was a damaged land she saw, and at its heart a vast chunk of rock rose up, leaning crazily as though it would topple on the lands beneath it.

'We see it!' called the triumphant voices of the Oibarene. From beyond Cmizen, in the swirling chaos of the portal back to the Warhive, long tendrils snaked out, as scarlet as the threads which held the Etrascu-creature to the tower. And they swung out over the abyss, drifting onwards into the distance.

Space had contracted in this terrible place, Jannovar could see. Distance meant nothing. These powers spanned such things with ease. They meant to link the Warhive with the World Splinter and with whatever it was that was slowly emerging from the depths of this world, the released

Malefics. Everything combined triumphantly, regardless of the oncoming wrath of Innasmorn, the armies who served her.

Pyramors met with no resistance as he hurried down the ramps of the tower. The wind shrieked about his ears, but took no notice of him. He was a mere fly in the chaos of the city. Events here were of such a magnitude that he was nothing. Or so he prayed.

He raced over innumerable spans, around several towers, knowing instinctively that he must reach the very heart of Umus Utmar if he were to find Zellorian. As he came to the last span, he could see the storms that gathered beyond the central towers. Zellorian was embroiled in the summoning, the awakening of the powers of the ancient past. Ignoring the fury of the wind, which threatened to blast Pyramors off the narrow span, he rushed to the tower and sped up its ramp, to the uppermost reaches of it. As he looked beyond, he felt his reason wavering.

The abyss opened out, like a massive rupture in the body of the world. Inside it, bathed in the lights of a dozen wild storms, there were several staggering sights, views into other worlds, other regions, that were somehow linked together. Monstrous shapes floated behind them all, the darkness of their thoughts serving as anchors for each floating vision. But the purpose was clear. Gates, Paths. World Cycles opened up and fused together, fragments of each knitting to make one awesome central power. To house the things that were already being dredged up from the pits of Innasmorn. The Malefics.

Across the chasm, Pyramors could see tiny figures on the far lip. Zellorian stood out sharply, his body lit by a stunning radiance. And in that light, gripped by two of his deformed retainers, Jannovar stood, eyes riveted on the endless nightmares before her. Pyramors sagged down. Nothing would enable him to get across to her. And even if he could, chaos would swallow him.

Ussemitus prepared to enter the city, watched by Asphogol and Gehennon, who had stood back as the waves of Zemoks and *moillum* had plunged on into the breach where the blasted gates had stood. Dazed, the two Openers were unsure what part they should have in the battle that was to follow. They could see the Windmasters and the Seers, both companies of which had deliberate purpose.

'It would serve no purpose if we were to enter the affray,' said Gehennon. 'We have no power here.'

Asphogol nodded slowly.

Ussemitus rode across to them and was about to speak, when he clapped his hands to his head and moaned as though he had been struck.

'What is it?' said Asphogol.

Ussemitus opened his eyes, but he seemed to be gazing at something far off, something that filled him with horror. 'The armies are too late! Zellorian has already opened up the Paths.'

'Then he cannot be stopped?' gasped Gehennon. 'Will he raise these Malefics?'

Ussemitus cursed. 'Auganzar's troops are storming the inner towers. The defenders are broken, smashed back, but Zellorian will have time – '

'Not if we act,' said Asphogol. 'Can you locate him precisely?'

'I can see him as clearly as I can see you – '

Asphogol swept back the folds of his robe, baring one thick arm. 'Then I'll lead us to his side.' He slipped out his blade of office and Ussemitus turned away as the Opener made his incision.

Almost at once Ussemitus found himself staring into a circular swirl of air and dust. He felt Asphogol grip his arm. 'Take us!' said the Opener. 'Use your mind to picture the place. My blood will feed on the image.'

Gehennon staggered back as both Asphogol and Ussemitus disappeared into the sudden vortex. He was about to follow, but put away his weapon. No, this was the ultimate madness, certain death. Instead he made his way towards the blasted gate of the city. The last of the warriors had ridden through to the battle within.

Zellorian could feel their coming. He shuddered, closing his eyes in delicious anticipation. The powers! They were unimaginable, the darkness swirling up from below. He let them course into his veins, slowly taking control of him. But it was so easy, such a joy, to let them have him, to be their instrument.

From the winds above him, a shape flapped down, skimming the heads of his immediate servants, the black gliderboat. Jannovar saw it and fell to her knees. It was monstrous, a parody of the machine it must once have been, with its one grotesque wing, its hellish face.

Behind her, something else moved, a swirl of cloud. Cries startled her, and she looked back to see an Innasmornian warrior driving his sword into the gut of one of Zellorian's guards. Had they broken through at last? But this figure was no ordinary warrior: he wore a white robe and was alone. But only for a moment. Behind him, from the mist, came a huge figure, and Jannovar recognised it at once. It was an Opener, and he was as large as any of the creatures she had ever seen.

Asphogol caught sight of Zellorian at once and smashed aside the thrusting spears of two guards, ignoring the ripping of his flesh as they bit into him. He made for Zellorian, an arm grasping him before the Prime Consul realised what had happened. But he swung round, fist blazing with light, directing it at the huge Opener. It glanced from the side of his skull with a bang that was lost in the din of the wind about them.

Asphogol staggered, releasing Zellorian. Ussemitus drove his weapon at the Prime Consul, but it was as though he struck out at solid rock, and the sword splintered in a burst of light. Zellorian lurched to one side, and as he did so, Asphogol punched out at him, knocking him off his balance. But then the guards closed in, and Ussemitus was forced back with the Opener. They picked up weapons that had fallen from the guards Ussemitus had killed and beat back a furious onslaught.

Pyramors saw something of the confusion on the distant ledge. As he watched, something tore from the skies towards him. He ducked down to avoid the rending claws, looking up to see the deformed gliderboat-creature swinging round in mid-air for another attack. Gripping his sword, he rolled over as the creature tried for him, chopping into one of its elongated legs. The thing flipped over in the air and crashed down to the edge of the tower.

At once Pyramors was upon it, about to drive his blade down through its neck. He straddled it, realising as he did so that although the thing was ungainly, it was extremely powerful.

'Spare me!' it shrieked against the wind, its voice distorted, but almost human.

Pyramors looked across to where Zellorian was defending himself from the unexpected attack. 'Take me across!' he snapped, gripping the neck of the creature and holding the cutting edge of his blade under its exposed throat. 'Take me over, or I'll open your neck from mouth to chest.'

The black gliderboat gasped as the warrior gripped it, knowing it dared not disobey, and Pyramors allowed it to lurch off the tower, gliding out across the abyss. As they went, something else came at them from the darkness above, a flight of other creatures. These were not the storm beasts of Zellorian's calling, but other gliderboats, though they had been modified and were like huge predatory birds, metal talons extended for the kill as they sought to drag Pyramors from the back of the captive craft.

As they swooped in, other shapes tore across the sky, driven by the winds, and Pyramors glimpsed shapes riding in them.

Gliderboats! True gliderboats.

Hold on to your strange mount, Pyramors, came a voice above the storm. It was Jubaia. *Hold on while we beat back these demons.*

Pyramors kept flat to the back of the black gliderboat as it swooped closer to the ledge where Zellorian was scrambling away from his assailants. The creature tried to land, but its feet scrabbled unsuccessfully on the stone and it was about to fall back. Pyramors leapt from it, meeting the wild stab of a spear as one of Zellorian's guards tried for him. He deflected the blow and smashed his fist into the neck of his assailant.

On the ledge, Zellorian drew back, and guards closed around him to protect him. Pyramors could see that the Opener and Ussemitus were sorely pressed, so he cut his way to them, trying as he did so to see where Jannovar had gone.

Zellorian saw her first and was about to grip her by the arm when something struck his shoulder, tearing him from the ground. He struggled free, toppling and landing close to the edge of the abyss. Again his warriors stood over him, shielding him. Jannovar had seen the dark shape that swept down from above. It was a gliderboat; she saw it turn, about to make another pass. There were other gliderboats here, engaged in a ferocious aerial battle with the gliderboat mutations that Zellorian used.

Before Jannovar could find Pyramors, the gliderboat that had prevented Zellorian from taking her appeared almost beside her. She heard its voice, its imperious shout inside her mind.

Get in!

There was no time to deliberate. She leapt, and almost at once they were swept up on a current of air, away from immediate pursuit. She gripped the side of the craft, looking down. Pyramors was beside the little Innasmornian warrior, and the two of them were beating back a mass of guards, the huge Opener with them, too. Looking out over the abyss, she saw Zellorian, who was now riding in one of his strange craft, aiming for the tower where the other monstrous beings had landed.

Zellorian dropped out of the black gliderboat on to the tower, landing beside the thing that had once been Etrascu. The Opener was now unrecognisable, body swollen to immense proportions, and on his back, the creature that had been Cmizen had also swollen up, the belly fused into the spine of Etrascu so that they had become one entity, one vast, slug-like monster with wings that pulsed limply beside them.

Zellorian used his sword to hack at the strands that held the creature to the tower, and as he did so, blood fountained outwards from the severed filaments. When his gruesome work was done, Zellorian leapt up on to the back of the creature and screamed something at it. Jannovar watched in fascinated horror as the bloated monster rose from its tower. And plunged downward into the abyss, into the dazzling light of the storms there, dropping away into the distance until, a tiny speck, it winked out.

She saw no more. The gliderboat that had rescued her tore over the city, away from the central towers, aiming for the mountains, and beside it an escort of other gliderboats materialised to protect her. And as they passed beyond the city, Jannovar saw other winged creatures arriving from the mountains.

Windriders, said a voice, the voice of the craft that had saved her. *Jubaia has brought them. They will harry the forces of Umus Utmar.*

Behind them, in the city, Auganzar had driven his Zemoks through the streets with devastating results, cutting through the defenders as powerfully as any storm. Zellorian's troops withered under the onslaught, and the tigerhounds broke the heart of any real defence. Vittargattus and Ondrabal were also cutting swathes through the defenders they met, closing in on the central towers.

Pyramors and Ussemitus worked their way up a ramp on to another ledge, and Asphogol joined them so that they were able to keep their immediate assailants at bay. But confusion reigned below them. On the ledge that wound round the abyss, the hordes of Zellorian's servants were screaming, many of them tumbling into the chasm. Storms raged below, and the light from the towers went out.

'What is wrong?' said Asphogol.

'Zellorian has fled,' shouted Ussemitus. 'Before the Malefics could take total control of him, we intervened. Human terror ruled him long enough for his mind to snap.'

'Fled?' said Pyramors. 'To where?'

'He has opened another Path.'

'The Warhive!' gasped Asphogol. 'I saw the Path to the Oibarene. Has he gone there?'

'No, nor to the World Splinter,' said Ussemitus. 'Both those Paths are mercifully closed. He has opened another Path, using that creature.'

'Path to where?' shouted Pyramors. '*To where?*'

'Outside this Cycle. Outside all those we know.'

Pyramors glared out into the abyss, where the storms were already beginning to subside, the crawling darkness below falling back on itself. 'No matter where he's gone, we'll follow him.'

Asphogol, looming over him, looked pale. But he had no time to think about the ominous promise of the Consul. The guards below them were about to renew their attack.

24

THE LABYRINTH

'Give me cover for a moment,' said Asphogol. 'I will take us out of this madness.'

There was no time for argument and Pyramors obeyed at once, shielding the huge Opener as best he could, with the help of Ussemitus. As they again defended themselves from the renewed onslaught of Zellorian's warriors, Asphogol made a Path for them. They heard the rush of the winds, and felt the opening behind them.

'It is done. Hurry,' called Asphogol, already moving down the Path. As Pyramors and Ussemitus followed, they saw the circular mouth of the Path close, brutally shutting off the pursuit like jaws of steel snapping against intrusion, killing the first group of Zellorian's warriors who were partially through the opening.

Moments later Asphogol brought them to safety outside the city gates, where the Windmasters and Seers were still concentrating their powers on the storms and sendings that were now focused deep in the city.

'Where is Gehennon?' said Asphogol, but no one knew.

Overhead they saw the graceful shape of a gliderboat as it came smoothly down to them, hovering close to the ground. Ussemitus recognised the tiny figure in its prow at once.

'Jubaia! But – surely that is not your craft – '

'No, she has gone up into the mountains.'

Pyramors was looking back at the city, face lined with anxiety. 'Jannovar,' he murmured.

Jubaia was shaking his head. 'Didn't you see?'

Pyramors swung round to him, sword gripped tightly as if he would use it on him. 'See? See what?'

'She has been lifted out of that hell. Up to safety in the mountains.'

Pyramors glanced at the mountains beyond them.

Ussemitus was looking at the city. And Aru? Where was she? At the forefront of the battle, no doubt.

The object of his concern was, as he had guessed, at the heart of things in the inner city. Together with Fomond and Armestor and several other Innasmornians, she had taken a group of Tremazon's knights and cut a swathe into the defenders of one of the main towers, and was even now forcing her way upwards. Chaos had broken out above. Apart from the maniacal anger of the storms and the furious combat that raged between Zellorian's elementals and the gliderboats and, to Aru's amazement, the windriders of Shung Nang, there was the screaming terror of the defending warriors. They had lost their cohesion, as though whatever leadership they had was in disarray, and Aru wondered what had occurred up on the higher levels of the citadel.

She led her assault out on to one of the wide ledges, driving back a last desperate defence, her warriors using all their strength and skill to despatch the enemy.

As they forced their way upwards, they knew nothing of the small group of beings who climbed after them from the lower shadows of the tower. Picking their way through the dead and the dying, ignoring the cries for mercy of the latter, the cloaked figures moved upwards stealthily, hugging the shadows.

'How many of them are there?' whispered one of the beings.

The leader turned to him with a grimace. 'They have all but cleared Zellorian's vermin from this tower. But it has cost them dear.' The figure pointed with disgust at the slain Human warriors, tangled with those they had killed.

'Then they should be easy for us.'

'Oh, yes. The Mother will give us the power we need to rid ourselves of these accursed intruders. We will deal with them all in time.' He waved his group on and they crept upwards towards the sounds of battle overhead.

Fomond stood, panting, at the edge of the curving ramp, near to the top of the tower. The last of the enemies here were above, the fight gone out of them. He could see they had slumped down. 'I think they are done,' he told Aru.

She nodded, her own chest heaving, her sword dripping. 'We need to rest.' She examined her company. It was sadly depleted, but both Fomond and Armestor had come through the struggle. Armestor had exhausted his arrows, much to his chagrin, but had resorted to a short sword.

'Mistress,' called one of the knights at the rear of the company. 'Someone is on the ramp below us.'

Aru walked back through the tired company, waiting to see who was following. From around a bend in the tower, a small group of cloaked figures suddenly emerged. In silence they spread themselves across the ramp, dropping their hoods to reveal their oddly coloured hair.

Fomond, who had followed Aru, gaped as he saw the figures.

'What is it?' Aru asked him softly.

'Windmasters,' Fomond breathed.

'But why aren't they with Azrand and the others?'

'That is Kuraal,' said Fomond, gesturing subtly. 'I have felt his hatred of us throughout this campaign.'

Kuraal may have heard. But he took a step forward. He could see the Casruel woman and the last of her followers. Fifty at most, including the Innasmornian woodlanders who had defied him for so long. The lap-dogs of the traitor, Ussemitus, were there.

'Begin,' Kuraal told his companions, and at once they did as he bid them, using their powers to call upon the raging elements about them.

At once there was a response as the Mother heard them, and Kuraal began to focus the energies of the wind, diverting part of the storm down towards the tower.

Fomond gasped. 'He intends to destroy us! He's calling on the Mother to help him.'

Armestor stood with them. 'Ussemitus cannot help us

here! We must flee.'

Aru called on her knights to regroup. They did so, but when they let loose the last of their arrows, the shafts fell uselessly from the air. And down from the skies came the first of the howling winds, obedient to Kuraal and his Blue Hairs, ready to wreak whatever destruction he intended. They were windwraiths, the terrible destructive agents of the Mother, and Fomond felt a wave of sheer terror rising up before him.

Ussemitus cocked his head, listening to every sound of the storm, as though he could single it out.

Pyramors, who had found a horse in the camp outside the gates, and who was preparing to ride into Umus Utmar again, saw the look of horror on Ussemitus's face. 'What now?'

'The Mother turns against her children,' he said, going to Azrand, breaking his concentration. 'Azrand! The Mother is being used against us – '

Azrand blinked, coming out of his own working with a shudder. 'Ussemitus, what are you doing?'

'Listen! In the city. The Mother *attacks* some of our people. Where are the rest of your Windmasters?'

'They are all here,' said Azrand, but as he looked over his shamen, he saw that a few were missing. 'Kuraal – '

'Kuraal! Yes, he used windwraiths against me once before. He has unleashed them again. We must turn them back!'

'We cannot break our working, Ussemitus. We are driving back the old darkness. We need every shred of concentration. You must not deflect me from my working.' Azrand turned away, closing his eyes.

Ussemitus looked up at the turbulent heavens, raising his fist to them. 'You are wrong!' he snarled. 'You will be your own undoing!'

Pyramors was stunned by the tenacity of the Innasmornian youth, as though he would defy the elements.

From the skies there was no answer.

Auganzar drove back the last of the defenders. Beside him, jaws dripping with the blood of their victims, the tigerhounds ripped into the last defiant warriors of Zellorian's central defence. The Zemoks and the *moillum* had broken through all defences and smashed their way upwards into the very heart of the citadel. The Swarm was inexorable in its power.

Such storms and aerial monsters as the enemy sent against them did nothing to prevent their onward march through the city. Csendook minds were impervious to psychic attack. The elements were countered perfectly by the gliderboat fleet brought by the allies of Man, and Auganzar wondered at these other remarkable creatures that dotted the skies, the winged beings who fought so ferociously with the storm demons.

Through the bloody streets and corridors of the city and its ruined buildings the armies cut their swathes, though Csendook fell, as did many of the *moillum*, beaten down by the sheer numbers of their opponents. And in that frightful carnage died the dreams of power of Fulvulus and Throcastor, killed before they could reach the goal at the heart of the city, though many were the servants of the enemy who had fallen to them as they fought.

At the end of it all, standing on the huge ledge that surrounded the abyss, Auganzar marvelled at the aerial combat. Innasmorn was unique: he had never seen the like of its storms, its elemental forces. And the things that flew in it now were like the visions of nightmare: the demented elemental forces and the warped stormgliders were equally as horrific, a ghastly fusion of powers of two civilisation, but serving one darkness. He gazed out across the abyss. It was obscured, though not lifeless, and whatever forces gathered themselves in it were subdued, somewhere far below. The living towers that rose up from it were shrivelled, as though seared by bolts of lightning from the raging storm.

But Zellorian was not here. Somehow he had fled. But was he still in Umus Utmar? Auganzar would pull apart every stone until he found him.

Kuraal drew back his lips in a feral laugh as he sensed the coming of the killing winds. They would rip this Human woman to shreds before the eyes of her followers, and then the hated woodland warriors would follow.

Aru and her group ducked as the wind clawed at them, supremely confident, shrieking overhead. Fomond dragged her aside, trying to get her knights to shield her, but they did not understand what was happening.

'Call Ussemitus!' shouted Armestor. 'Fomond! You and I must do it. It is our only hope – '

Again the windwraiths clawed at them and they saw the bestial fury of their faces, an irresistible force that would lift them up and tear them asunder when it came again. They watched as the snarling pack swung round, a tight vortex in the air above the Blue Hairs. Then the air beasts fell.

But they circled around the robed figures, and Fomond saw Kuraal's face change as he realised what was happening. The Blue Hair suddenly screamed, but it was too late. The elemental force closed in around the figures. They shrieked as they felt themselves gripped by invisible powers. Lifted like dolls, they tumbled in the air.

'Look away!' shouted Armestor above the sudden din, and every one of the knights did so, shutting out the terrible scene.

Kuraal was flung against the stone wall of the tower with such colossal force that he burst like a fruit, and his fellow Blue Hairs were shredded as they swung in the air, their blood showering the ramp. It was over in moments, the full fury of the windwraiths vented upon them. Then, as quickly as they had come, the pack raced away, leaving the tower in a sudden silence.

Aru opened her eyes upon carnage, gagging at the bloody remains of the rebel Blue Hairs.

'They did not serve the Mother,' whispered Fomond, his voice hoarse. 'She saw that. But it is no way to die.'

'Let's go down,' said Aru, dazed. 'Let's find the others.'

307

It was late in the day when the principals of the armies reassembled, joining Auganzar and his spearhead up on the ledge of the central tower. There had been great slaughter in the city, and overhead the skies had at last grown silent, though the grey clouds hung low, threatening more rain. The elements summoned by Zellorian and his rebel Windmasters and Seers had dissolved away. A unique silence hung once again over Umus Utmar.

Vittargattus had taken a number of flesh wounds, and was being tended to, though he tried to shake the physicians off irritably. Ondrabal and Tremazon had been less fortunate, but their wounds would heal well enough, given time.

They met on the upper turrets, looking down on the forces that ringed the huge chasm, a mixture of Csendook, Innasmornian and Man.

Ussemitus broke the grim silence that had settled over them as they weighed each other, studying the potential losses in their warriors. 'The Mother saw fit to bless the alliance,' he said. 'Though I fear for us.'

Auganzar put down his war helm, wiping the dirt and sweat from his face. 'These Malefics as you call them. What of them now?'

Ussemitus looked down at the darkness far below them. 'Such powers can never be destroyed. But they lack the power to focus now that Zellorian has gone. He was to have been their gate.'

'Gone he may be,' said Auganzar, his voice a deep growl, 'but he is not destroyed.'

'No,' said Pyramors. 'He must be followed.'

'I agree,' nodded Auganzar.

'He has left this World Cycle,' said Asphogol, with absolute assurance.

'You saw that?' said Auganzar, glancing at Asphogol.

The huge Opener nodded.

'Then we go after him.'

Vittargattus raised his voice. 'We owe you a great debt, Auganzar. The Mother has recognised you, not as an enemy, but as an ally. Thus I must tell you that Ondrabal and I are agreed, you have our support if you wish to pursue Zellorian. Even if it means travelling beyond Innasmorn.' He spoke stiffly, formally, trying to shut off the fears that the thought of such a journey instilled in him.

Auganzar smiled as Aru translated for him. 'I am honoured, Vittargattus. But this is a private affair now. My losses here are few. My Swarm is almost intact. Your world is safe. Look to it.'

Vittargattus listened to the translation, scowling but nodding. 'Very well. But the powers of the Windmasters and the Seers are at your disposal, should you need them.'

'I have my Openers,' replied Auganzar. Gehennon had joined Asphogol. Together they bowed.

'I trust you'll not object to my coming with you?' said Pyramors, a clear challenge in his eyes.

Auganzar studied him for a moment. 'Consul, of all Men, you have proven to be the strongest, a model for all your warriors. But I would not ask you to follow me now.'

'I have a mission to complete, just as you do.'

Auganzar nodded. 'Your people are decimated. This conflict has reduced your numbers further. There will be no contact with those who live among the Csendook in the cycle of Eannor. And the survivors here need capable leaders. Stay here, Pyramors. Help your people to grow strong again.'

Pyramors felt the anger rising in him, but controlled it as well as he could.

Aru was beside him. 'He's right, Pyramors. You've done enough. You've brought these alliances together. Between us we have to secure them. I need your skills. And there's another who needs you far more than I do,' she added softly.

'I could not rest until I know that Zellorian is dead. No world will be safe until he falls.'

'I will find him,' said Auganzar. 'But there is another reason why you must stay, Pyramors.' He pointed to the *moillum* he had brought. 'I will take only Csendook. Those Men are free, no longer my servants. I promised them that when they came. Many of them left families behind them to come here. They are well led, and Innasmorn will be their new home. They are fighting warriors, the best your race has ever produced, but it would take a warrior like you, Pyramors, to ease their acceptance here.'

Tremazon, leaning on a broken spear to support himself, spoke up. 'He's right, Pyramors. Our people are balanced very finely on a sword edge. We are all but wiped out. And we are from such disparate factions of the old Empire that it wouldn't take much to start us warring again. It would be the end of us. If you persist in hunting down Zellorian, in leaving Innasmorn, we are closer to that end.'

Pyramors closed his eyes. Once before he had put himself, his own desires, before those of his people. The Imperator Elect had taught him to show contempt for duty. But he would be a fool to scorn that duty now.

'I'll find him, Pyramors,' Auganzar promised him, and he saw in the Csendook's expression a conviction that could not lie. Yes, the warlord would find him.

'Very well. Take my curse to him.'

Asphogol stood alone on the broken tower that rose from the centre of the abyss. It was slick with the blood of the filaments which had held the creature that had taken Zellorian beyond the World Cycle. The huge Opener knelt and put his hands into the blood, watched by the Csendook who stood far across the abyss on its outer ledge.

Most of the armies were gone, back to the plain beyond the city, preparing to leave. There were gliderboats with them, and the surviving *moillum* who had come with Auganzar. They were exhausted, subdued, ready to talk about the future, though many of them would have preferred to remain with the Swarm as it made its last assault on their enemy.

Auganzar and Pyramors watched with Ussemitus as Asphogol tested the blood on the tower. At last the Opener stood up, as though he was satisfied with what he had found.

Gehennon also watched. He turned now to Auganzar. 'He knows where the trail leads, Zaru.'

'To the Warhive?'

'No, Zaru. Zellorian would be trapped there like a rat. The Oibarene's failure in this war has sent them deep into themselves. Zellorian would have no power on the Warhive. He has chosen a far more remote hiding place. There is an irony in it. For he has gone to the shattered Cycle. The Cycle of Quendai.'

Auganzar looked far down into the abyss. 'Quendai.' Formerly the home of the Csendook, once they had tamed it. Now destroyed by the extreme wars. A ruined Cycle, a tomb, filled with the debris of its worlds.

'It will be a fitting grave for him,' Auganzar said aloud.

Gehennon paled. Or for us all.

The Path had not been easy to open, even for the combined skills of Asphogol and Gehennon, but Ussemitus had prevailed upon the Mother to help them in the way that she had helped the spectrals to pursue Pyramors. It was not necessary for sacrifices to be made. But as Asphogol and Gehennon led the Swarm down the Path, quitting Innasmorn, the Openers felt themselves weakening. Around them the huge walls rose up, curving into a tunnel that grew smaller with distance. But it was not as other Paths. There was a suggestion of decay, of death, and in parts the walls were like grey stone, dark and solid.

As the Swarm moved on down the Path, it felt the closing in of the lifeless walls. The xillatraal and tigerhounds had fallen silent. But Auganzar refused to be intimidated by the place.

'How far?' was all he said to his Openers.

Asphogol pointed. 'We will emerge very soon, Zaru.'

Auganzar nodded, looking back at his Zemoks. He had no need to call them to arms: they were ready and eager for a further battle. They did not know the world they would visit, its history. It was as well for them, stoic warriors though they were.

As the Path came to its end, the walls were flaking, crumbling, as though the Swarm emerged from the rotting entrails of a huge beast, long since slain.

The world beyond the Path gaped at them like a cosmic wound.

Its lands had been twisted by unimaginable struggles, heaved up, broken, as though entire mountain ranges had been blasted, pulled down, reshaped by demented energies. Huge fissures rent the earth, and slabs of rock poked up insanely, ready to topple. Hung over them were endless miles of grey mosses, twisted into cables that clung like cerements, curling up into the clouds, suggestive of a land above that draped its dead roots over its parapets like the rotting limbs of long dead leviathans.

'What region can this be?' said Zuarzol, feeling his huge tigerhound, Raal, draw back at the dismal spectacle. It was the first time the savage creature had ever shown unease.

'It is called Quendai,' said Auganzar. 'A world that belonged to the Csendook, before Zellorian's ancestors did this to it. From the bones of this world and those of this World Cycle, Zellorian has bleached the last of the old secrets.'

'Is this desolation all there is, Zaru?' said Zuarzol.

'Yes. In world after world.'

'Then how will we find him?'

Auganzar called his Openers to him. 'Your masters, the Consummate Order, approved the aid you have given me,' he told them. 'They spoke for the Conceptors, is that not so?'

'It is,' said Asphogol, though he looked apprehensive. 'If you can speak to them – '

'The Conceptors, Zaru?'

Auganzar glared out at the hostile terrain, its mocking grey infinities. 'If that is what it takes, yes, the Conceptors themselves. They must want Zellorian as much as I do.'

'Zaru, they might not answer. And even if they do, they will ask a price of you.'

'Then it must be paid,' said Auganzar bitterly. 'But we are here to find Zellorian, *whatever the cost*.' He knew the

Zemoks could hear him, but there was no dissent. They were as dedicated to his cause as he was. He marvelled that they had not sought the truth behind the crusade: they must know it was not merely blind pride.

Asphogol said no more, but he moved away over the sand to where it curved away in a long dune.

'What will he do?' Auganzar asked Gehennon. 'Can he speak to his masters?'

'He is gifted with greater powers than any other Opener I have seen, Zaru. It is possible.'

They saw Asphogol shudder, his head thrown back in silence. The Opener held his position for long moments. Nothing stirred in this dead zone.

Asphogol was motionless, but at last turned, his face drained of blood. His hands gleamed by the light of the insipid sun of Quendai. As he came back to Auganzar, his fingers dripped blood on to the grey sands.

'Your sword,' said the Opener, his voice hoarse, as if he were speaking through sharp pain. 'Draw it out.'

Auganzar knew what he meant. He pulled the long sword of Hozermaak from its hilt, holding it out in front of him. He could feel the shiver of life within it.

'It will find him,' said Asphogol.

'How?'

Asphogol reached out with his bloodied hands and let the blood drip on to the blade. It hissed, the blood steaming as though the blade was red hot. Asphogol cried out as his blood ran, drawn into the blade. Auganzar stared at the hungry blade.

At last Asphogol turned away, slumping down on the sands. Auganzar could see that no drop of his blood remained on the blade.

'Can you feel it?' Asphogol asked, lips drawn tightly.

Auganzar held the blade up before him. It quivered like a serpent. And it turned of its own volition, pointing to a distant horizon.

'You no longer need me,' said Asphogol. 'The sword will open a Path for you. It hungers for Zellorian: he cannot escape you. But be careful. Evil has come in to the sword, shards of the dark Innasmorn. The weapon is at war with itself. You risk much in using it. Yet there is no other way.'

'How long before you can travel?' Auganzar asked him.

But the big Opener shook his head. His skin was very pale, grey almost, like the dust in which he sat. 'My work is done.'

'Then Gehennon will return for you.'

Asphogol nodded, feebly waving the Csendook away.

Auganzar turned, the sword guiding him. Before it the sands shifted, curling away in an arc that grew higher, eddying into the familiar shape of a tunnel, a Path to its prey.

The Swarm entered it, and as the last Zemok was swallowed by its mystery, Asphogol closed his eyes. He could hear a distant roar, the roar of his blood in his veins. But it was like the sound of a storm that subsides beyond the horizon, soon to be still.

25

QUENDAI

Jubaia took the craft up into the mountains. The air was very still, the storms having dissipated at last. There were a few hours of daylight left.

He had tried to contact Circu, but she had not responded. All he knew was that she had saved Jannovar from certain death at the hands of Zellorian in the citadel.

The craft is not far, said the gliderboat he controlled. It was not as sleek as Circu, nor did it respond the way Circu did, but he had been able to make it understand him.

'You speak to her?'

No, but I can feel its nearness.

'Then find her,' he said tersely, annoyed by the gliderboat's impersonal attitude.

The gliderboat swung away through a number of peaks, until Jubaia saw something down below, gleaming in the fading sunlight. Circu had selected a ridge that was well hidden from the skies, beneath an overhang of rock. The girl was huddled in the back of the craft. She looked to be asleep.

Jubaia took his craft down and was able to land it some distance from Circu's hiding place. He knew that she had sensed his coming, though she did not respond. The air of gloom still clung to her and he had begun to wonder if it was an illness, the beginning of a decline. But he forced such depressing thoughts from his mind and climbed out of the gliderboat, leaving it and clambering over the rocks above the precipitous drop.

He stood before Circu, hands on his hips. 'You did not make it easy for me to find you,' he mentally chided her.

I had the girl's safety in mind, was the almost sleepy reply. *Is it over?*

'At Umus Utmar? Yes. The Malefics will not rise, and

315

Zellorian has fled. Beyond Innasmorn.'

Then the pursuit goes on? Pyramors gives chase? She spoke the name with more than a little bitterness.

Jubaia stood beside the craft, his hand upon it. He studied it for a long time. 'What is wrong?' he said at last. 'You have closed me out for many days. What is this sadness that clings to you?'

Some things it is better not to know, was all she would tell him.

His attention was caught by movement in the back of the craft and he boarded her gently. Jannovar was stirring. She sat up, blinking her eyes. She looked startled when she saw Jubaia.

'This is not yet another abduction, my lady,' he said to her, grinning. 'I am not one of Zellorian's agents.'

Jannovar gasped as she saw the drop beyond the side of the craft. 'I was snatched from the city! Pyramors – '

'Safe enough,' chuckled Jubaia. 'And Zellorian is beaten. He has fled. The battle is over. We will take you back.'

She put her hand to her eyes, as though she could hardly believe what she saw around her. 'There was so much death about us. I saw – an Opener? How could that be?'

'You should rest, my lady. Sleep again, until my craft and I bring you back to the city.'

Jannovar looked down at the gliderboat. 'Your craft? But you are an Innasmornian! Can you control this gliderboat?'

Jubaia straightened proudly. 'I can. Though it is not control as you think of it. She and I share thoughts. I do not command.'

Jannovar smiled. 'You speak of her as if she were a living being.'

Jubaia frowned. 'But, my lady, she is.'

Jubaia, be quiet! came Circu's voice, and he jumped, wondering if the girl had heard. But she did not seem to have. *We should go back quickly. Don't let your tongue embarrass you. Prepare the girl for flight.*

The little thief was shocked by the harshness in the voice. What was wrong with her? 'Why are you so cold to me? What has hardened your heart, Circu?' He said the words softly, barely above a whisper, but Jannovar was staring at him.

'What did you say?' she asked him, no longer bemused, but alert.

'Forgive me, my lady. I spoke to the craft. She hears me.'

'What did you call her?'

Jubaia almost recoiled from the intensity of the girl's gaze. 'Well, she has a name, but it is a secret thing. Her past is a very private affair. She will not share her name – '

Do not tell her! came Circu's voice, a snarl inside his head.

Jannovar came towards him. 'I heard you speak her name. What was it?'

Do not tell her!

'My lady, she forbids me – '

'You called her, Circu. I heard you say it.'

Jubaia waited for the craft to speak, but she had gone silent as death, unreachable.

'You said it! Circu.'

'Yes, but you must not repeat it. It is a secret, precious thing.'

Jannovar's eyes widened and she staggered, gripping the side of the gliderboat. 'No, no you cannot have heard the name.'

'What is wrong, my lady?'

She sat, looking more dazed than ever. 'Where did you hear that name? How did you give it to this. . .craft?'

Jubaia looked embarrassed. 'Well, she told it to me. I am Innasmornian, and was once more than I am now. I can hear the minds of the gliderboats, understand what they may once have been.'

Jannovar closed her eyes. Something had shaken her very badly.

The little thief began to feel nervous. Why did Circu not speak? 'Does the name mean something to you?' he ventured.

She nodded, and to his surprise there were tears trickling from her eyes. 'I am not Jannovar.'

Jubaia was taken aback. 'But that's impossible! Pyramors has – ' But he stopped. 'Wait, though. Since he returned to Innasmorn, he hasn't seen you. By the Mother, have we brought the wrong girl out of the city? But, no, that can't be so. Zellorian had you up on the citadel – '

'You don't understand. I have taken Jannovar's name. Pyramors is my – ' She, too, stopped.

'You mean, you are not Jannovar, but you are pretending to be her? Does Pyramors know this?'

'Yes. We both thought Jannovar had died.'

'Then who are you?'

She looked away, more tears spilling down her cheek. 'I am Jannovar's sister. My real name is. . .Circu.'

'*Circu*?' he repeated. 'The name of my craft?'

'I took the name to confuse the Csendook. My sister was the lover of Pyramors. She and I were on Eannor when the Swarms came. Jannovar was to flee with Pyramors and the Imperator Elect, to this world. But Jannovar's husband, Fromhal, discovered her adultery and had members of our family sent to work under the city. In an effort to free Jannovar, I changed names and identities with her. Though I am younger, we are much alike. She was to be given to the Csendook by the slaver, Crasnow. But it was I who went to the Csendook, first on Eannor, and then on the Warhive.

'Pyramors found me there. He knew that I was not Jannovar, even though I had taken her identity. The Csendook knew no better and the men here know no better now. I have become Jannovar.'

'But what happened to your sister?' said Jubaia, his voice very low.

'We were separated when the Swarms came to Eannor. I thought she would be able to steal away with Pyramors on the Crossing. But she was taken to work in the gliderboat pens.'

They were both silent, and the air was very still. Jubaia tried to contact the gliderboat, but it had become like the metal that housed it, immobile and cold.

'You exchanged names,' he said at last. 'Circu.'

Suddenly the girl's eyes widened. 'But Jannovar must have died! This must have been a craft that she worked on – '

'Do you know what the engineers did when they created these craft?' Jubaia asked her very quietly. It had all become clear to him at last, the darkness within the gliderboat. She had *carried* Pyramors, had felt his touch, heard him speak of his new love.

The girl must have understood as well. She gaped at him. *Jubaia, you must hide the truth from her*

But Jubaia sprang up, his own eyes dimmed by tears. 'No! I will not hide the truth! Let her know. Speak to her! *You are her sister!*'

The girl shrank back, stunned by the vehemence of the Innasmornian's cry.

'This craft,' she began.

'They used the living to create them,' said Jubaia. 'They shut down their memories, other parts of their minds. Your Controllers cannot reach them, but I can. With my Innasmornian gifts! I woke her. She hears me. Just as she hears you, Circu.'

The girl recoiled, staring down at the lines of the gliderboat. 'She is. . .alive?'

'Tell her!' cried Jubaia. *'Tell her!'*

There was a long pause. But Circu heard the voice of her sister in her mind. *Yes, I survived, little sister. Part of me is trapped in this machine. Wyarne did his work well. Jannovar is not dead.*

Circu put her hands over her face, shaking her head as if she could purge the voice from within her.

You have become his lover.

'But how could I know!' Circu cried.

No. You could not know. And if Jubaia had been sensible enough to listen to me, you would never have known.

Circu's head snapped up, her eyes red. 'We must – '

'What?' said Jubaia. 'Undo what has been done? It is not possible. She would die.'

Yes, I am as I am, Circu. Let me remain this way. With your name. And you with mine.

'But Pyramors – '

Must not know! He must not. Circu, swear that to me! Swear that he will never know the truth.

'But he was yours —'

No more. I have another.

'Another?'

Jubaia, you, too must swear to keep this knowledge to yourself. I am Circu. She is Jannovar. Never change that, not now.

Jubaia nodded.

'What have I done?' gasped Circu. 'My sister, what have I done?' She began to cry and Jubaia put an arm around her.

You have done me no evil, Circu. I love you no less. Love him as I did, that is all I ask.

'And know this, Circu,' Jubaia told her softly. 'She, too, is loved, as much as ever she was.'

Little thief, said the voice inside him, for him alone, *it is all that I need.*

As they rested, too tired to move away from their high perch, they saw movements in the skies. Presently a number of winged shapes appeared close by, and Circu marvelled at them. She had seen the windriders of Shung Nang only briefly in the storm above the citadel, ghost-like and fleeting, but now as they dropped to the ledge she caught her breath at their magnificence.

'Jung-Bara,' said their leader, a tall warrior, his wings folding precisely behind him, feathers shining in the evening light. 'The battle is done. We are going back to our home.'

'Again I must thank you,' said the little thief.

'We have all served Innasmorn. We are all her children. The Aviatrix has spoken to me. There is a message for you.'

Jubaia stood.

'She says there is once again a place for you in Shung Nang.'

Jubaia caught his breath, his heart lurching at the words. But after a pause he shook his head. 'I am honoured. But my place is with Circu, riding the free winds of Innasmorn.'

'The Aviatrix knows this. But Circu is welcome in Shung Nang. She, too, will be honoured. She is your wings, is she not?'

Jubaia could hardly speak, but he nodded.

Yes, I am his wings, said a voice in the windrider's mind.

The windrider bowed, understanding. 'Then will you return with us?'

'We will,' said Jubaia. 'But you go on. We must take Jannovar back to her people. They will be concerned.'

'Of course,' said the windrider, suddenly spreading his wings with stunning grace. He lifted himself easily on the faintest of air currents. 'Shung Nang awaits you,' he called, waving as he turned. The windriders swept away as one, soon lost to view.

'Your people?' gasped Circu.

'Yes,' he said proudly. 'My brothers. Circu's also, now.'

You see, little sister, I have another life. You cannot conceive of what it will be like.

The girl nodded slowly. 'Then I'll go to mine.'

They found him after the equivalent of many days.

The world of Quendai was totally devastated, as they had feared it would be, and nothing lived either upon it or under it, save for the Man they hunted. The sword made by Hozermaak guided Auganzar and his Swarm, thirsting for Zellorian as hungrily as the tigerhounds that also picked up his scent.

He had taken refuge on a bare plateau of rock. Strewn about its feet were the remains of a city, machines tangled amongst the debris like dead monsters from another age, their spars poking up at the weak sun like black bones.

Zellorian was alone. Behind him, stretched out on the bare rock was the creature that had been his slave, the thing made in Umus Utmar, a fusion of Cmizen, Etrascu and other creatures. Like a huge balloon, it lay on its side, shrivelled, its belly split as if by a fall. Its life had leaked out of it along with its blood, its organs dried and hardened like stones within it.

'Supreme Sanguinary!' Zellorian shouted across the empty waste. 'I welcome you. Such a tenacious opponent. You have pursued me across countless worlds.'

Auganzar stood at the head of his Swarm. The tigerhounds snarled, desperate to be freed.

'Zaru, let them take him for you,' said Zuarzol, his own hatred of the Man no less feral.

Gehennon shook his head. 'Zaru, he is not simply a Man. All the power he has taken, the secrets he has plundered, are within him. As are the dark forces of Innasmorn. This is a trap.'

'Let loose your killers, Auganzar!' called Zellorian.

Auganzar motioned for his Zemoks to spread out, and they began the circling movements that would surround the Prime Consul. 'Prepare the beasts.'

Zuarzol grinned, speaking to his fellow Zemaals. The tigerhounds dropped to the ground, ready to crawl forward.

Zellorian turned to the huge carcass behind him. He may have spoken to it, no one could say. But it quivered, as though returning blasphemously to life. Something within it stirred, and from its already ruptured side, shapes burst forth, springing up beside Zellorian, a dozen dripping beings, half-formed, incomplete. They crouched defensively, headless but not without sentience. A dozen more stepped from the carcass.

'Come, loose your beasts, Auganzar!' called the Prime Consul. 'We must resolve our dispute here. There is so much to do beyond this cemetery of a world. Your world. Quendai. This is the beginning, the birth. Though Quendai was never your cradle.'

Auganzar gritted his teeth against what he knew was coming. His Zemoks would have to hear this. It could not be prevented. But it would serve only to fire them.

'But you know well enough where you began, do you not, Auganzar? Like that creature beside you, the Opener. Gehennon. Who made you, Gehennon? Who shaped your kind from blood and bone? Not Man. No. Csendook made you, helped by the Conceptors.'

Gehennon looked angry, but he spoke under his breath. 'It is no secret to me, Zaru. Unleash the tigerhounds.'

'Csendook made you, poor as you are. Man had greater skills than that. Man built with far greater precision. Something in his own image, but with magnified strength, killing drive. A destructive engine, faster, stronger and oblivious to so-called sorcery, powers of the mind.

'And you, Auganzar, are the finest example of that creation. You are the product of centuries of genetic engineering. But a strong slave will always turn on its master.'

Zuarzol and the other Zolutars stared at Zellorian in horror. 'These are lies to enrage us – '

Zellorian heard and snarled his contempt. 'You think so! Why do you think your master has spent so long trying to find me? To suppress the unacceptable reality.'

Auganzar turned to Zuarzol and the others. 'The secret dies here, with him. Now, let the tigerhounds go.'

It was done at once. The leashes were unclipped and the tigerhounds, a score of them, raced over the flat stone towards their prey. At once the creatures Zellorian had summoned from the huge carcass formed a barrier around him.

Zellorian's face twisted in a mirthless smile as he shouted something out, but it was drowned in the snarling of the tigerhounds. But something was happening to the hunched figures: from their shoulders, oval shapes mushroomed up, forming rapidly into heads. The tigerhounds ignored them as they raced forward, but the Csendook saw, and even they felt a shudder of revulsion. For each head had a face, and each face was the face of a Csendook. Those that had seen him recognised the face of Cmizen, once the Keeper of Eannor. A score of Cmizen simulacra gaped wretchedly at the tigerhounds, their expression pitiful, agonised, like that of a soul crying for release from inestimable torment.

The first of the hounds leapt, crashing into the chest of one of the Cmizen-things. They fell to the dust, rolling over and over, the claws of the beast ripping and tearing, the arms of the creature wrapping around it as its teeth sank into the thick pseudo-flesh. Other hounds sprang to the attack, until Zellorian was surrounded by dozens of them, all entangled with the ferocious tigerhounds. But as yet, none of the beasts had breached his defence. He watched calmly, imperturbably.

Auganzar motioned his Zemoks forward, and they began to close in. They watched in horror as one of the Cmizenthings, ripped almost in half by the savage attack, collapsed, pumping oily blood, only to reshape itself almost at once. It was happening to all the monsters from the corpse of the huge creature. As they were ripped up, they fell but reformed. Again and again the tigerhounds ripped into them, tearing off limbs, ripping out throats, but the fallen creatures melted and reshaped. But even their phenomenal strength was waning.

Zellorian saw the first of the tigerhounds smothered by two of his creatures and they began to squeeze its metallic torso. The hound bayed, teeth gleaming, flecked with blood. Abruptly its eyes started from their sockets as the pressure became unbearable, and there was a loud protest of metal, a grinding. The hound was flung aside, its side ripped open. It lay in the dust, long tongue hanging out, the eyes glazing.

Zuarzol screamed his fury. It was Raal, the great king beast of the tigerhounds, crushed like a puppy by these nightmares. The Zolutaal rushed forward blindly, his killing swords flashing, ignoring the groping claws of the Cmizencreatures. Zellorian saw him coming and waited without moving.

As Zuarzol reached him through the carnage, Zellorian ducked the first wild swing of a blade and reached out. To the other Zemoks who were closing in, it looked as though Zellorian had done no more than touch Zuarzol. The huge Csendook staggered back, clutching at his throat. He tried to speak, but no sound came. Instead his armour began to collapse in on itself, as though there was no longer a body inside it. It fell to the ground, steaming. Zuarzol was no more.

Zellorian waited for the next attack, eyes mocking the Zemoks as they paused beyond the circle of snarling tigerhounds. But the creatures that Zellorian had conjured were beginning to fall apart. They reformed over and over, but the ferocity of the tigerhounds never ebbed, and gradually they tore up the creatures, reducing them until nothing but a carpet of torn flesh and warped bone spread out from around Zellorian. Even so, he did not seem troubled.

One of the tigerhounds leapt for him, but he turned it aside almost contemptuously. The Csendook heard its neck snap like a twig. It tumbled and rolled, lying very still. The other tigerhounds abruptly went very silent, their eyes fixed on the Prime Consul.

'He cannot withstand their combined attack,' one of the Zemoks said.

But Zellorian spoke again, words that were not heard by any but the tigerhounds. Slowly they turned around, their scarlet eyes focusing now on their masters. Laughing, Zellorian waved them forward.

Appalled, the Zemoks saw the tigerhounds bearing down upon them. Zellorian had taken control of them, and he flung them into as vicious an assault as they had tried to make upon him. As tigerhound and Zemok met, there was a renewed battle, the sounds terrible in Auganzar's ears.

His warriors fought with all their skill and amazing strength, but the tigerhounds were maddened, filled with a new intensity of hatred. Already they were tearing the Zemoks apart. Auganzar met the attack of one of the hounds, driving his weapon up into its belly, splitting metal, flesh and bone, ripping the creature in half. It fell, twitching and writhing, snarling at its own spilled guts. Zellorian watched calmly. The Zemoks were trying to break through the circle of tigerhounds, but they were forced back. Even Auganzar, extraordinary warrior that he was, was forced to drop back. It was an equally matched conflict, for the tigerhounds were imbued with terrible strength, but even so, some of them were being cut down. Zellorian turned to see a lone figure standing apart from the battle. The surviving Opener. He must be left alive. There would be work for him after the slaughter.

Auganzar smashed the life from another of the tigerhounds, opening its head from skull to chin, and it toppled off him. He paused to look around him. The hounds were beaten at last, stretched out, or curled up, broken and bloodied. But he had lost a good many Zemoks. He tried to count the survivors. There were two score at the most, wounded and exhausted. The rest were tumbled among the dead tigerhounds, butchered.

'Supreme Sanguinary!' called Zellorian. 'It is almost over. Let your Zemoks rest. Come, you and I can settle this. Spare your warriors any more suffering.'

'Don't be fooled by him, Zaru!' called one of the Zemoks.

Auganzar shook his head. 'No. But if he invites a contest, I will give it to him. You wait until this is over.'

'Zaru,' said the Zemok, gripping his master's arm. 'Zaru, he is dangerous. You cannot – '

Auganzar shrugged himself free. 'Do as I say! You wait. All of you!' He looked up at Zellorian, then moved slowly up the slope towards him.

He was half way to the crest of the slope when a sound behind him made him turn. He heard Zellorian laugh, and down below the Zemoks gasped as they saw the tigerhounds twitching, staggering to their feet. The creatures were in bloody ruins, heads broken, backs snapped, limbs severed. But, like the Cmizen-things before them, they reformed, shaped by diabolical powers.

Auganzar turned to Zellorian, who again spoke to the air. There were terrible screams behind Auganzar. He knew what was happening, as the tigerhounds again attacked his survivors. He moved forward, a foot at a time, watching the Prime Consul for a sign of attack. But Zellorian merely pointed.

Auganzar turned again. To look upon utter destruction. The tigerhounds had collapsed once more, but not before they had completed their vile work. The Zemoks were destroyed, torn apart, flung this way and that as though a storm had burst among them. Not one of them lived. Beyond them, through the dust cloud thrown up by the final conflict, Gehennon stood, lone survivor of the mayhem.

'After this, it is over,' said Zellorian.

Auganzar faced him, yards away from him. He could see something in that face that spoke of many powers, many worlds. He was no longer Human, but a fusion of other things, other things that used him.

'A fitting grave, Quendai,' said the Csendook.

Auganzar pulled from its long scabbard the sword made by Hozermaak. He felt it throb in his hand, its life writhing within it, eager for release.

Zellorian's smile widened. 'Ah, you still insist on using a toy to match my powers. Auganzar, I can draw down power from the skies, storms, or pull up energies from the earth, no matter how corrupt they are. And I can drag out powers from within my mind: I can even enter yours and reshape it. Your blade is worthless.'

Auganzar moved forward, trying to ignore the words. He could feel something in the blade gathering itself, like a huge beast crouching, preparing to spring. Power. Hozermaak had spoken of power, of how this blade drank it. Took into itself the powers it cut down.

The blade was turning scarlet, but not with the blood of the slain. It was coming from within. Auganzar saw something move, as if deep down in a pool. That grim shape, rising up. And he knew what it must be.

Zellorian opened his arms as if to receive the attack, and light crackled about his fists. But Auganzar raced forward, holding out the blade of Hozermaak. He felt something before him, a wall of power, but the blade bit into it, ripping it asunder as if it were no more than a sheet. Zellorian's eyes opened in horror as he tried to bring his hands forward.

The Accrual! Auganzar could feel its power, stored in the blade that had sucked out its life. And its hunger was greater than ever before. Zellorian could not move as the blade reached out for him like a steel tongue.

Auganzar watched, almost in a dream, as the blade tore into Zellorian's chest, splitting him open easily, racing on through flesh, organ and bone. The Csendook lifted the Prime Consul up off the ground, letting him dangle on the blade. Blood gushed from the wound, but the sword drank it in thirstily, sucking all life from its victim. Zellorian's hands fizzed, blackening as if thrust into fire, but none of the powers he possessed came to his aid. They were all dragged into the body of the sword.

As he jerked and twisted, caught like a fish, Zellorian screamed his last defiance, and Auganzar could feel his life shutting out. He had not been prepared for this power, the power of the Conceptors, the hidden masters of the Five Cycles. This was their revenge, their punishment.

At last Auganzar tossed aside the blade. It sparkled with bright colours, scarlet and crimson, and the corpse it drained had become as wizened as that of an ancient Man. It still shook, and in the sword Auganzar could hear the roaring, growing louder like the birth of a volcano under him. He turned back to see Gehennon trudging up the slope.

'It's done, Gehennon,' he called hoarsely.

The Opener stared at the scene of death, eyes bulging. 'Zaru, we must get away from here swiftly. We – '

He had no time to answer. The corpse of Zellorian abruptly burst, and the sword itself, crammed with a thousand powers, shattered in mid air and flung its shards in all directions. Gehennon was sent tumbling into the dust, clasping his arms around his head to protect himself. He felt a wave of dirt fall over him.

It was a long time before he moved, dragging himself to his knees. The dust was swirling about in a miniature storm, but everything was silent. He crawled forward.

'Zaru?'

He could see a shape on the ground a few yards away. Crawling to it, he knew that it was the Supreme Sanguinary. Face down, motionless. Carefully he removed the war helm, setting it aside, then lifted the head. He sagged back when he saw what had happened.

A fragment of the exploding sword had entered the back of his neck and cut straight through the throat. The huge Csendook must have died instantly. Curiously there was very little blood. Maybe the fragment of sword had taken it.

Gehennon got to his feet, forcing back his misery. Beyond him he saw the pathetic corpse of Zellorian, like a crushed insect. The eyes stared up at him, their final moment of horrific realisation trapped vividly in them. Unlike Auganzar, there would be no serenity in death for him.

EPILOGUE

EPILOGUE

Pyramors stood on the outer walls of Umus Utmar, looking down at the armies as they came together on the plain. Men, *moillum*, Innasmornian, they made little attempt now to segregate. They had shed their blood together.

Jannovar slipped her hand into the warrior's, felt his fingers close gently over it. Jubaia and the gliderboat had already gone, following the miraculous windriders of Shung Nang. Pyramors need never know their secret, although it would always be an ache in her own heart.

Nearby on the parapet, Ussemitus also watched, and with him were Fomond and Armestor. He turned to them with a wry grin. 'Our forests seem a long way off.'

Fomond smiled, but even he could not repress the sadness he felt. They could never be as they had been. Ussemitus had another destiny, though who could say what the Mother had planned for him?

'I'll be glad to get back there,' snorted Armestor, though they knew his bluntness was hiding his own sorrow.

Beyond them, on the walls, Aru and Tremazon gazed outwards. The skies were clear, the light untainted, possibly for the first time in this bleak part of Innasmorn.

'The Innasmornians could sweep the last of us away with ease,' grunted the former Consul. 'Of all the companies in this war, Man was the most impoverished.'

Aru looked at him sharply. 'It will change, Tremazon. For us, everything will change. The Mother watches over us now. In her way, she has done for centuries.'

'Will the Innasmornians accept us, take our men for husbands, our women for their wives?'

Aru looked away, but she nodded. 'I am sure they will.'

'And you?'

'I just want to rest,' she told him, trying to smile.

'Of course.'

From the ramp behind them, they heard a shout. Presently Gladimyr came rushing upwards, a deep frown creasing his face. He found them all watching him.

'You must come, all of you,' he gasped. 'One of the Openers has returned.'

There was no need for him to say more, and at once the company followed him down the ramp, across the courtyards beyond to one of the many huge chambers of the citadel. Warriors had carried a body from the heart of Umus Utmar to this place, setting it down on a stretcher. Torchlight wavered in the huge vault, but as the company drew close, they saw that it was Gehennon, though he looked grey, his robes ripped and smeared with blood. Clutched in his arms was a bloody bundle that he refused to release to the men who had carried him here.

Ussemitus and Pyramors glanced at each other over the dying figure, but their eyes said what they both knew to be the truth.

'He is dead,' said the Opener, forcing the words out through bloodied lips. 'Auganzar is dead.' The weight of his loss struck them with a tragic force. No one had known what motives had driven this strange creature.

Pyramors felt himself stiffen with apprehension. Then the Prime Consul had again escaped them, was that it?

Gehennon lifted the bundle he held with a great effort. It, too, was caked with blood.

Ussemitus frowned at it as Gehennon pulled at the cloth wrappings. At length he revealed his grisly trophy. All those who were in the chamber stood back in horror.

It was the head of Zellorian. But the eyes were open. Dead, but fixed on some inner vision, the lips twisted in a malign smile.

Ussemitus took the head. 'So it is over,' he breathed. As he spoke, a tongue of vivid light shot from the mouth of the dead Consul, bursting like liquid fire over the head and shoulders of Ussemitus. He staggered back, dropping the head and clutching at his own.

Aru screamed and rushed to him.

Pyramors had his sword out in a moment and clove the fallen head in two neat pieces. Black fluid gushed from it, but no more light. It had performed its last deceit.

Aru had her arms around Ussemitus, speaking his name over and over again. But he sagged down, his body so small, so frail. Fomond and Armestor were beside Aru, gaping impotently. She set Ussemitus down on the flagstones. Already Gladimyr had rushed for medical help.

Beyond the transfixed company, a light began to glow beside Gehennon, shaping itself into human form. It put a hand on the forehead of the dying Opener, and on his face there was a sudden easing of pain. He closed his eyes. For him the suffering was over.

Pyramors had swung his blade round, as if the light-figure was yet another threat to them all. 'Ussemitus?' he whispered.

'You must lay the body in the earth,' said the voice of the spectral.

Aru studied it with tear-filled eyes. 'Ussemitus – '

'I go to the Mother,' he answered softly. 'She has claimed me, as I knew she would. Put the body among the trees of the northern forests. Armestor! Fomond! I charge you with this.'

They nodded through their own tears.

'Zellorian – ' began Pyramors, looking down at the grim relic on the floor.

'It was the last discharge of his powers, the last defiant act of the darkness. But Auganzar found them and has put an end to them.'

'Did none of them survive?' said Tremazon.

The spectral shook its head sadly. 'None. But it is over.'

Gladimyr returned with a number of surgeons, but they saw at once that both Ussemitus and Gehennon were beyond help.

'This is not a time to sorrow,' they heard a voice beyond the group saying. 'It is a time to rejoice.' It sounded like the Innasmornian mage, but as they looked, they saw only a glow.

As the light faded, Aru bent down, lifting the body of the

fallen Ussemitus, her tears splashing on his face, where there was no longer a trace of pain, only a deep contentment, an absolute serenity.

'Let me take him into the light,' she said.

Outside, as though in answer, she heard the whisper of the wind, its sigh of approval.

APPENDIX A

THE CSENDOOK MILITARY REGIME

The CSENDOOK are governed by the GARAZENDA, a body comprised of all the principal generals, the foremost of which form an inner council, the MAROZUL.

Subordinate to the generals are the military commanders, the ZARU, who have control of a unit of the army, or SWARM. Each Zaru would have under him a number of captains or ZOLUTARS, this number varying from Swarm to Swarm, dependent on the honorary standing of the Zaru, which would usually be calculated by victories in the field. The rank and file warriors of the Swarms are the ZEMOKS.

With the introduction of the gladiatorial system by the Supreme Sanguinary, Auganzar, who uses Men, or *moillum* as warriors to hasten the subjugation of rebels, new titles have been introduced. The *moillum* are trained in special schools, known as warhalls. Warhalls are put under the command of a Zaru acting for the owner of the warhall, who would be one of the Garazenda, and these Zaru are renamed ZARULL. Their Zolutars serving specifically at the warhalls become ZOLUTULLS.

The Zemoks are also renamed where they have specific duties in a warhall, or relating to *moillum*. Zemoks with a responsibility for training *moillum* are called ZEMOI, while the Zemoks with particular responsibilities for animals are called ZEMAAL.

There are periodic Games held, the principal of which are at the stadia on the Warhive, although all warhalls have their arenas. There are also the Hunts, which are held over a designated area of land surrounding the warhalls, which are built away from the city areas for just this reason. The principal Games are known as Testaments, the Hunts as Running Hunts.

APPENDIX B

CSENDOOK NAMES

Csendook names are generally family names, with rank or title built into the name, usually as a suffix. Thus a member of the Marozul would have a name ending in -MAR, such as Zuldamar; a member of the Garazenda who was not one of the Marozul, would have a name ending in -GAR, such as Xeltagar; a Zaru would have a name ending in -ZAR, such as Auganzar, and so on.

Certain Csendook who have not earned enough battle honours to give them the right to their full title do not have part of the title suffixed to their name, such as Cmizen, the Keeper of Eannor, although this tends to be something peculiar to the Zemoks as promotion through the ranks almost always depends on battle honours.

Apart from the Zemoks, Csendook are usually addressed by subordinates by their rank or title rather than name: thus Uldenzar is addressed by his warriors as 'Zaru' and less often by his name. Auganzar, the Supreme Sanguinary (a title unique to him) is also a Zaru, and is most commonly addressed by this title by his contemporaries.

In *Star Requiem*, loyalties among the Csendook are divided, chiefly between the followers of the two Marozul, Zuldamar and Horzumar, and those of Auganzar. The principal Csendook characters in LABYRINTH OF WORLDS are as follows:

ZULDAMAR,	A prominent member of the Marozul, and opponent of Auganzar
HORZUMAR,	A prominent member of the Marozul, close colleague of Zuldamar

VULKORMAR,	Marozul, neutral in the disputes with Auganzar
KAZRAMAR,	A young member of the Marozul, neutral
XELTAGAR,	A seasoned warrior, vociferous member of the Garazenda, suuporter of Auganzar
AUGANZAR,	A Zaru, the Supreme Sanguinary, warlord of the Csendook armies
VULPORZOL,	A Zolutull, personal agent of Zuldamar, on Eannor and the Warhive
ZUARZOL,	Former Zemaal, now Zolutar, chief handler of the tigerhounds
GUNTRAZOL,	Former Zemaal, now Zolutar, close colleague of Zuarzol
IMMARZOL,	Zolutar in the Swarm of Auganzar
QUENZOL,	Zolutar in the Swarm of Auganzar
VANDARZOL,	Zolutar in the Swarm of Auganzar
TORZARU,	A Zemok in Auganzar's Swarm
VARUZEM,	A Zemok in Auganzar's Swarm
HUNAR GADREEV,	wife of Auganzar
CMIZEN,	The Keeper of Eannor
ETRASCU,	An Opener, assigned to Cmizen by the Garazenda
GEHENNON,	A renegade Opener, serving Auganzar
ASPHOGOL,	An Opener of the rank of Ultimate, assigned by the Garazenda to Auganzar
GMARGAU,	a principal Opener, Voice of the Consummate Order

APPENDIX C

A HISTORICAL NOTE

After the battle of Umus Utmar, the Consummate Order of the Openers ensured that the World Cycles were again properly sealed. The actions of the renegade Opener, Gehennon, in returning from the Cycle of Quendai to that of Innasmorn had performed the last act in the ritual of closure. From then onwards, contact between the Five Cycles ceased altogether: only the Conceptors were able again to move along the ancient lines of division. There may have been similar movement by the last of the rogue creatures, the Accruals, but even they were aware of the events at Umus Utmar and the consequences of further tampering with the seals. The dissolution that had been spreading slowly through the Cycles as a result of the disruptions was halted, and a balance was preserved for a significant time thereafter.

On Innasmorn, the victorious armies of Vittargattus and Ondrabal returned to their own lands, and the union between Amerandabad and the cities of the south grew strong, trade increasing between the nations. The Vaza nations were no longer averse to visiting Ondrabal's huge and prosperous kingdom, and the northern continent became for a time the most powerful state on Innasmorn. Trade with the west also prospered.

Men who had fought beside the Innasmornians at Umus Utmar were gradually accepted by and drawn into the developing settlements, while the Windmasters and Seers spread the word of the Mother, her purpose. While many Human families had survived the fall of the Sculpted City and were brought down out of the mountains beyond its ruins, there were many Men without families of their own. Some took their own kind as partners, for many women among the Human survivors had been widowed by the war, while others settled with Innasmornian partners in one of the cities, or, after the fashion of the Vaza, roamed the vast forest lands seeking a new beginning. The Mother encouraged this spread of Man among Innasmornians. There were feuds, as there had always been feuds among Innasmornians, but for the most part the integration was achieved with minimal bloodshed.

There was for a time, a council set up, and Tremazon, former Consul to the Imperator Elect, was chosen to represent Man on this council, which met in the various principal cities. He married an Innasmornian girl, a cousin of King Ondrabal, while others of his knights married into the families of both Ondrabal and Vittargattus. Their children were to become the later rulers of the states of the new union.

Fomond and Armestor returned to their native forests in the north, and while the latter soon married and settled into the ways of a forester, Fomond took a party of followers and went far to the east, in search of new lands, a new life. What he found there and what he made of it, nothing is known.

Aru lived for several years in Amerandabad, contributing to its councils, and eventually married an Innasmornian warrior, Rennover, who took her to the mountains north and east of the Dhumvald, where new settlements sprung up. Aru became a legend among her new people, for she was visited by the revered warriors of sacred Shung Nang, the awesome windriders who were so rarely seen anywhere on Innasmorn.

Generally there was harmony, but where there was not, where the people for one reason or another became enmeshed in a dispute of any consequence, there were always the servants of the Mother, and with them the strange spirit-like spectrals to remind people of what had almost been, the darkness that had risen in its effort to devour them all.

The Garazenda never learned the truth of the last Crossing of Auganzar. Zuldamar gave the truth to his close friend, Horzumar, and certain others were told the truth, such as

Vulporzol and Csendook like him, who were absolutely loyal to Zuldamar. It was accepted by the Garazenda that Auganzar must have perished after leaving Eannor, along with the Swarm he had taken with him on what was, supposedly, his first major sweep of the rebel worlds of the Cycle. There was great mourning for the Supreme Sanguinary and all those who had fallen, and Zuldamar was instrumental in introducing the festivals in his honour. Later he was to take Hunar Gadreev, Auganzar's widow, for his wife, and their children served the Garazenda long and prosperously.

Vulporzol eventually became a member of the Marozul, and was given a responsibility for policing Eannor, now a closed world, alone with its many ghosts. *Moillum* were removed from it altogether, and such Csendook cities as existed there were far from the former zone of sacrifice.

Across the worlds of the Cycle, Man had come to terms with his defeat, and rebellion was very limited. Gradually the need for *moillum* was reduced, until eventually the gladiatorial schools disappeared almost entirely, though the tradition did not cease completely, nor was it ever fully outlawed. Man and Csendook did not mix well, but certain worlds were set aside for the survivors of the once proud Empire, although these were controlled by a central Csendook government.

Man's lost scientific arts remained forgotten, undisturbed for millennia. Nothing more was heard of the Oibarene, who brooded deep in the heart of the Warhive, powerless to free themselves since the defeat of the Malefics at Umus Utmar. The Csendook concentrated their energies for many years on the rebuilding of their war-torn Cycle, helped by the Consummate Order. There were internal wars occasionally, but no conflagrations, no destruction on the massive scale of the former wars with Man.

Only in Quendai did the silence flourish. Nothing stirred in the dead Cycle. And on its central world, a world of shifting grey sands, there were no visitors to the mound of the dead, where the great Csendook warlord, Auganzar, had fallen. Beside his body, the eyes of his war helm gazed up at scarlet skies as though in longing for a glimpse of the worlds it had known.